WINTERSMOON

HUGH WALPOLE

BOOKS BY
HUGH WALPOLE

NOVELS

JEREMY AT CRALE
HARMER JOHN
THE WOODEN HORSE
THE GODS AND MR. PERRIN
THE DARK FOREST
THE SECRET CITY

The London Novels

WINTERSMOON
FORTITUDE
THE DUCHESS OF WREXE
THE GREEN MIRROR
THE CAPTIVES
THE YOUNG ENCHANTED

Scenes from Provincial Life

THE CATHEDRAL
THE OLD LADIES

Phantasies

MARADICK AT FORTY
THE PRELUDE TO ADVENTURE
PORTRAIT OF A MAN WITH RED HAIR

BOOKS ABOUT CHILDREN

THE GOLDEN SCARECROW
JEREMY
JEREMY AND HAMLET

BELLES-LETTRES

JOSEPH CONRAD: A CRITICAL STUDY
THE CRYSTAL BOX: FRAGMENTS OF
AUTOBIOGRAPHY
SOME NOTES ON THE EVOLUTION OF THE
ENGLISH NOVEL

WINTERSMOON

BY

HUGH WALPOLE

1928

DOUBLEDAY, DORAN & COMPANY, INC.
GARDEN CITY, NEW YORK

"What of the Past?

Shall we make use of these grey-green lichened Palaces . . . or shall the spider-webs swallow them and we strike, out of this gleaming Quarry, this new white shining stone?"

HENRY GALLEON, *The Scarlet Emperor.*

DEDICATORY LETTER

DEAR ELIZABETH

You told me once that you were bored with sequels, both in real life and in novels—this, if I remember correctly, was when I begged you to give us some more of Fraulein Schmidt's history.

It would therefore be extremely impertinent of me to offer you a sequel—and this, in real life at least, I have hitherto succeeded in avoiding.

Now also I take no risk. This story of Janet Grandison, her marriage and her sister, is no sequel to anything save that it is, of course, like all of us, a sequel to everything. What I really mean is that you need read no other book before it in order properly to understand it.

But once upon a time, when I was young and credulous, I planned a Trilogy, called it "The Rising City" and published the first volume of it, "The Duchess of Wrexe."

So many people, older and wiser than I, told me that I was a fool to meddle with Trilogies, that I fancied myself Balzac, that readers hated presumption, and that novelists must be modest or they are nothing.

Therefore I pretended to kill my Trilogy, hid my Rising City under a green mist, and went my way. Trilogies, however, cannot be killed like that; they are the most persistent things alive. The Trilogy has grown into an unending sequence. After "The Duchess of Wrexe" came "The Green Mirror" and after "The Green Mirror" "The Young Enchanted," and now after "The Young Enchanted" this "Wintersmoon," and after "Wintersmoon"—who knows?

Here, at any rate, in these four books, is my idea of some of the England of 1900 to 1927, and behind this there is also something else that holds them, in my fancy, together.

And there are my four heroines, Rachel Seddon, Katherine

and Millie Trenchard and Janet Grandison. But, because an author sees a connection in these things and has the conceit to look on his four books as one continuous work no compulsion is offered to the reader. "Wintersmoon," indeed, may be read as though it had no ancestors and intends no progeny.

Above all, no compulsion is offered to yourself, dear Elizabeth, who rightly resents anything of the sort, anything that sounds too long to be borne.

So, if you will read this book simply as a story about certain people who appear for an hour or two to be alive in their own world you will have done everything that your faithful friend, the author, asks of you.

Yours affectionately,
HUGH WALPOLE.

CONTENTS

PART I. JANET AND ROSALIND

CHAPTER		PAGE
I	PARTY	3
II	THE SILVER TREE—I	14
III	BEAMINSTER AT HOME	23
IV	HALKIN STREET	41
V	WILDHERNE	62
VI	A FAMILY AFFAIR	73
VII	MARCH: LONDON	89
VIII	WEDDING	108

PART II. JANET AND WILDHERNE

I | DOWN IN WILTSHIRE | 121
II | UP AMONG THE BACHELORS | 133
III | WINTERSMOON: MORNING | 148
IV | A CARNATION IN A SILVER BOTTLE | 166
V | JANET'S HEART | 182
VI | ROSALIND PAYS A VISIT | 194
VII | WINTERSMOON AT EVENING | 214
VIII | ENGLISH HISTORY | 228

PART III. WILDHERNE AND HUMPHREY

I | BEAMINSTER PAYS TWO CALLS | 239
II | AT HALKIN STREET | 258
III | WHITE | 276
IV | ROSALIND IS ROSALIND | 289
V | THE STREETS IN SPRING | 303
VI | THE DUKE IS UNHAPPY | 318

CONTENTS

CHAPTER   PAGE

VII   PAGES FROM JANET'S JOURNAL 332

VIII A PUFF OF WIND 341

PART IV. JANET, ROSALIND AND WILDHERNE

I   AN OLD MAN IN A DRY MONTH 345

II   WINTERSMOON: AUTUMN NIGHT 363

III THE CHAPEL ON THE HILL 376

IV JOURNEY IN RAIN 390

V   THE MOON OBSCURED 401

VI JANET GOES NORTH 410

VII THE SEA-CAPTAIN WALKS HIS DECK . . . 423

VIII THE SILVER TREE—II. WATENDLATH . . . 437

PART I

JANET AND ROSALIND

WINTERSMOON

CHAPTER I

PARTY

"I AM asking you again to marry me as I did a fortnight ago."

Janet Grandison turned towards him and said:

"Yes. You've been very honest."

"I believe," he said, "honesty to be the only thing for us.
From the beginning I have always known that you valued
that—honesty I mean—more perhaps than anything. I
value it too."

She smiled.

"I believe you do. But we all do. We make a fetish of it.
It seems to me sometimes almost the only good thing that
has survived the war. Well," she went on, "I have had the
fortnight I begged for. A fortnight ago you asked me to
marry you. You said you weren't in love with me but that
you liked and respected me, that you thought we would get
on well together. . . . You want me to be the mother of
your children."

"Yes," he said. "I am not in love with you. I have been
in love for eight years with somebody, somebody whom it
is impossible for me to marry and someone who would not
marry me even though it were possible. With the exception
of this one person I would rather marry you than anyone
in the world. I like you. I admire you. I think we could be
good companions."

Her face was grave. "I don't know about that," she said
slowly. "I have been very little with men in my life. I don't
know how it would be. Giving you frankness for frankness

3

the other day I told you that I did not love you in the least.
But I like you. I would do all I could to make you happy
if I married you. But my sister comes first—she will always
come first. I loved my father—and I love my sister. Those
have been the only two emotions in my life. Love her! I
adore her. I am not exaggerating or using words without
thinking about them when I say that I would die for her
if it would give her what she wanted. And so if I marry
you to give her what she wants that isn't perhaps surprising so long as I tell you exactly how things are. And the
way things are can't go on much longer. We've been alone
now for eight years, she and I, and the last two have been
—well, impossible. You promised me that if I married you
she should always live with us. It should be her home."

"Of course. That is part of the bargain."

"Yes, it is a bargain, isn't it? Not romantic. But all my romance is for my sister. And yours——" She broke off, hesitating.

"Yes, mine is as I have told you. But how many marriages ever remain romantic? It is a platitude that they do
not. The best thing that comes of a happy marriage is companionship. That I believe we shall have."

He hesitated, then went on:

"I want to put it all fairly before you. There isn't very
much money. It won't be a gay life, you know, or a merry
one. The place down in the country, although I adore it,
won't seem very lively to you or to your sister, I'm afraid.
It's all in pieces, and I see no likelihood of my ever having
money enough to do much to it. One day perhaps—for my
son. . . . And then I am not at all what I should be in the
country. I moon about. I don't do any of the things I ought
to. I am an ass about affairs. And then so long as my father
is alive we would have to be a good deal in London. We
would have to stay in Halkin Street with them, and that,
as you know, wouldn't be very lively either. You know
exactly what life in Halkin Street is like. They'll be very
glad—my father and my mother—if you'll marry me. They
like you so much. You belong to the family. Your mother
was one of my mother's greatest friends. But it will be no

sort of escape for you—except for actual escape from money troubles. But we would all be kind to you and your sister. Everyone would be glad and would try to make you both happy."

"It will surprise everyone very much," Janet said slowly. "I have known you so little. You've been away so much."

"Yes. But we can trust one another. I'm sure of that."

"I believe we can."

Then, looking him honestly in the eyes, she said:

"I will marry you, Lord Poole, and I will be a good friend to you."

He took her hand.

"Thank you," he said. "You have made me very happy."

In old Lady Madden's vast and draughty drawing-room life pursued its decorous way. There were perhaps a hundred human beings in the room, but had you listened at the door in the intervals of music the sound proceeding from their conversation would have resembled nothing so much as the stealthy spinning of a bemused and industrious top. No more and no less. A very large painting by Sir Edward Burne-Jones of Grecian ladies gathered about a well, portraits of a number of glazed Madden ancestors, a huge fireplace of spotted marble, a great gold clock, a copy of Holman Hunt's "Scapegoat" (it gazed across the floor into the indifferent faces of the Grecian ladies), these held, as they had done for many a past year, command of the situation. No human being, however bold, however arrogant, would dream of antagonising them. And they knew it. All the guests of Lady Madden would also have known it had they thought of it. They did not think of it.

Little Felix Brun, seated uncomfortably on a little gilt chair, did not pretend to listen to the old lady with untidy white hair who was in the act of manfully demolishing Schumann's "Carnaval" at the enormous piano in the room's further corner. He was not listening. He was, as always throughout his life it had been his practice, observing. In earlier days he would have stood up against the wall whence he might more efficiently have taken his notes, but he was now seventy-six years of age and his legs too often defeated him. He was nevertheless intensely interested. He had seen nothing like this before.

He had not been in England for many years, not since the year 1911, and it was now the year of 1921. Ten years, and ten such years! The war had moved him to a patriotic participation that would have once seemed to him incredible. He had thought himself detached from his country—a cosmopolitan philosopher with Socratic vision. But the German invasion of Belgium had torn his Socratic isolation to ribbons, and for the next six years he had lived only in, and for, his beloved France.

Then with the disappointments and ironies of the Peace some of his cynical detachment returned. He was not wholly French—there was Austrian blood in his veins—and it was this same Austrian blood, perhaps, that led him, hating Germany as he did, to criticise France with a frankness that infuriated his Parisian circle. And so, rather happy that he had regained once more his impersonality, he returned to his once-so-beloved London.

The impression that he had had of it during his absent post-war years—impression gathered in the main from English novels and newspapers—was that his dear London was running swiftly to the dogs, the Upper Classes drinking cocktails and dancing eternally to the jazziest of music, the Middle Classes hopelessly and aimlessly impoverished, the Lower Classes rebellious, revolutionary, idle, and dole-fed.

He found, to his pleasure, his old rooms in Clarges Street vacant, and the stout, amiable Forrester, landlord, valet, and gossip, older but otherwise unchanged. The cost of living had doubled, of course, but so it had everywhere, and for the rest, in his first week's survey he could not, save for the congestion of traffic and the ruin of Regent Street, see that his London was very greatly altered. There were still the flower-women round the fountain in Piccadilly Circus, still the lions and Nelson, still the decent-looking fellows outlined against the freshness of the Green Park, still the sanctum by the fireplace under the stairs in St. James's Club, still Big Ben and the chastity of Curzon Street, the higgledy-piggledy of Shepherd's Market, the Christian Science Church, and the cloistered shabbiness of the Albany. His superficial landmarks were all there.

He was taken after the theatre to a place where they danced, and it seemed to him extremely English and decorous. He could find in it none of the dazzling wickedness and abnormality that the English novels of his reading had led him to expect. The Unemployed, bursting into music in the streets, struck him with their exceeding rosiness and physical vigour. He remembered faces seen by him recently in Berlin, Vienna, and Prague that had besieged successfully even his cynical indifference. He saw no such faces here.

And then coming out one day of Colnaghi's in Bond Street he encountered old Lady Madden, with her large spectacles and larger nose, her broad unwieldly figure, her hat a little askew, just exactly as she had been ten years earlier. She recognised him, told him in her deep, rather wheezy voice (she always talked like an old cab-driver whose life had been spent in rain and fog) that he was looking older, and asked him to her party.

So here he was to-night. He had realised at once on entering the room that for the first time since his return to London he was in the world that he had known before the war. Once in the old days of the South African War he had divided the English ruling classes into three parties —the Autocrats, the Aristocrats, and the Democrats. The Autocrats—the Beaminsters, the Gutterils, the Minsters— had been the people with whom, at that time, he had mostly lived. The old Duchess of Wrexe had been their queen, and for a time she had ruled England. She was long dead, and the Autocrats, as a party of power in England, were gone and gone for ever. The Democrats—Ruddards, Denisons, Funells, Muffats—there were plenty of them about, he supposed. The war and its consequences must have helped them to power. It was they, and the members of the old Autocratic party whom disaster and poverty had driven into their ranks, who danced and kicked their way through the illustrated papers. He didn't know and he didn't care. He felt in his bones that, at the present time at least, they were

unimportant whatever they might become. He dismissed
them with a shrug. They were food for the novelist who
wanted dazzling pictures with post-impressionist colours
and Freudian titles.

Remained then the Aristocrats—the Maddens, the Darrants, the Chichesters, the Medleys, the Weddons. He had
once said of them, "I take my hat off to them. All those
quiet decorous people, poor as mice many of them, standing
aside altogether from any movements or war-cries of the
day, living in their quiet little houses or their empty big
ones, clever some of them, charitable all of them, but never
asserting their position or estimating it. They never look
about them and see where they are. They've no need to.
They're just there."

He didn't remember, of course, that he had ever said
that, but it was what he still at this day, twenty-two years
later, felt. And they were of infinitely more importance now
than they had been then. They were all—positively all—that
was left of the old Aristocracy of England, that Class and
that Creed that, whether for good or ill, had meant a great
deal in the world's history. They were (he couldn't as yet
be sure but he fancied that he felt it in the air about him)
engaged now in a really desperate conflict. This might be
the last phase of their Power, or it might lead through vic-
tory to a new phase of Power, greater than any they had
yet known. If they were as poor as mice then, twenty-two
years ago, they were, they must be, a great deal poorer
than any reasonably fortunate mouse now. He fancied that
he could see something of that too as he looked about him.
But they would say nothing at all about it. They would have,
above everything else, their dignity and self-respect, qualities that the Democrats had lost long ago.

The possession of those qualities might make for dullness, but a little dullness was sometimes not a bad thing.

He had reached this point in his commentary when the
untidy lady buried the "Carnaval" with a sigh of relief and
everyone rose to the surface of the room. Brun turned to
discover his neighbour and saw (on the gilt chair next to
his) a nice young man whose face seemed familiar to him.

A moment later someone from behind them bent forwards and said, "Hullo, Seddon! How goes it?" and the young man, amiability all over him, turned back to talk.

Seddon . . . Seddon . . . Seddon. . . .

Little Brun swept his brain. The name was familiar enough, the face too. Ah! he knew. He had it. He turned to the boy, who was about to get up and go, and said:

"I beg your pardon. Forgive an old man a liberty. But I heard you addressed. . . . I have not been in London for many years; I am quite out of touch with everyone. But I once, twenty years ago, had two friends, Sir Roderick Seddon and his wife. You resemble her a little. My old affection for them, the memory of their goodness to me, makes me perhaps impertinent. . . . Pray forgive it. . . ."

The boy smiled.

"Yes," he said. "That must be my father and mother. I'm Tom Seddon."

Brun held out his hand.

"It's very exciting to me," he said, "to meet Rachel Seddon's son. It's a good omen for my happy return to London. You tell your father and mother when you see them that Felix Brun took this liberty with you, and that he is going to call if he may."

"My father's dead, sir," the boy answered. "He died before the war. But of course I know your name. When I was quite a kid I used to hear mother say that you knew more about European politics than anyone in Europe. At that time," he smiled delightfully, "I didn't know I was going into the Foreign Office, where as a matter of fact I am—the only thing I wanted was to play the Australians at cricket—so what mother said didn't mean as much to me as it ought to have done. But it means an awful lot now. You could tell me some things I most frightfully want to know."

The boy was so charming that little Brun was entirely captive. He had been so long away from England that he had a little forgotten how pleasant a pleasant Englishman can be. Young Seddon, with every turn of his head, every spoken word, every smile, brought back to Brun a world

of memories. Here was something that he could find nowhere else in Europe. He had been, yes, surely he had been
too long away.

"You know," young Seddon confided. "This is a jolly
dull party. Wasn't that woman awful on the piano? I
wouldn't be here if it weren't for a special reason . . ."
He paused for a moment looking eagerly about the room.
"There's somebody here I'm looking for . . . Ah! excuse
me a moment . . . One moment. . . ."

He was off, threading his way across the room through
the little gilt chairs. Brun followed him with his eyes. Two
girls were standing talking to Lady Madden. They were
striking enough standing there together. Striking even by
contrast. They were both tall, but one was very dark and
the other very fair. The dark one seemed to be the older of
the two; she was very tall, and held herself magnificently.
Her face expressed great sweetness; the eyes, the mouth
showed so striking a spirit of kindliness and gentleness that
Brun was arrested by this so strongly that for a time he
forgot everything and everyone else in the room. He would
like to know that girl. He was no sentimentalist, but kindliness and goodness of heart had their value in this world,
their positive international value. And this was English
kindliness (the girl was so English that it was almost shock-
ing), a little dull perhaps but restful, reliable in a degree that
during these late unstable years of his life had seemed non-
existent. He would like to know that girl—she would be
courageous, faithful, simple, perceptive of only a few things,
but seeing those things clearly without a tremor of her
dark protecting eyes.

The girl beside her was prettier, younger, far more sexu-
ally disturbing. They were sisters. That was assured by the
resemblance of the forehead, carriage of the head, general
pose and attitude to the world. The fair girl was beautiful,
which the dark girl was not. The fair girl had the English
beauty of a Reynolds or a Gainsborough. Everything was
fair and fresh and gentle, a little old-fashioned perhaps in
the abundance of the hair and the simplicity of the frock.
She was not naked, as now so many English girls were,

so much more naked than complete nudity. But then of course in this set, in this room, nudity would not be fashionable.

Young Seddon was talking to these two with great animation, talking to them both but looking always at the fair girl even when his eyes were turned to the older sister. *That* was his reason, then, for coming to this stuffy party. Little Brun felt a gentle stir of romantic, if rather cynical, pleasure. He wished him luck. They would make a handsome pair.

And then someone clapped him on the shoulder.

"Felix . . . Old Felix! It is! After these years!"

He turned round and looked up and there was old Johnnie Beaminster—Johnnie Beaminster, eighty or ninety or a hundred surely, but looking as neat and as round and as complete with his white hair and rosy unwrinkled face as he had been twenty, thirty, forty years ago! How these English people didn't change! It was, one must suppose, the lives they led or didn't lead, their baths and exercises and simple innocent minds! But Felix was delighted. There had been times, in the old past world, when he had found Johnnie Beaminster a bit of a bore, but now in this new, unfaithful, hysterical world old Beaminster was a pearl of great price, and it was a beautiful, round, shining, gleaming pearl that he looked, his smooth, good-tempered, stupid face crinkled into smiles.

"And you've been here ever so long and you've never told me. I call that too bad. You could have found me in a minute."

"No, but, Johnnie, I haven't been here so long. I'm only now settling in. I'd have bothered you soon enough. And I'm old. Mon dieu! how old! And snappy . . . You don't know how snappy. I'm kind to keep out of people's path."

"You were always snappy." Beaminster's chair leaned over to Brun's. He had his arm on the other's shoulder. "I'm damnably glad to see you. It's old times come back. I daresay they weren't really as good as we fancy them now, but it's an odd world these days. One would be lost in it if it weren't for a few good fellows. Still taking notes,

Felix? There's lots for you to be observing nowadays."

Brun laughed. "The old Duchess has gone, though."

Beaminster's face crinkled again. "Yes. She wouldn't work now. It's all too exposed. You couldn't carry on a mystery stunt like that these days. That's young Tom Seddon over there, Rachel's boy."

"I know. He's just been talking to me. Real English. None of Rachel's Russian complexities."

"Oh, he's a good boy. There isn't a nicer in town. I'm leaving him my goods and chattels. He doesn't know it, though. He's got brains. He'll go farther than poor Roddy ever did."

"And who are those girls he's talking to?"

"Miss Grandisons. Janet and Rosalind. Rosalind's a beauty and Janet's a treasure. Nicest girls in London. They are poorer than poor. Their mother was a Ludley. Can't think why they don't marry. They've been orphans for ten years now."

"And who is that—just joined them? Good-looking."

"That's Wildherne Poole. Old Romney's son. It's a pity he doesn't marry, but there's been some affair . . . The old Duke's always pressing him to. He's the only son and there's got to be an heir."

"Romney . . . Poole." Brun sorted the names. "I don't remember when I was here . . ."

"No, you wouldn't. Romney came into the thing very late. His elder brother had it. And he was always down at the place in Wiltshire. The present man doesn't cut any figure socially. They are poor and Church of England. Parsons, soup-kitchens, mufflers for the old women. Their house in Halkin Street is deadly. All the same he's a dear old boy. Too good and simple for these days."

The music began again.

After a sleepy while Beaminster and Brun stole away. As they passed down the stairs to the cloakroom the stir and whisper of the music faintly, wistfully pursued them. The hall-door opened for an instant and a vision of snow and a muffled amber lamp swept in with a rush of cold biting air. The door closed. Brun, fumbling for his cloakroom ticket, looked up at a huge, naked, badly-jointed Hercules that stuck out over the racks of coats and hats. It had its fig-leaf, but it had been pushed into that corner years ago because it wasn't quite decent. The only sound in the house was the faint tinkle of the piano and the unhurried ticking of a marble clock on the other side of the hall.

"It *is* jolly to be back," Brun confided to Beaminster. "Very touching. I could cry for two-pence."

CHAPTER II

IT was very good of the kindly old thing to offer the girls a lift in her four-wheeler. Four-wheelers were now remarkable and even romantic phenomena—you saw them so seldom and were in them simply never! But old Lady Anglish supported the old man with the side whiskers who drove this one, yes, and his whole family! As she explained to Rosalind when they were all settled inside, it wasn't only that she had never been in a motor-car yet and never would, but that Mussel's grandchildren were the sweetest children, and that when she went to see them she knew that there were at least half a dozen human things in the world who were glad to see her.

More people, Rosalind reflected as the cab crept like a sleep-walker over the snow, would be glad to see her if she looked less odd and didn't talk so continuously about herself and her plans. Her oddness was interesting seen at a dispassionate distance, but embarrassing as soon as you were in any way responsible for it. However, to-night the cab was positively a blessing. Otherwise they must have taken an omnibus. This disgusting poverty, this loathsome compelling of every reluctant penny to do its uttermost "bit"! And then the beauty of the night seen very dimly through the frost-dimmed panes of the cab drew Rosalind from those sordid thoughts. She was always easily drawn by any beauty—or by any ugliness for the matter of that. Life was what she wanted—to savour it, fully, utterly, to the last intensity, never to miss a thing, never to escape an experience that would be the ecstasy of enjoyment—if it were not for morals and other people's feelings. She had not, she considered, any morals herself. Nothing shocked her.

14

She had heard the most dreadful things and had never turned a hair. Nor did she care, when she looked into it dispassionately, very much for other people's feelings. Unless she loved them. There was the rub. This love. How tiresome it was, forcing you to be considerate and unselfish and yielding when you so definitely did not wish to be! Perhaps one day when she was older she would conquer this feeling and not care for anybody, only for herself. How satisfying that state would be!

The vast white space of Hyde Park Corner encircled them like a crystal lake. St. George's Hospital was black and forbidding like a jutting crag. The cab stopped to allow the motor-cars to pass, and with glaring fiery eyes like wolves out on the hunt they slipped by. Rosalind looked at her sister Janet, and saw that she was sitting back in her corner of the cab, her eyes closed. Something had happened to Janet! Rosalind knew it at once. The sisters always knew about one another. But something had also happened to Rosalind. Young Tom Seddon had as good as proposed to her. Only a few words, but they had been enough to tell her. And she didn't want him to propose. He mustn't propose, because if he did she would only refuse him and then all the pleasant friendly companionship of the last few years would be changed. She would refuse him because for one thing she didn't love him, and because for another and a more important thing he hadn't any money. His mother had just enough to keep herself and her son in that decent genteel poverty that Rosalind so thoroughly loathed. It was true that Tom was clever and might one day be an Ambassador, but all that was far distant. Moreover, there was something else about Tom. He was old-fashioned; he didn't believe in Socialism nor Freudian theories of abnormality nor modern painting, novels, and poetry. That is, when one said that he didn't believe in these things one meant that he considered them all and found them wanting, or, if not wanting, at least not perfection.

Especially with regard to Free Love he was too irritating for words. It was not that Rosalind desired lovers—far from it—but she believed in the theory of freedom, freedom for everybody to do just what they liked provided they left herself alone. But Tom had a hampered, restricted mind. He thought things "horrid" or "bad form." As a husband he would be too tiresome. As a friend he was charming, courteous, unselfish, humorous, gentle. He was intellectually "behind the times," a quite impossible thing for a modern husband.

They had arrived. Old Lady Anglish kissed them both and asked them to luncheon two days from now. They didn't know. They couldn't say. They would telephone. It was too kind of her to have brought them like this. They *were* grateful! The cab tottered off. They mounted the stairs to their little flat, and once in the sitting-room Rosalind sank into the arm-chair with the crimson peacocks, stretched her arms, yawned, and shivered.

"Of course Frances has let the fire go, although you especially told her."

"It's late. Nearly three. We'll go to bed and be warm in no time." Janet stood up, staring in front of her, seeing through walls and walls and walls far into Destiny.

"Ugh! How I detest this flat! It's shut in like a mortuary. Everything wants re-covering." Then Rosalind smiled. She had remembered something. She got up, disappeared into the next room, returned, a parcel in her hand.

She stood up against her sister smiling very prettily.

"Three o'clock in the morning is an absurd time to give you anything. But I can't wait. I got it this afternoon."

"For me? A present?" Janet's eyes shone, because like all good people she adored presents.

She took the little gilt scissors from the table, cut the string (a wicked proceeding), there was a thin wooden box with a lid, then cotton wool, then——

"Oh, take care!" Rosalind cried. "You'll drop it!"

But not Janet. Slowly, with all the eager awfulness of anticipation, she drew out the treasure. She held it out. She gasped.

It was the loveliest thing, *quite* the loveliest thing ever seen. It was a little tree, silver and white and green. Its leaves were of coloured metal, its flowers of silver, and it stood in a porphyry bowl. It was perfect. It was enchanted. Already, held there in Janet's hand, it had a life of its own, a magical life, gleaming, glittering under the electric light, but encased too in its own shining armour that held it apart, by itself, in its own natural and unstained beauty.

Janet gazed and gazed. She could not speak. Tears filled her eyes. That Rosalind should have given her this, Rosalind whom she loved so utterly, Rosalind——

She placed it on the table, then caught her sister into her arms and held her, cheek against cheek, held her as though it were for life.

"Why, Mops dear, you're crying!" Rosalind gently withdrew herself. "You *do* like it, then! I thought you would. I was at a little sale this afternoon—you know, Marie Haik's thing—and I saw one or two of these, and I had to get one. They were made by Mrs. Somebody or other, I forget the name, but she's married and got lots of money and just does them for pleasure. I saw it and I *had* to get it. It was too awfully sweet. I said to myself, 'That's just the thing for Mops!' "

She spoke a little eagerly, a little nervously. To see Janet in tears, controlled and wise-minded Janet, was embarrassing. And she didn't want to be thanked. It made her remember all the wicked selfish things she was always doing.

Janet wiped her eyes. But still she couldn't speak. The thing was too lovely, but lovelier still was it that Rosalind should have bought it, bought it of her own generous volition without any prompting and given it her now, of all time, just when she had *such* a piece of news to deliver!

"Oh, Rosalind . . . I'm so glad. It was wonderful of you, but more than that . . . just now . . . I would rather that you gave me something just now than at any other time in all our lives."

She turned round to it, gazing at it, drinking in its beauties.

"It makes me feel safer, your giving me that just now. It makes me feel that perhaps I've done right. It's a sign."

"A sign! Of what?" Rosalind was now watching her sister. "I knew all the time that we were coming home that something had happened to you. What is it? Have we come into money?"

"Yes, in a way." Janet's eyes lingered passionately on her sister's face. "But that's a horrid way to put it. I told Lord Poole to-night that I would marry him!"

"Oh! . . . Oh!"

It was Rosalind's turn. She threw her arms around Janet, kissing her, kissing her, kissing her:

"Oh, oh, oh! . . . Oh! How lovely! How beautiful! How perfect! I've been longing, been hoping, been aching for it to happen! You darling, you pet, you Perfect! Oh, Mops, you'll be a Duchess—my Mops will be a Duchess. You'll have everything you want and be happy for ever. And I'll be Wildherne's sister—good old Wildherne—and no more of this beastly flat. Oh, Mops! how heavenly!"

Then she saw, through her joy, the tears still standing in Janet's eyes.

"But you're happy about it, Mops darling, aren't you? You love him, don't you, and he loves you? It's all going to be perfect?"

"I don't know," Janet answered slowly. "Nothing's perfect ever, is it? And I don't love him. I love no one in the world but you. Perhaps it's a wicked thing I've done. It *would* be wicked if I didn't love him and he *did* love me. But he doesn't love me either. We were both quite honest about it."

"Oh, of course." Rosalind's voice was slow. "There's Diana Guard. I'd forgotten. But Diana doesn't care for him any longer. The whole world knows that."

"Yes, but he cares for her. The only one he's ever loved, and he will love her always, he said."

"Janet! Have you done this for me? Tell me—because if you have——"

"No, dear, of course not. A little for you perhaps, but a great deal for myself. I like him—better than any other man I know. And he likes me—better than any other woman except that one. I don't know that love's so important—not in these days. To be good companions is the thing. And I want to do something with my life. Here I am wasting away, getting old. I shall never love any man, not passionately as people mean by love. But I will be good to him and he will be good to me. And I can be of use to other people as well."

And Rosalind, reassured, was brilliantly happy again. Surely it was the most glorious, glorious event! No more this old flat, no more wondering where the next penny would come from. "We shan't be rich, you know," Janet put in. Lots of amusing people. "We shall have to be often in Halkin Street," Janet interrupted again, "and *that* won't be very amusing." Her darling Mops a Duchess. "They are both very alive, and long may they be so," Janet remarked again. Oh well, anyway, a Marchioness, and even if those things didn't mean very much these days, and nobody minded, still it was better than being cooped up in this hateful little flat. . . .

But at the end of her triumph she folded her arms around Janet.

"You are sure. You swear it isn't for me you're doing this?"

"I swear," Janet answered. "If I didn't like him nothing would induce me."

She turned to the little silver tree as though invoking its friendship.

Alone in her room, brushing her hair, gazing into her glass, Janet considered everything. Rosalind's joy had reassured her. There at least was happiness. But for herself? A little chill caught her body. She shivered, dropping the brushes, pressing her hands to her breast, staring into the glass as though passionately demanding from the face that she saw there a comforting answer. Marriage? And with a man whom she did not love? It was a reassurance to her that he did not love her; she would not have to submit to his passion, but he wanted children, and what would that intercourse be for them both deprived of passion? Would he not close his eyes and imagine that in his arms he held another dearly-loved woman? And she? Could she shelter herself enough behind her liking for him? Did she like him enough for *that?*

She had not met him so seldom. She knew his courtesy, his kindliness to others. She liked him best in his relation to his father and mother, to whom he was devoted. But then who could help but be devoted to the old Duke? No difficult task for any son.

Did she care for Wildherne Poole in any physical way whatever? Did she like him to be near her, was she happier when he took her hand, did her heart beat if he entered a room where she was?

No, none of these things. It was many years now since she had felt the stirring of her blood for any man. During these ten years since her mother's death all passion, all longing, all unselfishness, all ambition had been buried in her sister.

From the very first days when Rosalind had been carried out by the nurse on to the bright lawn at Sopover and the sun, enmeshed, had glittered in her hair, that passion had burned. Rosalind had always been so lovely, so amusing, so alive, so *packed* with charm. It had always been Rosalind whom everyone had noticed, and during that last awful week when Pamela Grandison had realised that she was leaving her two girls alone, and almost friendless, to fight their hard battle, it had been "Rosalind—Rosalind—Rosalind. . . . Look after her, Janet darling. She hasn't your character. She can't put up with things as you can. Look after her——"

Janet switched off the light, got into bed, lay down, staring into the darkness. It was true. Rosalind had not the character. Janet was no fool about her sister; she knew that she was selfish, comfort-loving, hard in sudden unexpected places. She, Janet, was never quite sure whether Rosalind loved her or no. Sometimes she did, and sometimes most certainly she did not. She was elusive, always just out of Janet's reach. And was not that very elusiveness partly responsible for Janet's passion? Do we not love the most those persons of whose love for us we are not quite sure?

But darling Rosalind, there was more, far more, than that in Janet's love for her. The struggle of these ten years, the increasing struggle as prices had gone up and up and the tiny investments had gone down and down, the sense that there was no one in the world who cared, no one but distant Luttrell and Grandison relations, no one at least whom proud Janet would humiliate herself to beg from. Her own best friends—Rachel Seddon, Mary Coane, Ada Danant, Constance Medley—all women, by the way, older than herself, had they ever realised *at all* how desperate the struggle was for Janet and Rosalind? And were not they themselves also hard up like all their set, like all their world? Wasn't the need for more money the one cry that nowadays you heard on every side of you? Hadn't Connie Medley her hat shop, and wasn't Ada Danant dressmaking, and hadn't Janet herself spent months of her life turning old shoes into new ones?

The same with all of them. Why should they then demand more charity than the rest?

Charity! No! Hateful word!

But wasn't it charity that Janet was about to receive from Wildherne Poole? Was she going to him for any reason but the mercenary one? Would she have considered marriage with him for a moment had she and Rosalind been rich?

Yes, she would. The answer came to her with astonishing clearness out of the darkness. She wanted to do more with her life than she was doing. She wanted (strangely, pathetically she knew it) to care for somebody who would quite definitely care for her. She wanted to feel affection for someone who would not, as Rosalind did, at one moment accept her, at another violently reject her. She wanted some sort of society in addition to the excitement of her love for Rosalind. This other thing would not be exciting at all—quite orderly, safe, rather humdrum. But always there and to be relied on. And she would be there for him too. He had his passion elsewhere and that would make him, as passion always does, restless and unhappy and unsatisfied. And she would be there for him to come home to. Someone upon whom he could absolutely rely.

She could not sleep. She turned on her light and lay, watching the pool of purple shadow encircling the little table, the three or four books, a photograph of her mother in a silver frame. Life! What was it? Why did she make so much of this step that she was taking? What matter it if it gave

Rosalind happiness, Wildherne Poole a son, the old Duke and Duchess comfort? She felt herself deprived of all personality. She lay there without body, without soul. Only a tiny impetus pushing others who were alive into more agreeable positions.

Then her life leapt back into her veins. She was *not* negative. She was as alive as they. For ten years, nay, for twenty years she had given herself wholly to others. Now her own time had come.

Then, as though there were disloyalty in this, she felt an aching longing for Rosalind. She must see her, know that she was there, touch her ever so gently.

She rose from her bed, found her dressing-gown and slippers, and stole from the room.

She opened Rosalind's door very gently and then stood there silently listening. From beyond the windows came that strange purring rumble of the London traffic. Once and again some heavier vehicle broke up the murmur and scattered it and the flat quivered, ever so gently, as though it were responding to the life beyond it. Above the murmur was Rosalind's regular soft breathing.

Janet moved forward very gently, felt the hard line of the bed, touched the pillow with her hand, then sank down on to the floor gathering her dressing-gown about her. She rested her head on the bedclothes without touching her sister.

Something deep, deep within her prayed. "Make her happy, God. Make her happy. If I'm doing wrong in this punish me but not her. Give her a lovely life. Give her everything. Make her happy."

She did not know whether she believed in a God. It was the fashion now not to. But sometimes it seemed to her that someone bent down and gathered her up and warmed her heart. A weak sentimental illusion, her friends would tell her. But to-night she was not thinking of her friends. In that dark murmuring room the outside world could not have its say.

She felt comforted and warmed.

Very very softly she leaned forward and kissed her sister's cheek. Then returned to her bed and slept.

CHAPTER III

LORD JOHN BEAMINSTER had had chambers for more than twenty years now at 90 Piccadilly, which is at the Piccadilly end of Half Moon Street, and the doors thereof confront the windows of that excellent haberdasher's, Messrs. Dare and Dolphin.

Lord John had lived there so long because he liked the view. He of course looked over the Green Park into the very eye of her late August Majesty Queen Victoria, and on the left of her there were the towers of Westminster and on the right Buckingham Palace. He stood, his legs widely planted, his thick back steadily set, like a captain directing his vessel, and for more than twenty years now had he thus sailed over that green misty sea, and always the farther he sailed, the farther did her August Majesty discreetly withdraw!

But he was not ruffled by this frustration. He rejoiced in it, and he rejoiced also in the spume and froth thrown up at his very feet, and felt as he looked down at the cascades and jets of humanity tossed fruitlessly at his walls all the pride of a good old mariner in his taut and seaworthy vessel.

To a visitor primed with his best cognac tossing his head he would say: "Just look at 'em! Pretty busy, what? And yet in here with the windows closed you can't hear a sound. And even with 'em open it don't worry you." And here he would look round upon his walls, upon the reproductions of Wheatley's "Street Cries"—the mezzotints, the "Ladies Waldegrave," and the others were in the little dining-room—and the old French clock with the naked Diana in gold, and the Louis XVI. sofa and chairs, and the glass book-cases with the bound sets of Madame de Sevignè and Sainte-Simon, and the ten volumes of *The Mistresses of the Kings of France,* and, primed also with his own excellent cognac, would feel kindly and amiable and entirely optimistic about everything.

That had always been his "note," that confidence in his own seaworthy vessel. Neither the little South African War nor the big World War which with all the social changes that followed them had at heart at all disturbed him, although for convention's sake he would complain of the "changed times," and that "things were not, dammit, at all as they used to be." But because his digestion was still so excellent, and because he had that best of all gifts the power to enjoy a good moment to its full consciously at the very instant that it was occurring, nothing but a collapse in his health would ever disturb him. It was not that he was selfish or hard-hearted. The sorrows of others grieved him, and he did many kindnesses in a quiet unobtrusive way, but life now in his seventy-seventh year was as good and rich to him as it had been in his seventh when his father had put him for the first time on his first pony.

When he did think of social conditions—and it was hard enough in these days to avoid them—he felt sure that the miseries of other people as recounted by other people were greatly exaggerated.

He had been told that he must read the novels of Mr. James Fossett, and faithfully he had read four or five of them. But he would read no more. Partly because they seemed so closely to resemble one another—there was a Policeman in all of them—and partly because the picture they presented did not at all resemble any life that he himself knew. The characters seemed to be in a sad repressed state, held down firmly by the cold hand of their author. He longed to watch them all out at play when Mr. Fossett had no longer his eye upon them.

Nor was it his experience that the Lower Orders were always unhappy. The Policeman on the corner of Half Moon Street—four to twelve one week and eight to four the next—was a good friend of his—he invited him sometimes when the weather was bad to the enjoyment of a glass of whisky —a very cheerful individual with a charming wife and two

handsome little boys. Old Fullerton—head man in these
Chambers for the last thirty years—found life anything but
depressing; and the old man who sold the *Evening News* by
the "In and Out" could be heard whistling to himself any
fine evening .

One morning he awoke, as ever, to the consciousness of
Fullerton's soft and unobtrusive entrance just as the clocks
in the sitting-room (the golden Diana) and the dining-room
were chanting the eight o'clock hour. Fullerton moved very
lightly for so stout a man, and always now for twenty years
Beaminster had wanted to snap out at him, "For God's sake,
Fullerton, you're not a cat!" A solemn notion, when you
looked into it, that this had been the first thought of your
day for more than twenty years!

But sleep had not vanished far enough for such daylight
energy, and also lying on the bed close to hand was the virgin
Morning Post, unravished as yet by the sighs, curses, aspira-
tions, triumphant discoveries of any vulgar reader.

He was older now also. He did not move so easily nor so
swiftly as he had once done; his body seemed to be cast into
the mould of the sheets and blankets that had cherished him
so lovingly all night. He might just lazily stretch his arm and
draw the *Morning Post* towards him, and this movement
coincided always with Fullerton's rasp of the cherry-
coloured silk curtains that once on a day Adela had insisted
upon, "because this room's so grisly—you *must* have some
colour," and was followed by the vision of Fullerton's broad
beam as he bent forward to gather together the discarded
evening clothes. Next step through the advancing hour was
the question, "What sort of a day?" and then Fullerton's
straightening body, the sudden projection of his round red
face, and the thick, rather husky answer: "Not bad, my
lord." "A little foggy this morning, my lord," or "Nice
bright morning, my lord."

Followed on this the bomb-like intrusion of the world
from China to Peru. The Himalayas leaned their snows
across the dressing-table, the torrents of Niagara tumbled
over the wardrobe, the rivers of China trickled across the
little rug from Teheran in front of the fire-place, the shout-

ing multitudes of Wall Street shattered the glass of the
Queen Anne mirror. Impassively Lord John surveyed chaos,
only once and again for Fullerton's benefit murmured,
"Those damned Balkans again," or "That feller that buried
his girl in a chicken-run is going to swing," or "No knowing
where these Bolsheviks are going to stop," and Fullerton
would reply, "Yes, my lord," or "No, my lord," or entering
more fully into the question would remember once when he
had been with Sir Asprey Fartingale or Colonel Meadows,
who had the floor above this in 1913, used to say that . . .
and to this no answer would issue from the bed.

Then the Bath and the Exercises. Beaminster was proud
of his body as, stretched on his toes, he slowly raised his
arms and counted ten. A decent, white, plump, symmetrical
body it was, everything moving a trifle more slowly than it
used to, but no rebellion anywhere, no refusal to function.

Once in a while there was a twinge of something, and if
this twinge occurred twice or thrice Barley Harter would be
consulted, there would follow perhaps a change of diet, port
would be dropped, or a fortnight at Bath or Harrogate
recommended; but for the most part things proceeded
smoothly enough, and soon there would be that slippery sliding into that bath with blue tiles so that your body like a
round white fish flapped and slithered and ever so gently
rolled. . . .

At nine o'clock precisely there came the best moment of
the day when, clothed and in his right mind, dark blue suit,
pearl pin in black tie, hair so snowy white that it seemed to
glow with some internal light of its own, face rubicund,
round, kindly and smooth in spite of its reputed years as any
baby's, John Beaminster sat down to his breakfast.

On this particular morning snow lay over the land and a
bright sun shone in the heavens. The landscape before the
windows lay in a whiteness unbroken save by gentle purple
shadows between the avenue of crystal sparkling trees that
stretched down to the Victoria Memorial, and the reflected
light of this whiteness shone into the little roof of the flat
with its ivory walls, gleaming tablecloth, and low white book-
cases.

Beaminster sat in this temple of glittering crystal before his coffee and eggs. He sat there smiling like the image of some Egyptian King of the 18th Dynasty—some Tutmose or Rameses—carved there in a crystal of ivory and purple for immortality. Then the egg was tapped, the coffee poured out, the letters opened, and immortality was shattered.

His thoughts, shot through with the sunshine, danced through his brain.

This was pleasant, this lovely morning, and he was in excellent health, and the coffee was hot, and the letters were agreeable. He opened them slowly one after another. Old Lady Meryon, Ball Hartop, a tailor, a wine merchant, a race-meeting, an invitation to dinner, to a house party, to Scotland. . . . Then a note from young Tom Seddon:

DEAR UNCLE JOHN—I shall pop in about four to-morrow (Tuesday) for an hour if I may. I've something to tell you. Just ring Grosvenor 4763 if that doesn't suit. I'm in till eleven.—Yours affectionately,

TOM.

He regarded this piece of paper covered with the big, boyish, sprawling hand affectionately, and when his breakfast was finished carried the letter with him into the other room, leaving the others upon the table.

He loved that boy. Standing motionless in a pool of sunlight, his white hair shining, he reflected upon how deeply he loved him. Now in his old age at last, when he might have yielded up all desire for human contacts involving as they must human trouble and self-sacrifice, this deep attachment had come to him. Come to him without his asking. He had always been interested in him, of course, Rachel's boy, but it was only during the last three years that he had been aware of this deep, yearning, unsatisfied affection.

Unsatisfied because the boy could not respond in that way. Why should he? He was not his son, no, nor his nephew, although he called him Uncle. His great-uncle. What an awful word, implying such a deadly distance of age and experience. How could they be friends with all those generations between them? And yet they had achieved something. The boy was a good boy, responding spontaneously, warmly to kindness, not selfish like so many of his generation, warm-hearted, and not afraid to show his feelings.

But—Uncle John! A good old codger, wonderful for his years, remarkable how he keeps up with things. Oh yes. Beaminster knew what the point of view must be.

Nevertheless the boy came to him for help when he was in difficulty. Here he was in love with this girl who, likely enough, cared nothing for him. Funny life was—you cared for somebody and somebody cared for somebody else, and that somebody cared for somebody else again. . . . Perhaps the point was in the caring, not in the returned affection. Look out, Uncle John! That's a platitude most despised of all creatures in this our wonderful age!

But Uncle John, standing in his pool of sunlight looking at the rough scribbled note with eyes of pride and affection, thought nothing of platitudes. By God, he was a good boy, and if the girl didn't like him she should be made to!

This girl (he sat down to continue his reflections), this Grandison girl, with what had she caught the boy? Well, she was good-looking, beautiful even, and John Beaminster had loved enough beautiful women in his life to realise what beauty could do. But had she anything else but beauty? He had talked to her but seldom, and on those occasions he had fancied that her eyes had been restless, searching about the room for others who were younger or more interesting. He had fancied that, perhaps. When you were over seventy, if you still cared for life you did fancy things sometimes. She was poor. Every one in London knew how poor were she and her sister. And she would be extravagant. A girl with that hair and those obstinate ambitious eyes!

But he fancied also that she did not care for the boy. She was flying, he fancied, after higher game, and if that were so wasn't the boy in for a bad time? Nonsense! We all go through it. It's good for the young. Teaches them self-control. The young, yes. But his own particular Tom! He did not wish him to suffer. He wanted him to have the happiest time! And that was not a boy to take things lightly! He would feel it. This was no passing fancy of his. The old man, looking back to an earlier evening, remembered how Tom had said to him, "Uncle John, I love that girl. I must marry her. I must."

And here a strange feeling, new to Beaminster, twisted his heart. A twist of jealousy. That was it. Jealousy of a girl like that, a light-weight? No, jealousy of love, wanting someone to love him, almost anyone, someone to whom he might still be everything . . . as he had once been, yes, and several times . . . but now, when you were old. . . .

The sunlight struck his chair, stroked his face. He chuckled. Why, he was like any old woman with his love and the rest. Straightening his shoulders he got up, crossed to the table, and sat down to write his letters.

Later on he went out.

As he turned the corner into Piccadilly the frosty air, the brilliant sunlight, confirmed him the more readily in the conviction, long held and never seriously threatened, that this Town belonged to him. Many men, passing along that same road, held that same conviction—and the conviction further that as this their Town was the finest, grandest, most beautiful, and most civilised Town in the world, that world also was theirs.

They held this conviction with no arrogance, and did not even know that they held it. Had you attacked their conviction and informed them that the slums in this Town were among the worst in the universe, that the streets were seething with extreme Socialism, that the organisation and Councils of the Town were incompetent and old-fashioned, that the ladies who paraded Jermyn Street from five in the evening until five in the morning were a disgrace and a scandal, they would have, pleasantly and courteously, agreed with you. Only had you attacked the Police Force of their stronghold would they, but yet courteously, have objected. And your objections, completely admitted by them, would only have confirmed them in their confidence.

Beaminster did not consciously think of London, but, taking his part in that admirable procession moving slowly and haughtily (but not arrogantly) on its way, his heart beat in unison with its every movement; every tree in the Green Park was his tree, every cigarette in every tobacconist's shop, every shirt in every haberdasher's, every stone in the Devonshire House wall (doomed so immediately to destruction), every flower in the florist's beyond the Berkeley Hotel—they were all his.

Once and again he would stop at a shop window and glance. His pause was slight, his gaze swift and comprehensive. Some daffodils, snatched from the Scillies, stirred his heart. They cost, had he wished to inquire, two shillings a bloom—but what matter since already they were his? He approved of their presence there, and that was enough.

From the corner of Bond Street to the Circus the procession of the possessors of the Town was democratised. Only here and there it appeared intermingled with other processions—the Procession of the Tourists, the Procession of the Hewers of Wood and the Drawers of Water, the Procession of the New Rich, the Procession of the Scavengers, the Procession of the Thieves and Vagabonds, the Procession of the Upholders of Morality, the Procession of Freudians, the Procession of the Thoroughly Married. With none of these did Beaminster have any concern.

He approved benevolently of the shop where they sold cheap stationery, of the haberdasher with the silk dressing-gowns, of Thomas Cook's Agency, and he glanced happily across the street at Mr. Hatchard's Bookshop, the establishment of Keith Prowse, and Prince's Restaurant.

Then came the sight that every day made his heart beat a little faster—St. James's Church, sheltered by its trees now crystal-silver against the sky, protected by its ivory-grey wall.

Always, every day, it was the same; he was drawn, as it were against his will, to cross exactly there, just when the picture shop with the sketch of the Prince of Wales in the window and Sackville Street with all its Tailors implored him to remain. No, just there he must cross, look up for an instant at the clock, and then pass on.

His church. It had been so for seventy-seven years. It was looking very well this morning, thank you. It did him justice.

The Processions tumbled into Piccadilly Circus, scattering

into tangled patterns only resolved into unity by the superb
Police Force under the tender beneficence of the Protecting
Eros.

But thence it was Beaminster's Town no longer. When he
had time he preferred to turn down St. James's Street, and
so along Pall Mall and up into Leicester Square again could
keep his Town around him for a little while longer.

During his walk through Coventry Street he considered
his affairs and looked no longer at the things and persons
around him. He did not feel himself now superior to his surroundings, but it was another world, a world that would not
thank him for his attention. Had he thought of them with
observation he would in all probability have felt them to be
superior to himself, because this was a working world and
his was not, or had not until lately been. But, lacking imagination, he did not perceive that these people were quite
real; they resembled the figures of the cinematograph which
on occasion he visited. They were all in one dimension, unac-
countably vanishing and reappearing, obeying no known law.

Down Leicester Square, past the little garden sparkling
white under the sun, he flung off on the one side the cheap
journalism of the newspaper shop and on the other the
gleaming canvases of the Leicester Galleries, and so reached
his bourne.

He stood, patiently, amiably, before the oak door, with the
grille unobtrusive like its superior members, of the Zoffany
Club.

He looked at his watch. Until a quarter to one precisely
that door was closed. He heard, gently harmonious across
the clear winter air, the chimes of Big Ben sounding the
quarter. The door opened and he passed inside.

The Zoffany Club is famous and precious because it is so
very ancient and so very small, and because the heart of London lies within its ebony and silver casket; this one of the
six Londons, London being divided under the six Poets—
Virgilius, Horatius, Catullus, Ovidius, Tullius, and Lesbia.
Here we are under Horatius.

There is but one room, long and lofty, of black oak, scattered with the gleaming silver of Georgian bowls and Caro-

turian jugs. There are Whistler etchings and Hogarthian prints and Baxter simplicities, and the wide, deep bow-window looks out on to the trees and traffic of that happy Square embracing the Alhambra, the Garrick Theatre, the National Portrait Gallery, and the best (if occasional) Punch and Judy show in England.

Young men who are fortunate enough to be elected to the Zoffany pass through three very definite stages; and this is reasonable enough, because the Zoffany, as everyone knows, is like a friend or a lover, and in every friendship and every love three stages of progess are inevitable. At first the young men are pleased because they are chosen, membership being difficult. They like the look of the room, the kindliness and discretion of the servants of the Zoffany (who are all called Edward, whether that be their name or no); they sniff the genial air with happy anticipations, that air of the Horatian London compounded of snuff and wax candles, cognac and fog, ancient leather and the most aromatic tobacco. They like to see the lights steal into the lamps beyond the bow-window, to watch the trees darken against the evening sky, and they may fancy if they please that Gainsborough and Reynolds, Hogarth and Constable crowd the windows of the National Portrait Gallery, and watch the sky signs of Trafalgar Square and the stiff German angles of Nurse Cavell with bewildered wonder.

They are pleased also maybe to sit at the long table with the most Ancient of Living Diplomatists, the most honourably battered of British Generals, the most beautifully silent of London Exquisites, and to find these great figures among the kindest and most genial of the human race.

But the Second Stage is swiftly reached. The world is full of a number of things; there are clubs not far away with cocktail bars and Turkish baths; the company of the Diplomat, the General, and the Exquisite may seem a trifle too monotonous in its regularity; there is but one room, one table, one Edward, one grill, one fireplace, one sofa. They vanish and pass away.

And then with some, but not with all (the Zoffany quietly chooses its own), the Third Stage is reached. Something draws them back. Other clubs may have their gaiety and splendours, their cards and diversions, their Point-to-Point and Golfing Gymkhanas, their guest-rooms and their Ladies' Chambers—there is only one Zoffany. For them there will be to the end of their long London club days no other club from world's end to world's end, no other grill, no other Georgian bowls, no other Edward, no other bow-window, and so, in their turn and in their own good time, they will become the most ancient of Diplomats, Generals, or Exquisites, sinking gently in the tender arms of the Zoffany to their eternal rest.

It was thus precisely that Beaminster felt about the Zoffany. But to-day, entering the room, he saw at a glance that he had no luck. Seated one on either side of the long table were the two men whom, of all the Zoffany Company, he liked the least, Pompey Turle and Charles Ravage. Pompey was not the Christian name given to Mr. Turle by his godfathers and godmother in baptism, but rather by his critics and detractors (of whom there were alas many) in his later years. He was a stout, heavy, lowering, over-moustached Foreign Office official who had written a small book on *Shelley,* reviewed a little in the more eclectic weeklies, and reduced the art of bad manners to a noble science.

Because of his self-satisfied pomposities he was christened Pompey, and because of his intolerable self-satisfaction and priggish superiorities men fled from before him as from the wrath of God.

Beaminster loathed him with all the loathing of one who had been taught to value courtesy before riches and kindliness of soul before intellect.

But Pompey Turle was important to no one save himself. Charles Ravage was another matter.

Ravage was the only child of Colonel Forester Ravage and Lady Evelyn Garth, whose history is public property and a very ancient story. Because of that same story Charles Ravage was now alone in a world that adored him, living recklessly on an income allowed him by his uncle, Lord Cairis, who loved him beyond reason.

Why the world adored him and his uncle loved him Beaminster had never been able to discover. He was nothing to look at, a little black man none too carefully groomed; he had never very much to say for himself, but stared at you with his blue-black eyes set like buttons in his blue-black face, as though he considered you too foolish to be possible.

He made many people uncomfortable, and especially old gentlemen of John Beaminster's age and tradition.

He had thirty years, a small flat in Mount Street, a loose reputation, and the adoration of his set and generation.

He was important to Beaminster because young Tom Seddon liked him.

Here, then, were the two men whom of all others Beaminster detested—the only two men in the long, mellow, sunny room. He made the best of it, sat smilingly down with them and listened to Pompey's oration on the present state of China. But while Pompey, like a complacent bluebottle, boomed his way along, Beaminster's thoughts were busy. He had come here to-day with a very definite purpose, and that purpose was to make sure that Tom Seddon was safe for election next month when his name would come before the august Committee. Neither Turle nor Ravage could be of any reassurance to him in that, but he hoped that someone —Barty Sonter or Monmouth or Felchester—on the Committee would soon appear and give him the comforting word. Not that he had any real doubt. No one had anything against Tom; he was a popular lad; they wanted youngsters in the club; he, Beaminster, was reason enough to ensure Tom's election, but the old man must catch the words from someone in authority: "Young Seddon? Oh, he's all right! Just the kind of boy we want!"

Then, as he sat there, ordering a steak from Edward and a pint of his own particular Zoffany claret, facing the dark countenance of Ravage, the strangest intimation crept over him that Ravage was, in one way or another, threatening his peace and security.

He had never been a man given to intimations or warnings, he had never before felt any especial connection with Ravage save that Ravage despised him (and, like the rest of us, he did not regard with favour those who despised him), but to-day there was something much more definite, something that made him physically uncomfortable, as though his collar-stud had slipped down the back of his neck or his shoes were pinching him.

He could not take his eyes from the other man's face, and he felt as though Ravage knew of this and was maliciously and contemptuously pleased at it. At last he asked Ravage some question or another, and on the man quietly answering it he went on :

"By the way, a young nephew of mine whom I think you know is coming up here next month—Tom Seddon—I wish you'd write your name on his page."

"Oh yes," said Ravage. "A nice boy. I like him."

He smiled at Beaminster.

"Isn't he rather young for this place?" boomed Turle. "Still got to win his spurs, hasn't he?"

Anger boiled in old Beaminster. Quietly he answered :

"We want some young fellows here, too many old fogies like myself. Club will die out if we don't take care."

"All the same, the Club doesn't want babes in arms," Turle pleasantly continued. Beaminster choked. Edward, alarmed, hurried towards him. Ravage amazingly came to his rescue.

"Glad you're not on the Committee, Turle," he said. "We'd have a nice lot of duds in here if you were. Young Seddon's just right for this place. No need for me to write my name. He's safe enough. And I don't know that my name's much help to anyone either."

He got up and went with his funny, rather lurching walk over to the Candidates' Book. As he stood there looking at it he revealed the odd shortness of his legs, short, thick, stumpy, out of proportion to his body. Better-looking fellow had he longer legs. Funny chap, with his short, black, scrubby hair, his blue-black countenance, his staring eyes.

Then Felchester came in. Beaminster was greatly relieved. He was in his own world once more.

But until Ravage left the room he was not truly comfortable. Something dangerous about that fellow! Something threatening!

About a quarter-past three he withdrew from his beloved sanctum where, half asleep, he had pleasantly listened to old

Porter Carrick's hunting adventures in Leicestershire, and
quietly proceeded to possess himself of a corner of Trafalgar
Square, half Pall Mall (including the Athenæum Club), and
the whole of St. James's.

St. James's was his own especial and inviolable property,
and never, he was pleased to see, had it looked better than
on this especial winter's afternoon—"all frosted over like
a cake," he thought appreciatively, "with a red sun cocking
its cheeky countenance over the Ryder Street flats, and all
the chimneys smoking like hell."

He was to-day greatly appreciative of Mr. Spinks's fine
array. Spinks's shop window was his favourite in the whole
of London—he gave it a look once a week at least when he
was in town. In other days he had purchased charming things
there, but now—well, there were not many women left now
to whom he cared to make presents. This thought, coming
to him quite unexpectedly, depressed him for a moment. He
stared with a sentimental fixity at the god Horus whose beak-
shaped countenance returned him stare for stare. Not many
women in his life any more, by God!—and Horus answered
him, "There's a time for everything!"

So there is! All his spirits were back again as he strode
off up the happy little hill towards Jermyn Street. Here indeed was for him a land of memories!

Every step was consecrated ground, consecrated to this
passion, that hazard and folly, this exquisite surprise, that
plot and plan, this discovery and that thundering disappointment.

And not only his own memories, but every masculine en-
terprise had here its consecrated triumph. Ghosts, recognised
by him from the long years of his own adventure, crowded
in upon him—dapper ghosts with their hats a little cocked,
their moustaches twirled, their canes fluttering, their eyes
boldly exploring. He could name them—Datchett, Cobham,
Harry Winchester, Fordie Munt, Tinden, Rake Lacket,
Borden-Cave, young Ponting Beaminster his cousin, poor
Will Reckets—yes, ghosts, and soon he too would join their
gathering and would hang like the rest about the windows of
White's, the chimney-pots of Ryder Street, the haberdashers

and bootshops of Jermyn Street . . . but what matter it!
Plenty of life in the old dog, and young Tom to carry on the
tradition after him when he was gone!

Young Tom was there already waiting for him when he
came in. The boy was quite at home, seated, his long legs
stretched out in front of him, his thin nose stuck in the
Evening Standard.

He jumped up at the sight of his uncle and stood there
smiling, and Beaminster also smiled, thinking what a nice
boy he was, the straightest and cleanest and handsomest in
all London.

Fullerton came in to draw the dark purple curtains, the
tea was placed at their side, they drew close to the happy fire.

"And now, Tom, what's your news?"

"Why, Miss Grandison, the older one, is engaged to Lord
Poole!"

Here *was* a piece of news! Beaminster, who had been leaning towards the fire, sat up with a jerk. His round pink face
seemed to swell with astonishment.

"To Poole! But——" then checking himself because the
boy was too young for current scandal. "When did you hear
this? Is it sure?"

"Quite certain. It was the night before last at Lady Madden's."

"Why, then, he—— But what will she—— The old Duke
will be pleased. Just what he would like. But I never dreamt
that Poole——"

He stared at the piece of buttered toast between his fingers,
slipped it into his mouth, wiped his fingers on his silk hand-
kerchief, felt blindly for the blue enamel cigarette-box at
his side.

"Poole! Good heavens!"

"Yes, don't you see?" Tom Seddon broke in eagerly.
"That leaves her sister all alone. While she's had her sister,
who adored her, she wouldn't want anybody else, but now
she's certain to marry."

"Who's certain to marry?" asked Beaminster, still thinking of Poole and his private affairs.

"Why, Rosalind—Miss Grandison, the young one. She'll

think of me now. She won't like being left. I'm sure sh
cares for me. She couldn't say the things she does—— Oh
Uncle John," he sprang to his feet. "She will take me. Sh
must. Why shouldn't she? She'll never find anybody wh
loves her better. I'll make a career. With her to work for
could do anything. Uncle John, you don't know what i
feels like."

Uncle John nodded his head.

"Don't I? Do you suppose because I'm over seventy I'v
forgotten anything? That's the time you begin to remember
And I've got plenty to look back to. Although I'm a bacheloi
it doesn't mean . . ." He broke off and looked up, his eye:
full of affection.

"Tom, my boy, don't set yourself on this too completely
Keep yourself a bit outside of it if you can until you know
she cares for you. It's easy enough for someone who isn'i
in it to advise you, but all the same you're yourself. Nobody
can touch you. I've learnt that from life. Life can hurt lik
the devil, and the more it sees it hurts the more it uses its
power. I remember there was a woman once. . . ." He broke
off again. "No, what's the use? You've got to take your own
medicine. If she did marry you what would you live on ?
She hasn't got anything, has she?"

"No, she hasn't, but I've got my Foreign Office pay and—
and—don't laugh at me, but I fancy I can write a bit."

"Write? That's a new idea. Write what?"

"Well, articles—politics. I'm frightfully keen on politics,
Uncle Tom. I mean to go into Parliament later on and
then——"

"Politics !" Beaminster shook his head. "It's a dirty game,
especially nowadays the way things are going."

"No, but that's just what it oughtn't to be. There are a
number of us—Forsyte, Harry Grendon, Godfrey Maule,
Bum Chichester, the Darrants, Humphrey Weddon—we've
formed a club of our own ; we all have the same idea."

"Oh! and what's that idea?" Beaminster inquired.

Tom Seddon began to pace the room. "It's this way.
There's all this class trouble, and then there's downing of the
Upper Classes, every book and paper saying they're no good

any more, that they're all rotten, never facing anything but dance and drink all night, and if they're not like that, why, then, they're so reactionary that they're right behind the times and selfish, only caring to keep their own class on top. We're all of us under thirty and we know that that's tommy rot. We aren't always drinking cocktails, and we believe that our class and its traditions means a lot to England, and that if you keep the fine side of it you'll be making better history for England than if you let it all go. What we feel is that we can do more for England, and for the world too, by being ourselves instead of pretending to be parlour Socialists and sham Bolsheviks. We *keep* our class with all that's been best in it for hundreds of years and co-operate with the other classes for the good of all of us. Of course, everyone's got to work now, and there's got to be co-operation instead of selfish prerogative, but we're not going to be ashamed of our class and our family and our tradition, and we won't be ashamed of England either. It sounds a bit vague," he went on apologetically, "but there's something real at the back of it. We all feel pretty deeply about it."

"Well, well," said Beaminster. He loved the boy so truly, as he saw him striding up and down the floor, his head back, his eyes shining, that he found it difficult for a moment to speak. What had happened to him, to his old selfish ways, his avoidance of sentiment? Sentiment? For two-pence he would have jumped up, flung his arms around the boy's neck and kissed him.

"What does your young woman say to all this kind of talk?"

"Oh, she's all right," Tom hesitated. "I haven't said very much to her about it yet, I'm a bit shy of boring her. But she's clever. She'll be as interested in it as I am. Of course she'll have her own point of view about it. She has about everything."

"I expect she has," said Beaminster rather drily. "But her sister, the older one who's going to marry Poole. Does she like you? She's going to be important now?"

"Janet?" Tom laughed. "Oh, she's splendid. She's the best sort in the world. Of course she isn't lovely like Rosalind, but she's the best sport anywhere. She adores Rosalind, and anything Rosalind wants she'd want too."

"Very bad for Rosalind," Beaminster commented.

"Oh, I don't know. Rosalind isn't spoiled, not a bit. They've had too hard a time to be spoiled, either of them. It will be grand for Janet now. The old Duke can't live very long and then they'll have a great time."

"That's right," Beaminster growled. "Push us into the grave. We're finished."

"No, you know I don't mean that. The Duke's splendid. Everybody loves him. But there's something rather fine in being Duchess of Romney even in these days. All that history behind you and power to make more. There *is* something in a family, and something in loving the same soil so many years you get something back—something your ancestors have given. . . ."

He stopped and prepared to go. He had to dress and be at the Carlton Grill by seven—going to a play.

"By the way," said Beaminster, his hand on the boy's shoulder as they stood by the door, "it's all right about Zoffany's. I went in there to-day."

"Oh, thanks awfully. Uncle John, you are a brick to me. I wish I could do something for you in return."

"You do, you do," Beaminster said hurriedly. "Just by coming in to see me. Now cut along or you'll be late."

Back in his room he stood, looking at the curtains, listening to the strange spider-like hum of the traffic beyond the windows.

Yes, he loved that boy. What was the use of it so late? What the meaning of it? What the meaning of anything?

He sat down slowly and heavily, pulled the *Evening Standard* towards him, read further details in the history of the young man who had buried his young woman in his own chicken-run, and in his ears rang persistently the tones, fresh and clear, of Tom's loves and ambitions.

CHAPTER IV

HALKIN STREET

WHEN Janet Grandison awakened on the morning after her acceptance of Wildherne Poole her first conscious sensation was one of indefinite, unsubstantiated fear.

She was afraid of something. Something had happened that would have for her appalling consequences. Her life was in danger, her sister's life was in danger. . . . She must act at once or . . .

The dim room swung like water about her, then settled itself. The familiar furniture stepped out from the mist and solidly contemplated her. She raised her head, looked across the room at the open window, a fragment of grey smoky sky, a twisted and ironical chimney. The room was very cold, but she liked that. She was reassured by the fresh sharpness of the air. She knew. Last night she had accepted Wildherne Poole.

His figure appeared before her standing just in front of the window, his head cutting the segment of grey sky. He was there, and he was a stranger, and she was going to marry him. He was so completely a stranger to her that she could look at him with absolute detachment, admiring his fine carriage, his dignity, his aristocratic sedateness that would have been complacency had it not been so entirely unconscious. She had seen him many times, and yet she had never seen him before this morning. Her soul was looking upon him for the first time.

How could she have given her word? She must go at once to him and tell him that she had not meant what she had said. She sat up in bed, her heart thumping beneath her thin nightdress, the cold air assaulting her like a sharp remonstrance. She felt like an animal, trapped. What had she done? How *could* she have pledged herself . . . ? Her normality rose like the shadow of an old friend reassuring her. There was no need for fear. What was life meant for if one was not to engage it boldly, challenge it; and what was one's own soul engaged upon if it shrank before circumstance? She had accepted Poole for reasons that were neither sudden nor ill-considered. And then again she shrank back. She had always been reserved, impersonal; her life had painted a back-ground for others. Now she must step forward and take her place. She would be an important figure in the lives of many people. The world would watch her to see of what stuff she were made, she, Janet, whose soul had always been shy and reticent and uneloquent save only when love had stirred her.

And now she would play a part where love could not help her. She had dreamt of love in her girlhood, and perhaps if Rosalind had not possessed her so entirely she would have known by now what love—sexual love, married love—might be, but she had never known, and now, by this action, she had shut it out of her life for ever. Sexual love, yes. But there were other loves—love of friends, of beauty, of high deeds—all these were open to her. She could love the old Duke very easily—already she loved him perhaps. And for Wildherne—it might be that constant companionship with him would lead to comradeship, and comradeship to a kind of sisterly love. They would both be tranquilly happy, wise, sensible comrades. Wasn't that the way that marriages were made in France, and were they not more successful than our impetuous, hurried, romantic affairs that had no basis of real understanding?

She understood Wildherne Poole wonderfully. And he her. Their mutual confidence and honesty was a marvellous thing.

The telephone bell rang sharply from the other room. She slipped out of bed, looking at her watch as she did so. Nine o'clock! She had no idea that it was so late.

Old Mrs. Beddoes, who came in the mornings to clean up, was in the other room busy with the breakfast.

"I was wondering whether to wake you, Miss. I thought

I'd leave Miss Rosalind. She's sound as sound. The telephone, Miss. I was just a-going to answer it myself."

Janet raised the receiver: "Yes?" she said. "Who is it?"

"Janet, is that you?'

It was Wildherne's voice. The colour mounted, flushed her forehead under her dark hair.

"Yes, Wildherne, good-morning."

"I do hope I'm not too early. I didn't wake you?"

"No, no. I've been awake some time."

There was a pause. She felt that she should say something. She was terribly conscious of Mrs. Beddoes.

His voice, level, kindly, unperturbed, went on:

"It is only that I have told my mother and father. They are so happy that it is good to see."

"I'm glad." Her voice trembled a little.

"They want you to come to luncheon to-day. Will you? I will come and fetch you."

"Of course. I will be delighted. What time?"

"I'll come about half-past twelve. We might walk, if you don't mind."

"Yes, I'll like that."

"All right. Half-past twelve. Good-bye."

"Good-bye, Wildherne."

She stood there staring in front of her. She was thinking of the Duke's happiness. That was one good thing that she had done, one splendid thing; she had made the finest old man in the country gloriously happy, and she would see that that happiness continued. If she were not happy herself, at least she could make others so.

And then, quite unexpectedly, happiness bubbled up in her own heart. She could be, on an instant, like a little child, naïve, pleased with the smallest thing, credulous, buoyant. That came from the simple sincerity of her character. She had always been much simpler than her sister.

After all, there would be very pleasant consequences of this affair—power and friends and comfort and ease from anxiety.

How often in that same little room she had stood there wondering whether she *could* surmount the difficulties that beat in upon herself and Rosalind, wondering too whether she were always to be alone, fighting her battles by herself without aid from anyone? . . . although there had been friends . . . and one friend. . . .

She went eagerly back to the telephone. Soon a sleepy voice murmured out of space: "Yes? Who's that?"

"Rachel, darling, I *am* so sorry to have wakened you. It's I, Janet. I have some news for you."

"Oh, Janet. Wait a moment. Now I'm awake. Anything the matter?"

"Well—not the matter exactly," Janet laughed. "It's only that last night Wildherne Poole proposed to me and I accepted him."

"Oh!" The little cry of delight pleased Janet, who laughed eagerly as though her friend were there in person in front of her. "You darling! Oh! I *am* so glad! How splendid! Splendid! . . . Wait, I'm coming straight round to you. In half an hour. . . ."

"Yes, that's all right. I'm not going out. He's coming to fetch me at half-past twelve." She turned away from the telephone still smiling, then saw Mrs. Beddoes' eyes fixed on her in a kind of ecstasy.

"Excuse me, Miss. I oughtn't to have heard, but I couldn't 'elp it. Oh, miss, I *am* so glad! That's Lord Poole, ain't it, the Marquis of Poole? Oh, dear, I *am* glad. You *must* excuse me, Miss, but you've been so kind to me, giving Beddoes that introduction and everything, and sending Janie to the 'orspital, that it isn't in human nature for me not to show a bit of pleasure when luck comes your way. And it isn't as if I was a stranger to Lord Poole neither, because my sister-in-law goes to that very church, St. Anne's in Wolverton Street, where all the Duke's people goes to, and she's seen Lord Poole there many a Sunday, and a fine, 'andsome, well-set-up young gentleman he is, they tell me. Oh, I am glad, Miss, and so heveryone will be because a kinder-hearted lady than yourself no one's ever set eyes on, and that I'd declare if I was 'ad up for murderin' my 'usband. You deserve to be 'appy if anyone does."

Mrs. Beddoes did not often express her feelings, and in the morning was inclined to be morose and mournful.

This was pleasant.

"Thank you, Mrs. Beddoes. I hope you will come to the wedding."

"Indeed and I will, Miss." Then she sighed, her original nature returning upon her. "This will mean losing another job for me. Always losing jobs through no fault of my own. That's what Beddoes says: Why is it, he says, that you're so unlucky, he says; you're the unluckiest woman I ever come across, he says—and so I am. It's gospel truth."

"Well, we'll see," said Janet. "Who knows what will happen? There may be jobs better than this."

"There may be and again there mayn't," said Mrs. Beddoes, wiping her nose with the back of her hand. "You never know your luck, of course, but it's been my experience to find things always worse than they ought to be, and so it'll go on to the end, I expect. That's what they call fate."

Janet departed to have her bath and to dress. She was speedy in all her actions (dawdling was abhorrent to her), and soon she was back in the little sitting-room expecting to find Rosalind, very beautiful, and still in spite of her bath only half awake, pouring out dreamily the coffee. "She's dressed and gone out," Mrs. Beddoes explained. "Wouldn't 'ave her coffee. Said she was in a hurry. She's left that note."

The note was there perched against the silver tree that had been arranged in front of Janet's place, and the note said:

DARLING—I'm in an awful hurry about something. Meant to have waked and didn't. Look at the tree as you drink your coffee and know that your wicked tiresome sister loves you and will let no Pooles whatsoever take her place.

ROSALIND

She had spelt "whatsoever" "watsoever." Janet smiled. She took up the little tree and caressed its stiff green leaves with loving fingers. The silver buds sparkled even in the dull light of the grey morning. Mrs. Beddoes smiled appreciatively, "Why, that *is* a pretty thing, Miss, I must say. Awful dangerous to dust, though," and she disappeared into Rosalind's bedroom.

Janet sighed. Rosalind might have stayed just for ten minutes on this morning of all others. How characteristic it all was! The haste, the affection, the ill-spelling, her room left no doubt in hopeless disorder, secrecy, impetuosity, unkindness mingled with the kindness.

As always when Janet thought of her sister that love, hot, tyrannous, jealous, yearning, tender, angry, arose in her heart, causing her to forget everything else. Why does love burn the fiercer from unfulfilment, why so passionately desired the fruit that is just without our reach?

Her coffee unfinished, she rose and walked about the room. She had forgotten Wildherne as though he had never existed. What was Rosalind about? Why had she not told Janet her preoccupation? Why must she always be so secret? Did Janet ever lecture or scold her? Did she not always understand, and if she gave advice was she not always tender and kind?

No, not always. When you felt such love and watched the loved one pursuing something or someone unworthy, how could you quiet that agitation and fear? She had not always quieted it, and Rosalind feared those moods when Janet's eyes were sad and reproachful and her silences minatory.

The little bell rang. Janet went to the door, and there was her dearest best friend, Rachel Seddon.

Rachel came in, and the two women held each other in a long loving embrace; then Rachel kept Janet at arm's length.

"Let me look at you and see whether you're changed. Not a bit. But you will be. Oh, you darling, I am so glad." Rachel Seddon was a woman of fifty, old enough to be Janet's mother. Therein had lain some of the charm of their relationship; Rachel was mother, sister, and friend to one who deeply needed such affection. And yet Rachel was strange. As she stood there in her dark furs, even in this moment of emotion, she seemed remote, apart. It was per-

naps the Russian blood in her, something sad and brooding
behind her vitality and fun. Her life, she said, was over.
Her husband, whom after a difficult early married life she
had come deeply to love (he crippled by a riding accident
and so drawing out of her that maternity that was by far
the most passionate element of her nature), after his death
she had rebuilt her life around her son, but there too there
was a remoteness and a final reserve. Tom was all English,
all his father; some of his mother's nature was so foreign
to him that she could not share it with him. She could not
share it with any one, and in the very moment of intimate
affection with Tom, Janet, Uncle John Beaminster, she
would withdraw herself and they would fumble blindly for
someone who was not there.

Janet knew this, and she knew also that there was another
barrier between herself and her friend. Rachel did not like
Rosalind, had never liked her. She would try to conceal it,
and of course could not. Rosalind, instantly perceptive of
all reactions to herself, had always known it. Rosalind did
not care for those who did not appreciate her.

But in spite of this Janet loved Rachel more than any one
else in the world, save only of course Rosalind.

Rachel had great influence over Janet; Janet was influenced only by those whom she could admire, and her own
modesty and self-abnegation were so deep that she could
admire easily. Even Rachel's dislike of Rosalind Janet could
understand. Rosalind was never at her best with Rachel;
Rachel did not understand her, Janet said, saw only her
selfish, pleasure-loving side. That such a side existed was of
course true; Janet was not blind about Rosalind. Her power
over Rosalind would have been greater perhaps had she not
seen Rosalind's faults so plainly.

The two friends sat down and talked, Rachel's hand in
Janet's. Rachel liked him, Wildherne Poole, so much. She
had known him for a long time and rather well. He was one
of the kindest and most honourable of men. He and Janet
were splendidly suited. They were alike in many ways,
Rachel thought, and yet their differences were enough to
make their lives together interesting and eventful.

Then a pause came, and Janet knew why it was there But she could not speak to Rachel of this love affair o Wildherne's. She knew that it was of that that Rachel wa thinking, and she knew that it would be of that that every one in London would be thinking when the engagement wa generally known. Only the old Duke and Duchess had hear nothing of it.

The little pause passed and conversation flowed again but Janet knew that that extra pressure from Rachel's hand had meant: "Janet, dear, if you are ever in any trouble, i anything is ever too difficult for you, I am there. I am alway at your side."

Then there was another thing. Rachel got up and, smiling at Janet, said:

"Tom is in love with Rosalind."

"I know," Janet said.

"We won't talk about it now. You have this other thing to think about. But sometime . . .?"

Then, with a little sigh, she added, "He's terribly in love poor boy."

They talked for a little while about anything, nothing Then, clinging together as though to assert against all the world and anything that it might do their mutual love, they parted.

The time passed swiftly. The little silver clock on the man tlepiece struck half-past twelve with so menacing a sudden ness that Janet sprang from her writing-desk and stood wait ing as though some voice had called her.

A moment later Wildherne Poole was in the room. He came straight to her and kissed her, not as though it were some duty that he must perform, but like a friend, someone who had known her all her life and cared for her dearly That action seemed at once to establish their relation happily She laughed, let her hand rest for a moment on the dark rough stuff of his coat, and said:

"Give me a moment. I'll have my things on and be back in no time. How punctual you are!"

When she came back in her dark furs (Rachel had giver

hem to her two Christmases ago) and her little round blue
iat he could have sighed with relief. She was fine in her
neight, her noble carriage, the good honesty of her eyes, the
strength and humour of her mouth. He had known that she
vas, but from the moment of her acceptance of him the test
hat, almost against his will, he must apply to her had been
wice as severe as before.

She would have much that she must do for him and his
amily. Would she be able to carry it off? He knew now,
ooking at her, that she would.

She too was reassured by his curly head of hair, the kind-
iness of his smiling eyes, the strength of chin and neck,
he slimness and fine proportion of his body, something
oyishly confident in his physical pose and something intel-
ectually mature in his mental assurance—why was it, then,
hat she felt no love for him, no slightest stirring of the
ulse, no eagerness, no physical response? Was it because
he knew that he had none of this for her and her pride pre-
ented her? No, she was aware how deeply she would have
ecoiled had there been any passion in his glance. There
vas only friendliness there, and that she could return to
im, full measure and brimming over.

So, as friends, they walked off. London was London in-
eed that morning, like no other city in the world. The tang
f the frost was still in the air; there was a thin slime of
iud over roadway and pavement, ancient prehistoric mud
s though in the night palæolithic monsters—dinosaurs and
cthyosauri—had invaded in vast clumsy cohorts the silent
treets bringing their forest slime with them. Everything
·as thick, grey, and muffled. There was as yet no fog, but
oon there would be; the snow was grey and dark, only
hining from roof to roof dimly as though under thin moon-
ght. Some light glimmered in shop windows, and all sounds
f traffic were hushed as though the world were straw-
overed because of the mortal sickness of some God. So
·day; and yet to-morrow the sun would return and all the
own glitter in a network of silver filagree. Eternal beauty
·nd wonder of the London moods—a city where ghosts and
ving men are both sheltered by that friendly spirit so that

time says nothing here. Buildings are for ever rising and
falling, streets for ever disappearing, but the kindly London
God stretches his colossal legs, murmurs sleepily his blessing
and all his children are included in his giant embrace.

Wildherne and Janet walked briskly, a splendid pair.

Janet, wisely, chose at once the impersonal mood that was
safe for them both.

"Wildherne, I want you to tell me everything about Hal
kin Street. Of course I have been there again and again
but it was always from outside. You have all been sweet to
me, but of course I wasn't one of you. Now I am to be, and
you must tell me certain things."

He was grateful to her for striking so exactly the right
note.

"I'll tell you anything you want to know. Ask your ques
tions."

"Well, there are your mother and father. Then who els
is there permanently?"

"Permanently? Let me see. There is Miss Crabbage
mother's secretary—very important. There is Beresford
father's secretary—not so important. There's Hignett, fam
ily butler, factotum, friend. If you are ever in a difficulty
ask Hignett, he has more common sense than all of us
There is the Reverend Charles Pomeroy of St. Anne's—
very important. There is my aunt Alice Purefoy—more im
portant than you would fancy. There is Dick Beresford
father's land-agent, not up in town very much but importan
anyway. There is Caroline Marsh, mother's protégé. I don'
like her, and you won't either. Watch her. She's dangerous
These are the permanents, I think, and of these Miss Crab
bage, Charles Pomeroy, and Caroline Marsh matter most
Pomeroy is a good fellow, sincere and true. But watch the
two women. Their lives depend on their power with my
mother. If you threaten that they'll try to make trouble."

"If they don't make trouble between you and me," Jane
said, "it isn't very serious."

"Ah, but it may be." Wildherne answered her more gravely
than she had expected. "This Halkin Street life is very queer
You'll see when you get into it more deeply. I love my

father passionately, and so he loves me, but my mother has always had a strange jealousy of us both—of his love for me and mine for him. My mother is not a clever woman, but she is deeply acquisitive. She wants to have everything absolutely for herself. She would cut herself to pieces for my father or myself, but she is not clever enough —she has never been clever enough to understand either of us. Don't think me unkind in this. I love my mother, but I find her very irritating to be with because she wants so much more of everything than she will ever have. My father has been escaping from her again and again all his life, and then reproaching himself for unkindness to her and so being over-tender and good to her. But still always escaping her, and she knows that. You have to pay her attention and deference, not because she is a vain woman, but because she is always wishing to be reassured of her power over people, a power of which she is never truly secure, as she knows.

"She is a strange woman, my mother. Apparently slow, unintelligent, conventional, and then, when you least expect it, dominating and overwhelming. The whole problem of Halkin Street and much of the problem of my life revolves round my mother's personality, and that is why I am emphasising her."

"I understand," Janet said in a low voice, following her own thoughts. "She is a lonely woman. She has never had either the power or the love that she wanted."

"Ah, but"—Wildherne broke in—"you mustn't judge my father in that. He loves her deeply, and has always done so. He understands her too better than any of us and, in her heart, she knows it. She need not be lonely. She would not be if she did not want so much more than any human being has ever been given on this earth, or ever will be."

He was silent a moment as they crossed Sloane Street, then went on again: "You have seen, of course, how tremendous a part religion plays with us at home. Church of England religion, Mr. Pomeroy, St. Anne's, and so on through a network of charities, societies, meetings and assemblies. The difference between my father and my mother in this is that

my father is a saint by the grace of God. He has the re
ligious beliefs of a little child, but they are utterly real t
him—they make him the happy, tranquil, gentle person h
is. Many of the Church affairs bore him. He does his par
for my mother's sake, but his religion is something deep with
in himself, something about which he is almost shy. M
mother is quite different. She loves all the offices of th
Church. She adores services and meetings, all the parapher
nalia of the external world of the Church of England. Tha
is where Miss Crabbage has her power. She has all thes
things at her fingers' ends; she manipulates with extraor
dinary skill. She is like a great general sitting in his tent, hi
maps before him, officers coming in and out for directions
She is a remarkable person, Miss Crabbage.

"Remember another thing," he went on. "As you mus
have noticed before now, my mother takes everything liter
ally. She has no sense of humour either about herself o
others. What you say you mean, and by what you sa
you'll be judged."

"I'm frightened," Janet said, putting out her hand an
touching his arm. "This is all terrifying."

He laughed and drew her arm through his. "It isn't terri
fying, because we're friends, because I shall stand by yo
through thick and thin, as you will by me. And you star
with immense advantages. They have longed that I shoul
marry, and that I should marry just such a one as your
self. We are gratifying their dearest wish. My mother think
the world of you, and you will perhaps be able to do for he
what no one else has been able to do."

"Oh, I will try! I will try!" Janet whispered. "Indeed
will do my best!" They were there. The dark, heavy, fade
door of the Halkin Street house faced Janet as it had ofte
faced her before, but now, waiting in front of it, her emo
tions were different from any that she had ever known
When that door opened her new life would begin, begi
far more truly than with her acceptance of Wildherne. H
scarcely seemed to count for her as she stood there, trul
terrified, waiting for her fate.

And yet when it did open and she saw in the doorwa

he cheerful rosy face of the young footman (brought up
robably from the place in Wiltshire), and behind him the
ark stony hall so familiar to her with its vast silly-faced
lock, its huge red picture of an eighteenth-century female
Romney, its dark shadows and dusky piece of tapestry, she
vas at home. Cold, shabby, echoing house, so bare and naked
ere, so overcrowded there, so destitute of all taste and
rtistic feeling and yet with so strong a personality, so un-
ouched by new crazes, fashions and habits, and yet so threat-
ning in its survival to the flimsiness of this chaotic post-
var age—she understood it, she knew how to approach it,
he belonged to it as she could never belong to Clara Paget's
lack and yellow bedroom or Althea Bendersby's drawing-
oom of cubic reds and blues.

In the dusk of the hall Hignett waited—Hignett, stout,
ound-faced, impersonal, thick in the legs, back, and brain,
eactionary, snob, drawing-room slave and kitchen tyrant,
aithful, conceited, ill-educated, intolerant, perfect servant
nd loyal friend of his master. And of his master's son.
His face lighted when he saw Wildherne as it but seldom
ghted for anyone. The Duke, Wildherne, his own child
Thomas Edward (aged eight) were for him the three per-
ect beings. He despised women (his wife most emphatically
ncluded), all other servants; he hated Socialists, Bolshevists,
Communists, and the clergy. He had no friends. He wanted
one. He had saved a large sum of money, but he would
ever retire until Wildherne, in his own time as Duke, dis-
nissed him.

He adored Wildherne. He would sacrifice every human
eing alive on the earth's surface in one vast holocaust (save
nly Thomas Edward) to please Wildherne. He loved him
nore, far more, than he had ever loved any woman. He hated
specially Miss Crabbage, and between himself and her there
vas pursued always an unceasing underground warfare.
These various emotions were visible to no one. He never
howed temper, surprise, disappointment, affection (save
nly to Thomas Edward), greed. His wife, a thin-faced
our woman who lived with the child in some dim street
n Bloomsbury, knew nothing about him but loved him. He

was not faithful to her, but she realised that his emotion towards women were ephemeral, trivial, and accidental.

Very little of the soul of Hignett was known to anybody He was to be of great importance in Janet's life. His lov of and fidelity to Wildherne she would one day know, know in a dark hour when she needed that knowledge.

Lastly, there was nothing about Wildherne of which Hig nett was not aware. Michael on his side knew that Hignet was a devoted servant, but that the man cared for hir personally never occurred to him. The man was devote because he had been brought up on the Wintersmoon estate had a feudal sense, was paid well, knew when he was wel off. Moreover, all the servants worshipped the Duke. O course they did. How could they help it? So much for Hig nett.

When Janet passed into the long green drawing-room sh saw three women standing by the wide open fireplace—th little, short, dumpy one the Duchess, the tall thin one with pincenez Miss Crabbage, and the fluffy flaxen one Carolin Marsh.

The old Duchess, mother of the present Duke, had know a spasm of artistic emotion, and under the influence of tha emotion had covered the long drawing-room with Morri wall-paper. Now that paper, green and faded, displaying when closely studied the unending pursuit by three elegan horsemen of a fleeing deer, was the background for Vic torian water-colours in heavy gold frames and two enor mous oil portraits of the last Duke and Duchess in the gor geous splendour of Court display. The long room was studded, as is the Ægean Sea by its islands, with gilt furni ture. The high windows looked out into Halkin Street.

There was very real emotion in the Duchess's voice as she came forward, embraced Janet, and murmured: "Welcome dear Janet, to your new home," and then in the funny, husky whisper that was so especially hers and suggested nothing so much as a kettle on the boil: "We are so glad. We are so happy. Nothing could have been better."

Had the Duchess ever been vain (she had never been so) she would have worn very high-heeled shoes and dicted

madly. Years ago when the Duke married her she was pretty
in a yellow blue-eyed canary kind of way. In those days
what she lost in height she saved in aristocratic bearing,
being the eldest daughter of Lord Medley, whose wife, as
everyone knows, was for so long lady-in-waiting to Queen
Victoria.

Now she was dumpy and shapeless, with pale blue eyes,
no eyebrows to speak of, and a strange round saucer of grey
hair that stood over her puckered face like a turban. But her
aristocratic bearing was still there. She never of course
actively considered her ancestry, her present position—those
were things too familiar to be thought of—but she was exceedingly quick to recognise anything that savoured of impertinence or discourtesy. Many a visitor ere now, resting
happily on the easy and almost fraternal kindness of the
Duke, had been arrested sharply by the sudden remote distinction of the Duchess. That turban of grey hair made up
quite sufficiently for the absence of eyebrows, and those eyes,
now so dimly blue, could be of a sudden terrible as daggers.

But Janet was of her world, and to-day nothing could be
fine enough for her. The Duchess took her off to a little
gilt sofa near the window, held her hand in her soft boneless fingers, and spoke straight from her heart. This thing
had made her happy as nothing had ever made her happy
before. Although she had not heard directly of Wildherne's
so famous intrigue, she was nevertheless more in the world
than was the Duke, and whispers, murmurs of something,
anything, had come to her ears.

Always she had been haunted by the fear that he, their
only child, the true hope of the world, would marry someone unworthy. In these dreadful godless democratic days
anybody might marry anybody. And now, after all her fears,
he had chosen of all the young women she knew the one
whom perhaps she herself preferred. A marvellous, marvellous piece of luck and fortune, and now, as she looked at the
girl, so tall, so graceful, so perfectly at ease and in her right
place, she was more than ever reassured. Moreover, the girl
would be easy to dominate. She had been poor, struggling,
with scarcely enough to eat; she would be so grateful for

everything, so ready to fall into any plans, to do what she
was told, to follow her mother-in-law's lead.

"Yes, when Wildherne told us last night it seemed as
though our most anxious prayers had been answered. You
can understand, dear Janet, our only boy, and the Duke and
myself the age we are. Before we went we wanted. . . ."
Her little fat underlip trembled. Tears swam in her blue
eyes. She was deeply moved. Janet also. Nothing stirred her
like the need for affection. She felt always so intensely for
lonely and unhappy and uncared-for people. The Duchess
was, most truly, not lonely nor unhappy nor uncared for,
but at this moment her religious and her family feelings were
both deeply stirred. She was therefore quite sincere.

". . . As Mr. Pomeroy said this morning we must from
our hearts thank God for His goodness. It is to Him that we
all owe this happiness."

At this moment the door at the far end of the room
opened and the Duke, followed by Mr. Pomeroy, entered.
Janet rose and, moving to Wildherne, walked with him towards his father.

As she was seeing, to-day, Wildherne, the house, the
Duchess in a new and more personal light, so now she saw
the Duke. He was a short thick-set man with a pointed beard
and hair of snow white. His sturdiness of figure and something of freedom in his walk would have given him a country
air had it not been for the perfect cut of his London clothes
—his black coat and waistcoat, his pepper-and-salt trousers,
his high white collar widely open at the neck, and the thick
gold ring that encircled his black tie. But you did not notice
these things, his glow of health, his exquisite neatness, and
his emphatic sturdiness—you saw only the kindliness, modesty, utter unself-consciousness that shone from his eyes
and formed the lines of the mouth above the beard. He had
not, perhaps, in his youth been handsome, his nose was too
snub, his mouth too irregular; the character of his life had
through the actions and thoughts of his seventy years written itself in his face.

Had he not come so late in life to the Dukedom, and had
there been in him some element of ruthlessness or vanity or

selfish ambition, he would have made more stir in the world. He had never figured in the public life of his country, he shrank from the personalities and falsities of politics, he was still a child in his perception of modern moralities and standards (or absence of them), but he was not a child in his wide tolerance, his warm charity, his negation of self. He had lived always for those he loved, his wife, his child, his tenantry, his servants, some friends. Above all for his religion, about which he rarely spoke and never argued. Unlike his wife he did not care of what sect anyone might be so that God was a reality; atheists, materialists he did not understand, but was sure that one day they would find the way. In God's good time everyone would find the way. "Not a sparrow. . . ."

He adored Wildherne. The boy had never given him a moment's unhappiness. He had sometimes wished that he were more practical and business-like, because one day, now not so distant, all the Wintersmoon estates must come into his hands, and in these days land was not easy, but he had carefully placed near him wise, honest, and capable men— Beresford the land-agent, Charles Robinson the family solicitor, and Lord Garnet, at one time Attorney-General and the Duke's oldest and closest friend.

These men would look after the boy when he himself was gone, and see that he came to no harm. And now Wildherne had done the one thing that, above all things, he had desired. He had not been anxious about Wildherne's choice as the Duchess had been; he was sure that his taste and fine feeling would guide him right, but of all the young women in London he liked Janet Grandison the best. He had felt from the beginning a father's affection for her, and now in very truth he was in that relation to her.

So now he came to her and caught her into his arms and kissed her. Afterwards he rested his hands on Wildherne's shoulders and, turning to the room in general, said: "You may as well all know—this is the happiest day of my life."

It was intended to be a family luncheon, and Mr. Pomeroy had for long been one of the family. He was an austere, dark, tall man, very neat and straight and silent. His sermons

had made St. Anne's the most fashionable church in London
he was immensely in request at social functions, ladies worshipped him, he had large private means, and a house filled
with beautiful things. Nevertheless he was entirely sincere
and faithful in his religion. He was not an ascetic, although
he looked like one. He liked beautiful women and good food
and wine and pictures and music, but he cared for God more
than any of these, and would have given them, all of them,
up immediately had he felt that God wished him to do so
He did not feel that God wished it. He gave away half his
income to charity, worked like a slave at his duties, neglected
nothing—and then enjoyed his Pissarros and Gauguins (he
had one tiny one), his month's holiday on the Riviera, and
the chamber music that Lady Rawlinson had at 12 Brook
Street every Tuesday evening in the season.

He had no interest in intrigue or gossip or the manipula-
tion of ecclesiastical strings. He left people like Miss Crabbage to do those things for him. He was the Duchess's best
friend.

Hignett said that luncheon was ready. They went in.

Janet had always felt this dining-room to be the coldest
and most uncomfortable room in London. The walls were
papered with squares of black and white imitation marble;
half a dozen portraits hung in gold frames of a desperate
heaviness. The elephantine marble mantlepiece supported a
huge clock of black marble, and between the two windows
was a marble bust of the late Duke in a Gladstonian collar
and a marble watch-chain. The high thick curtains that
framed the windows were of a dull lustreless red.

To-day this room depressed her desperately. It seemed to
step forward and say to her : "You were pleased and flattered
by their welcome of you in that other room. But make no
mistake, this is the life that you will have to lead. This
room holds the Halkin Street atmosphere. It is here that you
will be imprisoned."

The slightly chilled clear soup, water and fragments of
carrot, the heavy silver fruit-dish that blinked at her from
the centre of the table, the soft restrained movements of the

two footmen, all these things to which she was so thoroughly
accustomed seemed to have some extra meaning to-day for
her. She was sitting on the Duke's right hand; on her other
side was Mr. Pomeroy, and opposite to her Wildherne, but,
oddly enough, it was the women of whom she was so especially conscious.

Or perhaps it was not odd. Any other woman would at
that moment have felt the same. She had always been on
good terms with Miss Crabbage, but she did not like her,
and Caroline Marsh she had been tempted to despise. There
was a sycophant if you liked, with her pale fluffy hair, her
bad streaky complexion, her clumsy figure, and her swimming eyes fixed always eagerly on the Duchess's face, ready
to agree with everything, to anticipate the slightest wish, to
yield up compliment or reassurance or consolation the instant that it was demanded. But, poor child! Was it not
natural for her to be sycophantic? The Duchess had found
her, a miserable, frightened little governess to a band of
noisy impertinent children and, her heart touched, had
brought her to Halkin Street and to Wintersmoon that she
might read to her, run messages, be at hand on any and
every occasion. Was it not natural enough that this girl
should be watching Janet with apprehension, almost with
terror? If this wife of Lord Poole's did not like her what
might she not do, she with her power over both the Duke
and the Duchess? Poor girl. Janet would like to reassure her.
Soon she would do so, would tell her that there was nothing
to fear, that she had made another friend. Friend? No!
There was something about those weak watery eyes, that
loose supplicating mouth, that would make friendship impossible.

As the meal progressed Janet recovered some of her confidence. Her neighbourhood to the Duke warmed her.
Strange but true, and something to be faced by her, that
she loved the father more than the son. There was some
pulse of excitement in her thought of the Duke, over seventy
though he was; he was so fine, so noble, and so handsome,
with his white hair, his clear skin, his sturdy body. She was

his daughter now, and oh! she was proud of him! He turned and, bowing, raised his glass of wine to her. His other hand closed on hers, and it thrilled her to feel how warm and strong his grasp was.

"Janet, your health. And yours, Wildherne. Many, many happy years for you both."

They all stood up, and Janet and Wildherne, sitting, were isolated. They looked into one another's eyes. Perhaps with both of them there was the same thought: "We are cheating these old people. They think that we love one another and we do not. We are marrying each other for a reason of convenience. We mean to make the very best of this, for you as well as for ourselves, but it is not the glorious romantic affair that you fancy."

It was this recognition that drove her, afterwards, as though she was in a way putting all her cards on the table, to mention her sister:

"You haven't asked about Rosalind," she said, turning to the Duke.

"Ah, Rosalind," he answered, smiling. "No. I hope we are going to see her here very soon. How is the beautiful Rosalind? You know, I think she is the prettiest girl in London by far. I don't see a very great many, but however many I saw I should still think Rosalind the prettiest."

"You must bring her," the Duchess echoed, "to see us as soon as ever you can. What about luncheon to-morrow— or let me see, Mr. Pomeroy, isn't it to-morrow you wanted to bring Mr. Brixham and Mrs. Forster in connection with the Agatha Guild? *Was* it to-morrow? I forget."

"Oh, your Grace," Mr. Pomeroy answered, "any of these next days would do. There is no desperate hurry."

"It is rather important," Miss Crabbage broke in, addressing Mr. Pomeroy, "that the Duchess should *see* Mrs. Forster as soon as possible. That Agatha Bazaar is on the 22nd, and they are so *anxious* that the Duchess should be there that evening and just open it for them. And naturally the Duchess wishes to *hear* from Mrs. Forster first exactly. . . ." She had a habit of dealing terrific emphasis out to certain words as though she were hitting them on the head with a hammer.

"But really I think it's not so urgent," Mr. Pomeroy murmured. "Mrs. Forster can come any time, can she not?"

"I don't *quite* agree with you," remonstrated Miss Crabbage. "There is so *little* time, you see. Almost none at all, and if . . ."

Her voice always died into a murmur. The Duchess adored these little struggles over her so-to-speak recumbent body. She always waited for a while to see how things were going, and then sprang up to settle everything with a dominating word.

"Mr. Brixham and Mrs. Forster can come on Wednesday, Miss Crabbage. Do bring Rosalind to luncheon to-morrow, Janet, dear. We shall be so pleased to see her."

All this disturbance and then, perhaps after all, Rosalind might refuse to come. Rosalind had no liking for meals at Halkin Street. However, at this important time. . . .

"Thank you so much. I'm sure she'll love to come."

And, after all, in a corner of the drawing-room she had her word with the Duke. He put his arm through hers, and drew her to him so that they stood, body and soul, together.

"My dear, I'm over seventy. I have done nothing in my life to deserve that the desire of it should be granted like this. I have always loved you. I have watched you more than you have known. I have watched your courage, your unselfish devotion to others, your loyalty, the fun you've extracted from such little things. I have been proud of you. I have never said anything to Wildherne. I scarcely dared hope that it would be you of all others he would choose. But he has shown his wisdom. I'm proud of him too. But I only want to tell you, my dear, that as long as I live, and that may not be for very long, if there is any trouble of any kind in which an old man, who has known many sides of life, can help and advise you, he will give up everything to do so. God bless you, my dear child, and keep you in His charge and save you from all harm."

CHAPTER V

WILDHERNE could remember a day when, in the gardens of Wintersmoon, aged some six years or seven, he had waded into one of the ponds to look at a water-lily. The point had been that he had wanted to look at it, not to pluck it, and the point had further been that, pulled out of the pond by one of the gardeners, he had been sent to bed in disgrace and without his supper.

He had been in no way indignant with his sentence—he know that it was wrong for him to spoil his clothes with mud and disobey those in authority—but for the first time there had stolen into his mind wonder as to why the things that he wanted were always out of his reach. Then, as he grew older, there followed the further wonder as to why he wanted things that nobody else wanted.

At his private school at Rottingdean he learnt the first thing that little boys must be—to be like other little boys. He discovered that he was *not* like other little boys, and that he must hide this discovery, so he developed two Wildhernes, one that cared for football, sardines, and doughnuts in bed at night, and "scraps" with other boys, and the other that never knew what it cared for, had strange feelings about flowers, the sea, and English history, and a passionate devotion for everything that concerned Wintersmoon.

This second personality, he discovered, must be seen only by his father and one of the under-gardeners. The rest of the world laughed did he show any enthusiasm for anything that had not to do with games. At school above all he must appear to detest work of any kind. He liked work, but could not apply himself to it because thoughts about Wintersmoon and the spire of Salisbury Cathedral and the way the sea rolled in and strangled the pebbles on the long beach below the school would keep breaking in. Meanwhile he loved the under-gardener, who was called Mitchell and showed him how flowers grew, told him the names of birds, and was dismissed, in Wildherne's first year at Eton, for drunkenness.

At Eton he found that he could do what he liked, that nobody cared. Nevertheless the two Wildhernes continued to develop: he discovered that the one Wildherne was very useful for covering the other. He was good-looking, athletic, and amiable; it was not difficult for him to be popular, and he learnt that if he never showed enthusiasm about anything, never talked about anything that was "odd"—books, pictures, music, religion, scenery were things never to mention—he was popular and universally accepted as a "good fellow." When he was about sixteen he discovered that there were certain other boys in the school who cared for the things for which he himself cared. They made a set of their own, but they were all of them "odd," and some of them scandalous: he did not therefore join them, because his shyness about the things for which he cared caused him to detest publicity of any kind.

It was about this time that his love for his father acutely developed. He liked his mother, but it was his public personality with which she was concerned. She did not seem to be aware that he had any other. His father was as shy as himself, and their true communication with one another might have been long delayed had it not been for a serious attack of pneumonia that kept him prisoner during a whole summer at Wintersmoon when he was seventeen.

One summer evening, when he was convalescent, lying in a chair looking out over the lawns, the woods, the gently rising hills, he poured out all that was in his soul to his father, and from that moment they were companions.

He had always intensely admired his father, but until now he had never thought of him as human in the way that he himself was human. He was omnipotent, omniscient, something of other bodily make from himself. This evening it was as though his father's body stepped into view for the first time, blood and muscles like his own, the eyes real eyes, the chest with its breadth and thickness a man's chest, thighs and sinews of a man like himself—and when that night his father's hand closed on his he could feel the pulse beating through the strength of the palm. He twisted his fingers between his father's fingers. He kissed his father on the mouth. He had never kissed his father before, only been kissed by him.

Now he was alive to many things in his father's character that he had never seen before. He had always perceived his courtesy to others, his gentleness and yet his authority with the servants in the house and the men on the estate, but now he realised that this courtesy came from a deep modesty that would have been shyness had there been in the character more egotism.

He perceived another thing. On Sunday mornings they sat—his father, his mother, Aunt Alice, any guests—in the deep family pew in the old sixteenth-century church just outside the Wintersmoon gates. That had become a ritual so common as to inhibit consciousness. His second personality on these mornings would gladly swing itself free and he would be away far over England, far over Europe, lost in a beauty and a wonder that he had never had self-discipline enough to analyse.

But on this morning he was watching this new father of his. It was his first morning in church for months, the first bold step of his convalescence. Old Beatty, the white-bearded rector, was reading the First Lesson, and it was a Cursing Lesson—"I, the Lord thy God"—and the wretched Jews were cowering down on to their desert sand while the plague devastated them, fiery serpents assaulted them. . . .

On his father's face was written disgust, and at the "Here endeth" he moved his thick stocky shoulders as though he would shake some evil spell from off them.

Packed off to bed early Wildherne lay there wondering. He heard his father pass his door and called to him. He urged him to the bed, made him sit down on it, put his arms around him drawing him towards him.

"Father, you hate Jehovah. So do I. I loathe him, dirty bully." He was conscious that he was whispering this, and he know that he was whispering lest his mother should hear. They were drawn then into an intimacy more dangerous than any they had yet encountered.

Wildherne's mother had always dominated Wildherne's world, and in nothing more completely than in religion. His outer self had acquiesced utterly. When anyone was as certain as his mother was in these things, so sure about every detail so that no place in heaven was too distant for her vision, how could anyone as uncertain and wondering as Wildherne question?

But now, behold, his father questioned. His father had also his own private life sacred to him, reserved from all the world and from his wife. He let his son in. Loyal to her they were, both of them, but here they escaped her and they knew it.

Wildherne was only seventeen and, weakened by his long illness, looked the small child that, in many ways, he still was. His father held him tight to his heart that night. Who could know for how many years he had been longing with passionate desire for this?

"Remember your mother is the best woman I have ever known or am likely to know. Without her I should be nothing. I love her, Wildherne, as I hope one day you will love some fine woman—but at the end of it, in spite of the most perfect intimacy, we are alone—always, every one of us. It is the condition of life."

Wildherne went up to Balliol; his uncle died, and his father became Duke. He did all the things that his companions did. He was considered "a jolly good fellow. Not stuck up at all. A bit absent-minded." He rowed in his College boat, took a second in Greats. He came down having many acquaintances and not one friend. For his exterior self, which he gave readily to anyone, he cared so little that friendship could not possibly go with it. His interior self he gave only to his father.

In 1914 there was the war. He was wounded in 1916, and again in the spring of 1918—tiresome wounds involving pain of the wearying, irritating kind that seems to teach you

nothing but exasperation. He used to think about himself
during his long hours in hospital, and it surprised him to
perceive that if it had not been for his love for England
he would have been, long ago, a Conscientious Objector. He
loathed war, but he loathed the thought of a foreign-ridden
England still more deeply. There was, he supposed, an intellectual flaw in this somewhere. Had he been of the intellectual calibre of, say, Bertrand Russell, he would have
perceived that this love of country was exactly the thing that
held back the world's progress—this selfish clinging to one
small fragment of earth. But he could not help it. When he
thought of Boyton Church or Figheldean Village, or the
stretch of the Plain, or the old stones of St. Anne's Gate
in Salisbury, or the grey stretches of Longleat, or the lawns
of his own adored Wintersmoon, he simply knew that he
would fight to the last trouser-button to prevent this domination by German, Frenchman, or Spaniard.

He wished those Frenchmen and Spaniards all the luck in
the world, and he would gladly join with them to help them
keep their own pastures free, but Figheldean was like his
mother or old Aunt Alice—it looked to him with the love
born of centuries of association to keep it free from harm.

So he came out of the war with this dominating him
above all else—his love of England in general and of Wintersmoon in particular.

He discovered then that this same love of his country was
held by almost everyone to be old-fashioned and tyrannous.
His trouble was that two camps now were formed and he did
not seem to belong to either of them. The advanced camp
was international, Socialistic (but not Bolshevistic), anti-
Christian, anti-matrimony, and anti-sentimental. The reactionary camp was named Die-hard and cursed by everybody.
Certain old gentlemen with whom he talked at the Club
belonged apparently to this camp and were caught in a perfect mist of despair. The world was at an end, delivered
over to robbers, degenerates, and sadists. He was, he found,
neither socialistic nor reactionary.

He had no wish to go back to the old times when servants

slept in cubby-holes, when children were abused and terrified
with prospects of a fiery hell, when sanitation was in its
infancy, and science was considered blasphemous. But neither
did he wish to deliver Wintersmoon up to the first ignorant
band of labourers who came to demand it. Nor did he believe
that the traditions and heritage of England were so much
discarded offal. He was alone, as always. He seemed to fit
in nowhere at all.

He had always read a good deal but in a desultory fashion,
picking up what came his way. Now his love for England
directed all his reading energy—Chaucer and Spenser,
Shakespere of course, Marlowe, and Beaumont and Fletcher,
The Spectator, and Swift and Sterne, Fielding and Rich-
ardson, Jane Austen, and then all the Victorians, Macaulay,
Carlyle, Froude, Peacock, Landor, *Wuthering Heights* and
Henry Kingsley, Hardy and Meredith, and so to the mod-
erns. And the poets—Wordsworth first and best, Coleridge,
Shelley and Keats, Swinburne and Browning, Tennyson and
Rossetti—all of them for the things about England that they
could give him. But his great discovery was the accidental
finding in the library at Wintersmoon a volume of John
Clare. At that time in 1919 Clare was a forgotten poet. In
the following years, thanks to the generous enthusiasms of
Edmund Blunden, he was rediscovered and beautifully re-
issued, but to Wildherne that chance finding of a third
edition of the *Poems descriptive of Rural Life and Scenery*
seemed a miracle. He devoured the book, discovered then
that no one had ever heard of Clare, and further that no
one ever found the poems anything but trivial and commonplace. Even his father failed him here.

No matter. He would keep that to himself, as it seemed
to him he must keep almost everything that was of importance. Hunting discovered for him the two volumes of *The
Village Minstrel,* and this was of especial value to him because the first volume contained a steel engraving of Hilton's
painting of Clare. That strange, beautiful, pathetic face became now part of Wildherne's life. It seemed to him that he
had somewhere known him and been his friend. He knew

nothing as yet about his history, but he saw the tragedy in
those eager gazing eyes and that gentle mouth. To that man
at least he could have bared his soul.

He led now his public social life in London, and there
was no one to whom he could speak about his reading. When
he encountered, as he did at times, men who cared for the
Arts, they seemed to him to be so wise and to know so much
that his modesty prevented him. He felt, too, that there was
something about his social position which led them to dis-
believe that he *could* be interested in the Arts.

Some of his Oxford acquaintances moved among writers
and painters, but these seemed to care for things that he did
not understand. He was not modern at all. When your
favourite poets are Wordsworth, Arnold, and Clare, your
novelists Fielding and Sterne, your artists Cotman and
Bonnington and Girtin, what place had you in this other
world of eccentricity and revolt? The modern arts, when
he touched them at all, seemed to him all negation. His in-
comprehension seemed to him his own stupidity. He felt
himself slow, behind the times.

Meanwhile neither the social world nor the religious world
of Halkin Street realised that he cared at all for these things.
His good looks, the courtesy that he inherited from his
father, a certain gentleness that was never effeminacy, re-
tained for him in London the reputation that he had had at
Oxford: "Poole's a good sort. A bit absent-minded, hard to
know exactly, but one of the best really."

Then, early in 1920, came his meeting with Diana Guard.

Before this women had meant little to him. His love for
his father had been the only emotional experience roused by
another human being that he had known.

He fell in love with Diana Guard at sight. She was not a
beautiful woman. She was so fair as to be almost without
colour; she was not graceful, nor did she dress with any
special care. She gave, in general, the impression that she
was indifferent entirely to what anyone thought of her, and
that impression was the true one. She did not care.

She had married Charlie Guard when she was eighteen,
and he had been unfaithful to her within a month of the

wedding ceremony. They were quite good friends, and stayed
together for a week or two when they had nothing better to
do. Her father, old Prentiss Merriman, had left her plenty
of money; Charlie always borrowed from her when he was
in need. She had a beautiful flat in Charles Street, and a little
house near Reading.

She was in love with Wildherne for about six months,
and after that liked him very much.

He was swept by a storm of passion that blinded and
deafened him to the outside world save in this, his desperate
fear lest his father and mother should know of his intrigue.

Miraculously they did not. They lived, both of them,
quite outside the gossiping world of modern London, and
Wildherne was too well liked for anyone to think it his or her
worth while to carry tales. All London knew. He was by no
means Diana's first lover, nor would he be the last. Wildherne did not blind himself to this, nor did Diana attempt
to hide anything, but when the six months were over and
she loved him no longer, and told him so, he suffered tor-
tures only possible for the constant lover. She wished that
he would not be so constant. She was often bored with him.
And yet she liked him. She often wished that she did not.

He was on his way now to tell her about Janet.

He feared, most deeply, this interview. He feared it because he knew even now as he drove to Charles Street that
with every step nearer to Diana Janet's image was fading.
As he went up in the lift Janet vanished. There was left
only a promise, a message, a given word. And yet Diana's
sitting-room was as colourless as it always was. The wall-
paper was of a stiff dull bronze. There was only one picture,
a Walter Sickert oil of one of his Montmartre music-halls,
smoky grey with a spread of dingy red, out of which twisted
faces supported by crooked arms emerged. The only other
ornament was a dark Epstein bronze of a woman whose eyes
were full of longing, hatred, and chagrin. There was a piano;
there was a long book-case crammed untidily with foreign
books in paper covers. In a chair covered with a dark green
tapestry Diana was sitting. Her faint hair, pale face, and
dress of dark red-gold were as still and quiet as a pool in an

autumn wood. The eyes of the Epstein woman were the only
things in the room that had movement.

Wildherne came and sat down opposite her. No, he didn'
want tea. He smoked a cigarette. He didn't look at her. As
always when he was near her his heart hammered as though
it would beat him down on to his knees before her. He could
never be with her without instant memory of all the details
of the intimacies of the six months that they had had to
gether, as a drowning man is supposed to see his past life
Each separate detail flicked him with its sense of some
loveliness lost for ever.

"Well, Wildherne—you've come to tell me about your
engagement." She spoke very kindly; she liked him so much
and especially now that he was to belong to some other
woman.

"Yes, I have."

"Very right and proper. I've met her, of course, but al
ways with her sister, who is so pretty that she blinds one to
anyone else."

How like Diana! At once to make Janet obscure and
faded.

"Now tell me all about it, what you said to her, what she
said to you, whether everyone is pleased (which, of course
everyone is), that you're happy, that she's happy—every
thing."

"There isn't very much to tell," he answered. "When I
proposed to her I said that I didn't love her, that I couldn't
love her because I loved you."

At that Diana made a slight movement. "Oh, Wildherne
how like you! But why did you? Did you have to do that?"

"It seemed to me that I had. I couldn't marry her with
out telling her. Of course she had heard about us already, but
that made no difference. I had to tell her everything." He
paused.

"And it made no difference? She accepted you at once?"

"Not at once. I proposed to her three times. She was as
honest with me. She told me that she didn't love me either,
that the only person in the world that she loved was her
sister. It is partly for her sake that she is marrying me."

"I see. A thorough *marriage de convenance.*"

"No," he answered. "Not altogether. We are excellent friends. I like her tremendously. She likes me, I think."

"Most satisfactory," Diana said, "in this world where there is so little honesty. But there, you are an honest person, Wildherne. Too honest sometimes. I have told you so before now. You deserve to marry someone honest as yourself. You wouldn't be happy with anyone else."

He stood up, terribly agitated. "Diana—this is good-bye, you know. I can't see you again. That won't matter to you, but to me—it's something rather sharp—something torn out of me . . ." He broke off. He was trembling.

She looked up at him smiling. He looked very handsome standing there, with his yellow hair, the fine way that his head, thrust back, in its carriage and poise spoke of strength and courage and pride. Fine English. That's what he was. Dull as compared with Fine French or Italian or Spanish, but reliable in a way that no other aristocracy was. Diana liked him very much indeed.

"But, Wildherne—how foolish! Part? Why on earth? We're friends now, not lovers. We've had all this out over and over again. You know that you'll need me sometimes, just to talk to, to laugh with. Married men do need their women friends once and again. Part? What nonsense!"

"No! That's easy for you to say, but not for me. You are out of love, yes, and small trouble it has cost you, but I am as I was from the first. It must be broken. How often we've agreed about that! Haven't you told me again and again—'Wildherne, you must marry! You must marry! You must marry!'—We've repeated it, both of us, one to the other, like parrots. Well, now I'm doing it at last. And the condition is—I've told you always that it would be! I've told you. . . ."

He broke off, hesitated, then fell on his knees at her feet, burying his face in her lap. She stared out into the room above him, as so often before she had stared, stroking his hair gently and wondering, not about him but about herself —why she was for ever wanting what she could not have, why the savour went instantly from anything secured. An old wonder and eternal so long as the human heart beats

He raised his head, looked with aching desire into her eyes.

"Oh, Diana, help me! Send me away now and let me never return. You don't want me. You're bored with me. You'll be glad to be rid of me."

She took his head between her hands, bent down and kissed his forehead, then, moving, stood up, and he also, they both, side by side, before the fire.

She caught his hand and held it tightly in hers.

"No, Wildherne, I don't love you. That's true enough. But I love no one, and most certainly not myself. Love eludes me. At most I see it a room away, always out of touch. But friendship, that's another thing. Of all the nonsense this stupid post-war time has brought us *that* at least is our merit, that we've learnt the value of friendship between men and women, how to manage it and hold it so that it lasts. I want you as a friend. I can't trust anybody around me. They are false, and so am I. But you are *not* false. I can trust you altogether, and so I want you for a friend. Your Jane can't grudge me that. Besides, if all I hear is true, she's not a grudging woman."

"Well enough for you," he answered impatiently. "You will use me at the times when someone has deserted you or spoken ill of you or irritated you. Good enough. But for myself, no. I tell you I love you, with my body as well as the rest of me. That being so I will see you no more. Stop loving you I cannot, but stop seeing you I can."

She looked at him. Then something she saw in his face caused her to smile a little cynically.

"Well," she said, holding out her hand. "Au revoir."

"No," he answered her. "Good-bye."

"Oh, I never say good-bye," she said, turning carelessly away from him and looking into the little round gold mirror above the fire. "Things crop up again and people return. . . ."

He made as though he would speak, then swiftly, not looking back, left the room.

CHAPTER VI

A FAMILY AFFAIR

JANET was ready for the great family party.

In half an hour's time she would have surrendered herself to Purefoys, Darrants, Mellons, Medlers, Chichesters. In half an hour's time she would be standing there simply that they might gaze upon her, make their comments, deliver their judgments.

And she was *not* afraid.

That was the astonishing thing. Rosalind declared that were it her she would be *terrified*. Going as nobody at all—simply as the sister—of course she did not mind.

But Janet was surprised at her own absence of fear. She had been anticipating this event for many days; she saw in Wildherne's allusions to it that he was himself nervous. She had expected to be afraid and, with joy she knew it, she was not.

She was not afraid, because other things of a more serious nature were occupying her mind, and the most serious of them was Rosalind. She knew as she stood at the window of their little room and looked down at the pattern of lights threading the dusk below her that she was in one of those moods described by Rosalind as "melodramatic," those moods that Rosalind so deeply detested. She only knew these moods in relation to her sister, and they came always when she doubted Rosalind's love for her. There were times—and of late they had been frequent—when she seemed to lose touch with Rosalind altogether, when there was nothing to feed the hunger of her love. Calm, sensible, controlled as she could be with everyone else, with Rosalind she was sometimes like a desperate lover. She knew well when these moods were upon her and she hated them, but hate them as she might

73

they gripped her with a dreadful and torturing pain as though the fingers of some animal were laid upon her heart.

Rosalind came in, lovely in a white dress cut low enough to startle the Purefoy world. Janet was in black, a necklace of small pearls round her throat.

"Rosalind—you never turned up at lunch after all."

"No, darling, I couldn't. I'd have telephoned but. . . . How grand you look. Carrying yourself like a queen, the papers would say."

"Yes, you might have telephoned. Why didn't you?"

Rosalind's eyes were restless, saying, "Oh where can I escape?" She hated more than any other thing in her life these moods of Janet's.

"I don't know why I didn't. Oh, Janet, *don't* be tiresome. Not to-night. And I'm so sick of 'Where have you been? Why didn't you? What were you doing?' Can't you *see* how irritating it is?"

Janet's voice trembled. "And can't *you* see how selfish you are? Doesn't it occur to you that these last days— the last that we shall have alone—matter to me, that I want to be with you, and that you are always escaping me?"

"Yes, I *am* escaping you if you want to know. Just because you bother so. Why can't you let it all be natural? You are always forcing everything. You are natural enough with other people. Why not with me?"

"Because I love you so, because I love you more than all the rest of the world put together over and over again. That's why. Rosalind—darling—don't withdraw yourself now, now of all times, when I need you, when I *want* your love——"

"But I'm *not* withdrawing myself. You're so melodramatic, Janet. Always with me, never in the least with anyone else."

"But I'm *lonely,* Rosalind. Without you I haven't anyone. No one in the world. I *must* have you. I *must. I must.*"

"That's a nice thing to say a month or two before your marriage. Oh, I know you don't love him, but you're always telling me what wonderful friends you are. Surely you don't need me so much now you've got him."

"Not if you're happy." Janet drew her sister close to her. "You haven't been happy for ages. And you won't tell me anything. Of course I'm miserable when I see there's something the matter."

"There's nothing the matter." Then Rosalind went on more gently. "There's the bell. The taxi's there. Don't worry, Janet, dear. I'm quite all right, and you're going to be Queen of the Evening and I one of your humblest subjects. Now let's be happy. I'm sorry about luncheon. I am truly. But you know what I am, never in the right place at the right time. I'm hopeless."

They kissed and went together down the dark little stairs.

Inside the taxi Janet was miserable. Combined with her unhappiness about Rosalind was also the consciousness that she was being terribly unfair to Wildherne. It was true that he and his family, the Duke, the Duchess, and all the Purefoy world, might slip into the nethermost pit, and if only Rosalind were spared she would not care. Not at all? Well, only a very little. Oddly with that thought came the knowledge that she would miss Wildherne. He had been very good to her during these last weeks, and her heart, hungry for affection, always responded to any kindness. But one kiss from Rosalind outweighed all the kindness in the world from others. And this uncertainty. Why would Rosalind never tell her anything.

She made one more attempt.

"Rosalind, will you promise if there's anything the matter—even a little thing—to let me know at once?"

"Of course I will. You old goose, what *could* be the matter?"

"Anything might. There isn't anything, is there?"

"No, I tell you. No."

"It isn't Tom Seddon, is it?"

"Tom Seddon?" Rosalind laughed. "Heavens, no! It will be a long time before Tom keeps me awake!"

"He's most tremendously in love with you."

"Is he?"

"You know he is. Put him out of his misery, Rosalind, if you don't care for him. It isn't fair to leave him in doubt."

"Darling, you talk just like a Victorian novel. And here we are. Now for the fun!"

Wildherne, standing behind his mother at the top of the staircase, had a new impression of Janet. He was always just now receiving new impressions of her. It was as though someone were forcing him to realise that this affair of marriage was more complicated and subtle than he had as yet acknowledged to himself.

How many Janets was he marrying, and how many Wildhernes would marry her?

The crowd pressing up the staircase was very great. Janet, taller than most of the women, seemed, with her carriage and simple clothes, to be set apart from them. She looked proud, aloof, almost inhuman. He did not know that even now she was still thinking of Rosalind.

He had beautiful jewels waiting for her, but he was pleased to-night that she should be so simple. Her black hair, piled high, had no ornament; her neck and bust were superb. Yet she was not beautiful—kindly and a little remote —to-night she was finer than he had ever seen her, but at once she was always extinguished when you saw Rosalind. Rosalind's perfection of beauty did not mean monotony; she was saved from that by her delicate shell-pink colour and by the gold of her hair that, in its waves, hid shade upon shade of light.

As she came up the stairs, her eyes shining, her lips a little parted with her anticipated pleasure, her body moving with perfect grace and rhythm, she seemed to Wildherne the most beautiful creature ever seen by him. And yet not a pulse in his body beat the faster at the sight of her. Diana, if it had been she! And she would not of course be here to-night. Janet was speaking to his mother; with a little unexpected clap of pleasure he realised that he was *glad* that she was there, that she was his friend; there was already a sort of homeliness, a fireside feeling in his thought of her. Poor, dark Janet! lonelier, far lonelier than he knew.

The Duchess greeted her very kindly and then Wildherne came and led her into the long ballroom.

To Rosalind, following the happy pair, the party seemed at first sight a rather dowdy one. The room was very fine with its white walls, shining background to the family pictures and its glitter and sparkle of light, but nobody was very smartly dressed. Very few *young* people. No naked people at all. A great many old men with ribbons and orders. Faces stood out. The Prime Minister, the Archbishop of Canterbury. Of course there would be *lots* of clergy. . . .

And then it came to her slowly that the whole had something of an air, something rather grand, but something unreal as though it were a pageant. No one seemed to move, voices were low, very dimly from some obscure distance stole the murmur of a band, and the eyes of the stout mild gentleman and lady in the Purefoy Gainsborough stared down at Rosalind's golden hair and slim body and naked back as though they wondered what she was doing there.

Whether it were the Gainsborough or no she was aware, for the first time for many a month, that her clothes were unlike any others in the room. She did not care, but she did hope that soon she might find a friend, someone with whom she could laugh a little, just a little, at all these quaint old people.

Janet meanwhile had little time for observation. At the sight of the Duke, so square and sturdy, so aristocratic and at the same time so romantic with his square-cut white beard, piratical to-night as though this shining floor were the deck of his vessel and these all his captives, wearing his decorations with an air and yet also with an adorable absent-mindedness—she felt love for him flood her heart. The loneliness that all day had been so heavily oppressing her fled at sight of him. He drew her arm through his, nodding to Wildherne over his shoulder.

"I must capture her for five minutes: maybe we'll never return!"

She pressed her arm against his side and liked to feel his heart beating steadily through the stuff of his clothes.

Her love for him was growing apace. It was extraordinary how sheltered and protected he made her feel.

"Nervous?" he asked her as they passed out of the room.

"Not a bit. But where are you taking me?"

They had paused for a moment in a dimly lit alcove.

"First for this." He drew her to him, put his arms around her and kissed her on the lips. "I've longed to have a daughter —all my life—and now when at last I've got one I make the most of it. It had been almost too late, you know!"

She caught his hand, pressing it between both of hers.

"Oh!" she whispered. "Let me see you often, very often. There are going to be some things that will be difficult. I love you already so much. I think I could tell you anything."

"It's a compact," he answered, looking into her eyes. "We'll be together in everything.

"And now," he went on gaily, "this is the second reason I took you away!" He opened a door and led her into a little room, plastered so heavily with bright "marine" water-colour drawings that a large marble bust on the mantelpiece of Georgiana Duchess of Romney (1790–1822) looked extraordinarily solid and, beside so many waves and sea-horses, astonishingly static. Beneath the bust, sitting very straight and stiff in a cloth tapestry chair, was a little old lady in a lace cap. This was Lady Anne Purefoy, nearly a hundred, thoroughly alive and interested in everything.

Janet had never met her before. She kissed her. The lace cap nodded approval. She was a very gentle old lady, and had a voice like a musical-box, very sweet and true but distant so that you must bend your head to listen. Janet sat down beside her, and the Duke, in his favourite position with his thick legs squarely spread and his hands behind his broad back, stood over them benevolently.

"I have to stay in here, my dear. All those people in there rather too much for me. I'm ninety-two. So many relations. Fatiguing. And so you will marry Wildherne and the family will carry on. Take care of the first year. That's the difficult one. Never been married myself, of course, but have watched others. You've a sensible face. I like your hair. Forgive a very old lady her impertinences. The Queen said to me once, "Anne, you'll be impertinent to the last"—and so I shall be, to the very last. Shan't I, Geoffrey?"

"I'll tell you that, Aunt Anne, on your hundred and fiftieth birthday," he answered her.

"Ugh," she gave a little sarcastic shrug. "Don't threaten me. Lived much too long already. This noisy, distracting, adorable world. But tell me a little about yourself, my dear. Are you happy?"

"Very happy, Lady Anne," Janet answered softly.

"That's right. You should be. Wildherne is a dear. Are you economical? Can you run a house?"

"I haven't had a great deal of experience. My sister and I have been alone in the world for some years."

"Ah, your sister. She's very beautiful, they tell me. Is she here to-night?"

"Yes."

"Someone must bring her to see me, Geoffrey. I love to look at pretty girls. And are you very modern, deny God, and laugh at the King and Queen? You've plenty of clothes on your back, I'm glad to see. Not that I'm against a little fun. We old Victorians weren't by half as dull as they make us out to have been. Not by half. And do you rush about everywhere in a motor car?"

Janet laughed. "All my friends think me very old-fashioned," she said. "I'm quite ordinary, Lady Anne—ordinary and slow."

"Well, I'm glad you are—so glad you're not clever. We were just as clever sixty years ago, but we didn't make such a hullaballoo about it. If Mr. Disraeli and Huxley and Mr. Gladstone (although I never liked him) weren't clever, I wonder what they were. Show me anyone as clever to-day. Lloyd George and the rest. However, that's what we old people are for ever doing, running down the present. I don't want to, I'm sure. I find it very amusing but transitory. Selfish too. In the old days we believed in something greater than ourselves. A little too much in earnest, perhaps, but we had our little jokes."

"I must be taking her back, Aunt Anne," the Duke said. "She's the heroine to-night, you know."

"So she is. So she is. I like her. I like her very much in-

deed. Kiss me, my dear. May God bless you and keep you
and give you fine children worthy of their grandfather."

Her hot trembling hand rested for an instant on Janet's
cool forehead.

Soon she was standing in the long drawing-room, the
Duchess on one side of her, Wildherne on the other. This
was not an official reception; they stood there casually as
though accident had placed them, and yet in a moment it
was official, as official as though it were a Court Drawing-
Room.

And so, in its Purefoy world, it was. Yes, and further
than that, in its section of England ruled by the Purefoys,
Medleys, Chichesters and Darrants it had that significance,
for the Duke and Duchess were King and Queen of that
section and Janet bride of the Heir-Apparent.

She had not realised—she had had as yet no opportunity
of realising—how immensely self-sufficient, self-important,
and secure this world was. It was disregarded almost entirely
by the Press of the day. Its house parties, receptions, jour-
neys were scarcely recorded. The illustrated papers, the
novels of the time, the scandals, the fashions had no concern
with it. Any account of the England of the moment was
preoccupied with a Post-War Society, apparently conscience-
less, heartless, and creedless, and yet this Post-War Society
was numerically minute and potentially inorganic compared
with *this* unperturbed, resolved, static Society that, infinitely
poorer of course than before the war, yet carried on its
creeds, its ceremonies, its responsibilities precisely as though
no other Society existed.

And it was into this Society that Janet was now irrevocably to be plunged! Yes, irrevocably. She could see as she
faced them that they had claimed her for their own, that
she belonged now utterly to them, not they to her, and that
they had no doubt whatever that she was exceedingly fortunate to have been so chosen.

She caught the tone of it exactly from the Duchess. It
was her *luck* that she should know all these people and that
they should accept her so swiftly as one of themselves, and

she knew now that it had been from the beginning the root
of the Duchess's satisfaction, the foreknowledge that she
would be so accepted.

One of her deepest impressions was of kindliness. On
other casual visits either to Halkin Street or Lady Medley's
or Lady Blanche Chichester's or wherever she had not been
sure of that. She had been *outside* their world. And in the
society of Rosalind's friends she had known that there was
no kindliness at all. Camaraderie, perhaps, but always a
horror of sentiment, emotion, and above all a preoccupation with self that insisted on freedom at all and every
cost.

To-night again and again she caught that look of shy,
almost diffident friendliness. There were more young people than she had expected, girls with whom she felt she
could establish very pleasant relationships, but for the most
part her new uncles, aunts, and cousins were elderly and, as
Rosalind was surely somewhere confidently asserting, "too
established for worlds."

No one was difficult to talk to. They evidently had no desire that you should be clever; Janet did not feel, as always
with Rosalind's set, that she was two sentences behind and
that everyone was aware of it.

One fact gradually emerged from the tangled confusion
of words—her great fortune, they all felt, in having Wintersmoon for her home. Wintersmoon was *the house* in all
England. What a tragedy that in these monstrous days of impossible taxes some of it must be closed, but perhaps, as times
were better and we left the horrible war behind us, they
would be able to throw it all open again. Wintersmoon . . .
Wintersmoon . . . Wintersmoon . . . with its history and
stories and tradition and colour, with its great Oak and lovely
Minstrel's Gallery and Queen Elizabeth's bed and the wing
where Charles I. stayed for a whole fortnight before Edge-
hill, its three ghosts, and its Spanish Walk. She must indeed
be too gloriously happy in the prospect of such a home!

"And you'll suit it, my dear," said old Clara Darrant with
her bushy eyebrows and high lace collar (it was said that
she believed herself the reincarnation of Queen Elizabeth).

"I can see that you are going to be just right for it. Dear
Wildherne has chosen well."

She could see that there was something in her of which
they all approved. What this was she did not know, but in
the midst of all her preoccupation this private thought rather
miserably attacked her—that Wildherne had seen just this
same quality and had chosen her for that as you might choose
a chair or a table to go into a certain room because it suited
the Period!

And then *his* kindliness drove that thought away. Never
before, in her knowledge of him, had he been so right, so
exactly feeling for her and with her in all the twists and
turns of her situation, and when, at long last, she could move
away with him slowly to another part of the room, she
smiled at him her gratitude.

"You're tired?" he asked.

"Yes, a little—naturally. But they are all kinder than
kind. Wildherne, do you *approve* of me? Is everything all
right?"

"Everything is perfect. They all like you so much. Father's eyes are shining with pride. And mother's telling the
Bishop of London this very moment what a fortunate thing
it is that I've shown so much wisdom. . . ."

But it was odd with what an eagerness of discovery she
saw, a moment later, Rachel Seddon. It was like coming
home. The Duke, Rachel, Rosalind were the three in that
house that evening who could make her feel that. Not Wildherne.

She caught Rachel's hand with an impetuosity unlike her
accustomed gravity. Old John Beaminster, who was sitting
on the little gilt sofa beside his niece, wondered. He had
not seen Janet Grandison many times before, and never
like this with her head up so finely, her eyes shining, her
cheeks flushed. Why, she was almost a beauty! The old
man, a little a fish out of water to-night, the Beaminster
world being even in these degenerate days much gayer than
this Purefoy one, had just been murmuring to Rachel,
"Damned lot of parsons here—I'm going to clear," and then,
struck with the drama of Janet's presence, decided to stay on.

Rachel Seddon, looking more alien than usual in this so-English company, bent her dark eyes on her friend and then drew her close to her on the little sofa. "Janet, darling, you're much a success. I hear murmurs on every side of me: 'But isn't she charming? Just the wife for Wildherne. So quiet . . .' Oh yes, you're a success. You're doing it all to perfection. My dear, if you'd only seen me at my coming-out ball years ago. Do you remember, Uncle John, how terrified I was and how kind you were to me? That was the night I fell in love with Tony. . . . Ah dear! *Tout passe.* . . Tom's somewhere; have you seen him?"

No, Janet had not. Had Rachel been talking to Wildherne, because if not she must.

"Yes, we had a delightful time. I like him so much. I find that we think alike about almost everything, even about yourself. And his hair's such a nice colour. It would be a fortune to a woman. Ah! here's M. Brun. Do you know Miss Grandison? Janet, this is M. Felix Brun, one of my oldest friends, and the only man in Europe who knows anything about politics."

Little Brun was excited to-night. He had never before seen gathered together under the one roof so many of "the True English." Yes, in most of the other London houses to-day your companions might be of any European nationality, or at least American. But here, in what he called to John Beaminster "this rocky fastness," the English type was astounding. There was a foreign diplomat or two, but otherwise—all English. And, most amazing of all, not an American to be seen anywhere! Oh, but he was excited! And how odd they all were! So many clergymen in their black silk waistcoats and high white collars, so many old ladies, so many young ones without paint and powder, such dowdy clothes, and yet—something so fine and definite, something so unimaginative that it had all the clarity of a single-eyed vision.

Singled-eyed! That's what they were, with England right in the middle of the picture. No cheapness, no haste, and a pride that only the aristocracy of his own country could equal.

And now here was this tall, dark, plain girl about to marry
that tall, fair, handsome man, ultimately with God's grace
and the permission of the Bolsheviks to reign as queen of
this Purefoy country. A nice girl but stupid, he fancied.
Naïve at least. But then how naïf everyone around him
looked to-night! English naïvete hiding perhaps deep sub-
tleties. It was precisely of that that the clever people of other
nations could never be sure. It was precisely of that that
Brun could not to-night be sure. Was this great roomful as
simple as it looked? On the whole, he believed not.

Janet was able to spare but little attention on M. Brun.
Her eyes were roving everywhere for her sister. Never
for an instant through all the evening's happenings had she
forgotten her, but she had not been simply free to go to her.
Now she *was* free and she *would* go. Then she saw her—
slowly crossing the room with Wildherne. Janet knew instantly that things were going ill between them. She knew
exactly that expression of Rosalind's when, her temper
piqued, she was like a naughty insulting child. Wildherne's
courteous patience was easy enough for anyone to see. All
eyes were drawn to Rosalind as she passed. Her dress, or
lack of it, the lovely movement of her body, the easy almost
insolent gaze with which she honoured the room, it would
have been strange had she passed unnoticed. Then Janet saw
her eyes flash with relief. She broke away from Wildherne
almost without a word and in a moment was speaking to a
tall gaunt woman resembling a young friendly crocodile—
Althea—Althea Bendersley, a great friend of Rosalind's,
here to-night because she was a first cousin of Blanche
Chichester's. They greeted one another with eager laughter
and moved away. Janet's only too active imagination followed them into some corner where, eagerly ferocious, they
would pull the party to flakes and shreds.

Wildherne seemed for an instant bewildered by her so
precipitant desertion, then old Clara Darrant attacked him
and he was attentive courtesy once more.

Ancient M. Brun was talking, but Janet did not listen.
How could she ever have supposed that Rosalind would be
happy in this world? She had been so eager to extricate

Rosalind from the discomfort and unhappiness of their
struggling poverty that she had not thought at all of the
new life into which she was drawing her.

Her chief demand of Wildherne had been that Rosalind
should share their home, but how could she have been so
blind as to suppose that Rosalind would for a moment do so?
She had lost Rosalind by this step that she had taken, lost
her, not secured her.

A desperate restlessness possessed her.

"Excuse me, M. Brun, but I must find my sister. Rachel,
I'll be back in a moment. I simply haven't set eyes on Rosalind all the evening."

"I saw her with Althea Bendersley a moment ago," Rachel
said. Had Rachel seen Rosalind and Wildherne together?
Rachel saw so much. It was as though the Slav part of her
gave her some kind of second sight. She knew so constantly
just what Janet was feeling, but then this barrier of her
dislike of Rosalind came up between them and separated
them. Janet knew that Rachel was feeling that now—distrust, dislike that would quickly be hatred if Rosalind in-
jured her adored Tom.

Janet moved away, unhappiness in her heart. The people around her were all in an instant ghosts to her. Not one
of them save the Duke belonged to her. She wanted him with
a sudden desperate need that was only, as she well knew, the
precursor of many future needs. But she did not see him.
The room thickened and darkened around her. She had made
some horrible mistake. She would be punished all her life
because she was selling herself, body and soul, for comfort.
That it was not *her* comfort made no difference; and surely
she saw clearly enough to-night that it would not be Rosalind's comfort. Why had she done this thing? What crazy
impulse had driven her? The consciousness of her friendship with Wildherne had left her. Friendship when he was
madly in love with another woman?

She looked everywhere for her sister; then found herself
face to face with the very last human being whom at that
distracted moment she wished to encounter, the Duchess's
protégé, Caroline Marsh. The girl was standing against

the wall by herself. She looked plain and awkward in he
white dress, her pince-nez ill-fitting so that with a perpetua
nervous movement she was for ever pushing them bac
against her eyes.

At the sight of her lonely silent figure Janet's heart wer
out to her.

"Oh, Miss Marsh," she said, holding out her hand an
smiling, "how are you? I•do hope you are enjoying your
self."

"Oh yes, thank you, Miss Grandison," with great nervous
ness. "It's lovely, isn't it? I'm sure you ought to be ver
happy, Miss Grandison, seeing everyone so pleased. I'm sur
it's a great occasion. And Lord Poole's been so kind. H
brought me a cup of tea. I wouldn't have bothered him fo
the world, but he *is* so thoughtful, always thinking o
others."

"Let's sit down for a moment," said Janet, "here on thi
little sofa. You must have seen many friends here thi
evening."

"Well, Miss Grandison, friends . . . one can't expect t
have many of them, can one? But acquaintances, oh ye
ever so many! Trying to help the Duchess as I do of cours
I meet a lot of people. And may I ask when the day for th
wedding is fixed? Oh, I do hope you don't think me imperti
ent."

"Of course not. The wedding will be towards the end o
April, I expect. No one likes being married in May, althoug
of course it's only a superstition."

"Silly, isn't it? Oh, I do think superstitions are very foo
ish, don't you? And if I may say so your sister's lookin
perfectly lovely to-night. Quite a vision! Everybody's bee
commenting on it. Mr. Pomeroy thinks her lovely too. Don'
you think Mr. Pomeroy's a delightful gentleman, Mis
Grandison?"

"Well, really," Janet answered, laughing, "I have seen s
little of him so far."

"Oh, I think he's splendid! Everything he does is so fine
The Duchess wouldn't know how to get on without him, sh
wouldn't indeed! It just does one good to be near him."

And then Janet realised a strange thing. This plain, awkward, common girl, whom as she had fancied she had pleased by noticing, disliked her—yes, disliked her intensely. She did not know how she was aware of this, but she was quite certain of it. It emanated from the girl like a faint but unmistakable perfume. What was it? Jealousy? Or fear? Or hurt vanity? Had Janet done or said something?

Absurd how this knowledge added to her depression. This girl looked upon her as an invader, and there would be others, perhaps many others, who would do the same.

She got up.

"We must be friends," she said, smiling. "There are many things that will be difficult for me at first. I do hope you will help me sometimes."

Miss Marsh got up awkwardly, nervously pushing at her pince-nez.

"That's very kind of you, Miss Grandison. Of course if I can be of any assistance to you in any way——"

Mr. Pomeroy appeared, very elegant, very urbane. He had friends whom he wished to introduce, and then there were others. But people were leaving. Soon, ah soon, she would be able to escape. Wildherne found her, and together they moved into the next room.

Together Rosalind and she were in a cab. She was so tired that life—her life, all life, any life—jumped up and down before her like a Jack-in-the-Box. Rosalind said not a word.

They were in their little sitting-room. As Janet turned towards her bedroom Rosalind cried:

"Janet, how awful!"

Janet stayed. "Awful! What do you mean?"

"This evening—the people—everything."

"Oh, don't now, Rosalind. I'm too tired to listen. Make your clever criticisms in the morning."

But Rosalind flung her arms around her sister's neck, keeping her.

"Listen, dear. I know you're tired now. I won't be long. But if ever I was serious in my life, I am now. Janet, you've

got to give it up. You've got to tell him to-morrow that you
can't marry him. Never mind if they talk. Never mind if
we're poor. We'll go abroad together somewhere—Mentone
or somewhere—it will be after the season soon and cheap.
Anything—only you've got to give it up! You can't go on
with it."

Janet dragged herself from her sister's embrace.

"Rosalind, are you mad? What on earth do you mean?"

"I mean what I say. You've got to give it up, all of it.
You're doing it for me, and you can't make that sacrifice.
I won't let you. They are dreadful, these people—quite
dreadful. You'll run away from them in a week. Why,
they're awful! They haven't an idea in their heads! They're
pompous and stupid and impossible. And you don't love him,
not a bit. You're bored with him already, and as for that
idiot his mother——"

"Stop, Rosalind!" Janet's nerves, already strained to the
thinnest thread, snapped. "How dare you? I should have
thought it would be enough that on this evening, when it
was so important to me, you shouldn't take the least little
bit of trouble and should be rude to everybody. But it isn't.
Have you no sense of *anything* decent? Can't you see anything except your own selfishness and your own vanity? Remember, now and always, they are *my* people, and when you
laugh at them you laugh at me!"

"Oh well, then"—Rosalind moved to her room—"if they
are *yours* they are not mine, and, thank God, never will be!"

And she banged her door behind her.

CHAPTER VII

MARCH : LONDON

ROSALIND——JANET——ZANTI——WILDHERNE

JANET had no sleep that night. The sulky strokes of the church of St. Matthew's grumbled the quarters and then, with slow annoyed reiteration, hammered out the hours. She knew the little church with its grey-white walls, its tower like a candle-snuffer, its old woman who had a flower-stall a little to the right of its door, the hair-dresser, Emanuel Giles, just opposite to it, and, as she lay there, she could see these details as though they had all pressed forward into her room out of vulgar curiosity as to why she wasn't sleeping.

Her most vivid emotion was one of surprise that she felt so hotly in defence of those people whom Rosalind had attacked. She had not expected to feel that, but, as the ones whom she knew best, the Duke, Wildherne, old Lady Anne, Clara Darrant, Blanche Chichester, Mr. Pomeroy, yes and even Caroline Marsh came before her, she had a strange protective feeling towards them all. It was true, perhaps, that they were slow and stubborn and complacent, but she saw Rosalind's bright young horde advancing down upon them, charging them, sweeping them off the field and replacing them—with what? With carelessness, selfishness, cynicism, pessimism, intolerance.

And then in reaction her love for Rosalind surged up in her. What could she do to reconcile the two worlds? Some way she must find.

But to go back on her word to Wildherne never for an instant occurred to her. It appeared to her, she found, infinitely less possible now than three months ago when she had first given it.

And then she felt again the terror that had conquered her

89

towards the end of the evening. This job would be perhaps too much for her. Although she would not have them insulted, she could not have them acclaimed as hers. Her loneliness and her terror of greater loneliness came from just that, that she seemed to belong neither to the Purefoy world nor to Rosalind's.

But then neither did Wildherne. Her safety lay in coming closer to him, in helping him to understand her difficulties and in learning from him his own. And so at last, as it were under the protection of his friendly arm, in the grey ghostly morning she fell asleep.

When she woke Rosalind was sitting on her bed. She bent forward and kissed her. "That's right. Now you're awake. I've brought your breakfast, and while you're eating it we're going to talk."

Janet sat up and rubbed her eyes. Then she pulled Rosalind's head towards her and kissed it, burying her face in the fresh golden locks.

"I'm sorry I was cross last night. I was tired to death."

"Now don't you start that terrible humble apologising." Rosalind, one leg of her blue silk pyjamas over the other, puffed angrily at her cigarette. "I'm furious with myself. You were perfectly right. Last night I was as selfish and mean as I could be. I failed you at one of the most important moments of your life. I was disgraceful."

Janet knew that Rosalind always enjoyed these scenes of self-recrimination; but they were not the less genuine for that.

And, this time, there was something serious behind their difference. The quarrel could not be kissed away and forgotten as so many had been in the past.

"Yes, Rosalind dear, you did behave badly last night. Not so much when we came home but before that, at the party. You weren't nice to anybody. What happened to you? You were determined to be charming when you went, and then something changed your mood. What was it?"

"It was that pig of a Duchess. Oh, I beg your pardon, Janet. I forgot. But she was insufferable to me, Janet, really she was, patronising me as though I owed her the very

clothes on my back. And all the old women round me looking at me as though I were a prize mannequin! After that
Wildherne saw fit to take me in to see an old lady of about
nine hundred and ninety, who lectured me about the sins of
my generation as though *I* were responsible for them. She
spoke exactly as though Lloyd George were my little boy
whom, against the advice of all my relations, I'd sent to the
wrong boarding-school. By this time I was a little upset, and
then of course tumbled straight into Rachel Seddon and
Tom and that idiotic old Beaminster man—the last people
in the world I wanted to see. Rachel looked down her nose
at me, as she always does—how she hates me, that woman!
—and Tom made sheep's eyes until I could have throttled
him. Then Tom asked me to come and drink some tea with
him as though we were in one of Jane Austen's novels, and
I said I wouldn't, and turned round and tumbled—into whose
arms do you think, my dear—why, the Bishop of Polchester's—you know, that fat red man like a peony in full bloom
who was staying at the Conistons' when we were there last
year. *You* remember. The man who played tennis so ab-
surdly. So just to spite Tom Seddon I went off with the
Bishop to have some lemonade, and he made up to me like
anything, and asked me down to stay in the Palace at Polchester, and promised to play croquet with me. And then—
oh then I don't know what happened except that it was awful until, by a miracle of luck, I found Althea Bendersley.
After that it was better. We could sit in a corner and have
our little joke. But it's all very well; I don't want to excuse
myself. There's no excuse possible. I was disgraceful. I
meant so well when I started, but I can't endure to be
patronised, Janet, I can't indeed. It arouses everything evil
in me. And how dare they? I have never asked their charity
or indulgence! Oh, there I go again. . . . But, Janet, what
are we to do? That's the point. They're not my sort, and
never will be. I never can be happy with them. And you—
although you're so much better than me and so much quieter
—can *you* be happy with them, settle down with them, make
them your own people, *can* you?"

Janet, staring in front of her at the liquid blue March

sky beyond the window, waited a long while before her answer.

"That's my job, Rosalind," she said at last. "That's what I've got to do. Of course it isn't easy, but I think I like it because it's hard. I'll agree that I wouldn't have the courage to try if it weren't for two things. One is the Duke. I'm beginning to love him as though I really were his daughter, and I think he's beginning to love me. The other, of course, is Wildherne. You said last night that I don't love him and that already I was bored with him. The first of these things is of course true. Real love I feel only for you in the whole world, and I think that I am perhaps one of those who can only love one person at a time and that I couldn't begin to love Wildherne until I ceased to love you. I don't know how that is, but I do know that I am not bored with Wildherne, that I like him better every time I see him, that I admire him and trust him as I admire and trust no one else. You think him dull or slow or quiet, but then that *suits* me. We are alike, he and I, in many ways. We are old-fashioned perhaps, certainly we're slow and mean what we say. We have both given our word in this. It's our adventure. Of course we're taking risks, but that makes it more exciting. It may seem a tame sort of excitement to you, but it is not so really. There are great possibilities in it, and for more than ourselves."

"And Diana Guard?" asked Rosalind.

"Yes. I've faced that from the beginning. That isn't changed. He loves her, I suppose, just as he did. If I loved him I could not endure it, of course. But as it is——"

Rosalind got up and began to pace the little room, flinging back her head as she walked.

"All very well, then, but that hasn't settled the rest of them. Think of it. All the clergy and all the old women and all the long weeks down in Wiltshire. Wintersmoon may be a very beautiful house, but don't I know the kind of place it is! Half of it shut up with nice little ghosts with chains clanking up and down the empty passages, then the rooms that *are* lived in damp and mouldy, crammed with family portraits and armour. The garden and park overgrown and neglected, and the Duchess always coming down for the week-ends to see that you are doing as you ought to! Oh, Janet dearest, I didn't realise it until last night, but now that I do let me show you what you're in for! Give it up, Janet! Give it up! You're doing it for me, I know you are, although you talk so much about Wildherne and adventure. Wildherne and adventure! The two simply don't go together. You're doing it for me and I don't want it. I won't live in your mouldy old Wintersmoon anyway. Let's go on as we are. As I told you last night we'll go abroad to Mentone or somewhere. Perhaps I'll pick up a rich Spaniard or an Italian Marquis. I tell you, Janet, if you do this thing you'll just plunge me into temptation. Anything that happens to me afterwards will be your fault. I warn you."

"But, Rosalind," Janet said, "two months ago you were wildly delighted that I had done this. You were off your head with joy."

"Yes, but I didn't see what they were all like. I thought I could live with them, and now I see that I can't. I shall be all alone, and I'm not good when I'm alone."

"Darling, you won't be. You'll never be alone as long as I'm alive. You shan't go a scrap more to Halkin Street than you wish, and you won't find Wintersmoon so bad as you think. And then there's the Duke. You don't know him yet. You'll love him when you do."

"Old! old! old!" Rosalind chanted. "I've no use for anyone over sixty be he beautiful as Lucifer himself. It's no good. I haven't. I can't bear their hot dry hands and parchment skins. Sorry, Janet, but so it is. Well, there we are! You won't get out of it?"

"But of course not."

"It's your last chance."

"But, Rosalind, I don't get out of things. What I say I'll do, I'll do."

"Then you've ruined me. I warn you. I'm a ruined woman."

"Rosalind, don't be so idiotic. You can only ruin yourself. Don't pretend you're so weak."

"I am weak. Of course I'm weak. It's because of my adorable weakness that I'm so attractive." She looked back once more before she left the room. "I abandon you, then, to the Duchess and the Bishop of Polchester. Never say I didn't warn you."

Wildherne and Janet had arranged to meet that afternoon in the London Museum, a place to which she had never been. He said that it was pleasant because in the top rooms where the models and the old views were no one ever came and they could talk uninterruptedly.

Now this morning, thinking of Rosalind's words, it struck her that already she and Wildherne were fleeing from the family. Did he realise that? The wedding was fixed for the end of April, a month from to-day. St. Margaret's and wedding presents, small Purefoy cousins as train-bearers; it was all arranging itself into the regular ordained pattern. The March wind raced across the strip of blue sky dragging with it three discontented clouds who, busily engaged on their own private business, had been snatched up and worried off all against their poor wills. They tried to lag behind just as they passed Janet's window; all bulged and protesting they were. But no. Nothing to be done. They clung to a chimney and then, their skirts streaming behind them, were pulled away. Well, then, as Rosalind had said, here was Janet's last chance. To-day in that funny tucked-in Museum, buried in the heart of old grey buildings, she might extend Wildherne's eyes with horror by simply saying:

"Wildherne, I find that after all I cannot marry you."

Yes, and that little sentence quietly delivered, fine consequences there'd be! Everyone of course would say that, having discovered about Diana, she had thrown Wildherne over. The Duke and Duchess would hear with the rest—Wintersmoon ghosts would groan with disgust. The vast neglected garden would wail through all its grasses. No. And again No.

But, beyond that, she clung to Wildherne. She had never, in all her life, had a man friend, and already in these few weeks she had discovered that there were ways in which you

ould trust a man more than a woman. Simple men were
often indifferent when your spirit ached for some sort of
a scene, but certainly to be trusted. As a friend, of course.
As lovers she knew that they were most uncertain.

She had a strange fancy as she sat there—to stroke the
back of his neck where the hair grew short and lay in gold
parks of light against his fair skin. She knew why she
thought of that. Because his hair was like Rosalind's, the
same colour of glowing and glinting gold, the same fair gold
with deep shadows that passed and repassed as the head
turned. How many many times she had adored to busy her
hands in Rosalind's lovely hair, to pull the head slowly back
to her breast and then bend over and kiss the smooth forehead and the close soft eyelids! When Rosalind was weary
she liked that.

And so that was the physical link that Wildherne had with
Rosalind—the only physical feeling she had about Wildherne. How strange that in that same instant of discovery
of this feeling she should be conscious of a short quick stab
of jealousy of that other woman! The first. It passed as
quickly as it came. Had Diana Guard entered her room at
that moment she would have felt nothing but friendliness towards her. Nothing else? Well, only with it an increased
sense of loneliness because this Diana could draw human beings towards her so easily.

That power had never been Janet's. Rachel loved her,
and now, perhaps, the Duke. Rosalind at moments. But who
else in all her life? Was it her own shyness that kept them
away? Was it the absence in her of sexual feeling? Was it a
prudishness? Was it her own so long absorption in her
sister? ·

Whatever the reason, something had always shut her away
from other humans, and now perhaps this marriage with
Wildherne would open the door for her and give her freedom.

A letter fell with a soft thump into the little letter-box. She
went to rescue it and saw at once that it was in Tom Seddon's
sprawling, childish, but attractive hand.

"DEAR JANET"—she read—"I'm writing this so late a night that there'll probably be no sense in it. I'm writing after your party—I call it your party because it was for you, wasn' it, and anyway I shouldn't have been there if it hadn't been for you, if you understand what I mean.

"I'm writing of course about Rosalind. Oh, Janet, I am so miserable—so miserable and so ashamed. I am ashamed because I have broken down like this, but I have only to you, and you are so kind and understanding, and you love Rosalind so much that I am sure you will help me.

"If I knew that my case was hopeless I could, I think, bear it. *Of course* I could bear it. One can bear anything. But it is uncertainty that takes all my control away. I have asked Rosa lind twice to marry me and each time she has refused me, so that you would say that there isn't much uncertainty there wouldn't you? But although she has refused me she has spoken and behaved as though at any time she might change her mind. Sometimes she has been so kind to me that it has seemed as though she *must* mean 'yes.' But to-night at the Halkin Street party she would have nothing at all to do with me, until just at the last when I said 'good-night' she told me not to be angry with her and always to be her friend. I know that she doesn't love me, or doesn't most of the time, and then there are moments when I think she nearly does or would love me if she were with me a little more. Janet, tell me truly what you think. I can stand the truth. You must know what is in her mind. She must talk often to you. If you are certain that there is no chance for me at all, tell me. I must be more sure—my mother and old John Beaminster (who is a sort of Uncle to me) are so unhappy about it, and I try to pretend that there is nothing the matter, but it is very difficult when they know that something *is!*

"Then there is another thing. Of course she must have spoken to you about this man Ravage—Charles Ravage. Probably you know much more about it than I do. I don't want to be stupid and jealous. Rosalind has the right to make all the friends she wants to, of course, and for a long time I have tried not to worry about this. But now so many people talk that it is no longer a private affair. Everyone knows Ravage's reputation. To do him justice he does not attempt to disguise it and says frankly, anywhere and everywhere, that there is no code of morals to-day except the code of one's own pleasure. Rosa-

nd seems to like to be seen with him. I don't think that she
eally cares for him; it is a sort of bravado. But what is any-
ne so fine as she is doing with such a man at all? Forgive me,
anet, if I have interfered here when I have no business. I know
hat it is a dangerous thing to write letters as late as this. But I
an't resist it. No one but you can help me. Tell me if I have
ny chance. If I have, I will wait for ever. If you tell me that I
ave not I will conquer myself. I *will*. I *must*.—Your affec-
ionate friend,

Том."

The last words of the letter were scrawled across the
age.

She was dropping down the hill into St. James's, a clock
triking half-past two just behind her, when the name of
harles Ravage really confronted her.

Until then—through the last scraps of notes hurriedly
vritten in the flat, through a confusion of shopping and a
trange luncheon in Harrod's somewhere between the Daffo-
ils and the Dogs, Parrots and Monkeys—again and again
he thought had been, "Rosalind tells me nothing," and
hen, stepping forward and crossing with it like a figure in
dance, the other thought, "Poor Tom. I'll have to tell him
he doesn't care"—and it was only now that Ravage con-
ronted her. Perhaps it was because she was stepping down
nto his world—this funny men's world of silver clocks and
iding whips, mountains of tobacco, eighteenth-century pic-
ures, and red leather bedroom slippers. She was invading his
astle and so, ogre-like, he leaned out of his tower window
nd glared at her.

She had heard of him often—never in connection with
Rosalind—and seen him once. That "once" was very vivid
o her. It had been some two years before at a Sunday eve-
ing performance of the *Venice Preserved*. Rachel had taken
er.

At the end of the first act, when the lights had gone up, she
ad seen this short, dark, frowning man standing in the dusk
f the passage by the stalls' entrance. She had asked Rachel
vho he was. Oh, didn't she know? That was the famous

Charles Ravage. She was disappointed. She had heard of him
as a man of great fascination and impudent courage. Im
pudent he might be, but surely neither fascinating no
courageous. He seemed to her shabby in a grey suit, a dar
blue linen collar. His scorn of the play, the theatre and every
one in it, was manifest enough. She had told Rachel that sh
thought him disappointing. Rachel had asked her what sh
had expected, and she had been ashamed to confess to he
school-girl fancy of a modern Byronic desperado. Des
perado, yes, but not Byronic.

And then, as the lovely tragedy had proceeded, he seeme
to slip past her and take his place on the stage. She could hav
sworn that she saw him staring out from between the curtain
of cloth of gold, watching cynically the loyalties of the tw
devoted friends. He would not believe in that nor in an
other fine motive. All the evening he haunted her.

Rosalind had never once mentioned him to Janet, and ye
it was common London gossip that he was her familia
friend. Janet thought no longer of Tom—only this, tha
with every half-hour of passing day Rosalind seemed mor
surely to elude her. There was yet half an hour before he
meeting with Wildherne; she panted to hasten it that sh
might put her trouble to him. In Rosalind's urgency that sh
should break her engagement with Wildherne and that th
two of them should go abroad somewhere and hide, ha
there been perhaps a longing to escape from a situation tha
was rapidly becoming dangerous? Why had Rosalind tol
her *nothing?* Only surely because she had been afraid t
tell her, and if she was afraid. . . .

In her trouble she found herself staring, without seeing
anything, into an old curiosity shop. She did not know wher
she was. Although it was not yet three o'clock the Marcl
afternoon had wreathed the London streets in a brown sunny
mist that was not a fog, that obscured nothing, but trans
muted the old grey stone, the windows and doors with ar
amber light.

On such an afternoon London becomes of more impor
tance than its inhabitants. The geniality is that of an old

entleman taking his ease in his club window and watching
ie world go by. No other city has that masculine geniality—
Iew York moves too fast, it cannot afford the time; Paris
 too feminine; old Rome too conscious of modern Rome to
e light-hearted; Stockholm too physically material; Peters-
urg—alas, poor Petersburg, Petrograd, Leningrad, sink-
ig back into its marsh whence so recently it climbed!—but
>ur old, brown, smiling gentleman, rotund-stomached, clear-
yed, too unimaginative to be disturbed by the strange mut-
:rings beyond his window, he is still there, the guardian of
ie world's tradition.

Janet, looking into her window, was conscious dimly of
eautiful things—of porcelain and precious stuffs, of gold
id silver boxes, of a crystal bowl, a silver crucifix studded
·ith jewels, and ivory cabinet.

Absent-mindedly, thinking bitterly of Rosalind, she
epped back and saw over the shop only the word in large
old letters—"ZANTI."

These letters were stamped upon the front of the neat
ttle shop with its dark blue door, having in their simple
ievitability a kind of cheeky independence. No more words
ere necessary. You could take "Zanti" or leave him.

For the second time that day Janet had an odd sense of her
st chance being offered to her. She must escape from her
tuation within an hour's time or submit to it for ever, and
5 though a step or two forward would assist her decision,
:arcely knowing what she did, she walked into the shop.

Within the shop there was dusk, a dusk flung into radiance
. different points by splendid fragments of colour, gold and
irple and amethyst. Out of the dusk there emerged an
iormously fat man.

"Madame, how can I zerrve you?" he asked.

He was of course a Southerner, jet black hair fitting
ghtly his round, pale, many-chinned face like a skull-cap.
[e was not short, but rather tall and extremely broad. On
is stomach you could have laid a tea-tray. His eyes were
nall and sparkling like black diamonds. The effect of him
as, in spite of his stoutness, not unpleasant. His fingers

were slender for so fat a man. His black suit was clean an
well brushed. His smile friendly but not sycophantic. Jane
though that he was perhaps an Italian.

When he asked his question Janet was confused.

"There was—I thought I saw in the window a rose
coloured bowl."

"If you think you zee it, Madame," he answered her
"then it is there, but as a matter of fact there is no suc
bowl in the window."

Had she seen it? She now almost believed that sh
had a lovely porcelain bowl of the most delicate rose. "
am sure I saw it," she said, "a porcelain rose-coloure
bowl!"

"If you zee it," he repeated, "it is there. Madame is lucky
It is Madame's possession for ever. She will always hav
her rose-coloured bowl. I am glad my shop has been so for
tunate as to provide her with it."

"But if it is true," Janet continued, "may I look at i
please? Would you mind getting it from the window?"

"It is not there in the window," he answered her, smiling
"but certainly in Madame's imagination. How much bette
for Madame! No one can take it from her, no careless serv
ant break it—her lovely rose-coloured bowl!"

"Then," said Janet, "why do you have your shop? Wh
should anyone buy anything?"

"Why indeed!" He nodded his head gravely. "But alas
zo many people have not Madame's imagination! They can
not own anything unless they have it physically in thei
hands, unless they can touch and feel. Fortunate for me
otherwise I starve—unfortunate for them. They mus
pay. . . ." Then he added after a pause, "I can show
Madame zome beautiful unreal things, things she may touc
and feel and must pay for."

She sat down and allowed him to show her some things
very lovely things, a vase of crystal, some cups of jade, a
chain of old gold and pearls, a diamond snuff-box. She looke
at them gravely one after another. Once or twice she aske
the price; it was always enormous.

"You are very expensive," she said.

"For these things, yes," he answered. "I don't care whether I zell or no. I have enough money for my own wants."

"Don't you love these beautiful things? Don't you hate to part with them?" she asked him.

"No," he answered. "Nothing I can zee has so much value for me. Here am I, an ugly fat man—ugly, isn't it so? But this is not myself. I have learnt through a long life hunting for treasure where are the valuable things."

"Hunting for treasure?" Janet asked. "Do you mean real treasure?"

"Certainly. I have been everywhere. I am a citizen of the world. For a long time I was in Cornwall, then in London. I had a bookshop. That was in the days of the good Queen Victoria. Then I went to Spain, hunting for my castle, you know. In the war I fought for my country, Italy. That was treasure hunt, I can tell you. Then I came to London. It was not difficult for me to find things for my shop. I know where they are. And I settle here, resting. I am at peace."

"You have found what you were searching for?" Janet asked him.

"Not found, no. But I go now in the right direction. I waste no time over what I can see with my physical eyes. I have also a rose-coloured bowl." Then, smiling at her in the friendliest fashion, he said: "But excuse me, Madame, I bore you. It was when you asked for the rose-coloured bowl that I was tempted to talk. I hope if you ever wish to rest for a moment you will come into my shop. There is no need to buy anything."

She got up, looking about her at all the beautiful things. "Thank you," she said. "I will remember. Do you apply your philosophy also to people?" she went on. "Are none of the qualities and defects that we see in our friends real, but only the things that we cannot see?"

He shrugged his heavy shoulders. "Certainly they are real, our qualities and defects. Most tiresome their reality. Their reality obscures the thing behind just as, Madame, that vase and chain and cup obscure your rose-coloured bowl if you consider them too closely. We waste our time too much with

these realities when the true purpose of life is beyond then
Do not look too often at that crystal vase, Madame. It is no
worth your trouble."

"It is very beautiful," Janet said.

"Only for a moment, Madame. When you have bought
and taken it home and zee it on your mantelpiece, then yo
know all about it and your pleasure is satisfied. So it is wit
people. We must make it our business to search for the thing
that we shall never find. After the full summing-up some
thing always remains. It is only that that is of value."

"Do you always," Janet asked, "entertain your customer
with your philosophy? You must sell very little if you do."

"Ah no, Madame," he answered her. "But you came int
my shop in trouble. You did not intend to come in. You di
not come as a purchaser but as a fellow-traveller."

At that moment a lady and a gentleman entered the shop
The cup of jade pleased them. They asked its price. Bargair
ing began. Mr. Zanti was, Janet saw, sharp and extremel
commercial. A fine dust of haggling filled the air.

Janet said "good-day" and sped away to the Museum.

Wildherne was there waiting for her. They went into th
Museum together. A sight of wistfulness trembled and wa
gone. Even the large red-cheeked family coming in throug
the turnstile, then slowly wandering up the spreading stair
case, paused and listened a moment as though they had hear
something.

The dresses rustled ever so slightly in their glass cases
All the drinking vessels swayed a little, and the ink-hor
found in Threadneedle Street shivered. The death-mask o
Oliver Cromwell stirred not, nor did the extended hand o
the sewing wench in the old Inn waver, nor the fires of burn
ing London diminish.

But little ghosts were for ever troubling those floors, try
ing to find garments and furniture and pictures that had on
time been their friends. The old, old men who guarded th
rooms being themselves so nearly finished with this worl
were often disturbed by dreams, by whispers, by the touc
of eager fingers upon their dried old hands—hard for then
to distinguish between one world and another—all alike, a

alike, save for the sixpence pressed into the palm. The little ghosts did no tipping. Their coinage was of another sort.

So Wildherne and Janet found their way up the cold little staircase to the room where the cold little models were, and they sat there looking down on to the green trees of the Park that, hushed by the March wind down into the dusk of the afternoon, were shaking their feathers and preparing for sleep.

". . . because," Janet was saying, "he never pressed me to buy a thing, which you'll admit, Wildherne, is very unusual. Indeed, he would have hindered my buying anything had I wished. But I could not have wished, because everything was so expensive."

"And he talked philosophy to you?"

"Well, if you call it philosophy. Nothing very new, at any rate."

"And his point was——?"

"His point was that there are two lots of people, the lot who believe in the things they see and the lot who believe in the things they don't see."

"And he was of the second lot?"

"He was of the second lot."

"Did he want to sell you something he couldn't see?"

"Not to sell me. To give me."

"And did he give it to you?"

"My dear, I don't know. In any case I suppose I took it without asking him, a lovely rose-coloured bowl."

"Can I see it?"

"I don't know. It depends how our marriage goes."

She jumped up. "Oh, Wildherne, what nonsense we're talking! Or are we? I don't know. In any case we've little time and much to settle. Or *is* everything settled?"

"Everything? What?"

"Bridesmaids and their dresses, thankings for wedding presents, best man, going-away clothes, and 'I think, Miss Grandison, that a *little* looser in the sleeves—just the leetl-est——' I've been engaged in such things for weeks. No, it's something else that we must talk about here. Wildherne, I've been nearly as nothing running away."

He did not seem disturbed.

"So I expected after our party. I knew that Rosalind would urge you. She did, didn't she?"

"Yes, she did."

"Why was she so cross last night? We all tried to be nice to her."

"Your sort aren't her sort," Janet sat down beside him again. "It's no use. I ought to have seen it long ago. Oh, Wildherne, I'm going to lose her! I'm going to lose her! Oh, what shall I do? I must keep her. I *must*. I *must*."

She began to cry, she who never cried. The strain of the last weeks, the multitudinous movements that she seemed, by her own action, so unexpectedly to have started, the sense of her responsibility, the dim feeling that she was unjust and unfair to those she loved, all this broke down her discipline. He put his arm around her as a brother might have done.

"Listen, Janet, dear. Don't cry or, if it helps you, cry, but don't feel desperate about this. You haven't learnt to trust me yet, but you can, indeed you can. We are both, I think, shy people, and we haven't learnt yet to depend upon one another. And remember when we first determined on this we saw only the big issue. Now that we have gone further we see more in detail. I suspect that everyone is frightened before marriage, and just because we have been honest with one another we are not blinded by any evasions. . . . But the big thing remains. We are going to marry because we mean to make something fine out of our lives, for others besides ourselves. No big thing was ever taken on by anybody without big difficulties. But while we are true to one another and see something also beyond ourselves and our own happiness, all is well, no one can touch us."

"Well for ourselves, perhaps." Janet dried her eyes. "But for others. Who will look after Rosalind when I have you?"

"But you will be there to look after her."

"Not if she won't come near me. And as it is, she is keeping everything from me."

"What things?"

"Do you know a man called Ravage, Charles Ravage?"

"Yes, a little. Rather an outsider."

"She's a great friend of his. Apparently she goes about with him everywhere. She has never so much as mentioned his name to me."

"Of course she has her own friends." He took her hand and closed his over it. "She's different from us, from you and me. We are older, staider, more old-fashioned. She can't lead our life, of course, but we can show her that we care for her and are there to help her. If we try to tie her in, of course she will be off. But we needn't do that. She's not a baby. She knows life. Every modern girl of her kind can look after herself if she wants to, and Rosalind is fundamentally decent. She doesn't like me at present, but she will perhaps when she knows me a little better. Janet, I expect you've been fussing her a trifle. You've been living too close to her."

Janet sighed. "Yes, perhaps I have. Wildherne, I'm not very wise. I seem to know so little about people. And I'm not sure enough of myself. If someone dislikes me, I think they're right and take their view of myself. Caroline Marsh, for instance. She hates me."

Wildherne laughed. "Caroline Marsh! Is that worrying you? Well, really, Janet. I wouldn't have believed it of you. If she does dislike you, which I don't suppose is true for a moment, what *does* it matter?"

"But it *does* matter. She's going to be part of my life now."

"Caroline Marsh part of your life? Not if I know it!"

"Well, your mother is, and she's part of hers."

He put his arm around her again.

"Janet, dear, now be sensible. You've got stage fright, and I don't wonder. If you were alone in this there'd be some justification, but you're not alone in it and never will be again. We are together in this—and everything else."

"In some things, but not in everything." She spoke rapidly, looking down at the floor. "I want to tell you everything that's in my mind this afternoon. I feel as though in some way or another it is my last chance. Are we perhaps wrong after all, Wildherne, to take up this thing when—when you're in love with somebody else? Won't that make it after all something too difficult for us to manage?"

"I'm glad you've spoken about that," he said quietly. "I was going to tell you in any case. I went the other afternoon and said good-bye to her—finally."

"Oh, don't think," Janet broke in eagerly, "that I'm going back on my word. I said I would accept that. You can't kill your love for her, and I would not, except that I think it makes you unhappy and can lead to no good end. But I'm realising now, as I didn't at first, that as we grow closer to one another, even though it's only as friends, the thought of her will be more difficult to me. I have discovered that, and I knew that I must tell you."

He stayed quietly, thinking.

He said at last: "I can't promise you that I will not love her any more. I think that could only be killed in me by some other great love. Janet," he caught her hand again, "if you give me a son! . . . Oh, if we have a boy!"

His face was irradiated with a smile so beautiful that Janet, looking at him, caught her breath. It transformed him. It made of his quiet, rather uninteresting features something so strong and buoyant that he seemed someone new to her. Had he *that* ecstasy, might she not——?' She caught her breath again. There was not, and must not be, any thought of *that* love between them.

He went on: "Janet, I will always be honest with you. I will tell you of my temptations, and if they are too much for me I will warn you. That is an oath between us."

"Does she," Janet asked, "does she hate me?"

"Hate you? No! She doesn't care for me enough! And yet that struck her the other day. That you have something now that she has never had—my friendship."

"That she never had?"

"No, we were never friends. We have never trusted one another, never strengthened one another—always weakened and disappointed and estranged. That is what some love can do."

Janet stared about the room, slowly filling with dusk. "I have never known love like that," she said slowly. "Just think, Wildherne, no one has ever loved me with passion, no one in all my life, man or woman. Well, I must do my best with friendship."

She spoke against her intention with bitterness. It took her by surprise, as though someone had spoken those words for her. He put his arm around her and held her.

"Don't speak like that, Janet. Let's take on our adventure with glad hearts. After all, whether it is because we are old-fashioned or stupid, or whatever our reasons may be, we both believe in good things—we believe in our fathers who went before us and the England that they made. We believe, in spite of her faults and stupidities, that England is worthy of all love and devotion, and we believe that our class, in spite again of faults and stupidities, can do something for her by keeping what is good in that class and using it. And we believe in more. We believe in things unseen, and that life is a battle between good and evil, and that we can help one another to fight on the right side in that battle. These are things, Janet, bigger than our personal history. We may be making a mistake. We may spoil our lives by this. But it is worth the risk to try."

Janet nodded. "Rosalind would mock at you if she heard you," she said. "It is very old-fashioned to talk about good and evil. I'll do my best, Wildherne, I won't look back again. I'm with you in this whatever may come of it."

They kissed. One of the old, old men, a voice in the shadow, whispered that it was time to go. Closing——

Going—going—gone. . . .

CHAPTER VIII

WEDDING

MRS. BEDDOES, charwoman to Janet and Rosalind, knew before she opened her eyes that it was a fine day for the wedding. Resting her hand gently upon the broad sickle-shaped back of Mr. Beddoes, she raised herself on her elbow and looked about her.

The touch of the warm rough stuff of Mr. Beddoes' nightshirt seemed to tell her that it was a fine day. Early hours as yet, of course, to be certain, but on a wet morning he would lie with the clothes all huddled about him, right up to his chin, and now there he was lying over on his side with the whole back part of him exposed, victim to any merry little draught that might come his way. He was a cautious man even in his sleep; you wouldn't get him lying like that did he not know there was sun in the air.

The little tinny clock downstairs chirruped seven. Five was Mrs. Beddoes' accustomed hour, but to-day, being the wedding, was a holiday. *The* wedding—HER wedding —Mrs. Beddoes' wedding—one of the great days of all her life.

When that kind Miss Grandison had first suggested to her that she should be present at her wedding, Mrs. Beddoes had accepted it as one of that nice lady's ("a lady as *is* a lady") pleasant little jokes.

Present of course she would be, but present as she had been at many another (yes, she *adored* weddings), outside St. Margaret's near the railings, or facing the steps of St. George's, Hanover Square.

But no, there was that card propped up against the looking-glass as natural as natural :

THE DUKE AND DUCHESS
OF ROMNEY
REQUEST THE PLEASURE
OF THE COMPANY OF
Mrs. Beddoes
ON THE OCCASION
OF THE MARRIAGE OF
THEIR SON
WILDHERNE FRANCIS POOLE
TO
JANET
DAUGHTER OF THE LATE . . .

"The Duke and Duchess of Romney request the pleasure . . ."

Mrs. Beddoes at this point, had she been a charwoman in proper literary tradition, should have taken a gloomy view of social conditions, reflected painfully on ways and means, resented her husband's drunken habits, and sighed heavily. But she did nothing of the kind. She had no sense of social injustice at all, nor of injustice of any sort. She was a happy woman in spite of Beddoes' inability to keep his job (not through drunkenness, but rather through laziness). She did not feel that the world was an unjust place. She never pined to let birds out of their cages or to have a bath three times a week, nor was she tempted to steal her employers' silver, nor had she a fear of policemen. From her observation of situations in which she worked, it all seemed to her "much of a muchness," and it was as likely as not that you would be happier as a charwoman than as a duchess. Less cares, more freedom, fewer people bothering about what you did. She had a sore leg, and her charing frequently wearied her; on the other hand she had her cup of tea, her old man, and lying late in bed every Sunday morning.

What she *did* wish over and over was that Beddoes would allow her more of the bed. He was a large stout man, but, as she had told him again and again, there was no need for him to lie "crossways." She was for ever waking with the hard sharp edge of the bed pressing into her, and that gave her bad dreams, she couldn't but fancy. Nevertheless he hadn't treated her so wrongly during these twenty years. He had never so much as winked at another woman. For this his laziness was in the main responsible. He was half asleep most of the time; but indeed she was fond of him—yes, she was. She dragged his head round now and gave him a kiss. She knew that it would take a great deal more than that to wake him. Then slowly, for fear of hurting her leg, always at its most feverish first thing in the morning, she got out of bed.

It was not until she was on the point of departure that he realised what she was about. He was sitting there, last Sunday's *Lloyd's News* on his knees. He was resting between two jobs. She stood there in her black bonnet, the locket with the hair of their only child (Louis Allen died of croup aged four years six months) lying placidly on her bosom. She was wearing her black silk.

"Wot's up?" he asked.

She had told him over and over. She looked at him, broad and thick, his shirt open showing his hairy chest, his fat red face with the eyes half closed, his eyebrows like sand, his hair (what there was of it) like sand, his fat hands planted on his fat thighs. She loved him. Lord, how she loved him!

She came over and gave him a kiss.

"I've told you over and over. To-day's the wedding."

"Wot wedding?" He pinched her stout arm in the sleepy animal way he had, then he scratched the bald part of his head, leaning back with all his weight, tipping the chair on to its two back legs, and then yawning hugely.

"There you are!" she said, pushing him forward. "You'll 'ave that chair broke as surely as goodness! 'Ow often am I telling you, Louis . . .?" (Whenever she said his name, even to this day, it gave her a half-sensual, half-snobbish thrill, it was so foreign.) "Why, *the* wedding. . . . My Miss Grandison as is going to marry the Marquis of Poole."

"Well, she bloody well can marry him for all I care." He felt vaguely in his pocket for his pipe. "All the same I don't

ee why you should lose a day's work for it. Any excuse for
lleness with you women."

"I'm going inside," said Mrs. Beddoes huskily, the locket
ising and falling tumultuously. "Inside St. Margaret's."

"Oh, you are, are you?" He seemed to be roused a little by
hat. "And 'ow long before they shove you out again?"

"I've got my card." She had shown it to him already a
housand times. "I've as much right as the Prime Minister
mself."

Beddoes looked at her with admiration. He had always
dmired her from the moment of his first meeting her (in
he gallery of the Old Tivoli Music Hall). Everything she
id was admirable. And since the death of the boy he had
ived her. He did not know that, and his love for her was
ot so strong and powerful that it forced him to do anything
special for her. But it was love nevertheless. He was proud
f her, had tender feelings about her, was sometimes excited
y her, and had the fright of his life once when she was ill in
ed for a week.

He rose now, and, planting his legs wide apart, stretched
imself as a cat might.

"Well, so long, old girl." He caught her round the neck
id kissed her. "See you later."

As she went on her way she was vaguely disappointed be-
use he had not shown more curiosity. But he never did
iow curiosity about anything. It was not his way. Better
iat he should be like that than get excited and beat her as
red Simpson beat Eliza or Will Faulks kicked Clara. Some-
ing shameful. Yes, she was one of the lucky ones, only her
iots hurt her something cruel. It was fortunate that she
dn't wear them on ordinary working days. Should she
is it? Why no, it was only down Shaftesbury Avenue,
rough the Circus, Haymarket, and Whitehall. No distance
all on a bright day like this.

She forgot her boots in the general splendour of the morn-
g. There it was, striking eleven, and the wedding was at
velve. It was not often that she was in the streets at this gay
id busy hour. She liked to see people happy, and gay and

happy they all certainly were. What a difference a little b
of sun could make to everyone, and all the taxis—how cou
people afford them?—and half the steps not properly cleane
either!

But now she was passing the theatres, and was compelle
to stop and look at the photographs clinging like barnacles
the theatre walls.

Pretty creatures! Her heart went out to them all. Prett
dears! And after all it wasn't real, all that fuss and unhapp
ness! Why, there was a young lady being pushed back on
a sofa and a young gentleman in evening dress threatenin
her with a revolver! And here, only a few yards away, wer
at least a dozen young women with almost nothing on dan
ing round a short fat man dressed for golfing! You certain
could pick and choose—that is if you had any money to c
it with.

But in no time at all she was standing waiting for Pi
cadilly Circus to allow her to cross. She did not pause ner
ously like a country cousin. She did not know it, but Londc
belonged to her, Eros belonged to her, and the stout flowe
women, and the omnibuses that plunged like elephan
through the jungle of traffic, and the Criterion Theatre ar
the Pavilion—these all belonged to her, were of her fami
and she of theirs. When she moved quietly and with digni
on her way her world moved with her—London solemn
rose up and strayed after her, a family of children aft
their mother. Her thought was: "Nice fine day. I'd like
ride on top of a bus."

Passing the mighty buildings of Whitehall her heart ga
a bound. That was where the War was made—right insi
one of those gay buildings, and then inside again until yc
entered a room with a table in it, and then round this tab
several gentlemen, like the Hon. Fotheringay whose lady sl
used to char for, dressed in black tail-coats and top-hat
made the War. She didn't blame them. As she always sai
about the War, it was easy enough to criticise, but one thin
led to another; that she had often found in her own affair

Her idea of it was that first one gentleman in a black co;
had, feeling peevish in the morning, as so many gentlemen i

ack coats did, said something vexing to another gentleman
 a black coat, and he'd answered back, and the first gentle-
an had said, "I dare you!" and—there you were.

But although no one was to blame (except afterwards
ose dirty Germans sinking ships full of women and chil-
en without a word of warning), she did hope that it would
ver occur again.

She would never forget the way Lady Clara Manning
ied one morning after getting a telegram, or Bessie Ford
 the same house as herself when she lost her only boy, or
or Captain Frederick Somer, whose wife she still some-
mes worked for, coming out of hospital with his sight gone
d having to have his food cut up for him.

The thing was for everyone to keep their tempers and not
t hasty, which surely they would do now they'd seen what
e last time led to.

Then her heart almost stopped its beating. She was ap-
oaching St. Margaret's, and a crowd was already gathered
ere. Would she ever have the courage to mount those steps
d pass beneath those doors? The line of red carpet seemed
 rise and laugh at her. Had it been a wet day things
ould have been easier; everyone would have been under
nbrellas. She could have just slipped in. But here with all
is glittering sun and everyone staring. . . . She held the
rd tightly. After all it wasn't any good for people to look
 her rudely and ask her questions. Miss Janet was her
iend. Many's the time she'd talked to her just woman to
oman, and many's the time she'd been grumpy enough an-
ering Miss Janet back and saying to her quite sharply,
Vell, Miss, if you think I've got four pairs of 'ands."

Oh no, they were friends all right, and Mrs. Beddoes had
ven her word that she'd be there, so be there she would be.
Her feet were on the red carpet. She felt a world of eyes
on her, but once she had started upward it was easy
ough. There were gentlemen at the church door. She
owed her card. In another moment she was inside the cool
rk church.

There were, as yet, very few people present. A young
an, most beautifully dressed and wearing a large white

flower in his buttonhole, was walking up and down the cent
aisle showing everyone where to go, but Mrs. Beddo
escaped him, slipping round to the left up a side aisle ar
then, quite collectedly, as though she had been doing th
all her life, choosing a place where, obscure herself, she cou
see quite clearly the altar steps and choir.

She settled down, put her hand over her face for a momei
and said a prayer, gave a little pull to her bonnet and a jei
to her jacket, and then breathed freely.

She had a sudden dangerous impulse to shed tear
Churches always made her feel like that. They caused h
to remember her childhood, and her little brother who ha
been killed by an omnibus, and her mother who had died c
a decline after being beaten by her third husband one evenir
after a party. She loved to think of sad things, and that wa
why she liked churches. Why, also, she liked weddings, b
cause if weddings weren't sad, what were? A funny thir
when you came to think of it that funerals generally ende
in a lot of drink and laughter, and weddings in tears and
sense of disappointment. Funerals were more definite som
how.

The church was looking beautiful, the lovely glass of th
windows, the shining gold of some of the brasses, and the
the flowers! Such flowers! A pretty penny they must ha
cost! To think of Miss Janet, who had lived as poor as any
thing with her sister in those three rooms, having all thos
flowers! That came of marrying a title. They'd all come v
from the Duke's country place, she shouldn't wonder. She'
like Louis just to have had a sight of those flowers. If the
was one thing he cared for it was flowers, and he'd stare int
the flower shop windows as any other husband would star
into a public-house. They made her feel a bit sleepy. Indee
so tired was she after her work that whenever she sat dow
she felt a bit sleepy. Good thing for her the seat was so har
or she might have gone right off.

And now the people were beginning to come in! Th
church filled so quickly that it was as though they had a
been waiting outside for the doors to open!

Mrs. Beddoes regarded them critically. The first thing tha

e women stood for was whether they'd be good mistresses.
ou could tell in a moment. Characteristics hidden from the
st of the world were revealed in a trice to Mrs. Beddoes.
There is an old game that people in more tranquil days
ere fond of playing, a game in which you gave your
iends so many marks for their qualities. Eighteen, say,
ll marks—six for character, six for intelligence, six for
ysical attraction. In the same way Mrs. Beddoes gave the
dies who sat now on every side of her marks—six for good
mper, six for hoity-toity, and six for being a Real Lady—
d then something after that for paying wages promptly.
e saw no one near her who received very high marks, but
en they would be at their very worst at a wedding, pushing
e another, chattering in loud voices, giggling and laughing
-"like a lot of monkeys in a cage"—not as though they were
a church at all.

Mrs. Beddoes was especially indignant at a conversation of
nich she caught some fragments.

"But of *course!* Why, what do you think? Of course she
ows."

"Well, then, I call it disgusting!"

"My dear, you'd do the same if you hadn't a penny to
ss yourself with and lived in a poky little flat—not getting
y younger either."

". . . let him go . . . ?"

"Not she. She'll hold on to him tighter than ever. She's
at sort."

"Oh no. Of course the Duchess is delighted. She's always
en afraid that he'd pick up somebody who'd snap her
gers at her. But this Grandison girl is as meek as a mouse.
e'll be swallowed by the family before she's finished the
neymoon."

"The . . . Duke . . . like it."

"Oh, the Duke? He's an old darling, but of *course* he
ows nothing. Never has. He's too good for this naughty
rld, if you ask me."

". . . ——. . . —— ?"

"The sister? Oh, she's lovely! Oh no, really lovely. The
ettiest girl in London. *And* knows it. She'll give some

trouble before she's done. . . . Oh yes. . . . Didn't y•
know? . . . Charles Ravage. . . . She's everywhere wi
him. What people *see* in him. . . ."

At this moment Mrs. Beddoes turned right round and sa
in a loud voice, "'USH, PLEASE." Turning, she look
straight into the hard and glassy eyes of two beautiful ladi
whose clothes were exquisite, lips very red and faces deligl
fully pale. They stared straight through Mrs. Beddoes, b
their voices sank, and they had indeed little opportunity f
further conversation because the crush became now mc
turbulent, and on every side ladies and gentlemen were fo•
ing their way and urging that room should be made f
them. The organ was playing, and everywhere now the
was colour—pink and saffron and heliotrope, deep pur•
and palest cream, silky black and ivory white—and fac•
faces bold and impudent, faces mild and shapeless like t•
successful puddings, faces like birds, hawks and eagles a
robins and vultures, faces like dogs, Pekinese and bu
terriers and an occasional Airedale, faces like teapots a
door-knobs and candlesticks, faces like vegetables, cabbaǥ
and cauliflowers and turnips, and all of these faces lacking
something for beauty—the nose too large, the eyes too sm:
the mouth too straight, the forehead too low, but all of the
under the paint and the ambitions of the moment, hum•
faces with something attractive, something pathetic, son
thing lonely but endearing.

But Mrs. Beddoes was now in arms for her Miss Jan
That was the way in which they spoke of her? How d:
they, not knowing her at all? She knew her, had seen her
every circumstance of daily life, and watched her joys a•
sorrows, struggles with finances, struggles with her sist
struggles with all the little worries that were just like all •
worries that Mrs. Beddoes herself was forced to encount

Mrs. Beddoes, as she looked now about the church pack
and wedged with flesh and millinery, wished that she cou
find Miss Janet for a moment and put her arms round l
and tell her not to mind—that everything came all right
the end.

But the moment was approaching. Dimly beyond the h

d hair she could see Lord Poole's back as he stood at the
oir steps. A little rustle ran through the congregation. The
ide was approaching.

A rustle like the wind through corn swept the church.
veryone pressed forward and sideways. Janet Grandison on
e Duke's arm came, under the gaze of them all, to do her
ty.

At the sight of her—very tall and pale—Mrs. Beddoes
oked. What you saw were her eyes, which glowed with
st that same gentle kindliness that in ordinary day-by-day
siness they showed. She was a success because of them.
osalind, following as a bridesmaid, so much more beautiful,
is almost unnoticed. Janet was the success of the day, be-
use everyone who saw her thought, "She'd make a good
end if one's trouble became *too* bad. . . ." Everyone hav-
, of course, that one special trouble.

But she was Mrs. Beddoes' property. The church and
erything in it turned into soup for Mrs. Beddoes, because
r eyes filled with tears. That *kind* Miss Janet! And so
ten that grumpy, reluctant Mrs. Beddoes! Now Miss Rosa-
d—she deserved as good as she got. Mrs. Beddoes was
edding no tears for her, nor would she when her wedding
y came, haughty domineering thing, and all because her
se was straighter than some people's! But Miss Janet!
urmurs came from the choir steps. Something was going
. The church was hushed.

Dear, dear, the thing was done—only to be undone by
agony of complications and scandals. Miss Janet Grandi-
1 was the Marchioness of Poole.

Mrs. Beddoes settled herself more comfortably after that.
r heart ceased its thumping. While they were in the vestry
ning the register she could look about her. Ah! there was
e Duchess hurrying across the aisle, *and* the Bishop of
ndon. . . . There were other faces recognised by Mrs.
ddoes because of the illustrated papers. Then she saw
dy Hermione Ispel, for whom she had, at many periods,
ne a little bit of work. Lady Hermione, in purple and gold,
th her old face like an ivory mask and her eye-brows half a
rd from where they used to be. A good old thing, always

at her last penny and full of tips for races: "Now, my goo
soul"—that was what she used to call Mrs. Beddoes—"yo
tell your husband from me that Timothy Trot is a sure thin
If he's got a penny or two . . ." which was more than Lac
Hermione ever had! Oh, the trouble of getting wages or
of her!—blood out of a stone, as you might say—*and* th
mess her flat was always in—playing-cards and cigaret
ends, and those dolls that smart ladies stuck about their sofa
and liqueur glasses, and flowers done up in blue ribbon ar
all faded, and chocolate boxes. . . .

Hush! They were coming back. There she was on Lo
Poole's arm! And didn't she look happy? Really she di
smiling at her friends as she passed down the church, sto
ping for an instant here and there. The church was soup fo
Mrs. Beddoes once again, and she saw Lord Poole spread o
waveringly into an obscure haze.

A tear trickled down her cheek. Well, let it. Poor lam'
Little she knew! Mrs. Beddoes could tell her one or tv
things about marriage, and *she,* you might say, had been o
of the lucky ones. Oh, would he be kind to her? Would
now? Men! You could never tell with men. Tired of thin
so quickly, and of women quickest of all. But then at t
end, if you held on hard enough, they came back to you.
the beginning they wanted love, in the middle they want
change, at the last they wanted a home, and if only dri
didn't ruin them they always came back.

And now the scramble was beginning. Everyone was pus
ing to the door. What indecent behaviour, and in a chur
too! There was old Lady Hermione one of the worst. M
Beddoes could hear her cackle above the rest, that fun
voice like a jockey's!

Slowly Mrs. Beddoes went with the tide.

Slowly she faced the sun, the expectant crowd; slow
she slipped away between the cars, the policemen, and t
little boys.

Slowly she realised her boots again.

She was tired, but it had been a marvellous occasion.

END OF PART I

PART II

JANET AND WILDHERNE

CHAPTER I

DOWN IN WILTSHIRE

JANET POOLE looked up at the silver birch and caught without turning her head the pearl-grey shadow of the corner of the great house—the silver birch, the silver walls—should she pray to them for patience?

On the terrace on either side of her sat the Duchess, Miss Crabbage, and Caroline Marsh. The Duchess, Miss Crabbage, and Janet were in white, Miss Marsh in modest dove-grey. In the hot summer weather the silver birch moved its leaves very slightly, as though gently fanning itself.

"Therefore, Cecilia," the Duchess said, not raising her eyes from her work (something very small in white silk), "I think Wednesday will be the best day for Mr. Pomeroy."

"*Wednesday,*" said Miss Crabbage; "very good."

Janet looked at the silver birch and said, "I'm so sorry, but I'm afraid I shan't be able to have Mr. Pomeroy next week."

Everything followed as she had known, for the last half-hour, that it would. The grey turban seemed very slightly to circulate as though it were spinning in the sun. That was merely the effect that the Duchess gave when she raised her little head from her work and said very gently:

"Why, Janet dear?"

"Only because Wildherne and I are not going to have any-one down here just yet. It's still our honeymoon, you know," she ended, laughing. How she wished that her voice had not at that moment a little trembled!

"Mr. Pomeroy is hardly just anybody, dear," the Duchess said, her little fingers busy again with her piece of silk. "But

121

it's of course for you to say. Then, Cecilia, we must go up
on Tuesday. You must tell Hignett."

"Tuesday afternoon the *Blanchards* are coming over,"
said Miss Crabbage.

"Oh well, put them off. I shall be coming back—that is if
dear Janet invites me." The Duchess laughed, Janet laughed,
Caroline Marsh smiled. The silver birch smiled.

Conversation went on, but the challenge had been flung
down and accepted. Everyone knew it. Wintersmoon, over-
looking so superbly the four ladies, also knew it.

Janet after a while went into the house. She passed
through the long drawing-room, out through the high windows at the far end, down the upper terrace, along the green
walk, through the little wood, and was free and safe sitting
by herself in the little round temple that overlooked the
pond with the water-lilies. Through all these she must pass
to be free.

Sitting there, looking at the faint blue mirror of water on
which the flat leaves lay like thin plates of jade, she was
surprised to find that her whole body was trembling. The
words re-echoed again and again:

"I'm afraid that we shan't be able to have Mr. Pomeroy."

She had pulled Wildherne into it because he ought to be
in it, because during these last weeks he had not been in it
enough. Had she strength, even with his support behind her,
to carry it through? There had been times again and again
lately when she had been tempted simply to give it all up, to
lie down and let them run everything—the Duchess, Miss
Crabbage, and the rest. That abnegation was so easy. They
would all be so kind to her, they would applaud so warmly
her handsome recognition of the inevitable, everyone would
be pleased. Indeed, had it not been for the House she must
have surrendered. The coils within coils were too many, the
machinery too vast and all-embracing. But the House was as
strong as they; its roots went deeper than theirs. And the
House (she knew it beyond any question) supported her. She
would think, if ever she doubted, of the long high gallery
with its odd tessellated floor of white and grey, its forty or
fifty Purefoys, its windows with the view of the lawn, the

ake, the clustering trees, and the thin line of Down beyond:
all this supported her.

Supported her? Yes, but she needed something human.
Rosalind was not here—and Wildherne? Even while she
thought of him some stir made her look up and she found
him standing there.

"Wildherne!" she cried.

He came and sat beside her.

"Yes," he said. "I wondered where you were."

"I came here to think things out. I've told your mother
that we can't have Mr. Pomeroy next week."

He made the gesture that was now so familiar to her,
pulling a lock of his hair, dragging it down over his forehead, then pushing it back again.

"We can't, can't we?" he said, laughing. "Well, then, we
can't."

"It isn't as simple as that," she replied. "You know that
it is not."

They had been married now for five weeks, and the
physical intimacy that marriage had brought them had given
them an odd shyness of one another that they had not known
while they were engaged. This shyness had come because they
had both so thoroughly realised that in physical intimacy
kindness was not enough. They had faced that possibility before marriage, but the actual realisation of the fact had made
them more eager than before not to hurt one another, an
added tenderness because each had denied the other something that should have been there. They could not help
themselves. This absence had been an admitted part of their
bargain: nevertheless they were farther from one another
than they had been before marriage and desperately eager to
deny that added distance. Honesty was not so easy as it had
once been.

"Why isn't it simple?" Wildherne asked.

"Because it's rebellion," Janet answered gravely.

"My mother never expected," Wildherne said, "that after
my marriage she would have the same authority here as
before."

"Of course she expected it," Janet answered abruptly.

"She has always expected it. That was why she was so pleased when you married me. She thought that I would do exactly as she wished."

"She loves you very much," Wildherne said.

"Yes, if I help in the Great Cause. But I can't. I don't believe in it."

"And what is the Great Cause?" asked Wildherne.

In his voice there was the slightest touch of indulgence, even—her nerves already strained were eager to assure her —of patronage. She had noticed it before, and it had always irritated her.

"Wildherne, dear, I'm not a child. I know exactly what is happening."

"And what *is* happening exactly?"

She moved away from him a little. "You know that your mother is head, queen if you like, of a whole world. Mr. Pomeroy is her Prime Minister, Cecilia Crabbage her Home Secretary, Mr. Crawford her Minister of Foreign Affairs, and so on. Through her and her ministers, quietly, unobtrusively, a whole section of English life, social and religious, is moving. The organisation is immense. God is served: England is kept against Democracy, Bolshevism, America, Roman Catholicism, the Hun, Jazz, cocktails, immorality, and Christian Science. We are poor but strong. We recognise no element of modern evolution as anything but dangerous and of the Devil. There is no such thing as Time and Progress. There has been unfortunately a War, but we will disregard all consequences of it save those that help us back to where we were before the War. We are blind and deaf and dumb to everything that the so-called New World is concerned with. There is no New World. Vive l'Albert Memorial!"

She spoke bitterly. She rose and confronted him. "There are splendid things in your mother, splendid elements in her world, but her world is not mine—not ours, if I am to believe in all that you said once you meant to do with our lives —yours and mine!"

"Why, Janet, you're angry!" he said, looking up at her with surprise. "And you are talking like a *Times* leading article. *If* I believe in all that I once said . . . ! But of course I do. I haven't changed in the least. I'm behind you in everything."

She softened.

"We don't talk together as we did," she said. "We are alone so little. Do you know that your mother has been here for four weeks out of the five since we were married? And that Miss Crabbage has been here. And Caroline Marsh. And do you know that all the servants here, save only Mrs. Beddoes and Forster, do precisely what she says and never at all what I say? You must have noticed that during these weeks, but you have never said anything to me about it."

"Yes, there I've been wrong," he said. "I've been so accustomed to my mother. . . ."

"Of course. But it is difficult for me, isn't it?"

"That can be put right in a moment. I think the best thing would be to have Hignett here. He is longing to come. He is never happy when he is away from me, as a matter of fact. And, oddly enough, he likes you."

"Why oddly?" she asked, laughing.

"Because he doesn't care about women. He thinks them of no account—even my mother. He shall be our Major-Domo here, and he will serve you with a fidelity that will amaze you."

"And your mother?"

"She can find someone else. As a matter of fact Mrs. Persis, the housekeeper at Halkin Street, and Hignett fight cat and dog—it will be much better to part them. The only thing will be father—he is greatly attached to Hignett."

"He must come here more. Oh!" she sighed, "I wish he were here for ever!"

"You love him so much?"

"More than anyone in the world save Rosalind," Janet answered. "He knows me in a way that you don't, Wildherne; he always has from the beginning."

"Yes, I believe that's true. But it's easier for him." He broke into a tone which there was a curious note of passion. "Janet—you're unhappy!"

"Sometimes," she replied steadily. "I miss Rosalind."

"And then?" he asked her.

"I feel always that perhaps we have done a wicked thing Wildherne. To have married without love. . . ."

"Look farther! Look farther!" he cried. "Let's think o ourselves less and take our little troubles with a laugh. Wha does it matter if for a moment things need adjusting? W are both playing a longer game. And, Janet, you're m friend. I've never had a friend before. I find myself turning to you now at every step. I am always saying, 'I must tel Janet that,' or 'Where's Janet?' or 'Janet must know. That's new to me, and it's fine. If I'm blind sometimes anc slow to see how you are feeling it's because I've had sc little practice in friendship. It's an art. You are teaching me And, like every teacher, you must be patient."

Her eyes glowed.

"Oh, Wildherne, when you talk like that I am with you again, at your side, everything is well, everything is pos-sible! If I too am sometimes alarmed or lonely it is because this is new to me. You must be patient with *me*. And to-gether— Oh, together! What can't we do?"

With arms around one another, close, like lovers, they walked slowly up the soft sun-flecked path.

But, in this life of telephones, telegrams, and butchers grisly bills, the big moments yield so speedily to the smal ones. For Janet especially, who was moving now in a strange country, it seemed impossible to combine one phase of this life with another. At dinner on that same evening it seemec to her as though she was seated with human beings whc were all strangers to her, who, also, were combined agains her.

The dining hall at Wintersmoon, with its quaintly carvec Minstrels' Gallery, its Van Dyck of Sir Walter Purefoy, its torn flags from the Marlborough wars, its superb panelling was one of the historic sights of England, but it was not ar intimate dining-room for a small party of five human beings The table at which they were sitting was like a boat adrift in a sea of oak and amber lit with the reflections from the candles (there was no electricity allowed at dinner).

Janet knew of a little room at the end of the Long Gallery

hat would be perfect for herself and Wildherne when the
Duchess was gone, but meanwhile the Duchess was there.
She was there forgetting, as she always did, her food in the
nterest of the many arrangements that must be made. Nor
was she one to leave anything vague or undefined.

Any situation that arose must be settled and tabulated so
hat she might move swiftly on to the next one.

"Wildherne," she said, smiling, "I am going up to Halkin Street on Tuesday. I have to see Mr. Pomeroy, and
Janet doesn't want him down here."

"Well, mother dear, do what you have to do and come
back quickly," Wildherne answered cheerfully.

"I can't understand, Janet," said the Duchess, "what
you've got against Mr. Pomeroy."

"Got against him!" said Janet. "But nothing, of
course!"

"He wouldn't disturb you here in the least—you'd see
nothing of him."

"But I like him!" Janet said. "Only I want to have some
time alone here with Wildherne. I want to get to know the
house, the people in the village."

"Alone!" said the Duchess. "Then you'd rather, dear, that
just now I wasn't here?"

"For a week or two I want to be alone with Wildherne,"
Janet repeated, her heart thumping, her hands tightened on
her lap.

She knew enough already to be exactly aware that it was
characteristic of the Duchess to have conducted this little
campaign in the open. Anyone else would have fought her
privately. Anyone else would have hated her. Janet knew
that her mother-in-law admired and liked her.

"Well, that settles it," said the Duchess. "Cecilia, we are
banished."

"No, mother," Wildherne broke in, "of course not.
You're welcome here as often as you can come—always
and ever—save for these next weeks. Janet and I intend to
be hermits. Do you realise the crowds of people who've come
over lately? We've been invaded as though we were a Country Fair with the Fat Woman and the Man with Three

Heads. Janet's right. We want this place alone to ourselve
for a bit."

The Duchess nodded her turban. "You shall have it, an
we'll none of us come back until we're sent for—will we
Cecilia?"

Miss Crabbage smiled. "The *Duke* will benefit. And it wi
be *lovely* at Purefoy in this *weather*."

"Yes. We'll go down to Purefoy. And then we can ge
on with that Bankstead Crèche business." She paused, ther
looking up brightly, she asked, "But how is it, Janet dea
that Rosalind hasn't been to see you yet?"

Again, in spite of herself, Janet's voice trembled as sh
answered:

"Rosalind's been so busy. She's been moving into a ne
flat. And I think that at present she is a little afraid of you
She fancies that you don't like her."

"Afraid of me! Nonsense. Besides, Rosalind's afraid o
no one. A look at her's enough to see that. But what an ur
pleasant person I seem! In the way here, a bully there! Ar
I a bully, Caroline? You ought to know, if any one does."

Miss Marsh, drawn thus publicly on to the battle-grounc
blushed and murmured, "Why no, of course not, Lady Pool
was joking——"

"But," Janet broke in indignantly, "that's unfair. You'r
all kinder than kind. Rosalind doesn't want to push hersel
in too soon, that's all. It's natural. She'll be here ofte
enough."

"Of course, dear," the Duchess murmured. "You mus
miss her after living so long together. I understand per
fectly."

She did. She understood everything. Janet was her sor
Perhaps, after all, it would be a case of allies rather tha
monarch and subject. Better, possibly, that way.

That night Janet wrote to her sister:

DARLING ROSALIND—I got your note this morning, and
note it truly was. Hadn't you time for more than that? An
you tell one nothing. I seem to be for ever complaining, but fo
a week you hadn't written, and in a whole week in June in Lon

on surely *something* happens? News is news down here, you
now. Seriously, soon you have *got* to visit us here. Not for the
ext three weeks, because after a most public battle I've driven
ne Duchess away on the score that Wildherne and I want to
e alone, but at the beginning of July, even for a night.

Don't you miss me at *all?* Are you so gay and so busy that
ou never think of me? Whom are you seeing, what dances,
hat theatres? You tell me *nothing,* not even very much about
ne new flat.

What am I to do? If I preach to you, scold you, you are angry
nd push me away. Is pleading with you any good? It should be,
ecause I believe in your heart you love me. You *must*. What
ave we been through everything together for if we are not
) stay together to the end? Who cares for you as I do? I care
or you too much, I know, and worry you with my affection,
ut, Rosalind, I'm *hungry* now for love. Something has hap-
ened to me, something in my heart. I can stand alone no longer.
Wildherne is good to me and cares for me, but you must
ve me, Rosalind. Do what you will but love me—want me—
eed me. Perhaps I've made the greatest mistake of my life in
hat I have done, but I will carry it through as though it were
ly greatest success. That I swear. But you must stand beside
ne . Even though you find this new world of mine impossible,
ou must not find *me* impossible. Is all this incoherent? I dare-
ay. But your letters are so short that I seem to be out of touch
rith you altogether. You must come down here. Get to know
Wildherne. You will like him. He has magnificent things in him
–things that you especially will admire. Good-night. I'm tired,
nd if this letter sounds cross it is only on the top. Underneath
love you, love you, darling. And I miss you horribly.—Your
evoted sister,   JANET.

Her letter written, she went to the high windows of her
oom, standing wide open on this lovely June night, and
)oked out. The purple sky set with frosted stars lay in a
reat cup between the trees of the park to the left and the
igh Wintersmoon woods. Clear in front of her rose the
)owns, very gentle, lifting like a sigh, a murmur, in quiet
cquiescence to the sweeping heights of air. All around her
as the house. In the next room was Wildherne. At a mo-
nent he might come in to her. She wondered rather that he
ad not, after the little scene at dinner. It was like him,

though, that he should not. There was a certain weakness i
him that she well knew by now. He detested quarrels. H
liked, when people could not agree, to find some point o
agreement, suggest it to them, and then tell himself that the
had agreed. At any rate he had given them the opportunity
and he would stay away until all was well again.

He was loyal to her, and he would defend her always, bu
he liked her better, she knew, when she did not force him t
take a stand. That was why to-night she was lonely. She fe
that there was no one upon whom she could rely. She misse
desperately those little talks with Rosalind. Rosalind, wh
moved always with impulse, could yield herself generousl
and warmly when the mood was upon her. That mood wa
intermittent, but when it was there it had force and powe
Wildherne had, as yet, no force. She had fancied that sh
would not need it. She had not known.

The beautiful silence was broken with little sounds, th
whisper of a stream heard and then lost, the faint rustle o
trees as the breeze rose and fell, the multitude of hushe
voices of the night that could not be defined, that was secre
of their own world and apart.

All around her was the house, and in the night all the ol
life that the noisy day subdued had now its full existence.

She seemed as she stood there herself to reach back an
touch countless strange and inchoate things and persons. Th
Elizabethan pageant, with the famous Wintersmoon Dwar
with the yellow ruff; Elizabeth herself, gaunt face an
swearing tongue; colour, torches, flags, jewels, fountain
playing, the Satyrs in the Long Walk leering down upo
Elizabethan loves, the songs and the bawdy talk, the feas
with the famous pie from whose heart silver birds ros
singing into mid air, the minstrels in the gallery and th
madrigals, the torturing of the kitchen boy by three drunke
gentlemen of Elizabeth's Court who burnt out his tongue an
snipped off his nose in the merriment of the moment, th
marriage of Giles Purefoy to Eleanor Garden when th
festivities lasted seven weeks and the Grey Hunchback o
Wintersmoon appeared to seven astounded courtiers at th
same moment, the Masque of "Endymion" when twent

aked virgins bathed with twenty naked Elizabethan gentle-
nen in the lake where the statue of Pan still is at five of a
ummer morning and caused some (but not overmuch)
candal, Elizabeth herself flirting for her week's stay with
oung Geoffrey Purefoy, a boy of seventeen, and his splen-
id cloth of silver studded with rubies and his baby face and
is ruined character. . . . So they came, crowding into that
ld room with its dark panelled walls and silver mirrors
nd tapestry of Venus and Adonis. They pass, and for an
istant the unhappy Monmouth, haggard of face, peeps
irough the door and vanishes; Godolphin takes his evening
ieal and rides on to London. The young Francis Poole, an-
ther Henry Esmond, lives here alone, walking melancholy
bout the paths and woods, and soon is deep in the plotting
f '15. His face, shining through the still bright colours of
is portrait, yet seemed to dominate the house, so wistful, so
eautiful, so unhappy.

Janet to-night felt that unfortunate boy standing at her
ide. She knew every incident of his story, his life with the
esuits, his return to Wintersmoon, his love for a girl in
ie village, Jane Woodley, the family rage, the illegitimate
hild, and the girl's death in childbed, his own self-murder,
anging in the Wintersmoon woods on an icy snowy morn-
ig, that gentle patter of his bare feet down the Winters-
ioon passages, the sigh and the faint closing of a door that
as not there.

As he vanished he was followed by the Twelfth Duke, that
tout red-faced ruffian who in the last decade of the eigh-
eenth century gave Wintersmoon a brief record for orgies
iat Byron's Hell-Fire Club could not exceed. Here dark
olours stole upon the scene, hints of abnormalities and ter-
ors, of villagers debauched and shamed, of the Regency
akes, and the last orgy ending in that duel at dawn when
iree rascally gentlemen (one of them the Twelfth Duke
imself) vanished from this earthly scene to nobody's re-
ret.

Then lighter colours again—Lady Arabella Purefoy the
lue-stocking, with her published verses "The Looking
lass," "The Windows of Fashion," and her romance *The*

Baron's Keep in the Horace Walpole manner; the villag
genius of a week in the Bloomfield style with his volum
published by subscription, *The Village Green;* then th
Fourteenth Duke, also of a literary mind, correspondir
with Southey about "Roderick" and going to London
hear Hazlitt lecture; Thackeray's visit to Wintersmoon (ar
who knows how much the pages of *Esmond* owe to tha
visit?) ; the crinolines of the Purefoy ladies, and the gre
dance given for the coming of age of the Fourteenth Duk
the present Duke's father, and the appearance once agai
of the kindly Hunchback sitting cross-wise with his litt
yellow dog at his side in the moonlight on the Wintersmoc
lawn. . . .

And now? Janet turned from the window with a shive
She was to become part of this tradition. And what par
Had it been only fancy on her side that the House loved her
Had she strength and character sufficient to turn this a
venture of hers into success, even triumph? Success for he
self and Wildherne and the Duke, success for Wintersmoo
success even for England?

She lay in bed, looking out to the stars, praying to wha
God she knew not, but praying.

Was there someone in the room? Was that young Franc
Poole smiling good-will? Was that the Twelfth Duke wit
his little pig's eyes, his bloated cheeks, his sensual lurch
Was that, dim by the window, Arabella with her horse fac
and mildly intelligent gaze?

Before their questioning Janet sank down, down, and
she sank her last vision was of the little turban-heade
Duchess and Mr. Pomeroy showing her gravely her prope
seat in his church, somewhere at the back among his poore
parishioners, the ones who, alas, could not subscribe as the
would to his splendid financial efforts.

CHAPTER II

UP AMONG THE BACHELORS

THERE is an hour in St. James's and the summer when the guardian saint of all bachelors takes his evening walk. It is the hour when he can observe most pleasantly the happy doings of his devotees.

There is probably nothing pleasanter than this hour of the afternoon when the sun has done his hardest work of the day and is tempted to linger lazily among the twisted chimney-pots, crooked roofs, and odd angles of Ryder Street and Duke Street, when the smoke from those same chimneys is coloured with a faint plum-shadowed purple, when the sparrows as they sit in somnambulistic rows on the telegraph wires find their feathers flecked with colour, and when errant scraps of paper scattering over the tiles in the afternoon breezes glow with a sort of tinsel iridescence very satisfying to their almost submerged vanities.

During this happy hour or two St. James's is pleasantly and complaisantly busy. Doors are for ever opening and shutting. Unlike the Piccadilly world at the top of the hill everything of the motor savage hinterland is here softened and advanced a step in civilisation. Horns that have shrieked outside the Royal Academy are hushed to gentility outside Christie's, and Princes of the Motor Blood Royal are contented to steal modestly from street to street once they are south of Jermyn Street. With this result, that in St. James's at this hour you hear everywhere human voices. There are still many streets and squares in London where the human voice can be heard (in Paris, New York, Rome, Berlin it has gone the way of other outmoded functions), but nowhere can it be more pleasantly heard than here in St. James's. Page-boys, valets (either thin, spare and sharp-nosed or stout, purple-veined and complaisant), barbers,

newsmen, dog-fanciers, racing touts, and the white-haire
Prophet of a Newly Revealed Religion (he has a place al
ways at a quarter to five of an afternoon at the corner o
Ryder Street with his placard saying "WATCH AND PRA
FOR THE LORD COMETH"), all these have their proper place
functions in this afternoon hour. They step, they stroll, the
and wander, (all with the exception of the Prophet, wh
is stationary) from door to door. The public-house half dow
the hill in Duke Street knows them well: everyone in fac
knows everyone and social amiability is extreme.

Within doors, in and out of these warrens of chamber;
among these Master Bachelors, thousands of teas are takin
place; at any rate, even though whisky and soda is th
drink, the spirit of the hour is the Tea spirit.

Some of the Bachelors are having tea in ladies' houses—
Tea and Coffee and Macaroons—a kind of cake I much lov
—but many more are themselves entertaining ladies—or nc
even ladies, simply their own vulgar sex—or again not eve
that, simply their own vulgar selves. There is a sad amoun
of secret tea-tippling in St. James's just about this time

And in the world outside, as the sun slowly falls with
glittering profusion of sparkle among the roofs and win
dows, what a life there is! Nobody is busy, and yet there is
perpetual stir. All the newspapers outside the newsvendor
at the corner of Jermyn Street quiver with the informatio
about racing, cricket, and horrid murder that they have t
impart. The windows of the shops shining in the late su
glow with the pride of their eighteenth-century marines
their snuff-boxes, and their little figures of ivory and silver
The silversmith's at the corner of Ryder Street simply blaze
with his chains and watches. There is a twitter of birds, ;
distant ringing of bells, a patter of footsteps, a cry risin;
from the heart of London, sharp and piercing, and the
again, like a bell plunging into clear water, once more tha
melodious striking of the clocks, the intimate echo of a sma
country town hugging its own secure intimacy.

At this moment Charles Ravage was entertaining in hi
room two rather ancient gentlemen, one Mr. Felix Brun, an
the other old Canary Proffet, who founded the Selemite

Club in the sixties and has shaken hands since with more
Titled Hands than anyone else in England.

"That," thought Ravage, considering him gloomily, "is
your only distinction, and I wish you would gather your
miserable thin shanks together and take your departure."

Ravage had his rooms at the very back of one of the
Ryder Street warrens, so much at the back that it seemed
to hang on to the main building as though it had been slung
out from the wall like a cage. To reach it you had first to
satisfy the superior patronage of an elegant door-keeper,
then tread dark red carpets (if you disdained the lift) up
stairways between pots of ferns, all of the finest order—and
then, in a flash of time, on reaching the third floor you were
in a world of almost incredible shabbiness. Over the bannisters of the fine staircase hung innumerable pantaloons
waiting to be pressed or resting—after that for them so at-
tenuating process; little staircases like the entrances to
mouse-traps appeared mysteriously, and while you examined
them vanished; carpets dim with faded roses and emascu-
lated sunflowers were worn so threadbare that every step
was a danger. On chairs and shabby tables, among the
clothes, cleaning bottles, and brushes, dishes with battered
metal covers and plates greasy with fat showed that gentlemen had that day been lunching. Two cats mewed from door
to door, their eyes flaming and twisted with the eternal expectation of miraculous fish-bones.

At the back of this disorder Charles Ravage lived in a
mysterious silence. After stumbling over carpet holes and
black little stairs and the dust-pans of itinerant maidservants,
you came suddenly to his door. You entered, and at once
there was such a silence as perhaps no other spot in London could provide. It was a silence as in the heart of deepest
Africa (one can but imagine). It was a silence that had something of the impenetrability of a padded cell. You could
whisper and be heard clearly from one end of the place to
the other.

They were funny twisted rooms, four of them wriggling
out of a narrow and dingy little hall. Not much view. From
Ravage's bedroom, bathroom, and spare-room only chimney-

pots, and from the sitting-room a slanting furtive glimpse of Ryder Street (with everyone falling apparently on to their noses). This sitting-room was bare save for a shabby sofa, four chairs, a table, and a bad and very large photograph of Niagara Falls. There was one bookcase with books carelessly heaped about it rather than on it.

The three men were not well assorted. Felix Brun knew Ravage too slightly and Ravage knew Canary Proffet too well. That bag of bones, elegantly attired in black stock, high white collar, black braided coat, grey trousers, and little shining shoes sat perched up on one of Ravage's uncomfortable chairs, clinging on with his thin bony fingers to a world that was swiftly abandoning him. In the Merry Days of Merry King Edward he had been a fine social figure. His gaunt body, with its staring protuberant eyes, might often be seen standing at social attention in those handsome groups of Edwardian house parties.

He was everywhere—so ubiquitous that he was said to have solved the secret of perpetual motion. He had a "little place down in Hampshire," two plain sisters as bony as himself, and the Selemite Club. This last was the success of his life. He had founded it in those old dark days when club life was anti-social and he had introduced certain innovations—tea on certain afternoons for ladies and true shower-baths; he gave afternoon parties there at which foreign dukes from places with names like Schwellenburg, Mecklenburg, Strelitz appeared, and, on occasions, certain minor Royalties. It was the time after Lily Langtry and after the Duchess of Wrexe, when educated Society was reading the novels of John Oliver Hobbes and raving about *Pelleas et Melisande*.

That was Canary Proffet's period. His only one. The War had killed his world stone dead, as it had that of his friends old Absalom and Pretty Farquhar. Absalom and Farquhar had passed away under the stock of the change, but Canary was of sterner stuff and refused to pass away. He hung on anxiously with straightened means and a damaged liver. But so long as a duchess remained on the horizon he would be there waiting to be noticed.

Felix Brun surveyed this relic with serious attention. This London world seemed just now to be full of such relics, as the glittering sand is strewn with gleaming fish-bones. He had known so well the day when London was filled with Canary Proffets all exultant and important. A day never to return. Whatever was to be the future of this London world, there would be no room ever again for Canary Proffets. And yet who could tell? Might not Comrade XY 2343 be the Canary of 1965, wearing his red tie and Union badge with a super-traditional air and awaiting the gracious attention of the wife of the Minister of Public Works? It well might be.

Ravage, shabby, and listening indifferently to the talk of his guests, wished heartily that they would depart. What had induced them to invite old Brun he could not tell, but then he never deigned to discover the origin of his irrational impulses.

Someone was coming—Rosalind Grandison, in fact; and although, as usual, he did not care a damn what happened, nevertheless he would just as soon that these two old chatterers should totter away before her advent.

But Brun, as usual, was interested in the exposition of his own ideas, and took it for granted that, wherever he might be, he was wanted.

"This London of yours," he was saying, "intrigues me more than any of the old Londons ever did. You seem to have lost your spirits, all of you. On every side of me I hear and read nothing but complaints. Complaints of your Government, your morals, your workmen, your taxes, . . . *voilà*. There never was such a country for abusing itself!"

Ravage yawned, staring darkly through the bones of old Canary into the thin walls of his rabbit warren.

"What would you have?" he said. "It's all true enough. What they grandly call 'England's Day' is over. And so is the day of everyone else. Thank God for it. Now the private life has its turn. . . ."

"But over! Over!" Brun cried excitedly. "Where? How? Some few of you have lost your money and have learnt to work. Your women went to the War and there killed British

hypocrisy. And thank God for that! But your national character—that does not change. Your policemen. . . . Mor
Dieu, how I admire your policemen! And you grumble . .
because for the moment you pay high taxes and the papers
discuss Birth Control! Birth Control? An admirable thing in
this so overcrowded world."

Old Proffet sighed.

"My dear fellow, honestly you don't know what you're
talking about. Things are awful, positively awful. There's
no reverence left for anything, I assure you. One's shoved
about . . . why, it's too terrible. You should go in a Tube,
my dear fellow. . . ."

"I do," said Brun. "Try the Paris Underground if you
want to know what real democracy is. Besides, your governing classes *are* as strong as ever they were! Take a wedding
like Lord Poole's and the Grandison girl a few weeks ago.
There's your governing classes! In all their glory. And more
active and alive than ever they were in the old Duchess of
Wrexe's day. They have to do something to-day to keep
themselves alive . . . *and* they do it!"

"Yes," said Ravage sulkily. "The women set up hat-shops,
dance all night, play Bridge all the afternoon, and expect to
make the thing pay. They smash, and some fool of a man
pays the bill."

"Yes," said Brun eagerly. "You, like your plays and your
novels, are estimating the whole of English life by a small
crowd of people who are as abnormal as they are unimportant. I, who speak to you, have watched those people. I have
been to your Quadrant Club and The Pharisees and The
Dandy Lion and the rest of it. And what do I see? Always
the same young men and girls, the same six or seven old
women—and even then how innocent? You English, when
you are really depraved, play tennis and write memoirs of
eighteenth-century politicians and grow roses in the country
as you have always done. What is this immorality? The
same as it has always been, only now you come more into
the open. But not even now by half as much as you did before
the reign of the good Queen Victoria. When will you see that
that was a short interregnum of hypocrisy carried over from

Protestant Germany? Your Queen was a great queen and the Church of England a great church. They have had their time, and it was short enough as history goes. But you speak of that period, all of you, as though it had covered the centuries. You have jumped back to your proper character— Eighteenth Century."

Proffet sighed. "My dear Brun, I remember you twenty, thirty years ago. You talked in the same way then. The Eighteenth Century was the time of English Gentlemen. The English Gentleman is dead."

Ravage broke in. "Yes, and a damned good thing too. English this, that, and the other. Too much of this English. Have another whisky, Proffet, and cheer up. I should have thought you'd be glad to have finished with some of your climbing up staircases and kissing the fat hands of ridiculous duchesses. You should be, seeing what a long life of it you've had."

"Then England means nothing to you?" Brun asked. "Its lovely country, rivers and hills and castles? I'm international, perhaps, but yet when I think of a place in Normandy I know my heart beats."

"That's because you're never there," Ravage answered. "Our rivers and hills! Yes, and what about our climate, with its pretty fogs and its charming drizzle that lasts for months on end? My God!"

"And yet you live here," Brun answered. "I know your type, Ravage. There are millions here like you. You curse your country, but you love it; you despise it with your tongue, but in your heart you so deeply admire it and all that it does that your contempt for all other countries in comparison with it is unfathomable. You laugh at your fellow-countrymen, but you believe that there are none like them. You say that England's day is over, but she is for you the mistress of all the world, and you watch these changes going on around you with no doubt at all, but that through them she will be greater than ever."

"It may be," said Ravage languidly. "I've never thought about it."

How bored he was with these old men! They carried the

odour of the grave with them. He was waiting now for someone whose beauty and youth and freshness stirred him, in
spite of his will, his cynicism, his selfishness, to some new
bound of experience. Of what experience? He could not tell.
He had waited for many months now on the edge of things,
preferring it so. He believed that, with a wave of his hand,
the merest gesture, he could take possession and enjoy at
his will. But always then came satiety! With what remorse-
less swiftness! Perhaps, for once in his life, he would hold
his hand.

Not that he was any ruthless Don Juan. In spite of his
reputation the women in his life had been few. He did not
attract them in the way that rumour supposed. And ideas
were more to him, always, than human beings. Or, until
now, they had been.

He regarded Proffet with lowering gaze. For twopence
he would snap those bony members and rid the world of a
pestilent old fool.

The telephone bell rang. He went to it. "Yes, will you
ask her to come up, please?"

"I must be getting along," old Proffet mumbled. Then he
waited. Through many years of social effort he had acquired
the trick of pausing after he announced his departure because he expected then: "Oh, must you go, Mr. Proffet?
. . . Oh, if you must, won't you come to us on the twelfth,
only one or two people, all friends. . . ."

It was true that that agreeable sequence, once so consis-
tently regular, was now more honoured in the breach than the
observance, but habit was habit.

On this occasion there was no sequence. Ravage, who was
not noted for his manners, simply waited.

"Yes, I must move on. . . . I promised the Hartshorns.
. . . Well, well . . . Yes. Have you heard about the Lan-
grishes? Of course nobody thinks that the boy is his, and
the whole of the Langrish property. . . ."

Brun also made a movement. "Why do you allow your
papers to wash your dirty linen so publicly?" he asked. "I
can't understand it. It isn't like you. Columns and columns
of sexual abnormalities. . . ."

"Human nature, my dear Brun," Proffet murmured. 'Only human nature. Skeletons, you know. Other people's skeletons. . . ."

The door opened.

"Miss Grandison," someone announced.

Rosalind stood there, so young and lovely in her white clothes and shining health that the two old men were revenants from dead and dusty worlds. They did not feel that. They smiled with pleasure. They were as young and attractive as ever they had been, one look at Miss Grandison assured them.

"You know Miss Grandison, I think," Ravage said with ill-concealed disgust.

The old men smiled, bowed. Then slowly, reluctantly they departed, convinced that Miss Grandison would wish them to have remained.

"Pheugh!" Ravage threw the windows yet wider open. "I'm sorry, Rosalind. I did my best to get rid of them. To banish Canary Proffet is harder than keeping a bank balance. Never mind. They'll soon be dead."

But Rosalind could never think of more than one thing at a time. The old men were nothing to her.

"Charles," she said, "I wish I hadn't come. I'm out of mood to-day. I shall lose my temper, you will lose yours. I shall leave abruptly and so—one more day wasted."

"What's the matter?" he asked her. She was lovely. White and gold against his shabby, faded sofa cushions. Her colour and grace and form were so delicate that he could not believe in their reality. He was moved by beauty only when it touched his imagination more than his senses: he always felt the power of beauty most when physically he was not regarding it, but Rosalind had for him this especial quality that she was more imaginatively beautiful than actually, although the Lord knew she was actually beautiful enough.

"I've had a complaining letter from Janet," she said. "I ought to go to her, and I don't want to."

"Why don't you want to go?" he asked, watching her.

"The depths of Wiltshire," she answered. "Old house half

shut up, woods, ponds, peacocks, Salisbury Plain in the distance. And then I don't like Wildherne Poole, and he doesn't like me. I'm being disgustingly selfish. I adore Janet. I'm a pig."

"Of course you're selfish," Ravage answered. "You're one of the most selfish people I know. Certainly you ought to go. Your sister has done everything for you."

She looked up at him inquisitively. "Why do I spend so much of my time with you, Charles?" she asked. "I'm not in love with you. I don't even very much like you. Everyone thinks that I'm another of your victims. That's what distresses Janet so."

"We have something strangely in common," he answered. "Or we seem to have. Whether we should have after we'd lived together for a while I don't know. You're the only real companion I've ever had."

"That's what Wildherne says about Janet," Rosalind answered. "Janet takes it as a compliment. I don't. Besides, I don't think it's true. I'm too much frightened of you to be a good companion."

"Frightened?" he asked. "Are you?"

"Yes, of course. You've always known it."

"I would wish you not to be. There's nothing of me to be frightened of. Except my absurd reputation, which really does me altogether too much honour."

"Well," she said, speaking quickly and nervously, "I've come to tell you something. I think I'm going to be engaged to Tom Seddon."

He neither moved nor spoke.

"Why don't you say something?"

"What am I to say?" he answered quietly. "What you are going to do, you are going to do."

"And that's the end to our friendship," she went on.

"If you wish it—certainly," he answered.

She coloured angrily.

"Ah, you always provoke me so with your pretended passivity!" she cried. "You think it's the grand manner, I suppose. I wanted your opinion. But if you have none—well, I'd better be going!"

She got up.

"What kind of opinion do you expect me to have?" he asked her. "You know before I tell you. I never heard of anything more foolish, but—if it seems wise to you—do it!"

She sat down again.

"Foolish? And why?"

"You know what he is and you know what you yourself are. He is a boy with silly idealistic ideas. He is all enthusiasm and expectation. You are never enthusiastic and only expect things for yourself, never for people in general. He is in love with you, which bores you. He will remain in love with you because you don't love him, which will bore you still more. You detest his revered and widowed mother."

But she answered gravely:

"You don't know him at all. He is more interesting than you think. Perhaps he will do great things one day. And then he is safe. I shall know exactly where I am. With you and in this life I'm now leading I don't know where I am at all. And dear Janet will be delighted."

He laughed.

"You love your sister enough to sacrifice your whole life to her, but not enough to go and visit her for a few days in the country. . . . Well, if that's the way you see things, I'm not the one to stop you."

She beckoned him towards the sofa. "Come and sit down near me, Charles, and help me a little. You are the wisest person I know. Yes, whatever else you are, you are that. I want to climb out of this selfish, grabbing, ugly life I've been leading for months. Tom Seddon would help me there. Of course I'm not in love with him. I sometimes think that in spite of what I said just now you're the only human being I could ever be in love with. Don't we both know that one day that might happen, and haven't we both been holding back for months, and isn't there something wrong about us both that we can be so cold-blooded about a thing like this for so long?"

Her questions came out a little breathlessly. He came and sat down, near her but not touching her.

"Do you want me to make love to you?" he asked. "I could very easily."

"No." She drew back a little. "No, never! How unhappy we should be! So soon over and then hatred, disgust!" She shivered a little. "We are a poor breed, Charles, beside Janet—and Wildherne, perhaps. We are cleverer—and smaller."

"I deny that," he said lightly. "It is easier for them because they are old-fashioned. They believe in things that seem to us childish."

"For instance?" she asked.

"A benign deity, eternal love, the essential decency of humanity, England's destiny. . . ."

She looked up at him as he crouched in the corner of the sofa, huddled, his thin knees perked up towards his chin.

"Do you believe in nothing, then?"

He stared across the room.

"I don't know. I keep an open mind. But when you come to it, what have our generation left to them to believe in? A God? A first cause? At any rate not benign. Eternal love? We have reduced love to chemical equations. Essential decency of humanity? After the War? No, thank you. England's destiny? The words are so old-fashioned that they make one think of wax flowers under glass. There remains oneself. Also a chemical equation. . . . And yet. . . ."

"And yet?" she asked him.

"Yes. That's the devil of it!" he broke out, jumping off the sofa and beginning to pace the room. "That remains. One can't get rid of it. Or I can't. And you can't. Our resolve is to strip ourselves of all nonsense. But the nonsense remains."

He stood close to her, staring at her. "If I were to begin to make love to you, here and now, we should begin to believe in certain things—for a moment or two—certain beautiful things. And then—so quickly the disappointment! That's the matter with our modern kind. We can't stand the disillusion. We aren't brave enough to face it, and so we avoid, or laugh at, the things that produce it."

He stood looking at her. He bent forward, put his hand
i her throat, and very gently kissed her.

She said nothing.

She got up from the sofa, her hands, as he saw, trembling.
"I must go. . . . I have things to do. You shouldn't
ive done that, Charles. That isn't our kind of thing."

"It may be—any time," he answered huskily, looking at
:r.

"It mustn't be." She took his hand, held it for a moment.
Well, good-bye. I'll tell you what happens."

But he didn't reply. He had turned his back to her and was
anding at the farther end of the room.

She went out.

She was frightened. She stood for a moment in Ryder
treet looking about her, but seeing nothing. She felt as
ough she had been close to some danger that most nar-
•wly she had for the moment escaped. But only for a mo-
ent. The danger remained.

She had never, until now, been conscious of any peril, and
was for her a new emotion. The peril was within her. For
e first time she distrusted her own strength.

As she moved up the hill London seemed to threaten her.
he lovely evening was golden, suffused with that soft gentle
;ht that is so especially English, that was lying now bend the chimney-pots and pathways of the town, over fields
d hedges, hedges dark with purple shadows, and flowers
ere scenting the air, streams softly running through the
;ht with slumberous chatter, field animals gently stirring
om shade to shade, and the moon somewhere cherry-
•loured, horn-shaped, stealing over wood and hill.

But that gentleness nowhere touched her. She was angry
her own agitation, it was as though she were hurrying to
me place or person that would give her security.

At the corner outside Fortnum and Mason's she paused
:wildered, as though she had lost all sense of direction, then
:ard a gentle "How are you, Miss Grandison?" and looking
) saw the amiable features of John Beaminster.

She was delighted. She took his hand as though it wer[e] her only hope in a desperate world.

"Isn't it lovely weather?" he asked her.

"Yes," she answered gratefully, as though he had don[e] her some great courtesy. How charming he was! That so[rt] of courteous kindness was the best thing in the world. A[s] they moved towards the Green Park together she found her[-] self chatting to him as though he were her dearest friend.

"And where have you been, and what have you bee[n] doing?" he asked her. He was delighted with her friendlines[s.] She had always, he fancied, been impatient with him, think[-] ing him a tiresome old fogey, burdening an overcrowde[d] world with his presence.

And there was nothing he liked better than walking dow[n] Piccadilly on a fine evening with a beautiful girl. He had bee[n] to Hurlingham to see the polo: he told her about it.

"And how is your sister?" he asked her. "Is she in Lo[n-] don?"

"No, she's down at Wintersmoon."

"Ah! that's a place I should like to see."

"You must go down some time, Lord John. My siste[r] would love to see you."

"Yes," he said. "I don't really know Poole very well. [I] know his father better."

"We'll go down together, shall we? And it must be in th[e] summer. I'll admit to you frankly that I'm no good in th[e] country in the winter. I don't hunt, and otherwise wha[t] is there to do?"

"No. Quite." He smiled at her. How beautiful she was[!] Did he dare put in a word for his boy?

They were coming to Half Moon Street. He looked acros[s] the thundering tide of traffic.

"I cross here. I have rooms in 90 Piccadilly. Can I get yo[u] a taxi?"

"No, thank you. I shall walk to Hyde Park Corner."

His heart thumping he said: "Have you seen our youn[g] friend Tom Seddon lately?"

She looked at him, at the swinging strip of green flowin[g] beneath the trees, at the pearl-grey buildings opposite. Her was a crisis. She knew it. She knew that with her next words something most critical would be decided. On the one side the safety, friendliness, assurance of that green sward lit now with a saffron glow, on the other that road with its plunging traffic, roar, and ruthless arrogance.

She looked at him, her eyes searching his:

"Tell him to come and see me, Lord John— 39A Maypole Street—to ring me up. I want to see him."

"I will." The old man's face shone with happiness. He raised his hat and started across the street.

CHAPTER III

WINTERSMOON : MORNING — JANET
AND WILDHERNE

HIGNETT, as the Wintersmoon clock struck nin
stepped out of the long dining-room windows, stoo
on the terrace and surveyed the world.

This world was glittering and shining, dew-soaked, un
der the sun. Between the trees of the woods the light w
a sparkling fire and on the long green surface of the lawn
the sparks scattered from blade to blade. Birds, small an
dark in the shining splendour, hopped from hunting-groun
to hunting-ground. The great house spread fan-wise, clea
and sharp against the faint white-blue of the morning sk
Smoke curled in spirals, still, unflecked by wind, heave
wards. The peacock stood at the far end of the terrace,
sight of Hignett spread his fan, then turned and strutte
away, his greeting royally given.

Hignett sniffed the air, went back into the dining-roor
saw that all was well, then passed into the hall and, wi
an air of abstraction as though in spite of himself he mu
be a philosopher, stroked the slumberous gong. The soun
very soft and musical, stole up the broad staircase and gent
died away.

Hignett in fact, although his thick body showed no emo
tion, was well pleased with himself. He was pleased to b
here with his master once more. He had no objection
Halkin Street, but living was only half living when he wa
separated from the one and only human being who apa
from his son was of importance to him.

He would have been surprised had he ever thought of i
which he did not, at the indifference with which he regarde
the rest of the world. There was his work, and Lord Poo
and his boy. Nothing more.

148

But, as he saw Lady Poole coming in from the garden,
me faint interest stirred in him.

He had, in the beginning, disapproved of the marriage.
o one could say whether jealousy lurked in that disap-
oval, but at least here, as it seemed to him, was a girl
ho was nobody, no money, no position, arrogating to
rself the possession of the most perfect human being on
od's earth. That was how he saw it.

But these last weeks at Wintersmoon had disturbed a lit-
e that superiority. No one could deny that she was a
arming lady. All the servants in the place knew it. She
as mistress and friend, both relationships perfectly main-
ined. There was something, too, that appealed to Hignett's
ivalry. She was a little lost, a little desolate, and for the
st time in all his days Hignett questioned, ever so slightly,
s master's conduct.

This lady also recognised the quality of Hignett's devo-
n to his master. It was as though she had come to him,
ld out her hand to him and said: "I think your loyalty
d devotion to my master is one of the finest things I
ow."

Hignett was one of those who, disdaining flattery, like
eir best points to be suitably recognised.

Finally, there was nothing too small for Lady Poole's
tention. She never worried the servants, leaving every-
ing that ought to be left to Hignett and Mrs. Craddock,
e Wintersmoon housekeeper (a very submissive alterna-
e to the housekeeper of Halkin Street), but she was aware
everything and cared that things should go well. The
uble, for instance, that she took over that old Mrs. Bed-
es who was sometimes at Halkin Street and sometimes at
intersmoon and was never very useful anywhere because
r fat hurt her and she had spasms! There was not a gar-
ner's boy or kitchen maid of whom Lady Poole was not
vare, and always humanly aware, her heart being, say
hat you like, one of the largest. And Hignett, disdain the
en avowal of it as he would, placed a value on hearts.

"Had Lord Poole come down, Hignett?"

"No, my lady."

"Thank you. Aren't these flowers lovely?"

"Yes, my lady."

"Just put them in that bowl for a moment. I'll arrang[e]
them myself afterwards."

"Yes, my lady."

"Oh, I think Mrs. Craddock knows. We shall be six f[or]
luncheon. Sir Arnold and Lady Burnett and a friend [of]
theirs, a Mrs. Mark, are coming. They are motoring ov[er]
from Salisbury.

"Yes, my lady."

Janet went on into the sun-drenched dining-room. Sh[e]
stood at the window, looking out. She should have bee[n]
happy. She was not. She had now her desire. She and Wild[-]
herne were alone; but she was strange to-day. Something th[e]
matter. She was in a hysterical, emotional mood. Even no[w]
as she looked out on to the glorious garden her eyes fill[ed]
with tears. She did not know why.

Her letters were on the table and there was one fro[m]
Rosalind. She opened it eagerly and read:

DARLING JANET—Be happy. Last night I told Tom Sedd[on]
I would marry him. I am coming very soon to tell you all abo[ut]
it.—Your loving sister,

ROSALIND.

Wildherne at that moment came in.

"Wildherne! What do you think? Rosalind is going [to]
marry Tom Seddon after all! Isn't that splendid? Oh, I a[m]
glad! I *am* glad!"

He put his arms round her and kissed her. "So am [I.]
Delighted! That's the best news you could have. Tom Se[d-]
don's a capital fellow."

Janet's face darkened. "It's only Rachel. She won't li[ke]
it. She can't bear Rosalind. But she doesn't know her. Sh[e]
hasn't had a chance of knowing her."

"If Rosalind treats Tom well," Wildherne said, "it w[ill]
be all right."

The moment the words left his mouth he cursed hims[elf]
for a fool. The idiot he was! And whence came it th[at]

always during these last days he was saying something to hurt her?

"You're never quite fair to Rosalind," Janet said. "You don't know her."

"She hasn't given me much chance of knowing her," Wildherne said brightly. "She hasn't been down here since our marriage."

"That's quite natural," Janet replied, "when she knows you don't like her."

"Oh, come, Janet," Wildherne answered, "be fair. I'm ready to like her if she'll give me the chance."

"I don't think you are," Janet answered. "You are prejudiced."

Hignett was in the room and they were both aware of it. The pause between them was vocal with irritation. Then Janet said:

"Oh, by the way, don't forget the Burnetts are coming over from Salisbury for luncheon. You like him, I know."

"Yes. He's a good fellow.

"And I'm interested too because they are bringing over an old friend of Rachel's, a Mrs. Mark. Rachel has often wanted us to meet. She was a Miss Trenchard and made rather a romantic marriage, eloping or something. Rachel says she's a dear."

In her heart she was saying: "Rosalind engaged to Tom. . . Oh, I *am* glad! Am I? Isn't it dangerous! Why can't he be more sympathetic to me in this? He always hated Rosalind. . . . What's the matter with me this morning? I'm a bundle of nerves."

Hignett had gone. She went and stood by the window. Wildherne came and put his hand on her shoulder.

"I'm sorry," he said, "if I seemed unsympathetic about Rosalind. I want to be a true friend to her, and mean to be, if you'll let me."

"I know you do," Janet said, turning round to him and smiling. "I don't know what's the matter with me this morning. I'm nervous, disturbed—as though something were going to happen." She laughed. "I'll start about my household duties. That will set me right."

If Janet was unhappy, so too that morning was Wildherne. Unhappy and burning with a strange fire. As he
stood there in the library having his daily talk with Beresford the land agent, a little bow-legged man with a face
of brick-red, he could not tie his mind to the details of
the interview. He answered so absent-mindedly that Beresford showed his surprise.

"Yes, it's no use, Beresford, this morning. . . . I have
something on my mind. But there's nothing very urgent,
is there?"

"No, only the Planter's Row Cottages and they're not
really urgent. Only something must be done about them
soon."

"We'll have it out to-morrow morning, then."

Beresford gone, Wildherne stayed in the middle of the
room, his thoughts chaotic. What was the matter? He knew
what was the matter. For the last three days he had known
He was being urged to take the next train up to London
and from London a taxi to Charles Street, then the lift, the
ring of the bell, the little room with the dull bronze wal
paper and the Walter Sickert, and then. . . . He could see
nothing but this. For nights and days (and especially nights)
he had seen nothing but this. He had not wished for it
nay, rather he wished far otherwise. To be happy here
and tranquil with Janet in perfect companionship, loving the
house and the things to be done on the land and the English
country. Happy and tranquil! But he was neither happy nor
tranquil. This thing had driven down upon him like a hot
wind, enveloping him, suffocating him with his desire. He
must see her. He must see her. He must see her. Over and
over again the words clanged and clanged in his brain.

Each morning he had hoped that on waking the desire
would have died, but this morning it was yet fiercer and he
was stilling it with that old plea for vicious pleasure that
it must be satisfied to be quieted.

And after all, was he not honest with Janet? He had told
her from the first how it would be, but as, in his heart, he
heard the echo of this whisper he thought of her fine trusting
gaze, her frank carriage as she stood beside him shoulder

to shoulder—yes, she would accept it as part of the bargain, but how that acceptance would hurt her!

He was walking in the woods: they were black to him with a sort of fiery darkness. Even while he fought for all his decency he knew, as though he were watching the struggles of some other poor mortal, that he would yield.

He tried to fix his mind on Janet, on her goodness and kindliness and friendship, and he arranged round her his beloved English landscape with the Plain and the Downs and the lawns green at the foot of the house that here was a dead star, its lights all out, cold under sculptural moonshine, and to his right did he but turn his head a whistling fiery planet of aching passionate need.

When he came from the wood he felt as though he were crawling, his head hanging. The battle, that he had never truly fought, was simply lost.

They met, therefore, over the commonplace bodies of the Burnetts. The Burnetts were stout and cheerful, laughing at everything, eating and drinking everything, on her side surprised at everything, on his, fine English avoidance of agitation. It seemed that he knew about horses and tomatoes, and she about Madeira (the island) and Church movements. She knew, for instance, all about Mr. Pomeroy.

But it was Mrs. Mark who interested Janet. She interested her in the first place because she was a friend of Rachel Seddon's, but secondly because she resembled in certain ways, Janet fancied, herself. This was a quiet, gentle, kindly woman with at first not much sign of personality and character. This was because she held herself quiet behind the torrents of Burnett chatter and laughter. Then Janet secured a word from her. They talked about Rachel and Tom. Katherine Mark had not heard of the engagement and was deeply interested.

"My husband," she said, "has always been so fond of Tom. Philip, now that he is in Parliament, can help Tom in some ways. And then they talk about books by the hour."

Janet asked her whether she herself read a great deal, did she find time?

"Well, we are all in the middle of it, you see," Katherine Mark answered. "My sister Millie married a novelist and my only brother, Henry, is a novelist. With us novelists are as common as peas."

"What is the name of your brother-in-law?" Janet asked her.

"Westcott, Peter Westcott. I expect you have read some of his novels. *Reuben Hallard* is the name of his most famous one, although he wrote it years ago."

Of course Janet had read some of them. How interesting to know authors, to live in such an exciting world where people were really doing things! I am afraid that Janet said all the commonplace things.

"Well, no," said Katherine Mark, laughing. "I don't know that it's very interesting. I don't think that it's more valuable to create a mediocre novel than to create a bunch of fine tomatoes in your greenhouse—not so valuable. Peter writes good novels, though, and is a dear besides—but Henry. I'm afraid Henry's two productions are nothing to be proud of. Perhaps he'll do better later on. And Millie, my sister, is much prouder of her baby than of all the books Peter has written."

"It seems a wonderful world to me," Janet said. "Here we don't deal in anything so interesting as books."

There was more bitterness in her voice than she had intended, and she knew that Katherine Mark was aware of it.

"I suppose we all envy one another," Katherine Mark answered lightly. "You'd be surprised if you knew how I've longed to see this marvellous house. Will you show it me after luncheon? Or perhaps you are tired of showing it to people."

"No, indeed," Janet answered, ashamed of her depression. "I love this house, every inch of it. I feel as though it belonged to me entirely and had never belonged to anyone before—especially mine—and that's pretty arrogant considering that I've only just been brought into it."

"I understand that," Katherine Mark answered, "about places, I mean. We grew up in Cornwall, in a village with the charming name of Garth-in-Roselands, a large number of us, dozens of aunts and uncles. And I loved that old rambling house as I shall never love anywhere again. I haven't the courage to go back and see it, especially as I ran away with my husband from there, and I don't think it has ever forgiven me. Places are more alive than many people."

Meanwhile Janet was increasingly conscious of Wildherne. It seemed that even though people did not love one another it was possible, if they lived much together, to mingle spiritually—not in harmony but rather in discord—and so be bound together for ever afterwards in a dreadful jangling relation. She was jangling with Wildherne to-day. She saw his fair hair, his fine clear-cut nose, mouth and chin, heard his courteous, rather boyish voice with nothing but irritation.

What was the matter with her to-day? She seemed not to recognise herself. The real Janet was absent, and here was someone discontented, peevish, and, above all, uneasy with some undefined alarm.

Luncheon was over. The house was to be displayed.

They started on the familiar ground. There was not much in the occupied part of the house to be shown, the staircase, some pictures, the water tower, the famous painting in the long gallery by an unknown artist—"The Dark Knight in Silver Armour"—but soon the heavy black door at the end of the long gallery closed behind them, they were in another world, a world of science, shadow, and fading colour. As they stood there a moment before going on the shrill scream of the peacock came, penetrating the thick walls, through to them.

"You see," Wildherne explained, "the part of the house that we have left—the part we live in—has been rebuilt by the different dukes again and again, although the last one —my grandfather—had the good taste to make it fit in with the older part of the house fairly well. But the part that we are in now is exactly the building that it was in James I.'s day, and some of the rest is Henry II., and a very little of it Anglo-Saxon. Many of the rooms, of course, are empty and deserted—we simply haven't been able to afford to keep them up, but Elizabeth's room with the famous Peacock bed, James I.'s chapel, and the three rooms of Audrey Poole have been kept as they were. Audrey Poole was Elizabethan exquisite, Euphuist, courtier. He was a sort of minor Leicester; there is a story of a kind of Amy Robsart here—her name was Lucy Tourneur—and if the tale has any truth, he poisoned her in these same rooms and her wailing ghost may be seen any night at midnight about this very passage."

Lady Burnett shivered, and then in her hearty, cheerful voice cried: "Aren't these old stories too terrible? That brocade there, Lord Poole, must be worth a pretty penny."

But Audrey Poole's bedchamber hung with tapestry of grey and gold was exquisite. They all stood silent there. The small latticed windows looked out on to a little lawn of bright green bordered on one side by a thick hedge carved with the heads of birds and two grinning unicorns. The four-poster bed had hangings of cherry colour. On a chair was a lute, and hanging on the wall facing the windows Audrey's portrait, a pale lantern-jawed young man in cloth of silver.

Wildherne stepped out of the room and found that for the moment he was alone with Janet.

"Janet," he said, "I've got to go up to town to-night. I shall be back by mid-day to-morrow morning. I've told Hignett."

He had tried to speak quite easily, but at once he knew that she was aware of everything. They looked at one another. She dropped her eyes.

"Right," she answered. "Don't hurry back. Send me a wire if you're kept."

"Oh no," he said, "nothing will keep me."

They turned back to the others. They went on to James's chapel.

"Have you seen a ghost here yet, Lady Poole?" Lady Burnett asked.

"Oh no," Janet answered. "I don't think I'm the kind of a person to see ghosts. I'm too matter-of-fact."

"Well, I'm matter-of-fact enough," said Lady Burnett

cheerfully, "and I saw a ghost once. It was when we were staying at Poulteney Burrow with the Mannings. There's an old passage at Poulteney . . ." The story went cheerfully on. Janet heard none of it. Well, what had she to complain of? Had not this been always part of their bargain? Was he not free? Had not this very moment always been expected by her? And yet how it hurt! How desperately it hurt! Was it her pride? Was it her heart? Was it her pride in him or in herself? Was it her heart or his? Was it something maternal in her that longed to put her arms around him, as her mother her child, and to hold him back from something that would soil and hurt him? And what was this anger and indignation? What right had she to be either angry or indignant? She could analyse nothing. She was in a whirl of agitation and dismay. If he left her thus so soon after their marriage, and then, as the months passed, increasingly, what remained for her? What was this strange yearning desire that at this instant she felt, to hold him, to put her arms around him and, with that, anger so that, had they been alone, she could have attacked him, abused him? But what right had she? No right. . . . Nothing. . . . No hold on anyone. . . .

An odd feeling of faintness overcame her. She stayed behind in the dark light of the passage outside the chapel. She stood back against the wall, her hand over her eyes. Mrs. Mark was there.

"Lady Poole, aren't you well?" Her gentle voice was like that of an old friend.

"Oh no, thank you," Janet answered, smiling. "There's something stuffy about this part of the house, isn't there? Don't you feel it yourself?"

"Shan't we go back?" Mrs. Mark said. "Show me a little of the garden. I love gardens so."

"Yes. If you like," Janet replied. She went into the chapel.

"Wildherne," she said. "Mrs. Mark and I are going round the gardens for half an hour. Don't keep Lady Burnett too long in this dusty air, will you?"

She looked up at him, smiling. He caught her hand for a moment in his.

"No, dear. We won't be long."

She went back with Mrs. Mark. She knew what he had meant by that touch of the hand, that look into her eyes. It was as though he had said: "Don't judge me too hardly. This is too strong for me. Be patient." She fancied that he had meant that, but was there not something contemptible in that appeal for pity? Her anger was rising with every step that brought her back into the other part of the house. She would rather that he had defied her, taking stand on his bargain. "I told you that this would come. Well, why make such a fuss about it? Are we not modern husband and wife in a modern world? Have I pretended to love you?"

No, but if he had not loved her his arms had been round her, she had given him all that she could, she would perhaps bear him a child. . . .

She was glad that Mrs. Mark was with her. That would help her pride, her poor pride that was so nearly breaking that, had she been alone with Wildherne, she might have thrown herself at his feet, begging him to stay with her, not to leave her alone when she had no one. Hating her self-pity, her head up, as they turned down the long drive towards the walled kitchen gardens, she said to Mrs. Mark:

"It's odd, but I feel as though I had known you a long time."

"That happens, doesn't it?" Katherine Mark answered. "Every once and again someone comes who seems at once to belong to one's life. I felt the same about you the moment I saw you. And then Rachel is a great link."

"Yes. I wonder that we haven't met before. And now I hope that we will meet often. I am so seldom impulsive—not often enough. I enjoy the luxury of it when it comes."

"The great thing," Katherine Mark answered, "is to be natural about it, isn't it? We like one another at first sight—why shouldn't we say so? We have something in common, I know."

"Yes," Janet said. "I've heard of you so often from Rachel as Katherine. May I call you that? And will you call me Janet?"

"Of course," Katherine replied quietly. "I don't make

riends very often. My sister Millie is the one for that.
And after you've been married for a long time you're lazy."

"I don't make friends very often either," said Janet. "All
my life I've lived with my sister and we were orphans and
had very little money. Managing everything took up all
one's time."

"And now," said Katherine. "You have so much more
to manage. It must be wonderful suddenly to have the op-
ortunity to do so much. . . ."

"So much? I don't know," Janet interrupted. "I don't
think I'm managing very well. It was easier once, I expect,
but now these big places seem to have hardly the right to
exist. The world has changed so. Everyone is attacking
everything that this house stands for. And yet if it went
there is nothing that quite takes its place. It stands for something very beautiful. It ought not to be destroyed. It ought
to play its part in the new world. And that's what Wildherne and I——"

At those words she stopped. Wildherne and I! What
mockery! She turned round to Katherine:

"Tell me . . . Did you find marriage difficult at first?"

They had come to the little temple where some weeks
before Janet and Wildherne had had their talk. They sat
here, looking down at the pool with the water-lilies.

"Yes," said Katherine slowly. "Everyone does, I suppose.
Or, at least, not at first. When you are in love, as my husband and I were, nothing is difficult. But then there come
the more prosaic days. Compromise is hard for some people;
it wasn't hard for Philip while his romantic mood was on
him, but one can't be romantic always, especially when one
has to earn a living."

"Didn't you make a runaway match or something of the
kind? Tell me if I'm impertinent."

"Of course you're not. Yes, that was all very unhappy.
I was deeply attached to my mother, who was very strong-
willed and determined. She was jealous of Philip, and I
had to choose between her and Phil, and of course that made
me very unhappy."

"But your mother was reconciled afterwards?"

"No, never. She wouldn't even see me when she was d
ing."

"Ah, that I can't understand!" Janet cried. "That w:
selfish. That was wrong."

"She thought I was traitorous," Katherine answere
"She thought Philip had dangerous ideas—he had lived f
a long time in Russia—and would do me harm."

"Is he very foreign, then?"

Katherine laughed. "No, indeed. I'm afraid an Engli:
wife and English children have killed the Russian part (
him altogether. Besides, the Russia that he knew and lov(
has gone now so completely."

"In what way did you find marriage afterwards difi
cult? It will be a help to me, anything that you can tell me

"Well, Philip was ambitious—quite rightly so. F.
wanted to get on. He was clever and terribly hard-workin,
After a while his career was everything to him, and I thir
he forgot me a little. Then two children came, and I bega
to think more of them than of him. We really began '
drift apart. Then one summer in the Lakes we had it a
out. I said he cared only for his work, and he said I care
only for the children. We had a terrible quarrel, and in th:
quarrel found one another. We had never really know
one another before. Since then we have been wonderful
happy."

"Then you think that love can come through marriage?
Janet asked. "Might two people marry without love, do yc
think, and find love later—perhaps a long while later?"

"There are so many sorts of love," Katherine answere
"I'm not clever about these things. Millie and Henry, n
brother and sister, think they know all about it, but real
they know very little; but Peter, Millie's husband, is tl
wisest man I ever met. Life has taught him. Love, he say
is unselfishness, and simply that. He thinks that you don
begin to love anyone until the other person is much mot
to you than you yourself are. That's a commonplace and
platitude, of course, but in actual working life I believe
to be entirely true. Most people seem to think that love
only grasping, getting something."

"Yes. That's all very fine," Janet answered. "But you
ave to keep your own personality. You are somebody, you
ourself. If we all surrendered ourselves it would simply
ean that the Tramplers were always successful, and life
ould be horrible if the Tramplers had it all their own way."

"Of course," Katherine answered. "But that isn't quite
hat I mean. In an odd fashion it seems that if you love
omeone or something enough to live in them or in it,
our own personality grows and develops all the more. When
ou think of yourself you diminish; when you think of
hers you grow."

"All my life," Janet answered, "I have done what you
y. I have lived absolutely for my sister, given her every-
ing, thought always of her. Now I think that I have done
er only harm—and myself too. Now I want my own life.
want to be loved for myself. I want to play my part as
yself, not as someone else's shadow. But no one cares
hether I do or no. No one cares what I do. Perhaps I
ave sunk my own personality for so long in some other
at I have none left. I'm a shadow, changing with the light
the sun."

She rose.

"Let's go back to the house. I've spoken more personally
you than I meant, but you happened to catch me to-day
ther at a crisis of my affairs, and you've been so kind to
e that I let myself go."

"You're unhappy," Katherine said. "I saw it at once."

"Yes," Janet answered, "I'm unhappy. I'm on the edge
doing something very foolish. They don't want me here
less I do as they wish, unless I become part of their pat-
rn. They were glad when I married my husband, because
ey thought I would fit in. Well, I don't intend to fit in.
hey must realise it."

Katherine put her hand through Janet's arm.

"I'm older than you are. Perhaps I can help you a little
, in the old days, Rachel helped me. Our problems—
urs and my old one—are rather the same. But things work
it. One worries oneself and tries to make life do the thing
at one thinks it ought to do. That's never successful. Life

has its own way of dealing with us. I've learnt better no
how to be passive—not sluggish or lazy—but rather to tr
and make the best of each position as it arrives, not to tr
and force a square peg into a round hole. Of course I fa
again and again, but I know what the right attitude is
There is something bigger, grander than ourselves, some
thing that we must submit to."

"I can't see it to-day. I'm sure that what you say is true
but it sounds to-day copy-book. You've been through you
problems, I'm only starting on mine. I want something fc
myself. I've given and given and given. Now I'm out fc
myself."

"Don't think of me as always copy-book," Katherine an
swered, smiling. "I'm myself so often rebellious that it'
perhaps absurd that I should talk so primly. But althoug
I live selfishly and rebelliously I know that what I've said i
true. Millie is aways laughing at me for my slowness whe
I think I'm as energetic as an active volcano, but that's be
cause she's so much younger than I. And you are younge
than she. I was never very young. I was dominated by m
mother, as I've said, and then I had to act as her kind o
lieutenant in the family. Then came Philip, then the chi
dren, so I've never had my own way as I would have like
—save just that once when I carried Philip off. When
saw you to-day I thought to myself, 'That's what I woul
have liked to be—someone tall and grand, dominating, tak
ing one's place at the head of things.' And now you're no
that at all. How little one knows of people!"

They stood for a moment under the shadow of the tree
before advancing on to the brilliant, shining, sunlit lawn.

"You must be a friend of mine," Janet said. "You prom
ise? I want a friend terribly."

"Of course I will," Katherine answered. "If you'll hav
anyone as dowdy and ordinary for a friend."

They mounted to the terrace, where the others were wait
ing for them.

Standing in the sharp light they were unreal, figures blow
from glass in dazzling colours—Burnett purple-glazed, hi

ife a white sheen, Wildherne light grey, the colour of
air stonework.

Lady Burnett said: "It fits in so well, Lady Poole. Lord
'oole can catch the five o'clock at Salisbury if he goes with
s."

"That's very kind of you, Lady Burnett," Janet an-
wered, and looked at Wildherne. She had not intended it,
ut her look was challenging and hostile, and as it met his
yes it hardened. She saw him as her enemy.

She did not see him again—nor indeed any of them. She
tood there, spoke, smiled, waved her hand, but was autom-
ton save to the house, which swooped down in great white
olds, wave following wave. Then the walls stiffened, har-
ened even as her eyes had done, hemmed her in, coming
oser and closer with the courtyards, the long dark passages,
1e little rooms with their latticed windows, the Twelfth
)uke and the Fifth Duke, Audrey Poole and Lucy Tour-
eur, the jesters, the pastry-cooks, and the boy whose
ongue was cut out, dust rising on the deserted floors,
apestries tap-tapping against the cold stone of walls room-
1ick, the gay-nosed, apothecary with his squint and love-
hiltre, and, last of all, the present Duchess with her train of
ycophants. . . .

Well, what did it matter? She was alone in a vast silence.
he stood there, on the terrace, her hand to her brow. The
oneliness of this place was awful. Awful. Yes, she could
ot endure it. She had never bargained for this. Was she
ck to-day? What moved in her so that she saw unnatu-
ally, double-visioned, as they say men are before their
eath?

She turned and saw Hignett.

"I beg your pardon, my lady, but will you be alone for
nner to-night? Would you prefer it in your own room?"

Ridiculous man, final specimen of an obsolete tradition.
Jas he not a man with blood and bones and passions, and
et he stood there, thick, set-square, expressionless. If she
nched his stout arm would he not slap her face, and if he
apped her face would he not lose his job, become sottish
public-house piggeries, beat his wife and sell boot-laces?

And all because she pinched his arm. She was tempted
try. How indignant the Peacock would be!

Then her eyes met his. She realised that he liked he
"You can keep all your body in shape, Master Servant, sa
your eyes. . . . Your eyes betray you."

"No, Hignett," she said, "I am going up to town als
I shall meet Lord Poole later in the evening. We shall pro
ably come down together to-morrow morning."

"Very well, my lady."

"I shall want the small Daimler to take me to the 5.3
Tell Hawes. We shall both be back for luncheon to-morro
There won't be anyone else unless Lord Poole brings som
one down."

"Very well, my lady."

His eyes regarded hers. She thought that they saic
"You're troubled. I should like to help you. I know n
master so much better than you do. One day I'll be of son
use."

She was being rather clever about eyes to-day. She we
into the house.

She sat down and wrote:

DEAR WILDHERNE—If I'm not here when you get back
is only that I also went up to town for the night—to see Ros
lind.

Don't be anxious. I'm not quite the thing to-day and tl
Peacock is noisy. I can't see the Peahen anywhere—Yours,

JANET.

She went out again on to the terrace. Hignett was ju
coming in.

"If by chance I should be kept a few hours longer i
London," she said, "and Lord Poole returns before I d
will you let him have this note?"

"Yes, my lady."

She paused before going in again. "Do you miss Londo
Hignett? Don't you find it a little sleepy here?"

"No, my lady, I can't say that I do. I'm very partial t
Wintersmoon myself. London isn't what it was."

She stood looking about her.

"This is a very beautiful place."

"Yes, my lady, one of the finest houses in England."

"I'm glad you're here, Hignett. My husband can't get on ithout you."

"Thank you, my lady. I would do anything for Lord oole—or for you either, my lady."

"Thank you, Hignett. I'm sure you would."

She went up to her room.

CHAPTER IV

A CARNATION IN A SILVER BOTTLE

WILDHERNE POOLE sat alone in a first-class carriage and stared in front of him. He was aware at first of nothing save that the railway-carriage seemed of burning heat, and of a sentence of Lady Burnett's: "It was rash of me, considering how difficult it is nowadays to get a decent servant, but impertinence of course one can stand. . . ."

Impertinence of course one can't stand. . . .

No, of course one cannot. One can't *stand* impertinence. But why had Janet looked at him like that? She had no right. Had it not been part of their bargain? Was he to go on for ever with passion unsatisfied, with the fiery heat of life banked down?

His hands clenched, his heart leapt to that coming moment, that moment when, having first gazed into her very heart, he would sink on to his knees beside her, abase his head, and then feel the soft gentle touch of her fingers against his forehead, the cool clasp as the hands closed about his eyes, the drawing of him upwards to her breast. He saw nothing but that; he had for three days seen nothing but that. That he must have. He was parched for it, his throat dry for it, his eyes burning for it.

It was not his fault that Janet stood on the other side of that fire, not his fault that, with all their intercourse together, passion had never come to either of them.

Friendship, comradeship. Fine things. Now as he stared in front of him they were as distant as the shadowy ice of the spectral Poles.

But Janet's eyes were there. He moved uneasily. What right had she to reproach him? They were modern men and

166

women, and must learn, as other men and women were learning, to adapt marriage to modern needs.

He gave Janet something precious, something he had never given to any one before, friendship. He had told her, and had told her truly, that he had never known what friendship was before he knew her. That had made her happy. But he was healthy in all the vigour of his strength, and his body had needs that must be satisfied. In these days, thank God, we were frank about these things. But it was more than bodily passion. He had loved Diana for years: he could not be absolutely without her. And Janet knew that. Diana also knew it. With an upward sweep of shame he saw her as she had said "au revoir" that last time. Yes, she had known that he would return. . . .

He beat down his shame. He allowed the heat of his desire to lap him round. He bathed in it, staring into that room, seeing again and again that moment when he would sink on his knees and feel her thin cool fingers draw his head upward. . . .

Somewhere, in some novel by some Scandinavian, he had read that a lover thought of his lady as "a dark carnation in a silver bottle." That was Diana to him, and not only Diana, but all the world of passion and desire. "A dark carnation in a silver bottle." That dark crimson glowing above the frosted silver. What had Janet to do with that? Why should he not have her for a brief moment? Was he for ever to be tied to her and she to him? Was it not the power and glory of modern marriage that you were both free, tied only by mutual affection and understanding?

But the sense of shame swept upwards again. He wished to God that he had gone off without a word, just written a note for her. Why had she looked at him like that? She could not give him this. She knew that she could not. Well, then. . . .

Was it his fault that their last weeks together had not been happy? Had he not done everything that he could for her? Perhaps he had made a ghastly blunder in marrying her. She would never be happy in his world. Was it his fault if she was, at times, lonely? Had he not warned her?

Was he to blame if her sister was selfish and preferred her London life to the quiet Wintersmoon one? How was *he* to blame?

Shame still swept up as the wires beyond the window danced and rose. Far, far away, hidden beyond the vanishing landscape, a faint muffled cry tapped the window: "Wildherne—Wildherne. Where are you? Hold back. I'm coming to you."

The heat gathered round him. How he had missed Diana during these months! There was a room in Wintersmoon, empty, long deserted, where, as a small boy, he had gone once, escaping his governess, to play, and looking through the grimy window had seen into one of the kitchen pantries. On this same winter's afternoon it had chanced that, his nose pressed to the pane, he had caught sight of one of the grooms kissing and fondling one of the kitchen-maids—his first vision of that world. For years afterwards he had been haunted by the picture of the man, crimson-faced, pressing his lips into the girl's neck, her abandoned drooping form, the man's hands about her breasts. That small dusty room, quite naked, glowed always in his memory as though it were a blazing furnace of fire.

He was in that same room again now and Diana was with him. They two at last alone and together. The train, staggering and jolting, drew into London.

He found a porter and walked slowly towards the taxis.

For the rest of his life he would remember that moment— the summer's light filtering through the dusk and haze of the great station, the row of cabs huddled together like waiting cattle, the piled luggage and hurrying men and women, the shriek and blare and clatter of the traffic.

The cabman leant towards him: "Where to, sir?"

Someone else spoke (he would always swear that it had not been his voice): "Three Halkin Street."

Halkin Street! What had come over him? Halkin Street! The cab was already leaving the station, and he sat there, stupid, like a drunken man. Halkin Street! He made a movement as though he would pull at the window that he might lean out and give the man another direction. His hand touched the window and fell back. Well, what did it matter? He would see his father for half an hour and then go on. But perhaps his father was down at Purefoy. Then, most strangely, someone, other than he, prayed: "Let him be at Halkin Street! Let him be at Halkin Street!"

The cab had stopped before the familiar door and, a moment later, a meek-faced bony man (meagre substitute for Hignett) stood before him.

"West, is my father in?"

"Yes, my lord."

He stood in the hall.

"Will you be sleeping here, my lord?"

"Yes—I don't know. Take my bag up to my room anyway. Is my mother here?"

"No, my lord, she's at Purefoy. His Grace goes down tomorrow."

He crossed the hall to the library, opened the door, and then stood there, held by the familiar picture of his father, spectacles on the end of his nose, deep in the green leather chair, a huge tome on the reading-desk beside him.

"Father!"

The Duke looked up.

"Wildherne! But it can't be! You here? Anything the matter?"

"No, father."

Wildherne crossed the room, put his hand on his father's firm shoulder.

"Are you staying the night?"

"Yes, I think so."

"Lucky you caught me. I'm going down to Purefoy early to-morrow."

"Yes. . . . Look here, father." Wildherne's words came suddenly with a rush. "You've got to dine with me to-night. Yes, we'll have a tip-top dinner and go to the theatre."

The Duke sighed.

"What for? Dine with me here quietly. What have I to do with theatres at my age?" Then, looking at his son, he went on quietly: "What's up, Wildherne? You're excited

about something. Nothing wrong, is there?" Then more
anxiously: "Nothing wrong about Janet?"

"Nothing. Nothing. Only—don't think me an ass—I want
you to look after me to-night. We'll dine at the Zoffany and
go to a good show. I shall sleep in your dressing-room.
haven't done that since I was a kid. . . . Do you mind?"

"Mind?" The Duke slowly and reluctantly closed the vast
tome. Then he took his spectacles off his nose. Then he
stood up and shook himself: "Mind? No. If it pleases you.
I'm honoured at the attention. What time do we dine?"

"About half-past seven, I should say."

"It's half-past six now. I'll go up and dress. Sure Janet's
all right?"

"Absolutely. I'm going down again to-morrow morning."
They went out together arm-in-arm.

In his bedroom he undressed swiftly, as though his movements kept back his thoughts. Then, lying flat in his bath,
his eyes staring at the ceiling with the faded Early Victorian
cupids, some of that heat that had for three days invested
him withdrew.

As he looked at his long body, shadowy pale against the
gleaming white of the bath, he seemed after many hours
to spring free of it. This flesh that he could hold between
finger and thumb, this knee that as he raised it protruded
white and bony out of the water like a sudden sea-monster,
this wall of skin and bone, these thighs, ludicrous toes,
fantastic stretching arms: was it these absurd phenomena
that had during these last days subjected him to a kind of
witch-craft?

Fantastic, indeed, these cracking, creaking, slipping bones,
this heart hammering behind its wall! As he stood, naked,
his legs apart, the towel stretched across his back, he seemed
with that gesture to send the obscene spells that had held
him in a misty cloud to the rose-bottomed cupids! He was
free once more.

But he was not.

As the stiff crackling shirt enveloped his head, staring
into that starchy imprisonment he was aware that Diana

had returned. When his head was free again, looking about him he would see Diana standing there looking at him with her queer indifferent smile. Ah, but if he did! What could he do but go to her, crush her against his heart, kiss her hair, eyes, mouth, hold her, hold her. . . . He looked desperately about the room.

What was this farce that he was playing? Why was he here? He had come to London to see Diana. What if he were a cad and a false man of no honour? He had come to London to see Diana. What was he doing here in Halkin Street? To spend a long evening with his father when he might be with Diana? To have that trouble with Janet and then never to have seen Diana at all? And would Janet believe him? Of course she would not.

But there was no reasoning in him. With trembling fingers he tied his tie; he would be off. He would tell his father that after all he would not disturb him. He should have his quiet evening. Sorry to disturb him. Sorry to disturb him.

In the long glass he could see now his body, clothed in black, its fair hair crowning it, its foolish shining toes, its stiff bosom with one small pearl like a dead malevolent eye. Ah! but that was not the real body! The real body was Diana's—the fantastic limbs and bones and lumps of skin— these were for Diana. . . .

The door opened and the Duke was there looking the King of all the Sea Captains. "Your father," old Lady Anne once said to Wildherne, "sailed with Drake and has never, in his heart, forgotten it. He's never been quite happy since."

"Ready?" said the Duke.

Wildherne, then, realised that this stocky aristocratic adventurer had also some hold on his body, a hold as strong in its own way as Diana's was in hers.

Something physical. His instinct was to move towards his father, to put his hand on his shoulder. He liked to be near his father, and he knew that his father liked to be near him, and he knew too that because they were both Englishmen they were both shy of this. His father's power over him was strong and his power over his father. He had a power over his father that his mother had not, and the power was partly physical; it was as though there was some secret bone that joined them. It was out of his mother's body that he had come, but it was to his father's body that he belonged.

He knew now why it was that, to the Taximan at the station, he had said "Halkin Street."

Furthermore, as he looked at his father he was terribly proud of him. There was no man in England so fine in his bearing, so noble in glance of eye and carriage of head, so pure and true in colouring, in bone-shaping, in flash and turn of every feature. He should have ruled England had he had a wish. But he was more than that. His soul was finer than his body. As with all great men you could see that soul, gleaming like a shining fire behind the barricade of the imprisoning flesh. Dark heat within armoured strength. The dark carnation in its silver bottle again, but this time the colour of the flower was spirit not body.

"Ready then?" said the Duke again, looking at his son with pleasure.

"Yes," said Wildherne. "We've plenty of time. Is this an awful bore to you now? Not that I'm going to let you off it, all the same."

"It's not a bore, it's a surprise," said the Duke slowly. "Do you know, Wildherne, this is the first time since you left Oxford you've suggested our having an evening together?"

"Well, I don't know that you've ever suggested it yourself."

"No, I haven't. That's the truth. One gets in a groove." They stood in the hall waiting for a taxi.

"It's a wet night, your Grace," said West, whose eagerness to please struggled against oppressive adenoids.

"Poor Governor," Wildherne thought. "He'll be missing Hignett."

It *was* a wet night. As the doors opened the rain came with a wild fling to meet them, and all the rain pipes of Halkin Street were suddenly vocal.

In the taxi the Duke said: "Wildherne, I ask you only one question. I know you'll tell me the truth. There isn't anything wrong with Janet?"

Wildherne paused a moment, then answered: "No, father, I'll swear there's not. She's an angel. If anything's wrong, it's myself. I'm not terribly proud of myself, father."

"That's all right." The Duke pulled his beard. "Damned difficult thing marriage, especially the first year or two. But I love that girl, Wildherne. I always rather wanted a daughter you know. I don't know whether you're finding one another a little difficult just now. That will pass. But you can back one thing. She's at the top. Simply the best there is."

"I know it, father."

"Well, I'll ask no more. I'm pleased you came to me to-night. Yes, I am. Damned pleased. We'll have a good evening. I haven't been to a play for months."

They pulled up at the oak door of the Zoffany in a scatter of swirling rain.

Arrived upstairs in the long room the Duke's pleasure at being there shone out of every part of him. His wife was splendid, his married life as near perfection as married life can ever be, nevertheless it was astonishing, did you ever think of it, how seldom the Duke was free of his wife's interrogations. Had she a fault (which he would never allow), it was that she was invincibly curious, and did he spend the evening away from her he must always on returning endure a tempest of questions. Moreover, she had that gift, common to many superior women, of listening to your account and then reducing all the people and things for which she herself would not have cared to less than the dust.

To-night there would be no questions on returning. Yes, undoubtedly, however great a lover of women you might be, there were occasions when the company of men was a rest and a refreshment.

Wildherne meanwhile looked about him to see who were there. Dick Bennifer, up from Leicestershire where he was a M.F.H. *in excelsis,* for whom the summer months had no existence; Beryldon, an ancient peer, collector of Tang Pottery and four times married, known to his intimates as

"Bluebeard"; Carlyon, mountainous man, the only survivor of the old school of acting left to us, as kind as he was anecdotal; and that queer fish Ravage who had been playing around Janet's sister. . . .

No one was ever introduced to anyone in the Zoffany and two or three of Wildherne's most amusing club acquaintances were unknown to him by name. They had simply a "Zoffany" existence, never seen or heard of anywhere else bred of the silver and the Whistlers and the club grill; he met some of them with more pleasure than many of his outside acquaintances. That is what the Zoffany did for men made them human.

They had a delightful dinner.

Bennifer's pippin-apple face broke into a hundred wrinkles of pleasure, Beryldon moved his ancient wits to chuckles of good humour, Carlyon told some of his best stories, lamenting as ever that the real art of acting had so utterly abandoned the English stage. Only that odd fellow, Ravage, said little, and that little was uncomfortable.

Shabby saturnine fellow Wildherne thought him. And then remembered. Of course! This engagement of Rosalind's would hit him hard. Hurt his pride. Strange that a girl should care at the same time for two men so different as young Tom Seddon and this fellow. Dangerous-looking. But interesting. More interesting than young Seddon. Why was it that the decent, clean men were always less interesting than the rascals? Ravage was a rascal. You could see it in every inch of him.

But he turned soon from these less interesting speculations to consider his father. As always, in any company, the Duke had at once taken the lead. The Duke had a genius for human beings because he loved them. Had he not been guarded during his long married life by his wife, there is no knowing the mistakes he might have made. And yet, in all probability, no, because with his merry heart there went a shrewd and often disconcerting thrust of observation. The rules he went on were simple enough—"Five minutes' watch and a man's eyes and mouth will tell you everything. . . . The wise men should wear beards as I do."

Considering his thirst for human beings, it was astonishing perhaps that he had not mingled more with them, but t was probable that, in early life, he had realised that this warmth of heart of his might lead him into foolishness. Moreover, this very love of human nature had caused him many a sharp disappointment. His temper was fiery but swift. When he was angry he knew no compromises. He was, n his old age, often more positive than accurate. And he had certain bug-bears—Communism, athletic women, effeminate young men, motor bicycles, Lloyd George, books of reminiscence concerning dead people who couldn't defend themselves, and Prohibition were among them.

But to-night he was happy, enchanted, and enchanting. He would willingly have stayed there all night. "I've got to go," he said to them reluctantly as he rose, "my boy's a bully. Thank you for a delightful time."

He stumped down the room, humming a tune.

At the door he turned and in a rather husky whisper said to Wildherne: "What do you say to missing the theatre for once? . . . Very comfortable here."

"No," said Wildherne rather sharply. "If you don't mind, father, I'd rather go." The Duke remembered then that they were together that evening not only for enjoyment. He helped Wildherne on with his coat, and for a moment his hand rested on the boy's shoulder.

"Who was that rather dirty-looking individual opposite me?" he asked when they were in the taxi.

"That," said Wildherne, "was Charles Ravage. He's the feller who's been in love with Janet's sister."

"Hum," said the Duke. "Yes. Well, I didn't like him."

He began soon, confidentially: "I'm glad as it's turned out that you've got Wintersmoon. For a long time your mother hesitated between that and Purefoy. Of course Purefoy isn't half the house Wintersmoon is. Ugly barn of a place if you ask me. But it's more convenient for trains and things—easier to run too. Your mother never cared much for romantic things. I remember when we were engaged she thought me shockingly sentimental. So I was. Your mother was a lovely girl. Yes. Well. There you are. Janet's senti-

mental I shouldn't wonder. Got lots of heart that girl. Mo[...]
than her pretty sister."

"I don't like Rosalind," Wildherne said abruptly. "I'[...]
tried to and I can't.

"No. Well," said his father. "It's understandable. She[...]
too modern for you, Wildherne. But take her the right wa[...]
and she's a good enough girl I expect. Hum. Yes. It's [...]
funny thing, but I feel rather like a schoolgirl myself t[...]
night. Going out to a theatre, and those fellows at the Clu[...]
Very decent lot. Carlyon's been acting a long time. I r[...]
member him in those old plays, Oscar Wilde's time. Dirt[...]
looking fellow, Oscar Wilde. But clever talker. Yes. Hun[...]
Poor devil. And old Beryldon. Well, I'm older than he i[...]
I went to his wedding. Married one of the Stanbury girl[...]
Ugly girl like a camel. What sort of a piece are we seein[...]
to-night?"

"It's a musical comedy," said Wildherne. "That cha[...]
Bunny Hunter is in it. Little chap, makes jokes with carro[...]
and such. He makes me laugh whatever he does."

Five minutes later they were in the theatre.

The determined pessimists who delightedly find decaden[...]
in everything find it easily enough in the Gaiety Theatre ar[...]
hint darkly at the glories of Nellie Farren and the days [...]
old Burlesque. Thirty years hence the happy pessimist [...]
the day will be talking in the same fashion of Bunny Hunt[...]
and his fantastic world—a world of sofa cushions, soda[...]
water siphons, the male chorus, saxophones and eccentr[...]
dancing, a world of light come and light go, of jests vanishe[...]
as soon as uttered, a kind of Tweedle Dum Humpt[...]
Dumpty world whose centre remains always in the heart [...]
that small twisting body, shining cheerily one momen[...]
pathetically the next out of that crooked mouth, those thi[...]
fine nervous hands, that shock of untidy hair.

And how the Duke enjoyed himself! From the first me[...]
ment when, to a clash of discordant music, a whirling mo[...]
of young women clad in the brightest and scantiest of bath[...]
ing-dresses finding that they had the Plage at Trouville e[...]
tirely to themselves, proceeded to make hay under the shin[...]
ing tropical sun, he was enraptured.

It was long since he had seen these young women. The
tervening years had changed them not at all; they were as
ey had ever been, with their rhythmic movements, their
udied smiles that fitted so easily off and on, their shrill
scordant voices, their passion for the pink-faced hero,
eir inability to move about save in congregations of twenty
more.

Bunny Hunter was at once a personal friend. He seemed
have some important message for the Duke and for the
uke alone, and all through the persistent complications of
llapsing chairs, uneasily piled plates (his profession was
at of a waiter), and bathing machines with revolving
ors it seemed that, pathetically, he was endeavouring to
me to close personal quarters with the Duke. And this was
range because he had never met the Duke before. And yet
t so strange, because there was not a member of the
dience but had this same sense of private personal contact
ith him.

Wildherne was less absorbed and, as the fantastic game
oceeded on its way, it failed more and more to catch him
to its mazes.

At first the colour and the music pleased him, and then
wly the theatre with its light and heat and eager laughter
s removed.

He was alone: he was desperately unhappy. He should
t be there. This stupid game that he had played during
ese last hours was false and sterile. He knew where he
ould be, and once more he was waiting with beating heart
tside that door, the door opened, he moved forward in
ecstasy of excitement and happiness . . . the curtain
me down, the lights went up, his father turned to him.
xcellent. Excellent. Well, I enjoyed that. Most amusing."

He sat there in a chill sweat of terror. One word, one
ovement would be enough to send him outside. An excuse
his father. . . .

He saw and heard nothing. His father also fell into
ence, and they sat there, the two of them, like statues.
e lights went down again, once more there was the whirl
movement and the strange discordant music, but Wild-

herne held himself rigid. She was waiting for him. In som
strange fashion she had known that he would come. Sl
sat there, her eyes moving from the clock to the door, fro
the door to the clock. "Wildherne . . . Wildherne . .
Wildherne."

And in the second interval he muttered to his father: "
think I'll clear. . . . I feel as though I'd seen all this be
fore. Do you mind?" The old man did not turn, but h
hand fell on Wildherne's knee. "It isn't long to the en
now. But if you want to go I'll come. Let's watch a bit mor
of this. I'm enjoying it."

The pressure of his father's hand held him. Before thi
he could have left him, but now the abrupt movement tha
would be needed to shake off that pressure seemed more tha
he could compass.

He was angry. What was the foolish old man doing keep
ing him there? Time was slipping by. There, the accurse
thing was beginning again, those ridiculous women, tha
foolish little man with his so-ancient tricks. But he could nc
move. That hand seemed to hold him with its soft pressur
in some unaccountable power. From an infinite distance h
heard his father's laughter.

A kind of madness seized him. He would like to get u
there in his stall and shout to them all—anything, nothing—
something to break this icy stillness that bound him in, an
then after that shout he would be free. . . .

But, in an instant, with a kind of click as though a doo
had been unexpectedly opened, the thing was over.

The thing was over, and he was only conscious of a vas
deep, unfathomable weariness. All desire was gone fro
him. He was like a man dead.

They were in a taxi again and his father was talking
"I can't understand people being superior to that kind o
show. There was Bennifer at the Club to-night saying tha
there was nothing worth doing in London. Dull hole h
called it. Upon my word what do people want? And they'v
improved marvellously, these musical shows. Colours an
dresses and everything. Obviously don't mind what mone

ney spend. Must have cost a pretty penny that thing to-night, and I heard someone saying that that little man—what's his name?—gets six hundred a week. Well, he works for it, I must say."

He turned and put his arm over his son's shoulder.

"Tired, Wildherne?"

"Yes, sir, damned tired."

Inside the house Wildherne said that he thought he'd go to bed at once.

"I'm for it too," said the Duke, yawning. "Shan't do any reading to-night. Tires your eyes looking at all that colour."

He rang the bell for West, told him to lock up, and then, a little ahead of his son, stumped up the stairs.

Standing in the little dressing-room off his father's room Wildherne was conscious of an odd sensation.

The last time that he had slept there had been when he was about fifteen or sixteen. He had been sent home from Eton unexpectedly because of some fever scare. His own room had been occupied, and so he had slept in the little dressing-room. He had woken, he remembered, when his father had come up to bed, had called out to him, and then his father had opened the door between them and had come in and out as he undressed. He remembered vividly how funny his father had looked in his nightshirt, standing in the doorway, cleaning his teeth.

Just the same now, save that his father's hair and beard were dark brown then and he would be wearing pyjamas now. That was not so long ago when Wildherne had been a small boy; his father had taken to pyjamas reluctantly and complained of them still.

Wildherne remembered that he had talked excitedly about Thackeray. He was exploring *The Newcomes* for the first time, and his father had told him what a brave fight Thackeray had made of it with the tragedy of his married life.

"By Jove, that would be awful!" he could remember the young Wildherne exclaiming in awe-struck tones.

It was the same now. There was his father, half undressed,

standing in the doorway; how fine he was with his shoulde
set back, the snowy whiteness of his beard, and his de
chuckle as he recalled some of the jests of the evening. "We
you're tired, my boy. Mustn't keep you. Sure you want t
door open? I snore, you know."

"Yes. I remember. I don't mind." Wildherne went in
say good-night. His father was lying, his head in his ar
his eyes half closed. Wildherne bent down and kissed hi

"D'you remember the time," his father half-sleepily que
tioned, "when you slept in that room last? You had scar
fever at Eton. Autumn of Nineteen Seven that was."

"No, father. Nineteen Six."

"Nonsense. As though I didn't remember. Ninete
Seven."

"Nineteen Six, father. I remember because . . ."

The old man was furious—in a moment as was his cu
tom.

"Nonsense. As though I didn't remember. Ninete
Seven."

"It was Nineteen Six, because that was the year th
mother——"

"Good God!" The old man, his eyes flashing, leaped o
of bed. "The way you contradict. Always think you kno
everything. I'll prove it to you."

He paddled indignantly across to a cabinet near the fi
place, pulled open drawers as though his life was imperille
tossed little books about, found one, turned the pages i
patiently.

"Of course it was Nineteen Seven. Ah, here we are! Ju
September, November. . . . No, dammit, you're rig
Sorry. Can't think how . . ."

He dropped the little book on to the floor and sto
smilingly looking at his son.

"You've given your old father a splendid evening. Y
you have. Decent of you. Good night, my boy. God ble
you."

Through the open door came a succession of gigan
snores. Wildherne was a small boy again. He sank dow

own into a world of cricket bats, doughnuts and toffee; cross the shining Eton fields Colonel Newcome came towards him head erect, magnificent, benevolent . . . and the ace of the Colonel was the face of his father.

CHAPTER V

JANET'S HEART

JANET, crossing the hall to the car, encountered Mrs Beddoes.

"Well, Mrs. Beddoes, how are you getting along?"

"Very well, indeed, my lady. Thank you, my lady."

"Everything quite all right?"

"Yes, my lady. I'm doing a bit of work in 'Alkin Stree next week, my lady. It's kind o' convenient seeing as m 'usband isn't quite isself."

"Oh, dear. I hope it isn't anything bad."

"No, my lady. 'E don't seem to be able to rouse isself my lady. Doesn't take no interest in nothink."

"Well, I hope that you'll find him better when you ge home."

"Yes, my lady. Thank you, my lady."

It was when she was in the train that she asked herself "What am I doing? Where am I going to?" The trai seemed to know: it was moving forward with a very definit purpose. It was as though it had entrapped her and ha some plan of its own with regard to her. So for a while sh remained bemused, listening to the rhythm of the train' motion—swing—swing—burr—burr—swing—swing.

But Janet had never been one who allowed her mind to re main cloudy for long. She sat now, clearing everything a in despair at some other person's untidiness you clear room.

In the first place, Wildherne and she had arrived at crisis in their married life. The crisis had been actually pro voked because of Wildherne's action in going to London, bu that action had not truly caused it. There had been othe things. There had been the Duchess and her following. Ther

182

had been the isolation of Wintersmoon. There had been the absence of Rosalind. There had been the aloofness of Wildherne. There had been Janet's own wickedness and pride.

Yes, her own wickedness and pride. Would she not confess to herself now that she was seeing clearly into her own heart that it had not been only to help Rosalind that she had married Wildherne, but also because she had wanted to have the fun and splendour of "being Somebody"? Never before had she owned that to herself: now she saw it quite clearly. Then, very soon indeed after her marriage, she had realised that to "be Somebody" she must follow in the Duchess's train. Perfectly polite they would all be, amiable and kindly, but she must follow out exactly the line they had marked out for her.

Well, she had rebelled against that and rebelled successfully. She had fought the Duchess and, so it seemed, defeated her. The result of the battle had been exactly what Janet had wished it to be—the Duchess had vanished and all her train with her. And after that what? Had Janet been a step nearer happiness? Wintersmoon had been, all in a moment, wrapped in silence. It might have been the Palace of the Sleeping Beauty. Not a word from Halkin Street save an adorable little letter or two from the Duke. Neighbours, at first such a curse at Wintersmoon, were in a moment removed as though they did not exist.

Janet had what she had wanted, Wildherne and Wintersmoon to herself. The result of that had been that Wintersmoon had begun to terrify her and Wildherne had gone up to London.

She was more alone than ever.

It was part of the fineness of her character that she was able to take facts exactly as they were. She did not sentimentalise over them nor abuse them nor bewail them. Nor did she defend nor attack herself. Those were the facts. In one way or another they must be altered.

She had made this movement to London on an impulse of emotion that had no reason in it. She had made it because she was so exceedingly unhappy, and this unhappiness had to be faced and looked into just as the other facts had

been faced. Why was she unhappy? She was unhappy partly
because of her own crass failure in this job that she had
undertaken. She seemed to have failed in everything. She
had failed with Rosalind, and Rosalind's sudden engagement
to Tom Seddon did not mislead her. She had failed with
Rosalind because after all that she had done and sacrificed
Rosalind did not love her. If Rosalind had loved her she
would have come ere this to Wintersmoon. But you could not
make people love you. Janet did not share the common fem
inine illusion that if you do enough for people they love
you. It was, as she very well knew, generally the other
way.

Secondly, she had failed to take her place as Wildherne's
wife. It had seemed to her, before her marriage, that this
would be easy. She could make friends, she could play very
naturally the dignified but human hostess, she would have
money enough and a beautiful background. But she had
failed because she would not obey orders. She had expected
to give orders not to obey them.

She had failed, thirdly, with Wildherne. He had made her
very happy at that moment when he told her that she had
become the first friend that he had ever had. Yes, she had
been very happy, and then, a moment later, bitterly disap
pointed. Looking back now she realised that disappoint
ment. Why had she been disappointed? Was it because
Wildherne's friendship was beginning to be not enough for
her?

At that question she could have cried out there in the
railway carriage, "Oh no, no! Not that! Not that!"

She was seized with a strange dizziness so that the fields
beyond the window swam in a green haze and the carriage
itself and the stout gentleman alone with her in it lurched
and swung as though she were at sea. She controlled herself
and held herself rigid until everything was steady once
more. What was the matter with her? Was she going to be
ill? She who was never ill?

She drove herself back to her stern questioning.

If Wildherne's friendship was all that she wanted of
him, why was it that she had suffered so acutely when he had

old her of his visit to London? Why had she felt for him
t that moment so strange a mixture of tenderness and
onging and indignation and wounded pride? Why had she
fterwards known that if he had come to her she might have
hrown herself on his breast and begged him to stay with
er? Why this wild, impetuous flight to London? Wounded
ride. Yes, that had been her motive. But no, it was not
nough. She knew that it was not.

She turned, gazing out of the window but seeing no land-
cape, clenching her hands on her lap but not knowing that
he clenched them. . . .

Well, she had character, she had strength of will. If she
vas beginning to care for Wildherne with more feeling than
vas in their original bond, she would kill that feeling. She
vould submit to the Duchess. She would fling herself into
he Duchess's plans and be, for a time at least, her able
ieutenant. There was left to her at least the Duke. He was
oming soon to stay at Wintersmoon. Her love for him she
ould indulge to her full desire and his love for her (that,
hank God, was sure in this shifting world) would give her
ome warmth and fire. But that other. With a little shiver
f apprehension she turned from the window to see that the
rain was drawing into London.

She stepped from the train on to the platform and stood
here in bewilderment. The evening light spread in dusty
ilver shadow from space to space. The station was quiet
nd almost deserted. Some bell from some church in the
treets beyond was ringing for evening service. A porter
poke to her. She shook her head. Where was she going?
'o Rosalind? No. To no one whom she knew. As she stood
here the sound of the reiterated bell brought to her memory
little hotel just round the corner out of Jermyn Street
vhere once she had gone to have tea with some friend. She
ould remember as she sat in her friend's room that the
ells from St. James's had been ringing, striking a melo-
lious note above the rhythm of the traffic. The hotel had
een called Blanchard's. Her friend had told her that it was
ery quiet—it had had the air, she remembered, of being
lmost furtive.

"Blanchard's Hotel," she said to the taxi-driver, "of Jermyn Street."

He seemed to know it. When they came into the streets she saw that it was beginning to rain. There is nothing odder about London than the way in which it arranges itself to suit your condition. When you are rich and powerful it will seem to you a place full of spaciousness, dignity, decorum, and history. The people who serve you (and everyone is there only to serve you) will be fat, well-fed, and self-satisfied. You will walk on red carpets and all the towers will bend their heads in welcome and the bells ring for you. If you come as a brave and fearless adventurer with all your life in front of you, every side street will promise incident and every house-door a discovery. Strangers will beckon to you, windows mysteriously open, curious advertisements in newspapers will apply only to you.

But if you come to London, as most of us come, with money just not enough, health and strength just not enough and youth just not enough, London will see that she tests your courage. The skies will drizzle, the mud will gather about your ill-shod shoes, strangers will hustle you, shopkeepers pass you by, restaurants neglect you, every street will look like every other street and no street will be home.

So it was suddenly to-day with Janet. Even in the poorest days with Rosalind she had been somebody. There had been the places, posted like rendezvous about the town, where they could go and discover friends waiting for them. They had belonged to London. But to-day Janet belonged to no place and to nobody. Nobody was to know that she was in London nor why she was there. She did not herself know except that she was there to escape from her unhappiness.

She had had, perhaps subconsciously, an expectation that London would close about her with loving, friendly arms. That is exactly what it did not do. As the taxi jogged along the rain came down even more heavily; the mud splashed on to the pavements. The lights had an evil flare. They looked like the illustrations of diseases in medical charts.

As the cab splashed its way through the slanting rain Janet was aware of an odd sensation of relief. For one night she was to be rid of all of them—yes, of Wildherne, and the Duchess, and Rosalind, and Tom, and Rachel, and the servants at Wintersmoon (who from Hignett to Mrs. Beddoes were living, breathing creatures to her, each with a history as dangerous and dramatic as her own). She was no Marchioness of Poole—Janet Grandison perhaps still; at least she could not escape, even for this night, from that little twisted, desiring, lamenting, triumphing midge of a soul that had been with her from some unknown beginning and would go on with her, maybe, into limitless time, or maybe would not but would be snuffed out like a candle-wick between finger and thumb.

Of this small, queer, crawling creature she could not rid herself, but for the rest, for one night she was free, and a sort of melancholy peace, shrouded like the fading day in misty rain, enveloped her. In the impenetrable fastnesses of Blanchard's she would be able to think things out.

Impenetrable fastnesses they were. She stood in the little hall, misted with faint electric light and crowded with green-leaved plants in bright yellow pots. Within a sort of sentry-box a deep-bosomed lady with a most cultured voice and tiny green eyes considered the possibility of a room.

"Well, of course, we are very full at the moment, but we *have* one on the fourth floor, if that isn't too lofty. Some people like . . ."

She might have been reciting stanzas of Spenser's *Faerie Queene*. She closed her eyes tightly as she spoke.

"I like to be high up," said Janet brusquely.

"Very well, madam, if you wouldn't mind signing . . ."

A small Pekinese, sprung apparently from her violet silk bosom, yapped loudly.

"Quiet, Toto. . . . William. William. . . . Where's William, Mary? Ah, William, show this lady number forty-five, please."

Janet had signed her name "Mary Harrison, Bexhill," and going up in the lift considered how easily this might all be represented to Wildherne as the insignia of what the feuilletons call an "illicit adventure," then with a little shiver considered still further that Wildherne would not mind whether or no it were true. Yes, for the honour of the family he would perhaps be concerned—that good old traditional motive. And for her happiness? Yes, he would be concerned for that too. Whatever Wildherne was, he wanted her to be happy.

Her room was small and, it seemed, the target for all the rain in London. How it came pouring down! How the water pipes gurgled and sang! How the lines of water ran up and down the window-panes as though some gigantic composer frantically impelled by his genius, were writing scores on the glass!

She took off her hat, bathed her face and hands in hot water and sat down on the bed. She really was not well. That odd sensation of faintness and sickness still pursued her. She lay down. She faded away into a state of half-sleep when the ceiling of her room seemed to be dragged away by the wind and all the water came pouring down on to her face, but it did not wet her, only stroked her cheeks. She woke to the sound of St. James's clock. She sat up, her hands pressed to her forehead. It seemed to her that someone had waked her. Wildherne! He came to her sometimes at Wintersmoon and, finding her asleep, bent over and kissed her, so rousing her.

A shudder of unhappiness and desolation ran through her. He would be with Diana Guard now. They would be dining together. They would be smiling, laughing. They would have little jests. He would put out his hand and take hers. . . .

"This is your bargain. You agreed to it. Play your part."

Yes, she would play her part. She changed into a quiet black evening frock and went downstairs.

As she went she was conscious that the place seemed full of whispers, whispers of voices inside, of rain without. London was filled with these little hotels, she supposed—places where you could come quietly and not meet any one you did not wish to see. So many doors, so many little passages leading to nowhere. Nobody visible.

She was directed to the dining-room and here the whis-

pering continued. A little waiter with a high, intellectual
forehead but, unhappily, no chin whispered to her, "Would
she take thick or clear, and," a deeper whisper, "turbot or
sole to follow?" He seemed to be deeply relieved when she
decided on clear soup and turbot. That was apparently what
he had been hoping.

Mysterious couples, seen only in embryo because of the
thick yellow silk shades that guarded the lamps, protected,
too, by vases of flowers, drooping and languid, whispered
together and gazed into one another's eyes. Everyone was
very fond of everyone here. . . . Suddenly she could endure it no longer, but left it abruptly and returned to her
room.

She turned on the electric light and sharply turned it
off again. She sat on her bed, having flung open the window,
and stared out at the faint, fluffy light that came up through
the blurr of rain from the street below. The rain came hissing down and, mingled with the echo from the Piccadilly
traffic, had the personality of a voice.

There must be many others in London to-night who were
hearing that same voice and hating its cruel, sluggish indifference. What if she should find it impossible to continue
her life with Wildherne because she loved him? What if
her pride that she had always held as her most definite possession, the one that would never abandon her, did now leave
her so that she humiliated herself, giving him her love without wishing for any return, submitting to his absence, knowing where he was and tolerating it? Was she beginning to
feel love for him, or was it only that he had hurt her pride
by leaving her? Was this jealousy that now for the first
time had come to her? Did she hate this woman as women
hate when they are robbed of their lover?

No, she did not hate her, but she envied her—she who
could produce in him something that she could not produce—
the little things, the turn of the head, the pressure of the
hand, the mysterious smile?

Why had no man ever loved her? Was it because of her
absorption in her sister? Must a woman herself think of

men before they will turn to her? Or was it because of some lack in her that would keep her for ever outside that happiness? Oh, not that, not that!

At this moment Rosalind was nothing to her, her past life was nothing to her, she wanted only that Wildherne should turn to her with that flame in his eyes that she had never, as yet, beheld.

Then she knew that she loved Wildherne, and she abased her head and hid it in her hands.

After that she did not act quite sanely. She went out into the rain. She walked for a long time, not knowing her direction. And yet she must have known, for soon she was standing outside the building where Diana Guard had her flat. Janet had, for a long time past, known Diana's address, but she was not aware that subconsciously now she had sought it out. She simply found herself there.

She stood there under the street lamp in the driving rain and looked up at the windows. No one passed. She waited for a while staring through the wet mist at something that she could not quite see.

A taxi-cab passed her, and, feeling very ill, she hailed it and told it to go to Blanchard's.

Back in her little room again she undressed, was seized with violent sickness, and at last, in an odd state of languid weakness, was in bed. She pulled the bell at the bed-side and soon a diminutive, white-faced, large-eyed girl appeared.

"Do you think you could get me some tea?" Janet asked.

"I'll try, ma'am," the girl answered. "It isn't reely my job." Then, her eyes widening, she went on: "Why, ma'am, you do look bad! Would you fancy a fire?"

"Yes, I think I would," Janet answered feebly.

The child disappeared, soon to return with paper and wood and coal. She knelt down in front of the small grate and seen thus was an infant to whom the Marchioness would have been a grown-up sister.

When the fire was blazing she came and stood beside the bed again. "A fire's pleasant these wet nights, even in summer time." She stared at Janet and then smiled. "Is there

think I can get you?" she asked again. She had two large
ack smuts on her cheek from the coal.

"No, only the tea," said Janet, smiling back again.

The child turned then and moved about the room putting
ings a little to rights.

"Have you been here long?" Janet asked her.

"What? Blanchard's? Not 'arf. No one stays 'ere long."

"Why are you in service? You look so young. Do you
ke it?"

"Like it? No!" The child came close to Janet's bed again.
he put out her hand and stroked the quilt. She was sud-
enly confidential. "You see I 'ad a baby. Mother couldn't
and for that. Father's dead."

"What a shame!" Janet murmured. "Why, how old are
ou?"

"Sixteen and a 'alf."

"And isn't he going to marry you?"

She giggled. "Can't properly say as I'd know 'im again if
saw 'im. It was at a dance out Clapham. Catch me acting
lly that way again. But it's a proper kid, though. A boy.
ve got 'im kept out in the country."

Mysteriously in the distance a bell rang. "That's Mrs.
rench. . . . I won't be long with the tea." She vanished.

That child and a baby! The child's large eyes dwelling on
er with a look that was oddly friendly, oddly companion-
le, remained with her.

Then, with a fierce throb of her heart, so that it seemed
at within her something spoke to her, she knew.

She was herself to have a child.

She woke to find the room flooded with light and in her
eart a great ecstatic happiness. She lay still for a little
ondering why she was so happy. Then eagerly she looked
t her watch. She must return at once to Wintersmoon. She
ust be there before Wildherne.

Her watch told her that it was half-past seven. There was
train, she knew, at eight-thirty. She washed and dressed
nd went downstairs. Sun was flooding everywhere. She
id good morning to the little waiter as though she were

telling him some wonderful important news. She woul
wish to have seen the little maid-servant again. She left
note in her bedroom: "Thank you for being so kind to m
last night. You helped me so much." Then, considering th
matter, she rang the bell and waited. A stout untidy woma
answered it.

"Can I see the girl who attended to me last night?" sh
asked.

There was another pause, and she stood, hesitating i
great anxiety lest she should miss her train.

The child arrived wiping her mouth on her apron.

"I wanted to leave a note for you and give you this,
Janet said. "I was afraid that you mightn't get it, thougl
if I left it."

The girl stared at the money, then gasped. "Oh no, ma'au
you shouldn't . . ."

"What is your name?" Janet asked.

"Fanny Eagles."

"Well, Fanny, I have a friend who might help you. Whe
you leave here write to her. Her name is here. See, I'v
written it down. Wintersmoon, Wiltshire."

She bent and kissed the child's forehead, then hurriedl
went.

She caught her train and then sat in a dream. She ha
no thoughts. She was too happy to think. She had tele
graphed for the car, and at the sight of Hawes' round re
face she sighed with contentment.

Wintersmoon, standing up right in a lake of sunligh
was very silent. She found the note where she had left i
She tore it up. Then, coming into the garden, she saw Hig
nett.

"Hignett, has your master telegraphed about the train?

"Yes, my lady. He's coming by the one-thirty."

"Good. Will you ask him, please, to come to me as soo
as he arrives? I shall be down at the temple."

"Yes, my lady."

"And we'd better have luncheon at two, tell Mrs. Crad
dock."

"Yes, my lady."

She went down to the temple and sat there, her hands on
her lap, staring at the glassy surface of the pond.

There was apparently no interval between that and his
appearing. He came towards her, hastening, and she, smiling,
went to meet him. He began at once: "Janet, I want to tell
you. I spent last night at Halkin Street. I was with my
father all the evening. We went to the theatre and came back
to Halkin Street. He's gone down to Purefoy this morning."

But it seemed that she did not hear him. "Oh, Wildherne,"
she broke out. "I've wonderful news. We are going to have
a child. I'm so happy. Wildherne, I can think of nothing but
that. Hold me close. Don't let me go. . . . I'm so happy,
Wildherne, that I can't speak. . . . Just hold me. . . .
Closer. . . . Closer."

Hignett waited sternly by the luncheon table, but three
o'clock chimed through the house and still they were not
here.

CHAPTER VI

ROSALIND PAYS A VISIT

ROSALIND, on this lovely October day, looked abou her with pleasure. She liked fine weather: it alway seemed to her to be an especial compliment to herself. Sh was the only passenger to alight at the little station: tha also pleased her. No tiresome forced conversation on the wa up to the house. And there was Hawes, so chubby and clea coming towards her with that pleased and rather dazed ex pression with which men so often greeted her.

"Good afternoon, Hawes. Is there anyone else by th train?"

"No, miss."

"Splendid. What a lovely day, isn't it?"

"Yes, miss. We've been having fine weather this la week."

She had rather expected that Tom Seddon would be ther to meet her. She was relieved that he was not, but her vani was a little ruffled. He would have to have a splendid ex cuse!

As she settled herself in the car she was extremely please with herself. This was her third visit to Wintersmoon the last two months. No one could say that she was a neglec ful sister. As a matter of truth she had quite enjoyed he other two visits, but then the Duchess had been absent.

On this occasion she would be extremely present. How ever, Rosalind was not afraid of the Duchess. It was th Duchess's sad loss if she disliked her. The Duchess was to ancient to matter.

She had been herself surprised at her emotion when sh heard that Janet was to have a child. There came to her in flood one of those crises of feeling that sometimes attacke

194

er, that she found so inconvenient. She had reproached
erself bitterly for her recent neglect of Janet. Poor Janet!
o have a child, how dreadful, how tiresome, how irritating!
osalind did not believe that Janet cared very much for
ildren. There had never been any signs of it. Rosalind had
o feeling for children herself. She had been a horrid child.
ll children were horrid most of the time. And mingled with
is pity for Janet was also a sense of loss. Whether Janet
ked the child or no it would occupy her tremendously.
anet was just the kind of woman to be terribly conscientious
out her child. Her marriage with Wildherne had not
armed Rosalind, because Janet did not love Wildherne.
hat was the reason perhaps why Rosalind had not bothered
o go to Wintersmoon, because she was so sure of Janet—
ut now she could be sure no longer.

And so she had hurried to Wintersmoon and, on her visit,
ad been quite alone with Wildherne and Janet. That had
en most interesting, and for a quite unexpected reason.
 had been interesting because of the extraordinary change
 Wildherne.

Wildherne had always been to Rosalind the personifica-
on of superior dullness. That he had not liked her had not
ejudiced her at all. That had been his loss. She bore him
o malice for it. He had been dull because he had been so
rribly usual: the only unusual thing about it had been that
e had been able to put up with him for hour after hour!
is good looks, slim straight figure, honest good-natured
mile, charming pleasant voice, courtesy to servants, im-
erturbable English *savoir-faire*—oh, how dull that all was
 this modern, post-war, untidy, individual world! There
asn't anything about him that you couldn't foretell!

And then suddenly this!

She had noticed it in the first five minutes of her arrival.
e had not spoken two sentences to her before she had real-
ed that he was different now. He was dull no longer, he was
rdinary no longer, he was urbane and charming no longer—
 was somebody!

He liked her no better now than he had done before. In
r first quarter of an hour she had said something that

offended him. But what did that matter? He could dislike
her as much as he pleased now that he was interesting. What
had happened to him? Had he fallen in love with Janet?
No, it was soon clear enough that he had not, although he
was charming and attentive, keeping her indeed always in
mind, sheltering her, protecting her. . . . Why, of course
that was it! It was the child! That was what had altered
Wildherne. There was to be an heir (of course the child
must be a boy—God could not be so inattentive to the needs
of the best British families as to give the Purefoys a girl!)
The aching desire of Wildherne's life was to be fulfilled.

With this discovery there came to Rosalind another of
those tiresome romantic impulses of hers. Wildherne was
touching and moving to her. He was suddenly embarked,
she perceived, on a voyage of most desperate danger! The
perils that he was about to encounter! How likely that the
child would not be a boy, or, if it were one, how probable
that it would turn out badly, or die, or be dull and stupid.
To put all your eggs into such a basket! But he had. He,
now that this hope had come to him, was like some knight-
errant in quest of his Holy Grail! He was illumined with an
almost consecrated light.

She was touched, too, as she watched more closely, by
his treatment of Janet. How good and unselfish and kind
he was to her. Had he behaved thus to Rosalind she would
have wanted to smack his face, but Janet was different.
Janet wanted affection and tenderness—all those silly old
romantic Victorian things that everyone nowadays had discarded. Janet had always been old-fashioned.

In the immediate drama of all this Rosalind forgot, for
once, to consider her own personal history. Tom Seddon
had not been present on these two other occasions, and
Rosalind had thought about him as little as might be. With
regard to him Rosalind had hitherto been aware of swiftly
changing moods. She never tried to make her moods other
than they were. When she was bored with him and found
him tiresomely sentimental she told him so, and then he
would leave her with that pained dog-look in his eyes so

ften chronicled in fiction that has to do with the devoted
lovers of tyrannous females.

Rosalind *was* a tyrannous female! It was his fault did he
persist in marrying her, his fault entirely! Nevertheless
there were times when she almost loved Tom—he was such
a nice boy, so true and honest and safe—no fool either in
his traditional way. Going to him was putting into harbour.
Nothing drove her to him like her sense of danger, and
nothing irritated her so badly as his sense of safety.

He took it for granted, apparently, that now she had said
she would marry him all would be well! He couldn't con-
ceive that anyone would go back on the given word! When
he stopped his affectionate impulses he was unhappy, but
only because he felt that as yet he did not quite understand
her—marriage would put that right. There were times when
he felt five centuries older than he! Times again when he
seemed to protect her as no one else ever could.

This visit, then, would be an interesting one. The drama
was developing on every side. With three people—the
duchess, Wildherne, and Rachel Seddon—definitely hostile
to her; two people—Tom and Janet—utterly devoted to
her! Well, it would not be her fault if she did not get some
amusement out of it all!

There was, finally, something else. As they passed the
lodge gates and started up that marvellous historic drive,
the trees now amber and russet against the faint blue sky,
the lawns flowing like water down the little hills, the deer
seen and then vanishing like ghostly visitants, she was aware
that, in spite of its beauty, she hated Wintersmoon. Wintersmoon, the house, did not love her any more than did the
duchess and Wildherne. Rosalind was no sentimentalist
about places. Hills and houses were hills and houses to her:
she was not so foolish as to credit them with loving personalities. You might just as well believe in ghosts or do
spiritualistic writing! But there *was* something about Wintersmoon that, against her will, forced her to think of it
as separate, apart, having some sort of existence away from
the people who lived in it.

"Nasty, eerie old place," she had called it to Althea Ben-

dersley. "No, it isn't damp and mouldy, as I had thoug
it might be. Although they can only keep half of it ope
the rooms that are shut up are dry enough. Too dry,
you ask me! If houses could be people I'd say that it w
above itself, too conceited for words!"

She had stayed once in Switzerland and had loathed tl
place because the mountains made her feel so small. Wi
tersmoon would make her feel small if it could, it was th
kind of place!

"What do you do in the evenings?" Althea asked he

"Nothing," Rosalind had answered.

"Nothing!" Althea had cried, astonished.

"Wildherne plays Bridge so badly that it's a crime
witness it."

"I should turn up the carpet and dance," Althea had r
marked.

Then Rosalind had laughed.

"The carpets would refuse to turn," she had answere
"If they give a dance ever it will be a public one with S
Roger and the Lancers. Wintersmoon and Jazz! Little yc
realise!"

She found them, as she had expected, having tea in tl
hall.

She must herself have been of startling loveliness as sl
appeared there in her dark furs, her little hat not hidir
her shining splendid hair, something virginal in her poi:
her ardent daring readiness for any adventure, her smilir
challenge to them all to do their damnedest. Rosalind w
always more beautiful than anyone expected her to be, h
challenge always more daring. At every appearance sl
seemed to be standing *thus* for the first time—no one ev
before had seen her quite like this!

They were gathered about the big fire in the open sto;
fireplace, the tea-table between them. Tom sprang to his fe
with a cry: "Here she is!" Janet too rose as though tl
happiest moment of her life had come.

"Darling! How are you? Was the train very cold?"

"Yes! I'll have some tea right away!"

She came laughing into the middle of them, and there were some there two, when later events gathered shadows around that beauty, looked back to this moment and treasured it.

Everyone was charming—everyone always would be, no matter what occurred. Had Rosalind at that moment gone up to the Duchess and twitched the grey turban, no one would have shown displeasure.

Rosalind took them all in—the Duchess working at some silver-threaded embroidery; Wildherne close to Janet, his hand just touching her shoulder; Rachel Seddon talking to Brun; Miss Crabbage moving off on some important errand; that dear old maid, Lady Alice Purefoy, with her eager hungry look ready to break in upon anybody; the Duke broad and square in his quiet corner; Tom excited and happy, standing over her.

They asked her a few questions and then left her to her tea. She was pleased, because she knew that they all thought her lovely. Yes, whether they liked or no, they all thought her lovely. She felt that it had all been rather dull for them before she came in. She was glad that it had been.

She proceeded to bully Tom a little.

"I suppose you were too busy to come to the station."

He coloured crimson.

"I was coming, of course," he said, "but something stopped me."

She knew at once that "something" had been his mother.

"Oh, it didn't matter in the least. I didn't expect you."

"I'm most awfully sorry. I really am——"

Rachel broke in.

"Has it been very gay in London, Rosalind dear?"

"Yes—rather gay." Rosalind gave Rachel one of her most dazzling smiles. "But everything's so crowded. The world seems to be twice as full as ever it was before."

Alice Purefoy had something to say: "Yes, isn't it? London's so crowded. One can hardly move. I saw in the paper this morning that there were five deaths from motor-cars. One isn't safe anywhere, is one? Last week when I was motoring with Charlie Rockby down to Ockham——"

Nobody cared. Nobody ever cared for anything that Alice Purefoy had to say. Conversation, as though it had waited for this sign, became very general.

Soon Janet took Rosalind up to her room. When the door was closed behind them Rosalind gave her sister one of her warmest and most ardent embraces.

"Darling, how are you? You look splendid! You pet—you darling. Yes. You're happy. I can see it. I am so glad.'

Janet smiled.

"We're all very happy. Everyone is in the best of tempers. Tom has been in an agony of impatience all day. You mustn't be angry with him because he couldn't come to the station."

"Oh, I know how that was! Rachel wouldn't let him."

"It was her last afternoon with him. She has to go back to town to-morrow."

"Ah," said Rosalind, nodding her head. "That's because she doesn't want to be here with me."

"Don't be foolish, Rosalind. She's so sorry she has to go. You're a little strange to her at present. She's only half English, remember. She's lived so much by herself these last years. Tom's everything in the world to her, and now she has to give him up. It isn't easy for her."

"But Tom's so weak about her. He gives in to her in everything!"

They were sitting on the little sofa at the bottom of the bed. Janet put her arm around her sister and drew her closer to her.

"Don't be selfish about her, Rosalind. There are only these few months and then you'll have Tom to yourself for ever."

Rosalind laughed, then gave a little shiver. "For ever! Hasn't that a dreadful sound? I don't think I want any one for ever. Do you want Wildherne for ever?"

"Yes," said Janet quietly. "I think I do."

Rosalind looked at her, kissed her, and then said: "Why I believe you've fallen in love with him."

Janet smiled. "He's very good to me—better than I ever dreamt anyone would be!"

"And I should think he ought to be!" Rosalind burst out, jumping up and beginning to walk about the room. "You're the finest woman in the world, and you're going to be the mother of his child. What more can he want?"

Janet drew her down to the sofa again. "Never mind about me. Let me hear about yourself. Your letters say so little. You haven't been very good in writing to Tom either. The way he watches for the post is pathetic."

"Ah, now you're going to scold me. You're not to, Janet. I've come down here to enjoy myself. And I *will* enjoy myself. Every minute. And I'm going to make everyone love me. You laugh. But I can if I want to. Yes, even the Duchess. And I'll be adorable to Tom. Even Rachel will be satisfied."

"I know," Janet said. "You can do anything you like with people, darling. But," she hesitated, then went on, "Rosalind, if you don't really love Tom, if you know in your heart that you don't—break it off now, here and now. Never mind the scandal and the fuss. Wildherne and I will stand by you through anything. Better, oh, far better, do that now than marry him if you don't love him."

"Of course I love him," Rosalind said impatiently. "How preachy you are this evening! Why *should* I marry him if I didn't love him?"

"That's just it," Janet answered eagerly. "One doesn't know beforehand—one simply can't guess what it's going to be like. Even you with all your modernity don't know what it's like. Once you're married you're married. It's like being in a box. The intimacy's something fearful unless you love one another. And Tom—Tom would feel it more than anyone I ever met—if you didn't love him, I mean."

"I do love him," Rosalind answered, seriously and soberly. "At least one part of me does. The part of me that wants things to be built up and made beautiful. The other part of me is destructive. It would like to smash all this—Wintersmoon, British tradition, your mother-in-law. I hate it all. There's a fight in me, Janet, between the two just as there's a fight now in the world between the two. A part of me says, 'How lovely to marry Tom and settle down,

have a nice old house and a nice old garden, and look at English green fields and love England, and make it the leader
of the new world that's coming.' And the other half of
myself laughs at it all, says that that belongs now to a world
that is dead, utterly dead. That part of me wants to smash
everything up, to be selfish and individual, to believe in none
of the past, to hurt and break and mock. That part of me
loves no one, neither you nor Tom nor anyone. That part
of me belongs to the new world, and your old England is
an anachronism and absurd. That part of me believes that
when everything has been smashed perhaps there'll be a new
code and a new bunch of things to believe in, but it doesn't
matter if it doesn't. Life's a silly joke, and one pays it
back for its insulting cheek by snapping one's fingers at
it.

"But I'm not quite brave enough, Janet—that's the
trouble. Part of me clings to Tom and safety. And the
world's like me. It can't quite make up its mind. Shall it
still believe in those old words—honour, service, discipline,
restraint, unselfishness, duty—or shall it see them as tricks
and shams and fling them all away and be a nice new nasty
world full of selfishness and cynicism and each for himself, but also honest and clearheaded and without humbug?
People like you and Wildherne think there's no question as
to which is the better—but there *is* a question. Everyone's
been sentimental and traditional long enough, perhaps. Perhaps there's no plan in life, but it's all made up of little
pieces of interesting selfishness and coloured fragments of
personality—with the strongest on top. That's the question.
Dear me, how well I'm talking! You didn't know I could
talk like this, did you? And indeed I didn't know it myself."

No. Janet didn't know. She was absolutely surprised.
What had happened to Rosalind? With whom had she been?
Janet had a strange sense that here in the room with them,
behind Rosalind, there was a shadowy form, someone whose
face and figure she could almost discern but not quite. She
had a pathetic desire to hold on to her, to cling to her, crying, "Oh, Rosalind, don't go. Stay here. You will never be

happy where you're going. Stay! Stay!" But all she really said was: "Yes, that's all very clever. I know that that's the way people talk now, but what it comes down to is that Tom loves you more than I've ever seen anyone love anyone. You've got his life in your hands."

"How tiresome!" said Rosalind, laughing. "If I thought that I'd break it off to-night, but he's stronger than you think, Janet. He'll look after himself. Neither his mother nor you know him. And as to the rest, we'll see what comes. Anything may happen, I'm glad to say."

That night at dinner she was very happy. She had the Duke on one side of her and Tom on the other. She admired the Duke greatly: she admired his appearance and his sense of fun. She could not imagine how he had succeeded in putting up with the Duchess so long. She chaffed him and he chaffed her. She knew that he appreciated her beauty, and she liked to imagine that he would have been a regular dog in his day had he not married so early. In spite of his proprieties he was a man, and had good whirligig passions like any other strong man. She liked, too, his little sudden bursts of impatience and indignation. She would have married him with the greatest pleasure in the world had he been thirty years younger, and she wouldn't mind flirting with him now a little. How delightful to make the Duchess jealous!

But after a while she perceived that they were none of them—save Tom, and possibly Rachel—thinking of her very much. She was aware, almost with a sensation of frightened dismay, that she was quite outside their deeper plans and purposes. Before dinner was over she had realised with a sharp unbiassed apprehension that was one of her best gifts that nothing that she could ever do would upset the Duchess in the least!

And then she was aware, and admitted it to herself, with a funny little humorous shrug of "It serves you right," that it was Janet of whom they were all thinking. Janet counted everything, and she nothing at all.

Of course Wildherne would think thus, and the Duke

perhaps too because he loved her, but the Duchess and Miss Crabbage and Caroline Marsh and the servants—Janet was, for the moment, the centre of the world.

Well, Rosalind did not grudge it her, the darling. She had had a poor enough time for long enough, and of course it was not Janet herself, but the fact that she was to provide the great Purefoy family with a son and heir that obsessed them all so.

Nevertheless, before the evening was over, Rosalind was admiring her sister with all the warmth and generosity that was truly there in her heart. Janet was wonderful! How swiftly she had accommodated herself to this situation! How naturally she carried off all the difficulties of her rôle!

Rosalind had always known that she had had it in her How often in the old days in their stuffy, wicked little flat she had thought to herself: "Ah, if she only had her chance what wonderful things she would do!" And now she was doing them, living with an ease and graciousness and nobility that, Rosalind was honest enough to admit, would never belong to her younger sister!

Then, watching her, Rosalind was aware that to her, as to Wildherne, something new had occurred. What was it? Rosalind knew her so well that it was not difficult for her to detect this little flame of excitement rising and falling behind her outward serenity and composure. She was moved by some other secret life. It was not the coming of the child that had created it. It had to do with someone near her. Janet's eyes, in repose, were watching for someone. Her thoughts, privately working behind her outward duty, were engaged upon someone. Could it be Wildherne? Had Rosalind's shot in the dark that evening been a true one? Was Janet in love with Wildherne? Oh, but Rosalind hoped that that was not true! To be in love with Wildherne when Wildherne was not in love with her! There was pain, distress, even torture in store for anyone as sensitive and loving as Janet in such a case—yes, and jealousy of that woman in London. No, that must not, must not be.

But she was drawn away from Janet by a strange conversation that she had with Rachel after dinner.

Rachel herself arranged it, telling Rosalind quite definitely when they went into the long, dim Morris-shadowed drawing-room that she wanted to have a little talk with her. The older woman led the younger to a corner of a little sofa near one of the two fires, and there they were cut off from the others, and were able, privately alone, to give and receive challenges.

A challenge it was. They made a strange contrast on the little green sofa, Rachel, thirty years Rosalind's senior, so dark, so thin, with her impetuosity, foreign restlessness, and urgency, and Rosalind so fair and young and lovely, so triumphant in her assurance that her youth and beauty would carry her through anything.

"Rosalind," Rachel began at once, "you hate me—and you mustn't. If you are to be Tom's wife we must reach some sort of compromise. We must find some way to understand one another. I am a very lonely woman. I have only one or two friends in the world—Janet's one of them—and Tom's everything to me. You intend, when you marry him, to take him away from me. You must not do that. I throw myself on your pity. I don't care whether I seem to you silly, sentimental, melodramatic. It doesn't matter what you think, only you must think of me in this. You must use some of your power to help me."

Rosalind had a sense of tiresome irritation. This was the kind of sentimental appeal that women had long ago discarded, and behind that there was an uncomfortable feeling that it was bad for Tom to have such a fuss made about him! But she replied very sweetly:

"I haven't the slightest idea of taking Tom away from you."

This was, of course, quite untrue. She intended to take Tom away at the earliest possible moment.

"Yes, I see," said Rachel. "It's as I thought. You are determined not to come to any terms. I'm no fool. I was young myself once. I fought my own battles for my own advantage, and I was quite as ruthless as you are ever likely to be. I was a fool to appeal pathetically. I should rather have attacked your common sense. Let me put it like this then. I believe you'll be happier with Tom if you let me have, too, a little share in your life. Oh, don't think," she went on, as she saw that Rosalind was about to speak, "that I'm going to be the interfering mother-in-law. No, never that. But I want you to think of me one day as a possible ally. I am loyal and honest, and I've seen life for thirty years longer than you have, my dear, and was married for twenty of them. You think that I detest you and would do anything to stop this marriage. You are wrong. I admire even if I don't like you, and perhaps my dislike of you comes from my ignorance. I don't understand the modern girl. Tom is for ever telling me that I don't, and it's true. I have never perhaps quite understood English people. They seem to me cold when they should be warm, and impetuous where they should be cautious. You can help me there if you will."

Rosalind smiled. "You are wrong, Lady Seddon. We don't know one another at all, do we? But isn't that your fault? The advance ought to come from you. It is partly Tom's fault too. He is always reassuring me about you, as though you were some terrible opponent. I've seen so little of you. This is the first time, I think, that we've had a real talk. And then in your heart you don't believe that I love Tom? Isn't that true?"

(Did she love Tom? Oh, if she only knew!)

"Yes, that is true," Rachel answered gravely, "I do wonder sometimes. But then love is very strange—it seems to come and go. Tom is very simple: if he loves he loves, and if he hates he hates."

(So dull of him! Rosalind thought to herself.)

"I was like you in some ways. There were times in the first part of my own married life when I thought that I didn't love my husband. It's the fashion now I know to be entirely frank about things. If you dislike your husband you tell him so, and then when you like him again you tell him that too. For myself, I think there's a good deal to be said for reticences, but anyway, I believe I could help you sometimes, help you both. I want you to let me try."

Interfering old woman, Rosalind thought, but with a

mile she said: "Why of course! I shall love you to!"

Rachel sighed. "No, you don't mean it. I see that you
on't. You won't let me come anywhere near you. Well
hen, if you won't, you won't. Only, even at that, get it
ut of your head that I'm your enemy. I won't pretend that
ou're the kind of woman I had in my head for Tom's wife.
All mothers, I suppose, have their own ideas for their sons,
nd naturally their sons have other ideas. But I'm not your
nemy. I want to like you and understand you. I think you're
eautiful and clever and kind. Tom cares for you with all
is heart and soul. That's enough for me. Just remember
hat and give me a chance of knowing you a little."

Something in Rosalind's heart suddenly responded.

"Indeed I will," she said. "It must be hard for you to
ee somebody come along and make a snatch at Tom, but
t was inevitable, wasn't it? There would have been some-
ody in any case, and although she wouldn't have had my
aults she would have had some of her own. I'm sure that
ou can help me. You know Tom so well and I really know
im so little. It is very good of you to be so patient with
e. You don't know how impatient I am, over and over
gain, with myself. I have thought that you disliked me so
uch that it was hopeless to try and do anything about it.
 won't think so any longer."

They might then have made a movement towards one an-
ther that would have altered much later history, but at that
oment Tom came up to them. He sat with them a while,
hen Rachel got up and went away.

He followed her with his eyes for a moment, then turned
agerly to Rosalind: "You do like her better, don't you?
Now that you know her a little. She's so splendid and she's
ad such a difficult life, first with that beast of an old
Duchess who hated her, and then father being always an
nvalid. I do want you to like her so. She'll like you if you
nly like her."

"We're different generations, Tom."

"Oh I know! But what does that matter? Mother's never
rown really old. She's so clever and understanding."

Rosalind shook her head.

"She doesn't understand me—but then as I don't unde
stand myself it's not very surprising, I suppose."

But Tom wasn't listening. He was in that state of lov
when the eyes have so much work to do that there is litt
energy left over for thoughts.

He was gazing at Rosalind as though he had never see
her before.

"Oh, Rosalind, how beautiful you are! How beautifu
How beautiful! That silver dress. . . . And to think tha
I should have had the luck. . . . See, Rosalind, I'll tell yo
what we'll do. We'll creep off. They're all talking ther
They won't notice. Do you know the little room by Kin
James' Chapel, the little room where the two pages use
to wait while he said his prayers? You can see such a stur
ning piece of the garden from there, and there's a first clas
moon. Let's go up there for half an hour. What do yo
say?"

She looked at him and thought how good looking he wa
Much better looking than—than—oh well, than heaps o
other men! Tom's foreign blood gave him a distinction o
his own, and yet in spite of his dark hair he was very Eng
lish, with all that absolute unconsidered rightness of pos
and movement and dress that Englishmen managed so muc
better than the men of any other country. And how he love
her! No man had ever loved her as he did, and to-night i
this world that disregarded her and counted her as someon
of no importance it was pleasant to be reassured.

So she agreed to go, although she disliked the historica
unused parts of the house and had no great enthusiasm fo
the moon.

They slipped away.

The little room was bare and ivory white under the moor
which flooded in through the naked lozenge-paned windows
bathing the dull gold tapestry and transforming it with it
pattern of hunter and horses and red-brown trees into a
dim flowing unsubstantial dream. Tom had brought cushion
with them and they sat, close, on the little wooden plat
form under the window and looked out on to the stiff pea

)cks, ships, and lions of the clipped hedges. Behind were
ie woods velvet dark.

"I don't often worry you, darling," Tom said, "telling
ou how I love you. It's hard not to sometimes. If I saw
ou more often it would be easier, but I don't generally
ave you quite to myself like this. I don't want to force
iyself on you. I know I'm not worthy to kiss your shoe,
ut——"

"Oh, Tom," she broke in. "Don't be so modest. It's so
illy to make so little of yourself. You're worth twice of
ie: you're much cleverer and you have a far finer character
ind you're going to be a great man. You'll be Prime Minster I suppose, and I shall have lost my looks then and
veryone will be saying, 'I don't know however he could
ave married that stupid girl.' Don't you know me well
nough yet to know that I don't like you when you run
ourself down? I want you to look me in the face and say
'm every bit as good as you are. In fact, I'm a damned
ight better.' Don't love me too much, Tom. I'm not worth
."

"Well then," he answered, laughing, "I'm as good as you
re and a damned sight better." He caught her to him, kissed
er again and again, held her as though he would merge
er body with his so that they should never part any more.

That was better. She understood that. She responded with
ll the happy consciousness that with her senses at least she
ould give him all that he asked.

"I love you now," she whispered. "If it were always like
his."

"But it shall be," he whispered back to her. "It need never
hange. I will always be your lover. Marriage shan't make
ny difference. We will always be lovers."

"Ah! if we could!" She sighed, and slowly, gently re-
eased herself. "You mustn't be too good to me, Tom. That
vas what I was always telling Janet. I'm not one to treat
)o well. Don't give me everything. Hold something back.
reat yourself better than you treat me."

"As though I could!" He laughed. "Why, Rosalind, if I

had all the world I'd give it at once to you, and then there'
be the planets. I'd have to get them for you. I'd like t
give you things every moment of the day and night. I hav
nothing now. But I will have. I'm ambitious, Rosalin
doubly ambitious because I have you to work for."

"Work for yourself," she answered him. "You frighte
me if you put too much on to me. I would hate to fe
that if I ever failed you, you'd stop working or would car
less about reaching the top. It's far far better to do thing
for yourself. No one else is to be trusted."

"Trusted!" he cried triumphantly. "Why, I couldn't trus
you enough! You've given your word to me, and becaus
you're so honest you couldn't fail me after that!"

The moonlight seemed to drown her in a cold white floo

"That's silly of you, like a schoolboy. People aren't t
be trusted. No one. Or hardly anyone. Perhaps only yo
and Janet. And that's what's the matter with both of yo
You're so set. Because you've said you'll do a thing you'
do it. Because you've said you'll like somebody so you'
like them—for ever and ever and ever. Why, how can you
Everyone changes, everything alters. And especially no
when the world is changing so fast that we are all breath
less."

"That's not true of love," he answered. "Love doesn'
change."

"Love doesn't change!" she cried. "Why, it changes mor
than anything else! How can it stay the same when peopl
themselves change so? You love people for what they are
don't you? Well, if they're suddenly something differen
you don't love them any more, do you?"

He turned away from her, looking out to the moonli
garden.

"I don't like to think that," he said. "I'd be terribly un
happy if I thought that were true."

"True! Of course it's true," she answered impatiently
"And no one changes more than I do. I change every half
hour. You ought to have married Janet if you don't wan
any change. And even she changes."

"Do you mean," he asked slowly, "that you're not sure
hether you love me or not?"

"Of course I'm not sure. I'm not sure about anything. And
hat is love anyway? How can we tell whether we love
1e another until we have lived together? You think you
ve me now, but that's because you think my body is
eautiful; but when you've got used to my body——"

"No, no, no!" he broke in passionately. "That's not true.
hat's beastly. Love isn't only physical desire. That's not
ve. I love you because I honour and admire you—you,
our soul, not your body. If I didn't admire you——"

"Yes, if you didn't admire me?" she asked quietly.

"Then I shouldn't love you."

"Then love does change," she answered. "You've said it
ourself. How do you know that you will always admire
1e? You can't tell at all. You don't know me."

"I do, I do," he answered. "I know you as no one else in
1e world knows you."

She was suddenly touched. She drew his head to her
reast.

"Poor boy," she said. "Poor Tom. It's wrong of me to
:ke you. It's perhaps the wickedest thing I've ever done."

Alarm beat up in him in little waves, little waves that he
·ied vainly to quiet. "Rosalind, don't say that you've
ound you don't love me. If you don't, if you think you
on't—it's only a mood—wait until to-morrow . . . you'll
:e then. . . ."

"No, no," she said, reassuring him, stroking his hair,
·essing her hand against his cheek. "I do love you, Tom.
·he better part of me does at least?"

"And there's nobody else?"

"No," she hesitated an instant, "I love no one else—
1ly Janet."

"No other man?"

"No."

"Not—not Ravage?"

He knew how foolish it was to press such questions.
low often he had told himself that he at least would not

be like other men and ask these eternal never varying que
tions—those old questions of the poor unhappy never-to-b
satisfied lovers.

As the words left him his heart trembled. He had dor
a terribly stupid thing.

But she answered very quietly: "No, not Ravage."

He said no more. It was she at last who spoke, gent
and tenderly, a Rosalind whom very few in the world ha
ever seen, the Rosalind that kept Janet at her side throug
all tribulation and adversity.

"You know, Tom dear, it isn't wise to ask those que
tions. It's never wise. If I did love Ravage, nothing tha
you or anyone else could do would stop it. There is a pa
of me that you don't touch, that perhaps you will neve
touch. But isn't that true of all of us? Whoever knows an
one else however close they may seem to be?"

"Yes," said Tom slowly. "That's true enough. I ha
a friend once: he asked me to lend him three hundre
pounds. I couldn't. He wrote me a letter abusing me lil
a thief. After ten years' friendship too. No, one doesn
know."

He was frightened, frightened by the silence, by the moor
light, and by a strange sense that the house was trying t
tell him something.

"I want you to understand this about me," Rosalind wer
on. "It's important for both of us. I'm two people, Ton
and one belongs to a world that you will never understan
The future world perhaps. A world of negation and rebe
lion. Not better than this one—probably worse—but nev
Selfish, arrogant . . . I was talking of it to Janet to-da
She wouldn't understand it any more than you would. Yo
want to build up everything on tradition—to evolve thing
out of other things. This new world wants a clean brea
—snap—snap. . . . Perhaps you're right. Perhaps you'r
not. But whenever I'm impossible, selfish, and ill-tempered
remember that it is that other world that's working in m
I shall be restless sometimes. Be patient and wait for m
to come back."

"If you love me," he whispered, reaching up with his arm

ıd drawing her face to his and pressing his cheek against
ırs, "I will wait for ever."

But as they stayed so lovingly bathed in the moonlight,
her heart something whispered again:

"Poor Tom! Poor Tom!"

CHAPTER VII

WINTERSMOON AT EVENING

JANET, early on the morning following the day of Ros
lind's arrival, awoke suddenly, and in a condition
great panic. She sat up in bed, her heart panting with fea
her forehead beaded with sweat.

She was very conscious of her child; it was as thoug
from within her womb it had called out to her, itself afrai

She had been aware, during the last two weeks, that s
must guard perpetually against nervous irritability. She w
utterly unlike herself, and it seemed to her that the origin
Janet Grandison had crept away and deserted her ever sin
that day when, weeks before her impetuous trip to Londo
she had had a dim suspicion that perhaps she was going
have a child. She wanted that Janet Grandison back agai
She could rely on her, knew that she was controlled and no
mal. Of this present Janet Poole she knew nothing.
strange uncertain woman, prey to strange uncertain a
normal emotions.

But now, staring wildly about the dim room, she kne
only that she was terrified. The moonlight that had flood
the room when she went to sleep was gone, and in i
place was a strange smoky haze through which the furn
ture showed itself as though half submerged by water.
the whole house only the clocks were alive, and they we
ticking, clattering, whirring, jumping like mad things. B
surely people were listening everywhere? She seemed to
aware of their suppressed breathing and then, when
owl hooted from the wood, the passages and empty roor
seemed to walse into activity, as though that had been
signal.

What she wanted was that someone should be with he

She could go into the next room and wake Wildherne, and she knew how kind he would be to her and how he would seek to comfort her, how understanding and friendly he would be.

At the thought of that kindliness and friendliness she shivered. It was because he was always so kind and tender to her now that she was irritated. He was kind to her because of her precious burden: she was important to him not because of herself but because of the offering that she would make to him; any other woman, any other woman in the world would have done as well. Would these clocks never cease? Why was this house so vast and she so small? What would the house care if this thing that was coming to her killed her? Death! She had never visualised it as occurring to herself. She had never known a serious illness; the death of her parents had affected her deeply, but because they were her parents and because at the time of their death she had been very young there had been a certain inevitability in it. But Death for her—now—within a month or two! Many women died in childbirth, and why not she? And who would care? No one if the child lived.

So she lay there, and with every striking of the clocks the house seemed to step closer to her. She was a doomed woman.

The daylight chases away our fears. But all through that morning she felt as though she were pursued by some stealthy skulking figure. Rachel departed for London by the three o'clock train. It was a brilliant October day of amber sunlight. Wintersmoon basked in the sun, its grey walls dimly lit with a sheen of colour. Autumn silence was over everything. From the stables came the sound of men cleaning harness and the clatter of hooves on the stones of the courtyard. Within the walls some maid was singing at her work. The doves were gently cooing as though someone was stroking the air to music. And everything was amber coloured, the woods' russet seeming to stretch their shadows like a net over walls and lichened roofs.

Once and again the shrill scream of the peacocks stabbed

the air. The purr of the car that was taking Rachel to the
station, the last cries and laughter of the group on the
steps of the house bidding her farewell crackled into silence
like the sudden scatter of fireworks, then died. The sun,
low above the woods, flamed across the lawns, and a company of rosy clouds, close together as though clustered for
safety, floated westwards.

Janet, longing intolerably to be alone, found a book and
slipped away, as though she were engaged upon some conspiracy. She knew where they would never find her—in the
old rosy-walled kitchen garden where there was a small arbour with easy chairs. She took with her a fur coat and a
rug because it was already cold. When she reached the arbour she was pleased as though she had cheated all their
intentions. She snuggled down into her chair, warmly
wrapped, and opened her book, the most adorable of all
stories in English, *Persuasion*. Again and again in the past
Jane Austen had come to her rescue, reassuring her, comforting her, throwing over her that warm cloak woven of
common sense and humour and self-discipline and understanding tenderness. Surely it would not fail her now.

She read, with a little sigh of pleasure, the opening words
"Sir Walter Elliot, of Kellynch Hall, in Somersetshire, was
a man who, for his own amusement, never took up any
book but the Baronetage; there he found occupation for an
idle hour, and consolation in a distressed one : there his fac-
ulties were roused into admiration and respect, by contem-
plating the limited remnant of the earliest patent; there any
unwelcome sensations, arising from domestic affairs
changed naturally into pity and contempt."

She read on happily, warm and cosy within the defence
of the rose-red walls, looking out once and again over her
book to where the sharp line of the wall cut across the pale
sky, across the long straight rows of the friendly vegetables
to the group of little stubbly apple-trees and the clumps of
chrysanthemums and homely cottage flowers.

She read on, and then perhaps she dozed a little. She
seemed to carry the words of the book with her : " 'That you
are very likely to do very soon, I can tell you, ma'am,' said

Charles. 'Though he had not nerves for coming away with us and setting off again afterwards to pay a formal visit here, he will make his way over to Kellynch one day by himself, you may depend on it. I told him the distance and the road, and I told him of the church's being so very well worth seeing, for as he has a taste for those sort of things I thought that would be a good excuse.' . . ."

The words floated away with her. She passed into a dim dusk and stood groping, her hands feeling the air in front of her. Then with a start she awoke. The same fear was with her that had accompanied her in the night. The fear of sudden disaster, the fear that the child within her womb had seemed to arouse in her, a fear accompanied by a desperate final loneliness. The garden was dimmer now than it had been. The sun had fallen below the walls. The vegetables had strange writhing shapes, thin poles and waving tendrils pushing up like long dark fingers into the pale air. A musty stifled feeling was everywhere, as though she were in some room whose windows had not for many a day been opened.

Worst of all it seemed to her that someone terrible and sinister was approaching towards her from the house. Someone who wished to tear her child from her, or to strangle her and bury her there in the dusk beneath the vegetables, or to convey to her some awful news that Wildherne was dead or that Rosalind had been found, like poor young Francis Poole, hanging from a tree in the Wintersmoon woods.

Fantastic terrors crowded into the little arbour. She knew them to be fantastic, but could not beat them back. As the light fell the garden walls seemed to crowd in upon her, the vegetables to develop some awful life of their own, the cold and clammy potatoes, the damp and indifferent cabbages, the thin emasculate beans. . . .

Someone would come from the house, stealing through the dusk—Geoffrey Purefoy, beloved of the haggard queen, or poor young Francis with his hapless Jane, or the Twelfth Duke with his pigs' eyes and rolling belly, or the hatchet-faced Audrey, having watched with his pale eyes the last struggles of frail Lucy Tourneur.

She could not move. She sat, the book forgotten at her

feet; she was shivering with the cold of the evening, and every nerve in her was straining for the sound of the soft velvet-slippered feet.

Why could she not move? What had come to her old courage and fortitude? She clasped the sides of the chair and tried to pierce the shadows with her gaze.

Her fears were true. There were steps on the gravel path. With a cry she shrank back, covering her face with her hands. How ludicrous then to hear the quiet voice of Hignett:

"I beg your pardon, my lady. His lordship sent me to find you. It is nearly five o'clock."

She looked up, and as she saw his solid sensible figure she could have cried with relief. Once again she saw his eyes, kindly and human, waiting to help her. "Oh," she said with a little shiver, "I had fallen asleep. Thank you, Hignett. I'll come in."

Gravely he picked up the rug and the book and followed her.

In the lighted house this mood of strange disturbance was still with her. They were having tea in the hall; she slipped in through the dining-room and then almost furtively into the long drawing-room. She crossed to the farther fireplace, and there, quietly busy with her silver embroidery, was the Duchess.

The Duchess! The last person whom at that moment Janet wished to encounter. There was nothing to be done. "Ah, Janet," the Duchess said amiably, looking up. "Come and sit down. I shall enjoy a little talk."

The long room was filled with shadows that crept out from the leaping fires, and then hastily back into them again. There was only a small globe of light over the Duchess's head. Here, like a witch weaving her spells on the edge of a dark landscape, she sat.

"Sit down, dear. I'm sure you must be tired. Do you think you rest enough?"

"Oh yes," answered Janet cheerfully. "More than enough."

"Well, I don't know," the grey turban continued to murmur. "However, I prefer it to the other way—too much fuss. Before Wildherne was born you would have thought that the world was coming to an end."

"And yet," said Janet, "I shouldn't have thought that you've ever known what nerves were."

"Nerves!" the Duchess echoed scornfully. "When I was young the word didn't exist. I know you read in novels about young Victorian ladies for ever fainting, but that was before my day. Why, I'd have been shut up with bread and water for a fortnight if I'd pretended to nerves."

"It isn't always pretence," said Janet quietly.

"If it isn't pretence," said the Duchess, "it's next cousin to it. Losing one's temper's the same. I haven't lost my temper for thirty years. I don't know what the Duke would do if I did. He likes to lose his, although of course he never means anything by it."

The quiet little voice went on, the little boneless fingers moved in and out of the silk, the fire crackled, and the shadows crossed and recrossed. Once again Janet was listening for the step that was to bring her some awful news. The dark figure would stand watching her, then quietly move forward into the firelight. . . .

"I remember on one occasion," the Duchess continued, "when Mr. Disraeli was coming to have luncheon with us, the fish hadn't arrived, and my mother was greatly disturbed. At the same moment one of the footmen slipped in the hall and broke his leg. A most unfortunate combination of circumstances. Mr. Disraeli arrived in the middle of it all. 'There isn't any fish and the footman has broken his leg,' said my mother as quietly as anything, and it turned out that Mr. Disraeli liked a poached egg best of all."

"Don't things to-day," Janet asked, "ever disturb you?"

"What kind of things, my dear?"

"All this labour trouble. The unemployment. All the men who fought so splendidly in the War out of work. And the carelessness of everyone who *has* money."

"Why, dear me," said the Duchess. "It's always been the same. People are always out of work. And as for the suffering, the splendid things that Mr. Pomeroy is doing shows what *can* be done. Then they tell me that young women are very fast these days, dancing all night, and going out with young men in motor-cars. My dear, it was just the same when I was a girl, only there weren't so many newspapers and children were smacked more. I don't think, though, that there are quite as many gentlemen as there used to be, and I think the girls ought to wear more clothing. Now I don't want to hurt your feelings, Janet, but I did think that Rosalind was wearing very little last night. However, that's only fashion, I suppose."

"What would you do if there was a revolution," Janet asked, "a real revolution, the kind of thing they had in Russia?"

"Oh, a revolution!" said the Duchess. "Just pick up that silk for me, dear, will you? Why, what should one do? I'm sure all one's friends would behave splendidly, and it wouldn't last very long. There aren't enough foreigners in England to keep it going for long."

Janet felt her nervous irritation rising in a flood of rebellion. She would adore to stick pins into that .round plump arm.

"Sometimes," she cried, "it seems to me that everything is going, that our day is over, and England's day too."

"That's, my dear," the Duchess answered placidly, "because you don't trust in God enough. He knows what is good for all of us and will perfect His will in His own good time."

"Did he think the War was good for all of us?" Janet broke out. "What kind of world is my child to live in? What kind of love and charity will there be for him when all this hatred——"

She broke off.

"Oh, it's all right for you. Your trust in God makes you safe. But we are the younger generation, Wildherne and I. What sort of God is there for us to believe in?"

"Janet, dear, you're tired." The Duchess took the girl's hand in her own plump one. "I knew you were. Go and lie down for an hour. Don't come down to dinner. Poor child.

Your hand's quite hot. Let Miss Crabbage make you comfortable. I always find her wonderfully soothing."

Janet's rebellion died down. She bent over and kissed her mother-in-law. "Yes," she said, "I think I will go and lie down. But I don't want Miss Crabbage."

She had a ridiculous panic about crossing the long room. She did not dare to pierce those shadows.

"I'll come with you," said the Duchess, "and see you cosy." Perhaps after all, under that placidity, there was more understanding and perception than Janet's generation realised. They went through the shadowy room together.

At the top of the stairs they met Wildherne.

"Janet's tired," said the Duchess; "she's going to lie down."

Janet turned back to her smiling: "Thank you," she said, "Wildherne will look after me now."

He put his arm around her and they walked along the passage to the little sitting-room with the rose-coloured paper that Janet especially loved and had made her own. They sat down in front of the fire on the deep rose-patterned sofa, he with his arm still around her, she with her head on his shoulder. For a while she was comforted. They did not speak; she stared into the slumbering fire.

At last she said: "Wildherne, I've been so nervous to-day. Not like myself at all."

"I know, dear," he answered. "But don't worry about it. It's quite natural just now. We all understand it."

"You're like your mother," she said, sitting up and leaning forward, her face resting on her hands. "Does nothing upset her?"

"Nothing upsets her very much."

"I wish," said Janet, "she'd be upset just a little sometimes. Her placidity moves her such a long way from weak ailing mortals like Rosalind and myself."

He was immovably patient with her. "She feels more than you think."

"Do you?" She turned round upon him. "Do you feel more than I think? Do you feel, for instance, anything about me at all?"

The attack was so sudden that he had to prepare for a moment before he answered.

"About you? Why, Janet, what do you mean?"

"Yes—about me, me, me! Oh, I know you feel about the child, and therefore you feel about me because I'm the mother of the child, and unless I'm looked after properly just now the child is in danger, but that's not feeling about *me*—me, Janet Grandison that was, a personality all to herself."

She saw that he was deeply hurt and wounded, but the nervous apprehensions of the day were piling up now upon her; she was desperately, desperately weary; the calm imperturbability of the Duchess had throttled her like a piece of grey worsted. And because there was something that was true in her accusation, because during the last few weeks he had been thinking of the coming child for every waking and conscious moment, but also because he had, of late, done his utmost in every possible way to please her and thought he had succeeded—for all this, his pride and his conscience were alike stirred.

Then he remembered her condition, and with great self-control he answered: "I'm sorry, Janet, if I fail you."

But she had seen his self-control, and it was an added sting to her irritation.

"No, don't be sorry. Let's be natural, Wildherne. Forget for a moment that I'm in what the papers call an interesting condition. We promised once to be honest with one another. Let's try for a moment. All Wintersmoon is listening. Quiet —you can hear a pin drop or a beetle sigh through the house. They are listening everywhere. Audrey and Francis and stuffy Arabella, and poor Lucy Tourneur. Open the door suddenly and you'll see them all scatter down the passage. Now make your oath—before witnesses, remember. Wintersmoon at evening. *Their* time. They count more than we do after five has struck of an autumn evening. Your son is listening too. He'll remind you one day. Now for your oath. Swear by all their ghostly beards that your wife means something to you, that she is not just a child-

earer for the benefit of the great Purefoy family. . . .
wear! Swear!"

She was leaning forward, her eyes staring, her cheeks
rightly flushed, her thin straight body trembling. She seemed
o him in that moment unknown. He looked back to the
uiet, restrained, controlled woman to whom once (and
ow long ago it now seemed) he had proposed marriage.
Ie was here, shut in, with a stranger. Love could have
elped him; but kindness, pity, tenderness, admiration,
riendship all were there—only not love. And he was, for
is age, very young.

"I had thought," he said, "that we were still honest with
ne another. I have never been otherwise with you, Janet.
ndeed, I am speaking from the bottom of my heart when
say that I honour and revere you as my wife, my truest,
earest companion and friend. Because you are going to
ive me a child I have been very happy, and of course I've
hought of the child very much. It wouldn't be natural,
vould it, if I had not, but to think that you, you yourself,
on't mean everything to me——"

"Everything!" she cried. "Hush! I want them to hear
hat! Audrey, Francis—do you hear? I mean everything
o him—more than his family, his child, his father, his
nother—more than any of you. Everything! Isn't that
plendid? He has sworn. Now you may go. I don't want
ou any longer."

She sank back on to the sofa, closed her eyes, lay there
notionless. He bent over her. "Janet, dear, go and rest.
Have dinner in your room. I know that it hasn't been a
ood thing having all these people during these last days.
Soon they'll be gone and we'll have the place to ourselves."

Something very pathetic in her quiescence as she lay
here touched him deeply. Some shadow of an emotion dif-
erent from anything that he had ever known for her came
near to him at that instant.

"Janet, dear. Janet, dear."

But the kindness in his voice exasperated all her un-
atisfied need. She sprang to her feet. "You do your best.

Don't I see how hard you're trying? Leave me alone, Wil
herne. You're kind; it isn't your fault that you're not mo
than that."

He stood beside her, bewildered. He took her arm. "L
me go with you——"

"Oh, leave me, leave me!" she cried, breaking awa
from him. "Don't you see how you're driving me? L
you see nothing? Are you so blind? Will nothing sho
you?"

She faced him, her whole being stiff with hostility.

Someone had come in. They both turned and saw tl
Duke.

"I beg your pardon——" He was going. She stoppe
him.

"No, come in. Wildherne's been doing his best and I'
slapped him for it. Poor Wildherne——" She went up t
him and rested her hand lightly on his shoulder. "Try ar
forgive me. I'll do as you say, not come down to-nigh
Come up later on."

He turned and kissed her.

"All right. I will." Then he left the two of them togethe

The Duke put his arm around her. On the sofa she la
with her head on his breast, exhausted, her long thin hanc
tightly clasped, silent, her eyes veiled. He softly stroke
her hair; once and again he bent down and kissed her for
head.

She felt peace and confidence flow out of him. He kne
life, this old man, knew it in the only two possible way
by instinct and by experience. He had brain and heart an
passions all buoyantly active. He was child and man, love
and friend and father, master and servant. His thick stron
arms tightened about her; his heart beat against her chee
like the sure and benevolent marking of time. His hand tha
closed about hers was muscle and cool flesh, strength an
tenderness, duty and understanding forbearance. She be
gan to speak like a little child. "I've been wicked to-day
father. I've lost control. I don't know what marriage ha
made of me—something I'm not proud of."

"This is a difficult time," the Duke answered. "You

st child. You will fancy all kinds of things—and especially
at everyone is unjust to you."

"I'm frightened," she murmured, and a little shudder
n through her body. "I'm frightened—of something, any-
ing, nothing. I don't want this child to be born. Into what
nd of world am I bringing it? What right have I . . . to
is struggle, this unhappiness. . . ."

"Are you then so unhappy?" he asked her.

"Unhappy? Ah, that's a strong word. I've lost control.
m not doing this job as I had hoped to do it. I'm a fail-
e, father—a bad failure."

He paused before he went on: "Are you disappointed in
ildherne?"

She moved and then said sharply: "Why do you ask
e that?"

"Once or twice I have fancied that you were. And
hen I saw you together just now I knew that you had
en quarrelling."

"That has been all my fault," she answered quickly.
Wildherne has been an angel. I've exasperated him——"

"My dear—I love you so, and I know that you love me.
Je've both felt it from the first moment of our meeting.
ut tell me—don't be angry—or if you must be angry try
d understand beyond your anger. I've been wondering
ring these last weeks—do you love Wildherne enough?
re you finding perhaps that you don't love him as much
you thought you did?"

She turned round, slipping away from him. She stared
him, then without warning laughed. Laughed and laughed,
ftly, with very little sound, bitterly, her eyes stern and
ind.

"You ask me that?" she asked at last gently. "You think
at?"

She waited, then with bent head went on: "It is because
love him so much that I am so unhappy."

The Duke said: "Because you love him so much? Then
erything's well—when he loves you so."

"He doesn't love me," she answered. "He has never
ved me."

"He doesn't? But that's false." The old man frowne "You *are* seeing things falsely just now, Janet, dear. Wil herne adores you."

"He doesn't love me," she answered. "He never has. W married on that agreement."

The Duke turned on her sharply: "You—what?"

"We married on that agreement. It was to be a marria; of liking on both sides—but of nothing else. I married hi to give Rosalie comfort; he married me to give his hou a fitting hostess and family an heir. We were quite frar and honest. And all would have been well, but, unfort nately, after marriage I fell in love with him. I didn't wai to. I didn't mean to. It simply happened."

She had been selfishly (as how often afterwards she wa bitterly and with deep reproach to recall) thinking of h own distress—the Duke had been only to her a loving ar tender audience of that—but now the pain of his next word was so sharp that with a thrust of sudden awakened co sciousness she realised what she had done.

"What! Wildherne married you without loving you He told you that? Whom then"—the word was accusin in its attack—"does he love?"

"Whom?" Janet shook her head. "No one. He doesn love any woman. He loves you and his child that I ar bringing him—and I'm his friend."

"Janet, that isn't true." The Duke had caught her arn "There's someone else. I knew it, that other night when h came home. And you know it also, Janet. That's why you'r unhappy. He is living with some other woman."

"No! He is faithful to me absolutely. It is my fault, non other's. We made our bargain and I've broken it. But could not have known. He made me love him before I wa aware. He caught me . . . and held me. . . ." She brok off, struggling with her self-control. But she failed. Sh broke down, crying bitterly, her head in her hands.

He sank on his knees beside the sofa, leaned up caught her in his arms, drew down her head to his breas He strained her to him, stroking her hair, murmuring con solation to her as though she were a little child.

But as she cried there his eyes stared above her dark
ad into the room. He looked frightened, bewildered, and
rribly unhappy. Wildherne, the child of his life and power,
e heart of his ambition, the pride of his eyes, false, weak,
aying the blackguard like any other man . . .

His arms closed tightly about Janet as though he would
fend her against all the ghosts of evil and the deadly
wers of the obscene world.

CHAPTER VIII

ENGLISH HISTORY

"THE afternoons *do* draw in," said Mrs. Beddoes the shadow of Mr. Beddoes. She was on her kne at the end of the Long Gallery, scrubbing the floor. It was good moment for that early in the afternoon. No one can into the Long Gallery after luncheon, not for an hour least. The pictures had it all to themselves.

Physically Mr. Beddoes was in London, and (you mig bet your boots) at this moment fast asleep with the spor ing edition of the *Evening News* over his face, but spiri ually he was with Mrs. Beddoes—or, in absolute accurac she was with him.

This was Christmas Eve, and it grieved her sadly tha at such a time, she should be separated from him. Had h adored mistress been well enough (and how deeply Mr Beddoes adored Janet even Mrs. Beddoes didn't know) sl might have put in a word, Mr. Beddoes being one of tho men who really does miss his wife of a Christmas, but things were she couldn't of course think of bothering.

The child, by rights, should have been born in the midd of January, but during these last two days things had bee a trifle anxious (a way that "things" were always havir with "us poor women").

The London doctor had arrived that morning, and litt Doctor Bamfield from Salisbury was also here. Everythin in the house was as still as still.

Considering these matters, Mrs. Beddoes had rested fo a moment from her work and, looking up, had informe Mr. Beddoes about the drawing in of the afternoon. A though it was not yet three the dusk was creeping upon tl Long Gallery like smoke, and you couldn't see the pictur

cept for here a nose and there a chin and once in a way a
eaming eye. A shivery sort of place at the best of times,
d cold and draughty.

Mrs. Beddoes didn't care for galleries. But, looking about
r and out through the long high window, she saw, with
thrill of sentimental pleasure, the gentle hesitating fall
the first snow. She believed profoundly that there "should
a bit of snow at Christmas time," and the warm winters
at we have nowadays seemed to her part and parcel of
e general conspiracy to make food prices high, give
r pains in her feet, and Mr. Beddoes laziness in all his
nes.

When, therefore, she saw those grey flakes papering
ainst the heavy sky she climbed on to her feet and went
the window to look out. Yes, it was the right sort of
ow, the sort that was going to "lie."

At once before her vision danced a kind of Christmas
now of mince-pies, immense turkeys, red-nosed little boys
ith mufflers round their necks, snowballs, Christmas hymns,
e Christmas stockings you buy in the shop with a trumpet
aring out at the top, Christmas cards all glitter and robins,
aits and carols, London mud, pantomime with Dick Whit-
ngton's cat, burning raisins, plum puddings black as night,
ins in the stomach, the doors of public-houses opening
d shutting, country lanes with somebody's arm round
mebody's back, a bright silk bodice, after-dinner slumber,
d kind, polite ladies from the Vicarage.

This conclusion of early childhood's country memories
d later London histories came in one swimming pageant
fore her eyes. She was for a moment blinded by its glories,
en with a heavy sigh turned back to her work.

As she did so, she heard steps coming down the gallery,
d saw with a little flutter of alarm that it was Hignett.
r. Hignett was very much grander and more imposing
her than the Duke or Lord or Lady Poole—*not* so impos-
g as the Duchess, who was one of her several ideas of
od in female clothing. *After* the Duchess, but after no one
se, came Mr. Hignett.

However, she was not one to pretend that she had been

working when she had not, so she stood there waiting f
him.

"Any news, Mr. 'Ignett?" she asked in her husky, rur
bling voice.

He stopped and looked at her kindly. She saw that l
was greatly perturbed.

"Her Ladyship's not so well," he said. It was plain th
he was so deeply anxious that a conversation with anyor
was a relief.

"Poor lady," said Mrs. Beddoes. "It does seem 'ard. Tl
first's trouble enough anyway without 'aving things g
wrong."

"You're right," said Hignett, looking out of the window
"But it's his Lordship I'm anxious about. It's hit him som
thing terrible. If anything was to go wrong he'd never fo
give himself, feeling responsible in a kind of way." Higne
coughed. "It's snowing, I see. A bit cold in this gallery, Mi
Beddoes?"

"Well, yes, it is, Mr. 'Ignett, but workin' one sort c
forgets the weather. My mind's been on 'er Ladyship a
day, so that I 'aven't rightly been thinking of anything els
I was at the wedding, you know, Mr. 'Ignett, 'ad a speci
card all to myself, 'aving worked for Miss Janet and he
sister donkey's years." (A slight exaggeration in Mrs. Bec
does's narrative was pardonable.)

Hignett moved restlessly to the window and back again.

"It's a strange thing, Mrs. Beddoes, when you come t
think of it, that every man's mother had all this pain ar
trouble to bring him into the world, and nothing much fc
him to be grateful for when he is in. Being alive isn't muc
catch these days if you ask me, what with one thing ar
another."

To this, however, Mrs. Beddoes would not agree.

"There I'm not exactly with you, Mr. 'Ignett, if you'
forgive me being so free. Of course troubles come alike t
everybody, it wouldn't be natural without a trouble or tw
but what I've said to Mr. Beddoes many a time (and 'e
something of your way of thinking, Mr. 'Ignett), what I sa
is that there's always something *interesting* coming along

If it isn't one thing it's another. If it isn't a railway accident, it's twins, or a Royal Procession, or just a walk down the street to see the shops—if you live in London, that is. That's my meaning, Mr. 'Ignett. Life's always providing something for you."

Hignett allowed himself to smile. "That's a very sensible philosophy, Mrs. Beddoes," he remarked beneficently. He broke off. "What's that?"

Somewhere a bell rang. Doors opened and shut. There was a faint patter of echoing feet.

"My God! Something's up!" He turned, hurrying down the gallery. Mrs. Beddoes stood staring after him. The snow was falling now in a thick clustered curtain.

Wildherne had walked with his mother out of the dining-room in a bewildered uncertainty. He must do something and that quickly—but what? He was terrified with a fear that he did not dare to analyse. He tried to listen to what his mother was saying.

In the hall she put her arm around his shoulder, drew his head down and kissed his forehead.

"Dear, it will be all right. I know it will. God intends that it shall."

It was as though he were swimming in black underground water.

"It's her suffering," he said. "That she should suffer like this—it doesn't seem fair."

His mother drew him down to a seat near the stone fire-place.

"Be brave about it, Wildherne. That's what God has put us into the world for, to be brave. And soon, when the child is born, Janet will be so happy. I suffered very badly before your birth, and your poor father suffered still more, but as soon as you were born and were lying in my arm I was happier than I had ever been before. I thanked God then for my pain, and so will Janet."

"It was about two months ago"—he was fighting his way up through the darkness—"some time in October—that week-end when Rosalind and Tom were here—"

Her ears were sharp to hear whether any sound broke the upstairs silence.

"What, dear?"

"——that something worried her. Nothing went quite well with her after that."

"I noticed no change in her," the Duchess said, her little hand patting his knee.

"But I did. And there was a change in father too. Something's been the matter ever since then. Mother, what's happened to father?"

"Happened to him? . . . Why, nothing, dear."

"Oh yes, something has. He hasn't been natural to me for weeks. I've challenged him about it, but he won't have it out with me. There's never been anything between father and me before."

"Well," his mother answered slowly, "there *has* been something, dear. Something that will pass, I'm sure. I *think* that he had some talk with Janet . . . I don't know. . . . He won't tell me anything. But something about Janet distressed him. You didn't have any quarrel with Janet just then?"

"No, no," he answered eagerly, rising and walking about, "I've never had any quarrel with Janet, she's always been perfect——" He broke off. "Oh, the stillness of this house! Why isn't there something for me to do? It's as though the whole house were listening. There's nothing for me to do—nothing."

His mother drew him down to her again.

"Wildherne, dear, listen. Maternity is the grandest, finest thing a woman can know. However deeply she loves her husband, it isn't the same as her love of her child. Her husband *is* her child, but just because she hasn't suffered so terribly in bringing him into the world, so he isn't quite hers as her child is. There is no joy like that joy when you put your arm round your child and hold it close to your breast and feel its trust in you.

"I have sometimes thought that I haven't been quite the mother to you that I should have been. Always from a child

I've wanted to organise and manage things, and when that opportunity came to me I welcomed it. And sometimes, often perhaps, I've been so busy that I haven't considered your father and you enough. I don't know. The other is important too, and I always pray to God to direct me and try to do His Will, in which, of course, I continually fail. But at a moment like this God shows me that none of this other life weighs at all against my love for you. Believe that I would give everything up for you and your father. And so Janet will feel when she has her child. And be thankful that you love her so deeply and she you. There are many married people who have married without love, and then, at such a time as this, they have nothing to give one another. But because you and Janet love one another you are together in whatever you have to meet."

He bent down and kissed her very tenderly, then he got up and walked away.

He did not love Janet, even now when she was suffering all this pain for his sake. He was in a terror of distress for her, he would willingly have taken all her pain on to himself, but he did not love her. He knew, and the realisation of it was a lightning flash through the darkness, that in spite of all the longing in him for Janet's safety it was not love that moved him.

"Mother," he said, turning back, "won't you go up and see how things are? Perhaps there *is* something I could do. Anything but this idleness . . . this silence."

"Yes," she said. "Of course I'll go, dear."

As she went up the stairs Hignett came in from the garden.

"Oh, Hignett . . ." Wildherne stopped as though he had something to say. "No, no—it's nothing."

Hignett stood there beside his master, and there was something in the passive attention of his great bulk that seemed to say: "Yes. Nothing else matters to me but your well-being. If by tearing myself into small pieces I can help at all, I'm quite ready."

He only said: "There's nothing I can do, my lord?" The

two men looked at one another, and if friendship between one human being and another exists at all anywhere in the world, it existed then.

"No, nothing. Thank you, Hignett. It's all right, thank you."

"Very well, my lord."

Wildherne went out on to the terrace. He stood there and looked up to the grey, fathomless sky. He felt then the wet, gentle flakes of the snow caressing his face. He stood breathing in the cold, dun air.

He seemed to be utterly alone. He felt that he had no philosophy, no religion, no character with which to meet this crisis. If the child were born dead, and if perhaps Janet could have no more children, then the dream of his whole conscious, thinking life was ended. And if Janet died, he knew that bitter reproach would be his companion for the rest of his living days. Those were not mere words. That was true. He was of such a character that his conscience was persistent, unsleeping. It was true that he was young and old-fashioned for his time, but age would not change that in Wildherne. There was something of the Priest in Wildherne. He always saw things remorselessly with something of the revenging, inevitable chastity of clear running water. The only passion of his life had been that for Diana Guard and already (though he did not yet know this) that was supplanted by the passion for his son-to-be. His love of England, of his father, of his home, of such poetry as Clare's, of the long naked shoulder of the Plain, of the weedy rubble under foot in country lanes, of sudden streams, of riding, of early mornings seen from the windows of Wintersmoon—all these (save possibly his love for his father) had been affections, not passions. His feeling of friendship for Janet had been so easy; it was absolutely characteristic of him, characteristic of his loyalty, naïveté, innate purity, English unsexuality.

And so he had in him no recognized force to meet these two overwhelming emotions that had suddenly risen together to meet him—his sense of injustice to Janet, the threatened loss of his longed-for child.

He was torn with misery and apprehension. It was literally a tearing. He was sick with terror. At any moment some figure might approach, to tell him that Janet or his child, or both, were dead.

For the remainder of his life, then, he would remember that, at the most crucial moment of it, he had failed. And this sense of failure would not be to him as it would to many more callous men, a light thing. He was always ready to believe the worst about himself. It was the easiest thing to believe. And he was very young. Life had not as yet tested him at all.

He had never known before what it was to be utterly alone. Always there had been someone there. Now there was no one. There was above all not his father.

He did not know what had come between them, but something had. The old man was never clever at hiding his feelings, and Wildherne had in the last two months surprised again and again a strangely puzzled, deeply distressed look in the old man's eyes.

Suddenly, in a moment as it were, every kind of change had come into Wildherne's life. He was bewildered, just as the snow which was falling faster now was bewildering him. But he stood there without a coat, without any sensation of cold or wet—only the snow stole into his brain and lay there, filling every nook and cranny.

He came back, as in the last weeks a thousand times he had come back, to the child. Was that wrong of him—vile of him, perhaps—not to care finally, at the last turn of the screw, about his father or mother or Janet—to think again and again and again of the child?

He did not know it, but he was repeating over and over the words: "O God, give me a son! O God, give me a son!"

The snow beat him back, but it was as though he would press forward at every cost to that leafless wood and find his son there. His son! His son! What marvellous, magical words! He could not remember a time when he had been too young to have that ever before him. That had been the purpose always—to serve England by providing a fine son who would love and serve her. Also to serve Wintersmoon thus. Also to serve himself, his heart and mind and soul, thus.

If this purpose went, what went with it? What, for him, could replace it? What love or service were there worthy to be successor?

His heart ceased to beat. The snow swirled upwards in a blinding net. He saw a figure stand in the lighted doorway.

He didn't know then (he only knew afterwards in recollection), that it was the little round, pursey Bamfield.

The little man caught Wildherne by the shoulders.

"Lord Poole. It's a fine boy, and she's doing splendidly. She's taken it wonderfully. You can go up and see her very shortly."

He reeled into the hall, there stationed himself, looking up the wide staircase into the heart of the house.

Then, with long unsteady steps, he began to run up the stairs.

END OF PART II

PART III

WILDHERNE AND HUMPHREY

CHAPTER I

BEAMINSTER was never really quite the same man
again after an attack of rheumatic fever that he had
wards the end of nineteen twenty-two.

Although he had apparently quite recovered by the spring
nineteen twenty-three it was noticed by everyone that he
.d aged, that his carriage was no longer so upright nor
sprightly as it had been, that his spirit was at times sadly
oken, and that he had acquired the habit of talking to
mself.

People said that he would not in all probability live very
uch longer and speculated as to how much he would leave.
ey also said that his disappointment in the result of Tom
:ddon's marriage had a good deal to do with his breaking-
.

Johnny Beaminster was not aware that they talked like
is. As with all of us, he credited his friends with some
the pleasurable excitement about himself that he himself
ssesesd. He did not realise how dim and distant a figure
was to nearly everybody. He was aware, however, that
was neither so young nor so happy as he once had been.
; the months progressed the expectation that he would
yet again young and happy dwindled. The world seemed
have changed.

One thing that saddened him greatly was the departure
Fullerton, who was pensioned off. Instead of that cheer-
d sight in the morning of Fullerton's broad bending beam,
ere was a thin cadaverous young chap who was polite
d efficient enough, but with whom, for one reason or an-
her, Beaminster could establish no personal relation.

Then Beaminster was seldom now out of pain. Not bad

nor incapacitating pain, but twinges, shoots, and spasm
and, behind there, a kind of hovering fear as though som
thing very much worse was going to happen shortly.

Then the world was changing most sadly for the wor;
This London English world, which was after all Johnr
Beaminster's, was not at all as it had been. There was tl
Unemployment, this Socialist Menace, this perpetual pullin
down of well-known London landmarks, this ghastly Incor
Tax, this impertinence of servants, these masculine wom(
and these effeminate men, this perpetual talk of Bolshevis
(as though his beloved England could *ever* be ruled by Ru
sian Jews!), and, a real daily trouble to him, this rushir
and shrieking traffic so that he was almost afraid of goir
out into the streets of a morning.

Then the world was forgetting him. He would not ha
minded that in the least had he been able to keep arour
him his dozen dear old friends, male and female; but th(
were all dying or dead, and there was no one to take the
places. No one invited him out any more, and even in h
beloved Zoffany he had a suspicion that some of the m(
there thought him a dreadful old bore.

But of course none of these things weighed at all on h
mind in comparison with his distress and dismay at tl
consequences of Tom's marriage. These consequences we
the more disastrous to him because he could not discern e:
actly what they were. He was kept away from the truth. Ro
alind did not allow him to come within a hundred yar(
of her. No one told him anything. He only knew that h
dear Tom, for whom he would willingly give all the bloc
that still coursed through his wretched old body, was ur
happy and terribly altered for the worse.

Tom and Rosalind had been married in the autumn c
nineteen twenty-two, just before Beaminster had his attac
of rheumatic fever. It was now the autumn of ninetee
twenty-three. They had been married just a year, and thing
were as bad as they could possibly be.

The problem was to see exactly where they *were* ba(
Certain things were obvious—as for instance that Rosalir
got on with her mother-in-law, Lady Seddon, extremel

dly, that Rosalind was independent and selfish, that Tom
lked and seemed to have lost all his ambition. But definitely
 one would tell Beaminster anything.

Tom swore that "things were all right"; Rosalind said
at "Tom was a dear"; the world said that Rosalind "would
 off any day." But no one had any of those stiff, definite,
vkward things called "facts." It was only in the air that
e Seddon marriage wasn't turning out well.

In truth the two sisters, Janet, Marchioness of Poole,
d Rosalind Seddon, were very prominent figures just
w.

It happens every once and again in London that some
rsonality dominates, for a while, the scene. It is sometimes
 domination of deliberate intention, as it had once been
ith the Duchess of Wrexe. Sometimes it is a domination
 character, beauty, or position, the domination of a Dis-
eli, a Lily Langtry, a Gladstone, or (in the latter years of
e War) a Lloyd George. But it has happened sometimes
at a personality without any great gift whatever of intel-
gence, beauty, or wealth permeates the whole world of
ondon, permeates because of its moral truth and its pos-
ssion of some quality that is ardently desired by many
ople at the time.

It was something of this influence that Janet Poole was
ginning to have in London—dim, nebulous, but constant.
eople said that that world for which she stood—the quiet,
d-fashioned, rather shabby aristocracy—had a fuller and
ore active life than one supposed, and that Janet Poole
as a proof of this. She took no active part in public cere-
onies; she did not open bazaars nor crèches; she did not
eak at political meetings nor organise theatrical matinées.
ne was not, as was her mother-in-law, connected very def-
itely with a public and important movement. She spent
uch of her time in Wiltshire with her husband and little
n. She was not a woman with whom people made friends
sily; her picture appeared but seldom in the illustrated
pers; she had no publicly pronounced views on "The
odern Young Man," "Psycho-Analysis," "Should Di-
orce be made Easier?" It was simply that a great many

people were aware of her, were vaguely proud of her, a
prophesied that she and her husband would "be heard
one day." People liked the idea of her.

She may, of course, have been helped to some of l
fame by Rosalind.

Rosalind's beauty had grown and developed since l
marriage. Without becoming an actress in the Cinema,
appearing in every paper as an advertisement for somebod
Cream or Powder, without indeed being very greatly pho'
graphed or paragraphed anywhere, she was neverthel
known as the most interesting, beautiful woman in Lond
It was because she was "interesting" that people thoug
about her, because, without belonging to any particular s
she was known to be the friend of one or two curious a
rebellious personalities—Plan, the sculptor; Lamond, t
author of *Crust* and *The Blue-veined Monkey;* Charles Ra
age, and Hay Ferris, the negro Bolshevist—all men. She c
not care about women.

She was not seen often with any of these people—s
was not seen often with anyone. She never gave interviev
What she did give sometimes were little parties in t
Seddon flat near the British Museum. It was said that t
best talk in London was to be heard at these little parti
It was said that Tom Seddon never appeared at them.
was said, moreover, that they were extremely serious ar
one or two people asserted, excessively dull. Very lit
drinking, no dancing, no lovemaking. But no one knew ar
thing for certain. No one knew anything about Rosali
for certain—save this, that she was very different inde
from her sister.

The only other thing that was said was that Tom a
Rosalind Seddon had very little money, that they lived
the very simplest fashion, and that, from having been n
torious for her extravagance before her marriage, Rosali
since her marriage had become so economical that her enemi
(of whom she had a considerable number) called her mea

Of all these things old John Beaminster was aware, a
of some of these things he was thinking on this grey ar
misty afternoon, November 4, 1923.

He had finished his luncheon and had come into the little
ting-room to sit in front of the fire and have his half-
ur's nap. But to-day the nap would not come: he was too
eply disturbed.

He had not seen Tom for a week, nor had a line from him,
d, as was often the way with him in these days, a cloud
menacing disaster hovered above his head. This cloud
ngled with the thin wispy fog that had penetrated into
s room.

He knew that if he went to his window and looked out
 would see that wispy fog thinly pervading the trees,
nk with moisture, the Devonshire House gates (recently
aced just opposite his building), the long line of Picca-
ly, the figures of men, the bodies of motor-cars and om-
buses. He knew that he would be depressed by that sight,
d that the menacing cloud of his own fears would swell
d swell as he gazed. So he sat over his fire, aware that
ep would not come to him, aware of an occasional sharp
ooting pain in his right thigh, aware that he had eaten
) much luncheon, and that a glass of wine and a biscuit
re the best things for him in the middle of the day.

He must see Tom, and that as soon as may be, or if he
uld not see him in the flesh he must hear of him at first
nd. As often now, he spoke to himself aloud:

"I must see Tom. If he won't come to me I must go to
n. . . . Devilish chilly in here even with the fire. I was
fool to have that pheasant. Fullerton wouldn't have let
e. . . . That fog gets through the windows. Tom won't
 there this afternoon. He'll be at the Foreign Office. I
ght see her, though. . . ."

He had to confess to himself that he was afraid of "her."
ow many times had he struggled to throw off this fear!
 the old days he had been afraid of nobody, no, not of
e Duchess nor of dry-as-a-stick Adela—neither of man
r of woman nor of child. But to-day—he did not know
w it was—he was afraid of a good many people. He was
raid of the modern young man and the modern young
oman, who showed you so plainly that they thought every-
ing you uttered an idiocy; he was afraid of the people

who moved so quickly that they had not even time to
that you were there; he was afraid of the people who w
afraid, the men and women who were so nervous of the
ture that they made you also nervous. But he was afraid
none of them as he was of Rosalind. It was not that she w
ever rude or unkind, but she behaved to him as though
were almost dead, as though she had his little obitu:
laid out neatly there in front of her and, after consideri
it, happily flicked it aside.

Whenever he saw her he felt that he had advanced p
ceptibly nearer his grave; and although he did not ca
greatly about his death, yet he wanted to live. He clu
to life, to the warm crackling fire, to the bright sunny da
to the few friends who were still glad to see him, to t
pieces of fun that yet remained to him.

So he shrank from Rosalind. And, thinking of her, l
thoughts passed naturally to Janet Poole. Why shou
he not go and pay *her* a visit and tell her a little of l
trouble? She was devoted to her sister. She must hers
be distressed that this marriage was not proceeding happi
He did not know her very well, but when he had seen l
she had always been very kind to him. He liked her ve
much indeed. He was not afraid of *her*. Surely no o
could be that!

He resolved that he would, this very afternoon, pay tv
calls—one to Rosalind and Tom, the other to Lady Poo
From one or another of these he must surely learn son
thing.

He got up, walked up and down a little to feel confiden
in his limbs (he had sometimes a fear in these days l
one of his legs should suddenly desert him), went into t
little hall and put on his smart, rough, blue overcoat, fou
his bowler hat and gold-headed cane and started off.

Outside Dare and Dolphin's he summoned a taxi a
gave the man the Bloomsbury address. He sat back in t
taxi, confident and happy again. He always recovered ve
quickly his spirits; it needed very little to cheer him, but th
also it needed very little nowadays to depress him. Tha

1at he was to-day, up one moment, down the next. Very
olish.

When the taxi stopped in the rather shabby little street
1ere Tom and Rosalind had their abode he gave a dis-
1tented grunt. He knew that it was just now the fashion
r clever and extremely modern persons to find their resting-
1ce in Bloomsbury, but, upon his soul, he could not under-
1nd them! Dead-and-alive place! Nothing but cats and
licemen, and the odour of the British Museum mum-
es over all!

He climbed out carefully, paid lavishly the pinched-face
iver, and seeing at the side of the door the name Seddon
er two others, pushed the bell that belonged to it, found
e house door opened and entered the grimy hall.

They were on the third floor, so up the dingy stairs he
1mbed, but, arrived there, he found their door very smart
leed in shining white paint and a brilliantly polished
or-knocker. He was used to this, of course, having paid
1ny other visits, but the contrast between the house in
1eral and Rosalind's flat in particular never quite lost its
velty for him.

The sharp-faced maid, whom he thoroughly disliked,
cncd the door, and yes, Mrs. Seddon was in, Mr. Sed-
1n too, and they were both in the drawing-room, and there
another instant was Beaminster also, coming, as he was
mediately aware, upon something of a scene.

He fancied, looking backwards, that the maid, hating
r mistress (she left that very week), threw him in there
:entionally, hoping to make confusion twice confounded.
She did not of course do that, because Rosalind was far
) clever, but she did, terribly, confuse old Beaminster.
e, like all gentle souls, hated above everything a scene.
.s vision of Rosalind angry quite literally terrified him.
1d yet she was very beautiful. She was wearing a dress
silver grey, and it had a waistcoat with jewelled buttons.
1e was wearing a kind of Elizabethan ruff of stiff silver
)cade. Her hair clustered about her head in ripples and
adows of light. As she stood there in front of the green

Tang horse on the white mantelpiece, her hands on
hips, she was like a young St. George challenging
dragon. The dragon for the moment was poor Tom, w
was too fiercely enraged to be properly pitied. Yes, th
had undoubtedly been a scene.

Whatever she thought of the iniquities of the outrage
maid, Rosalind kept her indifferent charm. "Dear Un
John," she said, "that's lovely of you—to come at su
an unusual hour. And it's especially fortunate just no
because Tom and I have been having words, and I've
to go out and haven't time to cool him down. You can s
behind and do it for me."

Johnny Beaminster smiled and tried to appear happy.
looked, of course, abjectly miserable.

"I hope not serious words," he said.

"Not serious in the least," laughed Rosalind, going
and patting Tom on the shoulder. "We're arranging a co
promise, as all good husbands and wives should. I'm p
fectly ready to see Tom's point of view, but he won't
mine. However, you talk to him."

She came close to Beaminster, her lovely eyes gazi
into his.

"How smart you look, Uncle John. But then you alwa
are—smarter than anyone else in London—and young
Dear Uncle John, be kind to Tom. I can't bear him to
unhappy."

And she went out.

He sat down in the grand chair with its orange broca
near the white-tiled fireplace and looked up miserably at
Tang horse. Tom came and stood near him.

"'Fraid I came in at an awkward time, my boy," sa
Beaminster. "Maid ought to have prevented me."

"No," said Tom, "it's all right. We couldn't go on wra
gling, and we didn't know how to stop."

Beaminster's heart ached for the boy so desperately, a
he was so anxiously afraid lest he should show his sen
ment, that he did not know what to do, so he looked abc
the room.

"Pretty room," he said, as though he had never se

before. It was in fact a very pretty room, although there was almost nothing in it. There were orange curtains, a yellow Chinese rug, and a Chinese woodcut on the white wall. Also a piano.

"Oh, damn the room!" said Tom. He looked about him like an imprisoned animal. He went on: "Do you remember once, Uncle John, when I came to tea with you at 90 Piccadilly to tell you about Janet's engagement to Poole?"

"Yes," said Beaminster. "Of course I remember."

"And do you remember how happy and excited I was, and how I burst out with all my political and writing ambitions, and the wonderful things I was going to do with my life?"

"Yes," said Beaminster. "I remember."

"Fine, wasn't it?"

"Very fine indeed."

"Well, it may interest you to know that that's all completely finished and done with. I haven't any ambitions. I'm not going to do anything with my life. And I'm twenty-seven years of age."

John Beaminster raised his eyes to the boy's.

"Isn't that rather weak, Tom, my boy? To give up, I mean? Not like you really. But I'm glad you've spoken to me. I've held back too long—through a sort of shyness. And I've been miserable too—not as young as I was. You're everything I have in the world. If things aren't going well with you I'm upset, devilish upset. I've been a coward—I ought to have spoken to you long ago."

But the boy was just at that moment selfish. He cared for Beaminster more truly than for anyone else in the world, save only Rosalind and his mother, but just then he couldn't consider him—he could think only of his own misery.

"Weak!" he said, catching one of Beaminster's first words. "Yes, that's easy to say. I swore to make a success of this and I've failed. Yes, whatever way it goes now I've failed. And it wasn't as though I wasn't warned. Say what you like," he wheeled round fiercely upon the old man, who sat forward in his chair staring up at him, "but you can't be unfair to her. She warned me. She told me it wouldn't

be a success. I would have it. I longed for her, ached fo
her . . . and I ache for her still." It was terrible for Be
minster to see his distress. His heart seemed to stop i
beating with his pain and fear. But quietly and without ar
emotion he said:

"No, I won't blame her, but tell me, Tom, if you ca
if you wish to, what the trouble has been. I know som
thing of men and women. I'm old and have seen all sort
I haven't been married, it's true—but as good as marrie
you might say. Perhaps I can help you."

"The trouble? She's never cared for me, except phys
cally. She's found me a bore, sentimental, old-fashione
awfully stupid. She's been as patient with me as she kne
how to be, but everything that I say and do has seeme
to her idiotic."

"Idiotic!" Beaminster was astounded. "Idiotic! But you'
so clever. . . ."

"No. Not in her world. Oh, I'm cleverer than Rosalind
some things, but not at the things that matter to her ar
her friends."

"Her friends?" asked Beaminster, catching him up. "Wl
are her friends?"

"I don't know. In a way you might say she hasn't g
any, she's so by herself always. Even Ravage can't tou
her. . . . But they've got the kind of brains she likes-
better brains than hers. That's what she says she wan
At first I used to be here when she had her little partie
I thought I could join in and be one of them. But I couldn
They laughed at every single thing I believe in, and the
I would be angry, and then they'd laugh the more. So
kept away. And so I cut myself off from her more tha
ever."

He broke off, staring about the room as though here
the things about him he might find some help. "Then can
the worst thing. About six months ago I lost my temper ar
said that because it seemed that the only use I had for h
was a physical one I wouldn't have that, and that v
shouldn't live as man and wife again until she could ca
for me in other ways as well. Oh, as soon as I'd said it

gretted it, but she has kept me to it . . . and it's driving
e mad! I've implored her—begged her—humiliated my-
lf——"

He broke off, turned to the window and stood there with
wed head.

Beaminster clenched his hands. "That's bad," he said,
ying to keep his voice steady. "But doesn't she care for
u in any other way? Is that true?"

"She says it's not true. She says she cares for me in
any other ways. But she says that I made my demand,
d in return she makes hers. Hers is——" He flung out
s hands. "Impossible! Utterly! Hers is that I tell my
other that she and Rosalind are never to meet again, never
speak again unless other people are there. She hates my
other. She has always hated her. How can I tell my
other that? She says that when I do she will come back
me."

"Why does she hate your mother?"

"I don't know. She always has. She hates mother and
e loves Janet. Save for these two emotions she's aloof,
terly—by herself. And although she loves Janet she doesn't
ind hurting her—hurts her a hundred times a week. But
e isn't cruel, nor mean. She doesn't bear malice. Hate's
o strong a word to use about her feeling for my mother.
ie, like her friends, doesn't believe in strong emotions of
y kind. Cool—calm—unpassionate. They are all like that.
iey believe in Ideas."

He paused and then went on:

"And that's their world, the world that's coming. This
1 one has got to go, root and branch, to vanish off the
ce of the earth, and instead there's to be this new one,
ld, unpassionate, scientific, material, accurate, unfeeling.
o unkindness and no kindness either. Physical passion, be-
use the race must be continued, but eugenical passion. No
liculous generosities, but charity organised by the State.
ience the only religion. Not human beings, but ideas. . . .
h, I've heard them talk—Plan and Ferris and the others.
n not saying that Rosalind goes with them all the way—
ey are cleverer than she is. She is frightened sometimes.

And then she loves Janet, and even in a sort of way car
for me. She is apart from them—apart from me too."

He paused once more, then went on again with a rush
"She's so beautiful. If I didn't see her perhaps I could bea
it, but to see her and not to touch her——"

Beaminster, his eyes shining with indignation, said:

"I should ravish her. That's what she deserves. She
playing with you. Master her—whip her if necessary—
knock her down. All this rot. . . ."

"No," Tom shook his head. "I'd lose her altogether ther
She'd go off with Ravage straight. Not because she love
him—she doesn't, I'm sure—but because she's not goin
to belong to anybody. To nobody. She wouldn't resent m
beating her, you know—she'd admire me, perhaps—but sh
wouldn't stay with me."

Beaminster urged his plan.

"Try it, my boy, and see. Beat her and shut her up. It'
paid over and over again——"

"No, no," Tom broke in. "You don't understand. It
more subtle than that. Her body's not important enough t
her. It's her brain I've got to get at, and so, through tha
at her heart."

Beaminster shook his head.

"Well, perhaps you know best. I don't understand thes
young women. In my day it was plain sailing enough. I
they liked you they liked you, if they didn't they didn'
But all this talk about brains——"

Tom was better. Some of his trouble had passed. He rea
ised fully now the old man standing in front of him, an
with all the warmth of his young and impetuous hear
loved him.

"Dear Uncle John, it's splendid of you to bother. You'v
helped me too. I ought to have gone to you long ago, bu
I've been sort of keeping my troubles to myself. But jus
talking to you takes ever so much off my chest. I was wil
just now. I'll win this game yet."

"Of course you will." Beaminster put his hand on hi
shoulder. How fine the boy looked with his dark distinctior
splendid bearing, noble openness of brow and eye. "Thi

hustn't beat you. She's difficult, of course, but so all women
are, all women who are worth anything. You can take that
from me. But come and see me—oftener than you do. I'm
a bit lonely sometimes."

"I will," Tom said. "Indeed I will. I'll ring you up from
the F.O. to-morrow morning and we'll fix something."

Beaminster tapped the boy again on the shoulder, cocked
his hat on the side of his white head and departed. Half-
way down the dingy stairs he wanted to run back, just
to see the boy again, to say to him—well, what?—what was
there to say?

So, with a sigh of mingled affection and breathlessness,
he went on his way.

Seated, half an hour later, in the Morris-paper drawing-
room at 3 Halkin Street, talking to Janet Poole, he was able
to be himself. He had not been quite natural with either
Rosalind or Tom, fear of scorn holding back in one case
and fear of sentiment in the other. Now as he sat opposite
this tall, dark, quiet woman he was entirely reassured. He
was now in his own world, and with a woman whom he
could trust.

But how she had developed in these last two years! The
rather crude timid girl had become someone commanding,
assured, at her ease. He looked back to that party in this
same house when Janet had been introduced to the family.
He remembered how on that evening, when she had been
talking to Rachel Seddon and himself, she had sprung up
suddenly and left them, driven by some anxiety about her
sister. There had been something girlish and naïve in that
impetuous action, something immature indeed about her
whole appearance that evening. There was nothing immature about her now. Life had tested her since then.

And how kind she was! He thought that he had never
before in his life met anyone so kind. Goodness of heart
shone in her eyes, played about the lines of her mouth, expressed itself in every movement of her body. In the first
moment they were friends, and soon he was pouring out
all his anxieties and troubles before her.

First she had made him talk about himself.

No, he had not been quite so well lately. Rheumatis
had troubled him, and a little sciatica in the right thig
Oh, of course, he wasn't so young any longer. And he didr
know, but he fancied that the world wasn't quite so cor
fortable a place for old people as it used to be. Oh, he ha
nothing to complain of, but the traffic was difficult. You ha
to be quick when you were crossing a road, and it was rath
difficult for him to be quick these days. Then he brushe
all this aside. He hadn't come to talk about himself. Th
was of no interest to anybody. He was worried about Ros
lind and Tom.

He brought this out timidly. He didn't know. He migl
have no right to talk about this with her. She might thir
it impertinent of him. He soon saw that she did not, ar
he saw too that she wanted him to talk of it, that it wa
to her too a matter of grave and imminent importance. H
had just come from there. They had been quarrelling, ar
when he had been alone with Tom he had found that tl
boy was terribly unhappy and didn't know where to tur
for help.

"I don't want to be unfair," he said. "To take sides in a
affair of this kind is generally to do more harm than goo
Of course I'm prejudiced. Tom is every thing in the worl
to me. And then in a way I'm a little responsible. I was s
glad when she said that she would marry him. It was the or
thing in the world I wanted, and I helped it in every wa
I could. But I'm sure that Tom has been difficult. He's real
very young for his age, and he has some of his mother
foreign temperamental nature. . . ."

"Rachel," said Janet. "I'm afraid she's part of tl
trouble."

"Oh, she is," said Beaminster. "I fear that your siste
dislikes her very much. She always has done, I believe.

"Yes," said Janet. "She always has done."

"And then Rosalind's friends," Beaminster went or
"They think Tom very stupid. He isn't stupid. Not at al
But he's not one of their kind. He doesn't believe in th
things that they do."

"Nor does Rosalind," said Janet quickly. "If Tom would only realise that——"

"He does realise it," Beaminster broke in quickly. "He's very just to Rosalind, I think. He excuses her in every way. But he did a foolish thing——"

"Yes?" said Janet.

"No. That isn't for me to tell you. Your sister must speak of it to you. But they are not living as man and wife, Lady Poole. That is at the root of all the trouble."

"I knew that," Janet said. "I know a good deal, although Rosalind tells me very little. The difficulty is, Lord John, that nobody in the world understands Rosalind save myself. I thought that perhaps Tom would. But he doesn't. I've heard him say things to her again and again that I knew were just wrong, and I've longed to tell him, to show him. But it's so dangerous interfering between man and wife, even when the wife is your sister. But I've been too cowardly. I see that plainly. I'm so glad that you've come and talked to me."

"I've been saying the same thing to myself," said Beaminster. "I've not helped Tom enough. I've always said to myself— He doesn't want an old fogey talking to him. But I should have done something."

They both paused. They were both realising how infinite were the differences between human beings, how dark and lonely every human soul, how dangerous the task of stepping forward into that mystery.

Janet suddenly spoke with an intensity that surprised Beaminster.

"I know that you love Tom, Lord John, but I don't think that you can realise how I love my sister, how I love her and how little I seem to be able to do for her. I don't understand that about life. When one loves so deeply one should be able to have force, power that would carry you over every obstacle. But it isn't so. I have for a moment power with Rosalind, and then it is gone, gone like the wind. I believe that she loves me, but her selfishness drives me out. And it is not a base selfishness. There is nothing intentionally mean or cruel in it. It is as though she were conscious of some destiny, and everything must give way to it.

"That," said Beaminster drily, "is what many of th
young people of to-day seem to think, but they can't all o
them have destinies of such vital importance as they imag
ine. The world wouldn't be able to stand up under it."

Janet spoke, and it seemed to be to herself that she wa
speaking.

"I seem not to be strong enough or wise enough to carr
through the charges I have been given. I haven't the powe
. . . the power. . . ."

She got up and stood near to him, looking down upon hir
very kindly.

"At least we are together in this, Lord John. You fo
Tom and I for Rosalind. And perhaps both of us for bot
of them. When we love them so much we *must* be able t
do something for them. We'll try, won't we?"

She gave him her hand.

Before he could reply to her there was an interruption
Beaminster was conscious of the interruption before h
was visually aware of it. Janet made him conscious. Whe
she had been talking to him there had been something precise
almost stilted, in some of her words. She had talked t
him "rather like a book," and he remembered to have no
ticed that in her before—something old-maidish and old
fashioned.

But now, before his eyes, she changed to somethin
alive, merry, vibrating. Her face was lit with anticipation
She seemed for a moment to forget him, although sh
had been taking her conversation with him so seriously

She turned towards the door. It opened. The Duke cam
in leading by the hand a small boy.

The boy was short and sturdy. He was dressed in som
sort of white blouse and wide "Dutchman" trousers of dar
blue. His head was covered in the right sentimental tra
dition with bright yellow curls, but there was nothing senti
mental about him. His face was brown with health, and jus
as they entered the room he pulled his hand away from
his grandfather's and started to run to his mother. Whe

he had gone a little way he stumbled and fell. He lay flat for a moment, then slowly rose and sat back on his fat little haunches, looking up at the group in front of him with the oddest expression, his face half puckered to a howl, but behind the howl the beginning of a smile, and this smile was mingled with wonder as though he said: "That hurt. The right thing to do would be to cry, but I must have looked jolly funny tumbling like that."

He decided not to cry, rose to his feet, then looked up to his grandfather for comment.

Very slowly, and with a suspicion of experienced amusement, he remarked: "It 'urt."

"Hurt, darling, not 'urt," Janet said, coming towards him.

"Nanna says 'urt."

"I know, dear. She says 'urt and you say hurt. You mustn't say everything that Nanna says."

"Because why?"

"Because Nanna is one person and you're another."

This seemed to amuse him greatly. He produced some chucking and gurgling noises which were to him complete and very satisfactory sentences.

Then he saw Beaminster. He smiled at him a most engaging smile. He looked up at him, his whole face alive with interest.

"How are you?" he asked, then at once, as though he had for ever settled that question (the question of manners), he turned round to his mother and cried:

"Oh, mummie, the heluphunt's been sick in the stummick cos it's eaten itself full."

"I'm afraid," said Janet, laughing and looking at the Duke, "that he's got that from Nanna too. She's an excellent woman, but she seems to be teaching him some terrible words."

"What a lot he talks," said Beaminster. "He isn't two yet, is he?"

"In a month," she answered, sitting down and taking him on to her lap. "Poor child, he was born on Christmas Eve,

so that people will always be cheating him out of birthday
presents. But he hasn't realised that tragedy yet—have you,
Humphrey?"

But Humphrey was still working hard at his story.

"The Heluphunt," he said, "had jam. Nanna said she
could, because why she was a poor Heluphunt. Poor little
boys don't have jam Nanna says. Because why, mummie?"

"Because poor little boys haven't enough pennies to get
jam at the shop——"

But his attention had wandered. He was absorbed by
Beaminster, who was sitting on the sofa opposite him. He
sat rigid on his mother's lap, his eyes staring in his head.

Then wriggling, he tried to get down. "Nice old man," he
said. He struggled over to Beaminster.

"Coming up?" Beaminster asked him, stretching out
his arms. Humphrey considered, his face twisted with that
same humorous speculative expression. Then he decided
that the adventure was worth while, climbed on to Beaminster's broad thigh and sat there, straddle-legged, his wide
Dutch trousers standing out like wings.

He considered them with great satisfaction.

"Do you like my trousies?"

Beaminster said that he did.

He felt deep in his pocket and produced two marbles, a
pencil, and a very minute, naked, black doll. One of the
marbles he presented to Beaminster.

"You have that."

"Thank you very much," said Beaminster.

He put up his hand and stroked Beaminster's smooth
soft cheek, still regarding him with wide speculative eyes.

"Don't bother Lord John, darling," Janet said. "Put him
down, Lord John, if he bothers you."

But the old man was delighted. He held the child tightly
to him. Humphrey laid his head back on Beaminster's
waistcoat then shouted with delight. "Oh!" he shrieked,
wriggling all over.

He plunged his hand into the pocket, and after some
mighty efforts he pulled out a large gold repeater. Here
was ecstasy! The gold cover flew open with a click, then

the little distant silvery voice sounded, paused, sounded again. He was in an ecstasy. He sat, the watch pressed closely to his ear, his face now intensely grave in the importance of the glorious experience.

"More! More! More!" he cried, and with every chiming of the little voice his whole body wriggled.

He was absorbed. They were all absorbed. But suddenly, before any of the others were aware, Humphrey had tumbled off Beaminster's knee and was running, staggering, almost falling, running towards the door.

"Daddy! Oh, Daddy!" he cried.

Wildherne had come in. He caught the child to him and held him as though he were defying anyone or anything to touch him.

"Oh, Daddy! There's an old man . . ." He began, in incoherent excitement, his story, words and little gasps for breath and chuckles of laughter and sudden little sighs all mingled together. His arms were tightly fastened round his father's neck; his knees dug into his father's body as though they were planted there for ever. The eyes of father and son seemed to mingle together in their complete mutual adoring absorption.

Then, at last, coming forward carrying his son, Wildherne, as though he were pulling himself out of some deep dream, recognised Beaminster.

"Hullo, Beaminster! How are you?" he said.

CHAPTER II

KATHERINE MARK was told that Lady Poole was expecting her and would she wait in Lady Poole's room and Lady Poole would soon be in.

Katherine knew Lady Poole's room well enough and had waited there on other occasions. It was her habit—it had been from childhood her habit—to be punctual to the second, and Janet had in these days many things to keep her. It was not her fault in the least and Katherine never bore her a grudge.

But as she waited in the little softly-lighted room, conscious of the house on every side of her, the silver clock on the mantelpiece beating like that pulse of the room, she was aware that she was oddly excited. She reflected further that she was always excited when she came into any sort of contact with this strange family. For strange to her they were!

On her way up to this room she had been passed by a little woman in deep black and a widow's veil, and having in her hand a little pile of devout-looking books. Then, at the turn of the stairs on the first floor, a door had for a moment opened, a clergyman had appeared and vanished again. On the second floor, on the way to Janet's sitting-room, another door had opened; there had issued a buzzing whirr of talk and Katherine Mark had seen through the open door a long table round which a number of very earnest ladies were seated.

She had the sense that although Number Three Halkin Street was outwardly so quiet, it was inwardly buzzing with active, energetic life.

258

It was not this life that was strange to her. In her father's house in Westminster, when she was young, there had been as much packed, compressed life as though they had all been confined in a beleaguered camp. What *was* strange to her was the contrast this devout, eager, clerical business made with the lives and characters of the Duke, Wildherne, and Janet.

Her own family—that is, her husband Philip, her sister Millie Westcott, and her brother Henry Trenchard—had all wondered very much at this friendship of hers with Janet Poole.

It wasn't, they declared, the kind of world to which Katherine in any way belonged. Philip, who was socially ambitious, approved of it, but wondered why, while Katherine was about it, she hadn't made friends with the really smart, powerful aristocracy, not with these old-fashioned and behind-the-times Darrants, Medleys, Purefoys, and the rest. He was not a snob, but he liked to be in the middle of things. The Duchess of Romney and her Purefoy clan simply weren't in the middle of things at all.

Millie and Henry were much more violent. They were bored at the mere idea of Katherine spending her time with such uninteresting people. They were amazed at Katherine for standing it.

It was, as usual, Peter who understood the matter. "If Katherine's made a friend," he said, "that's enough. I'd live perpetually in the middle of a musical comedy if I was going to get a real friendship out of it. Yes, I'd even be the waiter who drops the plates."

He liked the "sound" of Janet Poole. He was a little wistful about it. His marriage was a very happy one, but he seemed always at the end "to walk by himself." So did Katherine. They were alike in that.

She was thinking of these things as she sat there waiting for Janet. Funny room with its old-fashioned wallpaper and furniture! Janet had done a little to it, but she had never been able to make it hers. The room had never surrendered. Three Halkin Street had never surrendered; it remained the Duchess.

Katherine's friendship with Janet had grown wonderfully during the last year. She had taken—and very sad the knowledge made her—Rachel Seddon's place. As soon as Rachel and Rosalind became so unfriendly Janet's position between them was impossible. She could not be disloyal to Rosalind, and she saw in every meeting with Rachel reproach and criticism.

She was terribly sorry for Rachel, and for Tom, too, but Rosalind came first. So Rachel had visited Wintersmoon less and less, and in London came very seldom to Halkin Street.

At last not at all.

Katherine Mark had not really taken her place. There would always be for Janet something especial about Rachel that no one else in the world had—her foreign beauty, something tragic in that, something tempestuous in her loves and hates, something tragic in her hopes always foredoomed, something terrifying in her maternity. Katherine, so quiet, and sure, and domestic, was very different, but in her slow determined way she was beginning to love Janet as no woman had ever loved her before. Rosalind had loved Janet in spasms. Rachel had loved her when she was not absorbed by her boy or with a kind of desperate Slav self-preoccupation, but with Katherine her affection seemed always there, steady, unchanging, unflinching. Janet was beginning to feel it as a flame, clear, dauntless, unswayed by any breeze.

Katherine, on her side, found Janet's life, with all its problems and possibilities, of thrilling interest. She never went to Halkin Street or Wintersmoon without a forewarning that something quite extraordinary was about to happen. She found the Duke and Duchess, Wildherne and Janet, Rosalind and Tom, characters wrapped in some dramatic atmosphere that other people she knew never possessed. She watched them and the development of their histories as she might watch a play. The beauty of Wintersmoon might have had something to do with this, but around the stories of Janet and Rosalind there was some symbolic air.

She did not know why she watched them so intently. Every movement they made was to her dramatic.

The clock struck four: Janet was ten minutes late. The door opened. But it was not Janet. It was that funny girl Caroline Marsh.

"Oh, I beg your pardon," Miss Marsh said. "I didn't know there was anyone here."

"How do you do, Miss Marsh?" Katherine went up to her smiling. "I'm waiting for Lady Poole. She's nearly quarter of an hour late."

"Oh, is she?" said Miss Marsh, giggling. "That's very wrong of her, isn't it? She *is* rather unpunctual. It isn't quite right is it when you have so many important things to do as Lady Poole has?"

Katherine had never liked Caroline Marsh. She didn't like her appearance, her fuzzy untidy hair, her large spectacles, her pink complexion. "Oh, I don't know," she said, stiffening a little. "I wouldn't have said that Lady Poole *was* very unpunctual." Then, making it plain that she did not want to discuss her she went on: "How are you, Miss Marsh? Very busy?"

"Oh, I'm all right, thank you, Mrs. Mark—quite all right, thank you. Yes, quite all right. It's too bad of Lady Poole to leave you like this. The Duchess was saying only the other day——"

Katherine interrupted stiffly.

"Is the Duchess in London just now?"

"Oh no, Mrs. Mark, she's at Purefoy. I'm going down to her to-morrow. She needs me pretty constantly." Her eyes were really spiteful as she added: "I do hope Lady Poole hasn't forgotten about her appointment. That *would* be a shame," and so departed.

"Why, I believe she hates her!" thought Katherine. "The nasty creature. She'd damage Janet if she could."

The thought was quite new to her and held her standing there in the middle of the room. Janet always seemed to her so charming, so courteous, so kind that she couldn't believe that anyone would dislike her. But here was an enemy,

and perhaps there were others, and others again. Janet had
never taken Katherine altogether into her confidence. On
her side Katherine had always been very shy of intrusion
and Janet in her turn was proud.

Katherine knew something of Janet's troubles, but now
suddenly, saw the situation quite freshly.

She was aware of a strange new inrush of feeling and
affection for Janet. The poor dear! What was she having
to encounter here? There had been times when over Janet's
face there had swept shadows of unhappiness that Kath
erine had seen but had not dared to question.

She determined that this afternoon she would take a step
forward and demand more of Janet's confidence. If Jane
did not wish to give it Katherine would understand, but per
haps for months past Janet had been needing her help and
had not allowed herself to ask for it. What was going on
here? How lonely *was* Janet? . . .

As Katherine paused there the door was flung open
and Janet, her face flushed above her dark furs, hurried
in.

"Katherine dear, I *am* so sorry!" They embraced. "Come
close to the fire. We'll have tea in a minute. I thought tha
I'd be punctual. It took longer. . . . No, this chair. This is
the comfortable one. I've been with Rosalind."

She took off her furs, then pulled her chair close to Kath
crine's. She caught Katherine's hand between her own.

"Are you cross with me? Don't you *hate* people to be un
punctual! I do."

"No," said Katherine slowly. "Caroline Marsh has been
entertaining me."

"And abusing me?"

"No, she wouldn't dare. But I could see she doesn't like
you."

"No, she never has. And I'm sure I've always tried to be
nice to her. She thinks that I'm suborning the Duchess."

Katherine laughed. "A difficult thing to do that."

"Yes, indeed, but the poor creature—Caroline Marsh I
mean—lives in a state of perpetual terror. At any moment
a wave of the hand and she's thrown out into penniless dark

ness. Poor thing, I'm sorry enough for her, but I'm afraid that that doesn't make me like her any better."

Someone came in with the tea. They waited until they were alone again.

Suddenly Janet said:

"Katherine, I'm at my wits' end this afternoon. People are coming to dinner—Mr. Pomeroy and the rest—and unless I have an outlet for an hour first I don't know how I'll get through the evening. I've had an awful time with Rosalind—exasperating, maddening—and no good done at the end of it."

Katherine said quietly: "Let yourself go, then. We're friends, aren't we? I've been feeling lately that you're holding yourself in too much. You know that you can trust me."

"Indeed I know," said Janet, nodding her head. "But I've got to hold myself in—in general, I mean. Because I didn't—once—last year I've suffered badly and others have suffered too."

She stretched her body forward to the fire and rested her head on her hands, staring into the caverns of crimson and gold.

"You know—I suppose everyone knows—that Rosalind and Tom aren't getting on. The other afternoon Lord John Beaminster—he's Tom's kind of father, you know—came here to see me. He had just been with Rosalind and Tom and they'd been quarrelling and this had upset him very much. So he asked me whether I could help. I have been a coward about Rosalind for a long time now. I hate a quarrel with her—detest it. No good ever comes of her anger. Just because I know her so well, I've no right to say anything. . . . One's relations are always the most exasperating people simply because they see one with no illusions. . . Well, to-day I ventured. Worse than useless of course. She blamed nobody, said that she was very fond of Tom, but that she couldn't endure his kind of mind—and that he wanted to be left alone."

"Tom's mind?" asked Katherine. "Why, is he very stupid?"

"No, he isn't stupid, but he isn't very modern. He's old-

fashioned. I think the Russian Revolution has given him
kind of horror of disorder, and then he has a lot of hi
father in him. His father was a dear, but reactionary Eng
lish, no imagination, perhaps."

"Doesn't Rosalind care whether she makes you unhapp
or not?" asked Katherine.

"Yes, she cares," Janet answered. "But her caring onl
irritates her. She doesn't want to care, she doesn't want t
have any feelings, she would cut them right out of her if sh
could." Janet paused, then went on: "I can't do anything.
must just wait till she needs me. She'll stay with Tom, I'r
sure. If she went off—if she went in a sort of rebelliou
mood with some man who was handy, then I don't know
. . . I think it would break me. . . . 'I'd be so ashamed
. . . You see, Katherine, ever since we were tiny childre
she's been my sort of baby. There was never anyone els
to look after her. Why, Humphrey has grandfathers an
grandmothers and fathers and nurses! Rosalind never ha
anyone but I, and if anything really bad happened to her, i
she did some irrevocable thing, it would be I who was re
sponsible—my blame . . ."

"No, Janet," Katherine interrupted, "that's wrong. W
are each of us responsible for ourselves. That was m
mother's fault. She wanted to be responsible for all of u
she wouldn't let any of us alone, and so we all escaped her."

"Ah, but I'm not forcing myself on Rosalind," Jane
cried. "That's just what I'm not doing. It's only because
love her that I am afraid for her. And afraid for mysel
too," she added softly.

She hesitated, looked about the room as though she feare
something, then, still staring into the fire that was now du
molten gold, continued:

"Katherine, you said just now that you'd noticed ho
lately I'd been holding myself in, and I told you that it wa
because of something that happened last year. Well,
wasn't last year. It was just two years ago.

"I don't think you've ever known—I've at least never to
you—but Wildherne and I married without any love fo
one another. It was a bargain, he wanted a son and

wanted comfort for Rosalind and myself. Very bad of us, you'll say. Perhaps. But in any case we were honest with one another. No pretence at all.

"After we'd been married three or four months I fell in love with him. I didn't want to. I didn't expect to. It simply happened. It wasn't perhaps very remarkable really when you consider that because of my absorption in Rosalind I had never known anything of men, never considered them or realised what friendship with a man might be. Moreover, Wildherne has always, from the first day of our engagement until now, been kind and good to me beyond words to express. It simply was that after I began to love him I didn't want his kindness—that irritated me. I wanted his love. And he, of course, hadn't got it to give.

"When he knew that I was going to have a child his kindness to me redoubled, but it wasn't for me, it was for his child. I knew that and my irritation grew. I got into a strange, hysterical, nervous state—one's first child is an odd and upsetting experience, isn't it?—and one day, worked up and ridiculously nervous, I told the Duke that Wildherne and I had married without love but that unfortunately I had grown to love him since. Oh! it was a crime! The wickedest thing I have ever done. The old man adored Wildherne, and this shocked him terribly : he had already been made uneasy by things he had noticed about Wildherne. He suspected that everything was much worse than it really was. He has never been the same to Wildherne since. Some ridiculous shyness keeps them apart. Wildherne knows that something is wrong but he won't have it out. I've tried to do what I can, but the Duke simply won't talk about it.

"On that evening I learnt my lesson. I swore that whatever else might happen to me, for the future I'd guard my tongue."

She paused. Katherine looked up at her and smiled.

"Then," Janet went on, "Humphrey came. You know the kind of sentimental nonsense you read in novels about a child bringing father and mother together. I think that it's sentimental nonsense because it's generally false. In our case, when Humphrey came my love for Wildherne seemed to enter a new stage.

"As I lay there getting well I made a vow to myself, a solemn vow which I called the ghosts of Wintersmoon to witness. I swore that, come what might, I would live now only for Wildherne and Humphrey with as little of selfishness in my love as I could manage. That, however deeply Wildherne loved Humphrey and in that love forgot me, would not complain, would not try to have it otherwise. think, Katherine, I began to see dimly what real love might be, began to understand a love quite different from the possessive passion that I had felt for Rosalind.

"That is the especial peril of good mild women, that possessive love, that clutch on the beloved object. I had been like that, first with Rosalind and then afterwards with Wildherne. Now I was determined to beat myself into something else, to try and lose myself and my selfish desires in love outside myself. Well . . ."

"Well?" asked Katherine as she paused.

"Oh, my dear, I'm managing so badly! I am truly a poor specimen. I wouldn't say that to anybody but yourself—people always take you at your own valuation, and I've got to keep my end up here—but, standing outside oneself and looking at oneself, what an absurdity! What a ludicrous, pitiful object! I don't think I'm worse than anyone else, more or less average, better than some, worse than others—worse than the Duke, for instance, and worse, if you will allow me, than you, my dear—but better—oh yes, certainly better—than Caroline Marsh.

"There isn't a motive, an impulse in me that isn't suspect. If I love Humphrey, it's my egotism; or Wildherne, and it's my horrible sensual nature; or the Duke, and it's my sentimentality; or Rosalind, and it's my pride; or the Duchess and it's my conceit. Never mind—what's the good? But see my little soul, Katherine, fluttering like a broken-winged unfledged bird in a dark cellar full of broken glass and spiders. Dear me, yes. That's picturesque, isn't it? But the point is, Katherine, that the worst item in my account is jealousy—wretched, mean, green-eyed jealousy."

"Jealousy!" cried Katherine.

"Yes—when I was a kid I was jealous of Rosalind, jealous of every friend that she made, jealous of everything that she did without me, of every place that she went to that I didn't see. Then when I first knew that I was in love with Wildherne I was jealous of a friend of his, desperately, meanly jealous, and now—oh, Katherine, how dreadful even to say it!—I'm jealous of my own child."

Katherine didn't speak. She nodded her head.

"Now, isn't that awful? Isn't that something to hide yourself *from* yourself over? I love Humphrey—of course I love him, the darling—but I love Wildherne more. Yes, I love Wildherne more than I could have conceived that I could love. And I have to go on day after day, day after day, seeing him devoured by another love, devoured almost to madness. Those are perhaps absurd, melodramatic words, but they are true. The passionate wish of his life has been granted to him, and granted to him wonderfully, because Humphrey is everything that he could ever possibly have wished his son to be. Isn't it natural that he should forget everyone else in his love for his son? He never has loved me anyway, he has never pretended to. But is it easy for me, do you think, loving him as I do, to watch how he gives it, how wonderfully he gives it, and to get none of it myself? And there's fear in it too. If anything now were to take Humphrey away from him, I think he would go mad."

"Oh, Janet," Katherine cried, "I understand. When I had to choose between my mother and Phil, loving them both as I did, I suffered something in this way. Oh yes, I understand."

"There are some women," Janet said slowly, "who seem doomed through life to miss love, who give it and give it, but never—God help them—never through life receive it back again."

Then, unexpectedly, she turned to Katherine, laughing.

"A sense of humour, my dear, helps. Last night when Humphrey was being bathed, Wildherne must assist, and he rubbed soap into Humphrey's eye. Humphrey tried to bite him, and Wildherne was as cross as a bad-tempered

monkey. For five minutes *I* was the one who mattered, I ha
to nurse them both, Humphrey cried on one side of me
and Wildherne wanted petting on the other. Patience! Pa
tience! It will all come to me one day, I know it will. Bu
sometimes when Rosalind's in a mood, the Duke peevish
Wildherne fussing like an old woman about Humphrey, th
Duchess bullying Mr. Pomeroy, Caroline Marsh blinking
evilly behind her glasses, and Miss Crabbage arranging m
life for me, I could bang all their heads together, shut then
up in the cellar, and go off with the key! . . . There, I fee
better, much better! *What* a darling you are, Katherine, and
how glad I am that I have you for my friend! You sit ther
with your wise eyes and grandmotherly attention and lister
like the angel you are!

"Katherine, dear, am I very wicked? Is there any hope fo
me? To be jealous of my own child, aged one and three
quarters, isn't that awful?"

"No," said Katherine. "Very natural." She put her arm
round Janet and drew her towards her and kissed her
"There, I've been wanting to do that for weeks! But I've al
ways been a little afraid of you. You've never before hon
oured me as you have to-day. I'm shy. I always have been
I've never been able to believe people liked me, and unless
know they do, I'm dumb. Now I know you're my friend
You've trusted me splendidly, and it makes me very happy
Don't worry, Janet, but be, as you have said, patient. I'n
sure that you're right about Wildherne. Friendship slips into
love very often and nobody recognises the change until som
crisis displays it. Go on caring for them both, the father
and the child. They need you more than they need anyone
else in the world, and that's something for any woman. And
don't let your conscience be too active. More people, I be
lieve, have been ruined by overworking their consciences
than by overworking their stomachs, and you know how
devastating dyspepsia can be."

"Yes, dear," said Janet. "Thank you." She sighed. "Yes.
I'm better—much better. I can face dinner and Mr. Pom
eroy quite confidently. I want you one day to come with me
to a friend I've made who keeps a curiosity shop. He's a

very fat man, and his name is Zanti. He's like you in some
ways—calm and unruffable. He has a nice philosophy the
point of which is that nothing that you can see is real—
very comforting when you see Caroline Marsh, for instance.
I simply say to myself, 'Caroline, you don't exist,' and she
doesn't. She positively doesn't. It makes me feel so superior."

There was a knock on the door. "Oh, bother, we're interrupted! Come in!" Janet turned impatiently. The door
opened and it was Wildherne.

Katherine had the same romantic sense about Wildherne
that she had about the Duke and the Duchess. It was not
because he was fine and handsome. It was certainly not because she was a snob. It was perhaps because of the power
that he had and, yes, even in these democratic, levelling days,
the power that he was going to have. In her own world no
one had any power at all to speak of. Her husband was making a sensible income and knew sensible people, and her
brother-in-law, Peter Westcott, wrote books which moved
certain souls here and there towards happiness and idealism,
but her class was, on the whole, impotent, that famous
British Middle Class, the most impotent because the most
unimaginative and thought-lazy of any in the Western
world.

But Wildherne was, in her view of him, more powerful
than his ancestors were a hundred years ago. Then their
power had been shown externally in their grabbing of every
sort of pleasant and important thing—leisure, food, sport,
parade, politics—but now, because this aristocratic class was
shorn on every side of its external importance, it must, if
its powers were to appear at all, exercise its finer virtues—
its self-control, forbearance, knowledge of men, traditional
courtesy, code of honour—and this, it seemed to her, a man
like the Duke did. And Wildherne also in his younger, less-
experienced way.

This was not to say that Katherine liked Wildherne. She
knew him very slightly; he was a little too polite for her
comfort and she was irritated with him for not loving
Janet. But she watched and listened to him as she would not

watch and listen to many cleverer and more interesting peo
ple.

He stopped in the doorway.

"Am I interrupting? Shall I go away?" Then he came
forward. "At least I'll say how do you do, Mrs. Mark—
and then I'll vanish."

"No, it's I who must be going," said Katherine. "I've
stayed as it is longer than I should have done. I've got a
family, Lord Poole, and it needs attention."

"So have I got a family," he answered her grandly
"Won't you stop and see it?"

He looked to Katherine then the happiest and most confident human being. This pleased her: she had seen him on
occasion when a sort of puzzled unhappiness had accom
panied him. She loved to find other people happy so she
loved to behold him now.

But she did not stay. She kissed Janet quietly, gave Wild
herne her hand with a smile, and departed in her usual way
without noise or fuss or any demonstration.

Wildherne came and sat on the arm of Janet's chair. He
bent down and kissed her.

"Well, dear. I hope I didn't drive her away."

"Not at all. She was going anyway. What sort of an
afternoon have you had?"

"Oh, so-so. Bothering about rents and cottages and such
Janet, dear, I'm no business man, and that's the truth."

"Why should you be?" She looked up at him, smiling
and as she looked at him her heart began to beat violently
His hand lay on his knee just above her. She had to call in
her control (as though it were some keeper of her own
particular private asylum), because what she wanted to do
was to take his hand and hold it close to her, and then to
reach up with her other hand and pull down his head and
press his cheek against hers. And as she felt this emotion
in her she was aware, in an instant panorama, of the
strange succession of experiences that had come to her. It
could not be such a little while since that moment in that
little London hotel when she had first realised that she loved
him! Odder yet to look back behind that and remember the

days when he had aroused no feeling in her at all save only a mild friendliness and companionship!

But she did not move. She said very quietly: "Katherine Mark is nice. I like her."

"Yes," he answered. "I like her too. I'm glad she's your friend."

"I've been with Rosalind this afternoon," she went on. "That's difficult. Rosalind's so hard to get at. She simply says she's very fond of Tom but that he's stupid."

She saw him begin to say something and then call the words back. She knew that he had begun to attack Rosalind and then, remembering, prevented himself.

"Isn't it," he asked, "some of Rosalind's friends who are doing the mischief? That man Plan, for instance—well, really, you've only got to look at him!"

"No," said Janet, "I think it's something deeper than that."

But how odd! She was scarcely thinking of Rosalind at all. Wildherne possessed her body and spirit. She suddenly —and the impulse in her was moved by some mysterious, insistent compulsion—leaned back and laid her head against his body.

"Let me rest a moment," she murmured. "I'm tired."

"Poor dear," he answered, "I expect that you are."

And as she lay there, feeling the rhythm of his heart beat against her, her eyes closed, how she longed for him to bend over her, to take her head between his hands, to stroke her hair, to kiss her eyes! It was as though to some unknown God she sent up a prayer: "Oh, let me have this. Only this. One sign. One tender, loving movement. I'll ask no more."

But he did not move. He went on talking about Rosalind, about the weather, about politics, the Labour party, his affairs at Wintersmoon. . . .

She did not hear his words. They were like the irritating tick of some clock when you are straining your ears for the approach of someone you love. It seemed to her that if she only wished it enough he must make some movement. She surely had the will power to move his body to her desire. But she had not. She had no power at all. He did not move.

She raised her head. Then he said, eager excitement in his voice: "Janet, isn't it time for Humphrey? Shan't we ring and have him sent down? I've got something I've bought him."

A hot impulse of shame and anger constricted her heart. She scattered it. But she had to pause before she answered "Yes, of course. I'll ring."

As she moved towards the bell he asked eagerly: "Has he been all right to-day? Nothing the matter?"

"Well, I haven't seen him since luncheon. He was splendid then."

Wildherne waited, his eyes on the door. When the footman appeared he said quickly:

"Ask Mrs. Bone to bring Master Humphrey down, will you, please?"

They were now far apart, he standing near the door, she sitting back loosely by the big fire playing with her string of dark blue beads.

"And so I think I shall go down to Wintersmoon at the end of the week. Will you be able to come? And we can take Humphrey down with us. The country's much better for him than London."

Wintersmoon! How that House dominated her! How oddly she both loved it and feared it, and, behind that love and fear, the sense that it lay with Wildherne and herself as to the future of its power—whether for good or for evil. That House—hung as it sometimes seemed to her in tapestries of glittering silver, hemmed in by trees of jade, haunted by spirits in cloth of gold and crimson damask—a place of magic, a spell cast upon herself and Wildherne but a spell that they could themselves transform were they but good enough, but strong enough!

But good enough, but strong enough! She hung her head.

"Yes, I could come down. Your mother spoke of bringing Mr. Pomeroy down for two or three days next week."

"Would you rather she didn't? You've only got to say." Wildherne spoke in that voice that in those days, tried Janet hard—promising eagerly to gratify her slightest wish and, in reality, denying her everything!

"Oh no, I like him. I admire him. At least he knows his own mind. I wish mine was so clear."

There was a respectful knock on the door then, a moment after, rushing in, tumbling in, the wide Dutch-blue trousers, the shout of excitement, legs and arms whirling.

Wildherne caught him up. You might fancy, Janet thought, that he hadn't seen Humphrey for years. She watched them, smiling. Humphrey, from Wildherne's shoulder, crowed to her:

"Mummy, clack clack—tick, tick—bad Abram, broke him in little pieces," came out.

"He means, my lady," Mrs. Bone interpreted, "it's his black doll, my lady, and I'm afraid he's broken his water-jug—and it's very fortunate he didn't cut himself anywhere."

"What happened?" Wildherne asked, anxiously looking at his son's bare knees.

"Well, my lord, he was trying to wash his black doll, although I've told him not to go near the washing-stand, and of course he can't really reach up to it, but he stood on his tiptoes and reached up to it and brought it all down just when my back was turned," she ended a little breathlessly.

Humphrey watched their faces anxiously to see what the verdict was going to be, then, after looking at his father, he was happily assured that all would be well, so he smiled broadly and brought out quite clearly and with great satisfaction:

"It broke all in little pieces."

"Yes, but, Humphrey," said Wildherne, trying to speak sternly, "you shouldn't have gone there when you were told not to. That's naughty. You mustn't ever do what nurse says you're not to."

Humphrey's face was instantly grave.

"I'll kiss nurse," he said reluctantly.

"He's said he was sorry, my lord," said Mrs. Bone, mollified. "He knows it wasn't right. I don't think he'll do it again. He's a very obedient little boy as a general rule."

"I'm glad to hear it," said Wildherne, as deeply relieved

as though he had himself been exonerated. "Are you really sorry, Humphrey?"

"Sowwy. Sowwy," said Humphrey quickly. He was now entirely absorbed in the minute black doll Abram, whose skinny body he was stroking over and over again.

"It's a strange thing, my lady," Mrs. Bone continued, "what a feeling he's got for that doll there. He'll hardly look at his other toys in comparison with it."

"Thank you, Mrs. Bone," said Janet. "We'll look after him for half an hour. Come for him at half-past five, will you, please?"

"Yes, my lady." Mrs. Bone withdrew.

"Funny little beggar," said Wildherne, holding him tightly to him. "What are you fond of that old thing for? Now I've got something here for you. What do you think Daddy's got?"

Humphrey looked up at him, down at the doll, and then up again:

"A helephunt," he said excitedly.

"No. Try again."

"A loppilopp."

"A what?"

"A loppilopp."

"He means," said Janet, "a lollipop. He heard Mrs. Bone say one day when I was there, "Oh, I *do* like lollipops!" Some one had sent her some sugared almonds. The word's fascinated him ever since."

"Here it is," said Wildherne, pulling something out of his pocket. There was paper, and then paper. Humphrey's hand tore at the parcel. Abram fell neglected to the floor. Finally a beautiful highly-coloured negro doll, cap of red, tunic of bright blue with gold buttons, trousers of red, and long, shiny, black boots. He grinned and grinned. His eyes rolled in his head; his tongue worked backwards and forwards. His right leg stuck out, and then his left.

Humphrey rolled on his father's knee. He screamed with pleasure.

"Again! Again! Again!" he cried. The tongue came out, the eyes rolled, the legs strutted. He took him and held him aloft, he turned him upside down, he felt his jacket and cap and boots.

He laughed, gurgling like water choking in the tap. He squeezed his hands into fists and shook them in the air.

Suddenly his face was grave.

"Abram!" he cried. He slipped off his father's knee, picked up the naked little doll, looked up at his father.

"Abram's mine!"

"Yes, but so's Solomon," said his father, holding out the grand negro.

"Abram's more mine." He began very gently to stroke the little doll's shining body. He held him close to his chest, even as his father so lately had held himself.

Wildherne bent forward.

"Come up again, Humphrey. Bring Abram with you."

The child, as though he were suddenly shy, his hand tightly clutching the small doll, hid his face deep in his father's coat. Wildherne bent down, whispering in his ear. The two heads touched.

"Wildherne," began Janet. But he did not hear.

"Wildherne," she said again.

Then very quietly left them together.

CHAPTER III

WHITE

H UMPHREY was, for the first time, aware of snow on waking up this morning of his second birthday.

He was aware at once, on opening his eyes, that there was a strange light over everything, and with that awareness there was an odd happiness and excitement as though he had just eaten something new and extremely attractive.

His impulse, as always when there was a new experience, was to find Abram and tell him about it. Abram was hard to find. Last night when they had both gone to sleep he had been, as he happily preferred to be, clenched in Humphrey's fist. Now he had vanished. He was inside the bedclothes somewhere. He was just under Humphrey's right foot.

He was dragged out, wiped over, and then shown this strange light that penetrated the green blind and lay, like a colour, over everything.

The room was still. The door between the bedroom and the nursery was a little open and, because the blinds in the nursery were already up, a thin shaft of sunlight shone through. The crackle of the nursery fire could be heard, and someone in there was moving about. But his own room was still sleeping; everything in it was sleeping—the green Cock-yolly Bird on the mantelpiece, the clock with the moon and the stars, the brown cupboards, the large armchair and the little armchair, the carpet with the red-breasted robins, the pictures with gentlemen riding horses, the blue glass bowl that sometimes had flowers in the daytime but never at night.

All these were sleeping in this strange white light.

He climbed out of bed, ran over the robins in his naked

feet (although he had been told never to) and, standing on tip-toe, raised a piece of the green blind.

He was amazed. He didn't know what had happened. Everything was white—the grass, the hedges, the distant trees—and not only white but sparkling. He nearly tumbled over in his excitement. He had to hold on to the blind with both hands, and was so much on tip-toe that he was nearly off the carpet.

There were also flowers and trees on the window pane, and when he rubbed his nose against the glass it was very, very cold, like some round white sweets that his grandfather had given him that left everything cold behind them when you swallowed them.

Everything that was white was cold—Mrs. Bone's apron when it was new, the inside of his bed, the outside edge of the nursery fireplace, the little sparkling things on his mother's Fairy Tree that was on her writing table (the thing that he wanted most in the world to have as his own). Everything that was white was cold. He knew several colours —red, green, white, blue, black. He liked blue best. Then he saw, hopping across the white ground, finding their way as it were among the sparkles, two large fat blackbirds. They had all the white ground to themselves, and they seemed to know this because they moved about very proudly.

Then an astonishing thing happened. The big fat tree all alone near the Lodge shook itself, and a cloud of white hung against the blue sky and scattered like smoke. That was marvellous. Humphrey held his breath waiting for it to happen again. But the big tree seemed to be satisfied, as though it had scratched its forehead and once was enough. Nothing now moved anywhere. Even the two birds hopped no longer.

He was aware, without moving, that Mrs. Bone was in the doorway.

"Why, Master Humphrey, whatever are you doing? That's a nice way to catch your mortal cold on your birthday, standing there in your naked feet, and an hour yet before your breakfast-time, and a cold morning like this too. Back to bed now *at* once. . . ."

He obeyed, although it was a pity, because that wonderfu
sparkle would be gone soon. He was sure of that, becaus
it was already his experience that anything very pleasan
was gone before you could touch it. He obeyed, because h
was naturally obedient and liked to please people.

"White," he said. He liked most especially those words—
white, red, green, blue—and used them as often as might be

"That's snow," said Mrs. Bone, tucking the clothes i
around him.

"What's snow?" he asked.

"It's frozen rain," she answered. "When it's cold the rai
turns into snow."

"Because why?" he asked.

"Because it's cold."

He was finding now with every minute of his life nev
words. Some he liked and some he did not. He thought h
would use all the words he liked best.

"Why isn't it red and blue and black and green?" h
asked.

"Why, because it isn't," said Mrs. Bone, suddenly impa
tient. "Now you just go to sleep for another hour, Maste
Humphrey. It's your birthday, and you'll be tired enoug]
by the evening, I warrant, without all this fussing an hou
earlier than you ought, Christmas Eve and all."

She left him, and he lay looking at the white ceiling—
which would surely be very cold if you could touch it; h
said over and over again to himself, "Red, blue, black, green
white," murmuring them to Abram, who lay on his back o
the counterpane listening.

Sleep! With all that sparkle outside and the strange ligh
in the room! Everything in the room was waking. Th
Cockyolly Bird blinked its eyes and shook its feathers. A]
the gentlemen on horseback began to jump their hedges and
ditches. . . .

He realised to the full—as it were down in the very pi
of his stomach—that something especially was occurring
when, seated like a king in his high chair, a stiff crackling
napkin tucked round his neck, his yellow curls all crinkly

nd shining from Mrs. Bone's brushes, he surveyed the
reakfast table.

Yes, something especial was occurring. The blue glass
owl had floating in it the heads of white flowers. In front
f his porridge saucer was a white furry animal with beady
lack eyes, and around its neck a stiff piece of paper with
vriting on it.

A spoonful of porridge half raised to his mouth, he stared
t this. Mrs. Bone bent and kissed him—unusual for her.
That's from Nanny," she said, "to her dear little boy be-
ause this is his birthday, and he's a good little boy and does
vhat Nanny tells him, and Nanny loves him. It's a polar
ear, ducky." White again! He put out his hand and took
. It was charming to the touch—warm and friendly—and
o, although he understood nothing of what Mrs. Bone had
aid, he looked up at her, giving her one of his adorable
miles and rubbing his spoon full of porridge on his napkin.

"There's a dirty boy," cried Mrs. Bone in a flurry, "and
is father and mother and all coming soon to see him, and
orridge all down his bib and everything. Do you like it,
ucky? It squeaks if you push it. There! Isn't that funny?"

It *was*—very funny. And also you could push it so that
ne upper part of its body moved backwards and it stood on
s hind legs. As always, Abram must be shown the sensa-
on. Abram was pulled out from the inside of Humphrey's
louse, and Black and White were introduced.

Bacon followed porridge, a most unusual proceeding. All
ecause of Master Humphrey's birthday.

"Burfday? Burfday?"

What was this odd funny word that continued to appear?

"Burfday?" he said, poking the polar bear's stomach.

"Yes, it's your birthday, darling," said Mrs. Bone, "and
any more of them."

"Because why?" he asked, stroking the polar bear's coat
ith Abram's legs.

"Because everyone has to have a birthday," Mrs. Bone
ontinued. "There isn't anyone in the world hasn't got a
irthday, although some ladies like to forget it. Your birth-
ay's the day and hour you came into this world of sin and

shame without by your leave or for your leave, and it's luck
when they're like you, ducky, and not rubbing their poor lit
tle noses in the gutter with nothing to put in their stomachs
It's enough to make one a Bolshie just to think of it," sh
ended indignantly.

It was one of Mrs. Bone's characteristics that when sh
began a speech she had no idea where she would end. Bu
this did not matter with Humphrey, because he never lis
tened. He was now engaged in assisting Abram to hit th
polar bear in the squeaky part. And every time the pola
bear squeaked, Abram smiled darkly his jealous satisfactior
Then the bacon arrived, beautifully crisp and delicate. Hum
phrey was as greedy as he could be. He adored his food
Mrs. Bone helped him with the crinkly bacon, and he helpe
himself with the thick buttered toast. Wonderful! An
then, as always when something excellent happened, h
thought of his father.

"Daddy!" he said, smiling up at Mrs. Bone.

"Yes, your Daddy's coming in half a second," she as
sured him. "Why, just to think of it, your birthday an
your Daddy not coming! Never fear! As soon take a vis
to Hegypt in the summer time!"

(Mrs. Bone had been once with a family in Luxor i
April and had never forgotten it.)

Humphrey looked around the room. The sun streamed i
soaking the red-breasted robin, and from his chair he coul
see the breast and arms of a large tree virgin white an
glittering with crystals. He didn't know what all this shir
ing was, but he must inspect it more closely. He must g
out.

"Down," he said, pushing against the arm of his chai
He was liberated, and then, just as he reached the floor, wa
arrested by a pool of sunlight. The door opened. In can
his mother, his grandmother, and his grandfather.

They were all carrying parcels. He ran to his mothe
shouting something unintelligible. She bent down an
kissed him. Then he was kissed by his grandmother and l
his grandfather. He liked at present men better than wome
The order of his affections was:

DADDY
HIGNETT
GRANDFATHER
HAWES

Grandmother
Mother
Mrs. Bone
Mrs. Ferris
Forster

Not Mrs. Craddock
Aunt Alice
West
Miss Crabbage
and—especially *not*—
Caroline Marsh
whom he LOATHED. . . .

(I have forgotten Mostyn the head gardener—very old, very
wrinkled, very earthy, very ill-tempered, very wise about children and flowers.)

His mother, his grandmother, his grandfather, all had
things in paper. The things when they were unpacked were
—one beautiful boat to sail on the lake in the farther wood,
one large box of hussars with prancing horses, and (from
grandmother) one purple leather prayer-book which was, as
yet, meaningless.

His mother sat on the floor in her lovely grey dress, and
he sat on her lap.

In his heart he was puzzled. He was just the same gentleman now as he would be at forty, fifty or sixty, and he was
quite well aware that these friends of his (composite com-
binations of scents, movements, noises and hard and soft
places) were being good to him and trying to make him
happy. He did not know why they should take this trouble,
but he did know that he must be nice in return. So he smiled,
and smiled, and smiled again. He hugged the boat to his
blouse, he politely assisted his grandfather to arrange the
hussars on the sunny carpet, but all the time he wanted his
father. All this was well enough, but where was his father?
Why wasn't his father here?

At last, smiling at his mother and catching her silve
chain, he said:

"Daddy."

"He's coming in a minute, darling," Janet told him. "He'
talking to Mr. Beresford. You don't think he wouldn'
come and see you on your birthday, do you?"

"Burfday? Burfday?" Here was this odd word again.

"Because why?" he asked, looking at the Duchess. He ha
discovered that she answered his questions quickest.

The Duchess looked back at him adoringly. It is a pity t
record the fact, perhaps, that at this moment Mr. Pomeroy
Miss Crabbage, and the whole paraphernalia of the Gran
Cause would have been flung into the nursery fire to sav
Humphrey's little finger.

"Darling," she said. "You came to this world from heave
just this day two years ago."

But Humphrey was once more aware of the silver
breasted tree now shining in a glory of splendour beyond th
window. "White," he said, and got up and moved toward
the door.

At that moment his father appeared. With a loud chirru
of joy he proclaimed his triumph. He was caught up hig
in the air, he rubbed his cheeks against his father's, he pu
his hand into his hair and pulled it—he saw all the other
in the room "as ghosts walking."

They went a little apart by themselves.

"What have I got you do you think, Humphrey, for you
birthday?"

"Burfday?" That strange name again. Humphrey giggle
and gurgled and plunged his hand wildly in and out of hi
father's hair.

"Here—I'll put you down. Now, look!" But Humphre
couldn't look. He was absorbed by his father. He put hi
arms round his father's thigh and held on for all he wa
worth, looking up and laughing and laughing. This wa
where he wanted to be. Something held him to his father s
tightly that when he was removed from that contact he wa
dissatisfied, as though he were not having the right food.

And Wildherne too, seeing those large round eyes gazing

up at him in an ecstasy of pleasure, forgot for a moment
everything, present and people and all. Father and son
seemed in that instant to have some private personal communication with one another.

Wildherne broke away.

"No, but, Humphrey, look. See what I've got for you."

He went down on to his knees, splashing into the sunshine. He undid the string about his parcel. It had an odd
shape, like a house, and then when it stood all sturdy and
square upon the floor, behold it *was* a house!

This was a house entirely white save for green trees round
the windows. It was a house, too, with a wide door that
opened, and up to the door slanting white steps which you
looked on, and then, miracle of miracles, the top of the
house (roof and chimneys and all) lifted off, and inside the
stomach of the house were heaps and heaps of animals,
every animal wrapped in a separate piece of paper, and every
animal shining white like the house; and the animals—although this, of course, meant nothing to Humphrey at the
time—were, severally, one and all, made of ivory.

The family gathered around to admire this beautiful
thing. Every animal was taken out of its paper separately
by Humphrey himself. There were elephants, rhinoceri,
lions, tigers, caterpillars, cows, sheep, hens, dogs, wolves,
camels, eagles, donkeys, horses, crocodiles, cats, and many,
many another. And there were two of everything.

They went in procession up the slanting steps. The sun
poured down upon them, and their bodies glowed with a
burning white radiance.

Humphrey shouted with joy, and with his body taut with
ecstasy rushed at his father's thighs. . . .

The clock in the tower struck half-past two, and Humphrey in a white jersey, thick white muffler, and round white
woollen cap, entered, under the guardianship of Mrs. Bone,
the wood. He entered on tip-toe, holding his breath.

This was his favorite wood. It was the one that he knew
the best because it was nearer to the house than the others.
Now his feet crunched on the hard, shining, white snow, and

little balls of it gathered under his boots, and once and again
one of the trees above his head would give that glorious
shiver that he had first seen from his window.

He said nothing to Mrs. Bone. He did not, as was his
usual custom, prance about, hide behind trees and pretend
to be a rabbit. But he *was* like a little animal snuffing with
his nose, and often he would stroke the snow on the tree
bark.

Once he tumbled down. He lay there kicking with his
heels, and Mrs. Bone thought that he was hurt and was crying, but he got up smiling at her rather shyly. She wiped the
snow off his face. His eyes shone like little bright fires. He
stamped with his feet on the ground as though he were as-
suring it of something. A little wind blew through the wood
and all the trees tumbled down their snow.

Mrs. Bone stopped for a moment to speak with Hignett;
Humphrey made instantly for the Little Door.

He did not mean to be disobedient; he had been told often
enough that when he was out with Mrs. Bone he must stay
by Mrs. Bone, but now he went in through the Little Door
as though he were obeying the orders of someone much more
important than Mrs. Bone.

Through the Little Door you went up some black curly
stairs, and up these Humphrey went on his hands and knees,
then a little way along a passage, and almost at once you
were in a room, an empty place, and all around the room
dogs and horsemen were running. This room was filled with
a white dim gloom. Humphrey found there, as he knew he
would, the man in the cloth of silver; for him this man
was, as always before, in shining stuff that was stiff around
his neck and stiff over his hands. Humphrey and he were
old friends. The child in his woolly white hat stood with
his feet apart and looked up at the long pale figure dim there
in the snow light.

He had tried several times to tell his father, Mrs. Bone
his mother, Hignett, about the white man, but *he* could not
explain and *they* could not understand.

There were others as well—the fat red man, the kind

ady who cried, the little man in yellow, but the man in
white was the one he knew best.

The room was very chill. Outside the snow had begun to
fall again and was beginning softly to pile up in little drifts
outside the window. . . . The white man went away. Humphrey scrambled down the crooked stairs, and outside the
Little Door there was Mrs. Bone very cross, looking for him
everywhere, but when he smiled at her she knew that he
was none the worse. He had been gone only five minutes,
and his knees were all dirty scrambling about at the bottom
of those filthy old stairs . . . and she'd told him not to
. . but what a child he was for exploring, and all the
little village children were coming now for the Christmas
Tree, and Master Humphrey had to give them their presents. . . .

So Humphrey saw his first Christmas Tree. There had
been one on his first anniversary, but he had not realised it;
he had been allowed only a short glimpse of it lest he should
be over-excited, and there had been no children from the
village. But to-day it was placed at the end of the long
drawing-room. It glittered and shone with its candles and
coloured balls and frosted silver, and the children danced in
a ring round it.

He loved the colour and splendour of the Tree, but still
more he loved the village children. He had never seen so
many children together before, and he was intensely interested in them. He would not leave his father's side, and indeed during most of the time he stood with one hand in his
mother's hand and one hand in his father's. He was glor-
ously happy; he had never been so happy before.

He could not look at the children enough. Their hair so
carefully brushed, their shining faces, their stiff best frocks,
the way that one little girl was for ever jerking downwards
to pull at her black stocking and another little girl was
pushing the yellow hair off her forehead, and a little boy
was so small he could scarcely keep his feet, and, most exciting of all, the shy glances that every moment they darted
at him, glances of shyness and excitement and almost of
pleading.

He would like to run into the middle of them, but some
thing kept him back. He looked up into his father's face an
smiled, and then up into his mother's and smiled. His whol
body was quivering like a hound at the hound trail whe
the man runs in dragging the scent behind him. . . .

The great moment came when, standing on a chair, h
delivered the presents. The Duke took them off the tre
(or, with the bigger ones from the table) and then hande
them to Humphrey, who gave them to the children.

He couldn't smile enough, and then suddenly he woul
laugh, stamping with his feet on the chair. The trouble wa
that he wanted always to see what was inside every parce
and, eagerly inquisitive over one, would forget the next. On
little girl stood on tiptoe, put her arms around him, an
kissed him.

Her mother and aunt, large stout women, came forwar
nervously horrified. Humphrey laughed as though there ha
never been such a joke, and then, as always, looked up t
his father to see what he felt about it.

He was suddenly tired. He sat down upon the chair an
yawned.

He wanted Hignett. Very often when he was tired h
wanted Hignett if his father was not available. He had a
times an odd shyness about his father, and this especiall
when other people were there. He would not care at all hov
many times he demanded the patience and attention of hi
mother or his grandmother or Mrs. Bone. It seemed to hin
that it was their business to serve him. But instinctively, an
with a miraculous intuition for such a baby, he respecte
his father's preoccupation.

Now was such an occasion. His father was talking ver
busily with an old black man something like Abram, but no
nearly so charming (the Vicar). So he sat on his chair
looked up at his mother, and said very distinctly:

" 'Ignett."

That firm and massive man was not far away. Humphre
liked that firmness. Wherever you pushed at Hignett he wa
strong. The thing that at present Humphrey disliked mos
about his elders was the disposition suddenly to give wa

when you did not expect it. That was why, above everything else in the world, he disliked the lap of Caroline Marsh. The foundations upon which one rested would quiver, wobble, subside. She was *never* to be depended upon.

But Hignett was both strong and tender, and he smelt of an especial soap that had tar in it. (But Humphrey did not know that it was tar.)

"Hignett," said Janet, smiling in a fashion of which he especially approved. (He described it to Mrs. Bone: "Why I like 'er, Mrs. Bone, is because when she asks you to do something it's like one human to another, and yet keeping her place at the same time. If people 'ud talk more about masters and mistresses keeping their places, and less about servants keeping theirs, there wouldn't be so much of this bloody Bolshevism 'anging about.")

"Hignett," said Janet. "Will you carry Master Humphrey upstairs? I know he wants you to."

As a rule he hated to go upstairs. It meant bread and milk, being bathed (intolerable had it not been for Abram's company), bed while the birds were yet singing; but to-night he was very weary. He knew that his father would come soon. He was kissed a good deal, waved his hand to the children, pulled his grandfather's beard, and then his head was against Hignett's stiff white shirt, his arm around Hignett's thick red neck.

Hignett adored him. He would have adored any child of Wildherne's, but this one, so manly and strong on his feet, such a proper little gentleman, always laughing!

When they were alone, mounting the staircase, he talked to him. Quite silent with most people, he always talked to Humphrey. His theory was that it was never too early to begin, and that you never knew how much a child might take in be it ever so young.

"You see, Master Humphrey, all these little boys and girls they're sort o' looking up to you now and thinking you're something wonderful, something made of different clay from themselves; but in these days when they get older they'll be told they're not different clay at all, but just the same, and it might be something better, and then when they see all the things you've got and they haven't they'll be grumbling and complaining, and then'll be the time for you to remember that because your people 'ave been English gentlemen for 'undreds and 'undreds of years is no reason that you're better, but it *is* a reason that you behave better and are kinder and wiser and more generous thinkin'. It does give you an advantage, let the Labourites say what they please, but only when you behave like a gentleman just as your father does. You can't do better than follow your father, Master Humphrey, and I'm telling you this whose been with him most of his life. He's the properest gentleman. . . ."

They were at the top of the stairs. Humphrey was asleep.

Hignett carried him through the nursery and laid him on his bed. He bent over him and then, seeing that no one was there save the leaping crackling fire, he bent down and kissed him.

Mrs. Bone was coming. He straightened himself. "Tired out," he said and then, with a cough that had in it indifference, aloofness, and responsibility he withdrew.

Nevertheless, half an hour later, Humphrey, in bed now, was wide awake. His father was there. His father, as usual, sat on the bed, and Humphrey, his lower half under the bedclothes, the rest of him leaning on his father's breast, recounted in his at present confused fashion the adventures of the day. He sighed and lay still. His hand grew tighter about his father's. It seemed as though to-night he wanted to be especially loving, and Wildherne feeling the light clutch of the small fingers about his hand knew a sudden odd little breath of dismay, of fear blow about him. It was almost as though someone had entered the room. There was only the firelight jumping and leaping.

Wildherne pressed the boy to him. He held him as though he were defying someone.

"White man," said Humphrey sleepily. But Wildherne did not hear him.

CHAPTER IV

ROSALIND IS ROSALIND

THERE are winter days in London when a kind of terror is abroad. The streets have devilish faces, houses bend to the wind and yet there is no wind that you can realise. In squares and places where four streets meet human beings pause as though summoned to hear some ominous news; their faces raised to the grey sky express their timid expectation; the windows, empty shining eyes, leer down; and the rattle of the traffic is a sneering repetition of a bogey cry: "They're after you. . . . They're after you. . . . They're after you. . . ."

And all the skeletons come out of all their cozy cupboards and go rattling along the paving stones. It seems to you that in all the rooms piled above your head the fires are dwindling down to ash and cinder, telephones are ringing and finding no answer, taps are dripping, and the postmen showering overdue bills. All the honourable plays are in their last nights and the dishonourable ones sold out for weeks to come; the crematoriums are all ablaze and the flowers lying faded in the cemeteries; the streets wail with the trumpets of the Unemployed; and the old man who has stolen the bag of the elegant young woman of fashion is, with head hanging, on his way to Bow Street, and the "Punch and Judy" outside the Garrick Hotel for Gentlemen Only hasn't a child to laugh at it.

On just such an afternoon in January Rosalind returned to her Bloomsbury refuge from a week at Wintersmoon and found Charles Ravage waiting for her.

He shouldn't have been there; she was angry with him when she saw him, but she was pleased as well.

She was in the strangest of confused moods, and he would understand her better than anyone else in the world.

That was always his final claim on her—that he understood her better, far better, than did anyone else.

He looked oddly shabby and saturnine after the smart and handsome healthiness of the Duke and Wildherne. But she was tired just now of healthiness, cold baths, shooting and riding—very tired indeed. But what a little insignificant nit of a man he was, although his eyes were fine. Yes, his eyes were very fine indeed, but why was his linen never quite clean, and why did he always look as though it was yesterday that he had shaved and never to-day?

The best of it was that he never cared in the least what you thought of him. You could die at his feet and he wouldn't mind—a great comfort that!

"What are you here for?" she asked, looking, all in russet-brown as she was, like the loveliest Fire-Bird ever dreamed of by Stravinsky.

"You told me the train you were coming by," he answered indifferently. "But if you're busy I'll go."

"No," she answered, going to the fire and warming her hands, then flinging off her furs on to the chair behind her. "But you can't stay long. Tom is coming back from the Foreign Office at half-past three."

"Is he? Well, why not?"

"Why not?" answered Rosalind. "Dangerous. He doesn't like you and I've promised Janet to try and be good." She sighed. "Charles, I'm pretty miserable—more unhappy than I've ever been."

"Yes?" he said without any interest.

"Yes. I know you think that ridiculous. You despise me for having any feeling—about people I mean. One should be moved only by Ideas. Ugh! on a day like this too."

"No," he answered quietly. "There you do me an injustice. I have plenty of feelings about people—yourself for instance. But when one's feelings are sentimental—as yours are—one should deal with them calmly. I like being sentimental, but I won't let that interfere with my real purposes."

"Well," said Rosalind, "when all's said and done what *are* your real purposes?"

"Not very important," he answered calmly. "But much more important than myself and my personal history."

"Words are easy, aren't they?" she answered scornfully. "I haven't risen to your heights. I would like to be as free as you are. It is one thing I think I really want, but can't get free of my affections. I love Janet. I'm fond of Tom. Everything they do, everything they believe in, everything they stand for maddens me."

She paused, but he said nothing. "This week at Wintersmoon has been so infuriating that if I had the strength I'd pull every stone of the place down. All of them sitting round like mummies in a museum. The Duchess adoring the Duke, the Duke adoring Wildherne, Janet adoring Wildherne, Wildherne adoring the baby."

"Very pleasant—so much natural affection," said Ravage.

"Yes, and in the evening we sit in the long drawing-room filled with the mist of all the Ages, and the Duchess embroiders while a charity girl she's picked up somewhere reads to her out of a novel all about county families in the seventies. Janet and I sit in another corner and look at one another. The peacock suddenly screams from the terrace outside, and the footman brings in barley-water and lemonade."

"Very good for the nerves," commented Ravage. "I should like a week or two of it."

"Ah, but that's not it," Rosalind went on. "It's the sentiment behind it. Wintersmoon. Wintersmoon. Wintersmoon and beautiful England and Wildherne so excited about his boy that he can't forget him for a second, and Janet so deeply in love with Wildherne that it gives her agony every time she sees that he doesn't care twopence about her. . . ."

"Doesn't he?" asked Ravage.

"No—only as a sort of agreeable housekeeper. And then all of them looking at me as though I were some kind of wild animal who might break out at any moment and pull the furniture to pieces and run away from Tom and so disgrace them all for ever. That's Janet's fear. She thinks I'm going to run away with you!"

"You're not, are you?" asked Ravage.

"No, of course I'm not," answered Rosalind impatiently "But they are all feeling so much and wanting so much and trying to drag me in and make me feel too. And I do feel. That's the worst of it! I love Janet as much as ever I did. But she's so old-fashioned, so sentimental, so self-sacrificing, so romantic about Tom and his devotion to me, so sad about my never speaking to Rachel. . . . Oh, it's disgusting!"

She broke off and then added with the oddest sigh:

"But that baby's adorable!"

Ravage watched her but said nothing.

"You know," she went on, flushing and turning a little away from him. "I should love to have some children if—if I could leave them whenever I wanted to. Oh, I should adore it, a baby like Humphrey . . . but that perpetual responsibility! It isn't oddly enough the hard work that I'd mind. I don't believe I'd mind any amount of hard work ever. It's hard work, real work, that I'm wanting now. But that responsibility for their happiness—it's *that* that I can't stand. I don't want anyone to be responsible for mine, why then should I be responsible for Janet's and Tom's and Rachel's?"

She turned towards him. He laughed. "You're not—not at all responsible unless you make yourself."

"But I am! There's Janet, 'Oh, Rosalind, don't hurt Tom!' And Tom, 'Oh please, Rosalind dear, don't hurt mother!' And Rachel, 'Rosalind, do be careful about Tom!' "

Ravage answered her.

"You're not ruthless enough."

She looked at him, pausing as though she were considering this remark.

"Ruthless! Yes, that's all very well. But how far can one go? If everyone were as ruthless as they wanted to be——"

"Most people," he broke in, "don't want to be. Most people mean to be generous and kind and unselfish and warmhearted. They're not. They end only in sentimentality. But that isn't their intention. That's where we have the advantage, or ought to have. We're honest both with ourselves and others."

She moved restlessly away from him. "Well, I can't go on for ever like this. That's certain. Things are reaching a crisis. As regards Tom, I'm to blame. I should never have married him, and I knew it at the time. If only he didn't love me! Isn't there something ironical in it, Charles, that I would give all I have for Tom to care about me as Wildherne does for Janet—to feel that we're friends and are only together as friends, and that Janet would give her soul for Wildherne to care about her as Tom does about me? If Tom and I were only friends, if there was none of this awful kind of pound-of-flesh bond, I could put up with his stupid sentimental opinions and he could put up with my selfish indifference to other people's feelings. We like one another, we admire certain things in one another, but this love of his makes all our relations false, makes me say things I don't mean, makes him lose his temper. One day there's going to be an awful row and I shall go off. Tom's heart will be broken, his mother will rave, and Janet will be terribly unhappy. I—who am I to do these things? I am nothing, nobody. Pretty, yes, but nothing more, neither clever nor fine nor faithful. Honest, if I can be, and hence these tears."

"Go off?" Ravage asked. "Where to?"

"I don't know. Only to be free. Never to be bound to any living soul I swear, and to work—to help someone somewhere towards making things a little less sentimental and false and muddled."

He said nothing and she went on.

"I tell you, Charles, there are going to be awful ructions soon. Both Janet and I have got ourselves into positions that are beyond us. I might have guessed that she'd fall in love with that man—the first man that she'd ever had anything real to do with and he nice looking too. And Janet's so sweet and unselfish that she's always too good for anyone she cares for——"

"If you went away from here," said Ravage pursuing his own ideas, "every one would think that you'd gone away to somebody."

"They'd be wrong." She turned almost viciously upon him. "I tell you I don't want anyone else. I want to be alone—free—by myself. Like a man. Aren't women free nowadays? Isn't it the one thing that, through all this hullabaloo, they've won? I don't say they're any the happier for it. I don't believe they are. But they're more useful. They can do more. They aren't, at any rate, such priceless idiots."

Ravage got up and stood beside her. "Rosalind," he asked, "do you like me?"

"Like you?" she asked. "What do you mean?"

"I mean exactly what I say," he answered. "Do you like me? Most people don't. I don't as a rule care. But I should prefer that you did. And I should like to know."

"Of course I like you," she answered, her voice troubled. "You know perfectly well that I do."

"How do you like me?" he pursued. "As a companion? As someone to talk to?"

"Yes."

"And that's all?"

She moved away.

"How absurd you are! What's the matter with you to-day?" But the question was not answered.

The door opened and Tom came in. There was a moment's pause.

Rosalind said lightly: "Tom, you know Charles Ravage, don't you? I must go and change my things. . . . Farewell, Charles. Ring me up sometime."

She nodded to him and went out.

The two men waited, neither speaking. At last Ravage said: "Well, I must be moving along."

Tom did not stir, did not speak.

"So long, Seddon," said Ravage by the door.

"Good-bye," said Tom.

He sighed when he found himself alone. He moved to the window and looked out at the dirty-water sky across whose surface whisps of green lawn were dragged wearily as though by bored and weary angels. Two chimneys, like impertinent but rather friendly demons, cocked noses at him. He sighed again. He was struggling to find securely his self-control.

He had hurried back from the Foreign Office passionately eager to see her. She had been away for a week. She had not written to him. She had been removed far enough from him so that he saw only her beauty as one sees a fire burning with lovely amber flame in a clear field. As always when he had been parted from her for a little while he felt that this next time it would be all right and, as with all of us when we love very deeply, he was ready to lay all the blame on himself and say that now he would take care that he did not make those mistakes that he had made before —taking it for granted that she would be this time as she had been last time when, because she was a woman, she would almost certainly be something quite different.

In any case, hurrying home, he had been all ready for a "new start," one of those "new starts" that are so illogical because they ignore entirely fundamental conditions of character, circumstance, and surroundings.

He came back ready for every submission, and he found Ravage. He hated Ravage, hated him for his appearance, opinions, reputation, and for the power that he had over Rosalind. He would have hated him less perhaps had he known certainly that Rosalind was in love with him; at least he could then knock the fellow down. But now there was nothing to be done. Rosalind must have her friends. But, Lord, how he loathed the fellow!

And to find him here, waiting for her. He must have known when she would return. Rosalind must have written to him.

Nevertheless, he would not lose his self-control. Of what use to be angry? She must have her friends. But why was it to be always *her* way? Why was a rotten fellow like Ravage, whom everybody knew to be rotten, to be allowed to come and go as he pleased, and then if Tom did object—Eugh! the stir, the cry for feminine freedom. Whereas if he asked for *his* rights!

Rosalind came in. She kissed him and stood beside him, her hand on his shoulder.

"So I'm back. And very glad too."

"Did you enjoy yourself?"

His voice, do what he would, implied restraint. He must be restrained *first,* show that he had a right to a grievance;

then he would throw the grievance out of the window. But at the note in his voice hers also drew in. She took her hand away.

"Enjoy myself? Not very much."

She moved to the fire and, sitting down, stretched out her golden shoes towards it.

"Why?" he asked, following her slowly.

"Why? Well, in the first place I detest Wintersmoon. You know I do. That's why I think it's so unkind of you always to be forcing me down there. Great barn of a place—full of ghosts—and so pleased with itself."

"And what else was tiresome?"

"Oh, everything! Janet didn't really want me a bit. She's only got time for Wildherne and the baby. The baby's a darling though. A great sense of humour. Sarcastic."

"What did you do all the time?" in that very polite voice adopted by us when we want to show that we are justly hurt but are perfect gentlemen in spite of it.

"Oh, I don't know. Knitted with the Duchess, discussed the probable sex of the kitten, went to tea with local nobility, learnt a very clever Patience that almost no one can do, watched Janet being perfectly sweet. . . ." She broke off, laughing. "Tom, how ridiculous you look! Standing on one foot like a stork nursing a grievance!"

"What do you want to have that man here for the moment you come back?" he asked huskily.

She smiled and put out her hand to him.

"Tom, don't be such a baby! That man! Why, you talk like a dramatist. And are you going to be jealous? Are we going to have a scene with heroics, and am I this evening about midnight to take refuge in Charles Ravage's bedroom? Tom, dear, please don't be so silly. I'm tired, you're tired, the weather's damnable. Let's have some tea and rest ourselves a bit."

But he wouldn't take her hand. He moved away.

"Yes, that's how you always go on. I'm a silly fool to make a fuss about anything and you're always so wise and superior. All the same I hate Ravage. Everyone knows he's a lousy swine. He oughtn't to be allowed to touch even your hand."

"Look out, Tom!" she said quietly. "He's my friend."

"No, he's not your friend!" Tom answered. "You may say it as often as you like and I simply won't believe it. He *can't* be the friend of anyone of your sort. He's dirty to look at, dirty to listen to. He thinks himself God Almighty for no reason on earth. He's a swine and he shan't come here again."

Rosalind half rose. Then, with a little shake of the head, settled down in her chair again.

"Tom, I warn you," she said quietly. "Let's not have a row just now. I'm tired and bothered. You're tired and bothered. If we *must* discuss these things, let's leave them until we're unruffled to start with. I don't want us to quarrel—not until we must. Leave Ravage alone just now. You don't know him, you don't understand him. Of course you're not going to dictate to me who my friends should be. I leave *you* quite free, don't I?"

He had apparently not been listening to her. She was amazed at that, but how good-looking he was, especially when he was angry as he was now, his dark face flushed, his slim body carried tautly, as though it were the physical expression of his rising temper. Yes, if only he wouldn't be so stupid!

"And there's another thing," he went on in the same husky, childish voice: "you never answered my mother's letter."

She tapped the chair with her hand.

"No. I asked you to tell your mother that it was much better that we shouldn't meet or write to one another any more."

"Yes, but she thought she must make one more try, so she wrote the very kindest letter . . ."

"How do you know?"

"She told me the sort of thing that it was."

"Then you know more about it than I do." Rosalind looked up at him, laughing. "I didn't read it."

"That was unkind of you, Rosalind."

"No, not unkind, merely prudent. If I had read it I should
have been driven to answer it. My answer would only have
led to more trouble. Remember, Tom, that what, in a letter, would seem sweet and kind to you might only be irritating and provoking to me. That's just our trouble all the
time—we don't see things alike."

He turned to her, flung out his hands. "By God! I don't
understand you! I understand you less than the first day I
met you. Granted that I'm stupid and exasperating, granted
that my mother is old-fashioned and foolishly fond of me;
granted that Janet is, by your standard, sentimental; and
that Wildherne, the Duke, the Duchess, and the rest are
so outside everything that seems to you real, that they're
like tiresome ghosts to you; granted that all that Wintersmoon stands for is to you narrow and hopelessly conserva-
tive—granted all this, why shouldn't you, all the same, take
some steps in our direction, try to realise that there are
other people in the world beside you and your set, come
outside yourself for a minute—why not?"

He broke off breathlessly. He hadn't intended to be oratori-
cal, but his foreign blood often made him so, and then
Rosalind laughed at him, imitating him, and then things
were worse than they had been before. This time, however,
she did not laugh at him. She nodded her head, looking
thoughtfully into the fire.

"Yes, there's a lot in what you say, Tom. Why shouldn't
I? If I'd been smacked properly when I was a kid I dare
say I should. Half the trouble with women like me to-day is
that we *weren't* smacked. But facts are facts. We can't
change our views of things. We ought perhaps to pretend
that we can, but we don't like pretending about anything.
We would rather that you didn't pretend either. We aren't
indignant with you for leading the life that you want to,
why should you for ever be so indignant about us?"

"Yes, you are," Tom interrupted hotly. "You can't bear
what you call my stupidity. You are for ever girding at
it."

"Of course," she agreed frankly. "I think you're after

old dead things and I think it's a pity, you being as nice
as you are. But I don't get excited by this as you do by my
friends and opinions. You'll grant me my calmness, Tom."

"Yes, and I hate your calmness," he went on. "It's as
though we none of us mattered to you at all. Janet and I
love you passionately. You don't consider us in any way
whatever. I'll leave myself for a moment outside it. There's
Janet, who's given nearly all her life to you. She wants
love terribly. She's one of those people—there are some in
the world—who are only alive when they are needed and
loved. Even her baby doesn't need her. There's a sort of
bond between him and his father—that happens sometimes
too—that keeps everyone else outside. If you gave her a
little love it would help her over this difficult time marvellously. But you don't. You say that I'm always driving you
down to Wintersmoon. I do nothing of the sort. You are
hardly ever down there. And now you've spent a week there,
and come back grumbling about the dull time you've had
there instead of considering Janet and whether you've given
her any fun."

He was on dangerous ground now. Had he been less intent on his own argument he would have watched her more
closely. He might have at any rate known that with Rosalind
it was when her conscience was uneasy that she was unjust.

She answered him quietly enough. "What do you really
know, Tom, about Janet and myself? You don't know
very much about me although you've lived with me for a
considerable time, and you know nothing at all about
Janet.

"I don't think, as a matter of fact, she'd thank you very
much for your defence of her. You picture her as a kind
of sentimental old maid who is longing to be loved. She
isn't anything of the kind. And I, as a matter of fact, am
counting very little to her just now. Her whole mind is
centred on Wildherne and the baby. I can't help her there
and she knows it.

"As regards your mother, Tom. I'm very sorry, but
we're simply hopelessly incompatible, and there I don't

altogether blame myself. She'd have been jealous of who-ever it was you married."

A new hardness came into her voice. "I know you blame me, Tom, for everything that has gone wrong with our marriage. I was to blame at the beginning for agreeing to marry you. I knew then that it wouldn't do, but I liked you then as I like you now, and I was guilty of having that romantic, sentimental idea that people change one another. Superficially a little perhaps, but basically never. Yes, I was wrong in that, but since then—well, examine yourself a little. Are the faults in these things ever only on one side? Haven't you taken your mother's view of me a little, per-haps without knowing it? Come now. Be fair."

The sudden coldness in her voice alarmed him out of his anger. He was shot through with that old, old fear that he was going to lose her, a fear that struck straight to his heart, piercing it with a sharp, constricting pain. If he lost her, if she left him—a ghastly, shivering blackness opened then in front of him, something acidly nihilistic that came from his Russian strain.

He knelt beside her chair.

"Rosalind, darling, you're right. Only to-day as I was coming along I was thinking how much of it all had been my fault. It isn't that I haven't tried, but the more I try the more I seem to irritate you. You say that you oughtn't to have married me. But you ought, you ought. I couldn't live without you, Rosalind. I know that that's a cowardly thing to say, but it's true. If you left me——"

She broke in upon him.

"Oh, don't say that, don't say that! It *is* cowardly and weak. We oughtn't to depend on people like that. It isn't fair on them. You're yourself, yourself! If I *did* leave you, you're a man with your own life, your own courage. It's that sentimentality in you, Tom, that's always coming between us. Snap your fingers at me, be free of me, and then we'll be friends as we ought to be."

"Free of you!" He put his arms around her, drawing her to him, burying his face in her lovely hair. "Never! So long as I live I'm yours—my life only exists because you are there. Once I had ambitions. I've got them still, perhaps, somewhere, but only if you want me to have them, care for me to get on. I love you so that I'm your slave, and I'm proud that I am. At least there's been one thing in my life that's real and true. Leave me! That is the end of me if you do."

She pulled herself away from him, dragging her body from his hands. "Ah, no, no, no! It's just this that I can't bear! Why must we behave like children still? Can't you understand me a *little?* After all this time are you so blind? Don't you understand that people don't matter to me, that I can't help it, that I'm made like that? Give me an idea that's interesting and there's something to catch hold of—but people, people—one's relation to them, their relations to oneself, whether I love Janet or she me, whether you adore me or I don't adore you, whether one day I'll run off with Charles Ravage or perhaps I won't—I tell you, Tom, it all means nothing to me. I like you, but I want to get past you to something real, some ideas about life, some work that shows results, and you tie me, you hold me back. We've slept together for over a year—is it any novelty for us to create scenes over? My body. I tell you I'm sick of my body and all this constant talk about it. What's my body? A knock from a hammer can turn it into something odious, disgusting. We must be meant to get more out of life than that. We *are* meant to and I will.

"Go on with your work, Tom, and I'll get hold of mine. Then we'll be friends and respect one another. But all this clinging, holding, depending—I detest it—and so, by this time, should you!"

"I love you," he said very low. "I can't help myself. Love isn't what you say. Love *is* personal, the need for one another. You don't love me at all if you can talk as you do."

She was near the door. She turned.

"Well, then, I don't. Realise it and we'll get along better."

"You don't love me?"

He moistened his lips with his tongue.

"Not if you mean all this sentimental nonsense by love."

"You never have loved me?"

She shook her head impatiently. "Oh, leave me alone, Tom. I warned you not to have a row to-night. Don't go on with these ridiculous questions."

He came nearer to her.

"You have never loved me?"

"No. Nor anyone. We're talking like a cook and her policeman. Our silly talk has made me all sticky. We're friends, Tom, but I warn you that if you try to hold me as you do, to hedge me in with sentiment and reproach me and make scenes every other hour—one day you'll find me gone. I warn you."

"Very well, then," he said staring at her as though he had never seen her before. "Go. Go. . . . I won't keep you."

She left the room, quietly closing the door behind her.

He stood there, still staring in front of him; then, his body quivering, he went to the mantel-shelf and held on to it to steady himself.

"Oh, my God," he said, whispering. "What can I do?"

CHAPTER V

THE STREETS IN SPRING

WILDHERNE stood for a moment outside the Garrick
Theatre, slipping, as it were, from one suit of clothes
to another. The clothes that he had just been wearing had
been supplied for him by Ruth Draper who, for two hours
and a half, had enchanted him so completely that he had not
considered himself at all. Enchanted was the word!

Leaving the theatre like a dark velvety hole behind him,
a cave that had flung him out into this trembling, translucent pool of shifting light, he could swear that that stage in
there had been peopled with moving and gesticulating figures—that trembling Italian peasant in the black shawl,
the old Eastside New York woman before the magistrate, the
fashionable English hostess displaying her garden, the crowd
of noisy children around their mother's bed, the wounded
tottering into the station on the Western Plains. Had there,
in the midst of all these, moved that quiet, dark, reserved
little figure, so utterly without ostentation, so entirely without self-importance?

On the busy pavement people jostled him. The cars swung
by, flashed and swung again. He moved to the shelter in
the middle of the street and looked up at the windows of
the Zoffany opposite him. Should he go up there for half
an hour or back to Halkin Street and at once, at that question, other figures superseded those of the theatre, figures
not more real but more insistently dependent on his own
activity—his father, mother, Janet, Humphrey? Should he
go up? No, he would return to Halkin Street—yes, even
though Humphrey was down at Wintersmoon.

As he walked past the Leicester Galleries into the wider
waters of Leicester Square a figure insistently kept pace with

him. This was the waitress whom just now he had en
countered in the theatre—the waitress of that Western
Plains station, busy in her duty but torn with agony about
the fate of her lover—never for an instant relaxing, taut like
a bow-string, but tender, maternal, mother to the little
broken, tragic world around her, so much for them, for
herself the lover only, fierce, strong, unyielding.

This figure had become, in some odd sort of way and
quite against his will, Janet. He did not, just then, wish to
think about Janet.

He was yet young enough to imagine that by banishing
something unpleasant or ungrateful from his mind he slew
it. But banishment is the most dangerous of all insults and
the banished always return.

Everything was all right with Janet. That was the final
word. But this figure walking now beside him, silent, un
challenging, but unflaggingly eloquent—with her all was no
well. She was simply an image created for him by a great
artist. He did not slay her by that artifice; she was still there
persistent, at his side. What, anyway, had this girl of the
Western Plains to do with Janet? What in common? The
question then leapt up at him—Janet is unhappy. Why?

"Why?" asked the little waitress, staring up into his
face. "Why is Janet unhappy?"

"I don't know," he answered her. He went into the little
square and sat down beneath the statue of Shakespeare
upon whose head two pigeons, perched, looked like a Scots
man's bonnet.

Next to Wildherne was a down-and-out with holes in
his boots. His eyes were fixed on the pigeons. Shakespeare
pirouetted, one leg straight, one knee bent. The sun softly
glinted through a vapour of silver gauze, and there was
a sniff of flowers in the air. The traffic rumbled very softly

Why was Janet unhappy? How did he know that she
was? She gave him no sign. He had taken it for granted
He had been perfectly comfortable about it? How did he
know? He moved restlessly, and the faint, dim blue patches
of sky played hide-and-seek with Shakespeare and the
pigeons. . . .

He had kept to his side of the bargain. No one could reproach him. She could not have had a better companion
and friend than he had been to her. He had been on her
side in everything. He was careful not to leave her alone
when his inclination was always to go to Humphrey. He
yielded Humphrey up to her on every possible occasion. He
was good to her friends, that little woman Katherine Mark,
for instance; he was as polite as possible to sister Rosalind
(difficult this); Janet had only to ask for things and she
got them (only she never did ask for things) . . . yes, yes,
yes . . . he gave her everything except love, and that he
could not give her. But as she did not love him, his love,
had he had it to offer her, must have been an affront to
her.

He had loved, in all his life, only his father and Diana
and Humphrey, and the last of these had killed the second.
But Janet? Could he ever feel for her the heat and desire
and longing that he had known in such different fashion
for these others, his father, his mistress, and his son? He
moved once more uneasily and the flecked palely-silver blue
moved with him. The pigeons, motionless on Shakespeare's
head, were observing him. Could it be that they were laughing at him? Wildherne, of course, did not think so. He
was thinking too deeply even to notice them. But the down-
and-out rubbed his stubbly cheek reflectively. That was no
end of a toff sitting next to him. Should he press his little
story upon him? The pigeons made him uneasy. He knew
something about birds.

Were they giggling together there? Is not a solemn, rather
priggish young Englishman something to smile at? Something touching too. For Wildherne, though he were solemn
and ignorant of life, was also warm of heart and eager for
justice. But now he was being moulded by a new experience,
moulded by his love for his son. He would not have believed before this that he could be so enchanted, so enraptured!

Before the child came he had tutored himself to every
possible caution. He was not to think his child the wonder
of wonders as so many parents did. He was not to be dis-

appointed because it was unbeautiful, unclever, uncharming.
He would not abuse it too harshly nor pet it too warmly.
And then, behold, when it came, from the first instant when
from Mrs. Bone's arms it had looked up and gurgled in
his face, it had belonged to him, been part of him, body and
soul. There was something exceptional here. No one could
deny it. From the very beginning the child had gone to
him. The baby had recognised the peculiar bond between
them from that first glance. Everyone was aware of this.
Something strange in their union.

It was a kind of triumph for Wildherne. No one had
ever thought of him as remarkable. His father had loved
him, but had perhaps been a little disappointed in him.
Diana had kindly tolerated him. His wife had emphasised
again and again that she did not love him. But the child
found him perfection, worshipped him, waited always for
him, wanted only him.

Was it unnatural, then, that Janet should be hidden a
little behind this glorious happiness that he and Humphrey
were creating together? He was devoted to her, she was
the best companion a man could have. Why should she not
be contented, then? Perhaps—and the idea was a new one—
she wanted more of her child? She was jealous because
Humphrey went to him instead of to her? And yet it did
not seem like that. She seemed often to prefer to be alone
with Wildherne.

Women were odd. How could you tell what was going
on in their minds? For ever wanting something that they
had not got! Yes. "Damned odd," he said aloud, considering for the first time the pigeons.

"Beg pardon, sir," the down-and-out began, but Wildherne got up and moved on. He was smiling. He had not
even seen the down-and-out. He was thinking of Humphrey.

"Bloody toff," said the down-and-out. "It's this kind
of thing makes you a Communist——"

He shuffled off. The pigeons trembled their feathers in the
sunny, silvery air.

But moving did not rid Wildherne of his trouble. The

ttle waitress from the Western Plains was yet at his side
sking him about Janet.

He had set in motion a complicated tangle when, on that
ight at the old lady's party, he had once again asked Janet
o marry him. How many lives had he involved with that one
imple sentence? His father's, his mother's, Janet's, Rosa-
nd's, Tom Seddon's, and Tom Seddon's mother's, young
Humphrey, Caroline Marsh, Miss Crabbage, Mr. Pomeroy
—and through these how many others, and through the
thers how many more? You might say that, if you liked,
bout every action in life, but in his own case he had an
dd impression that his marriage with Janet was leading
ertain lives towards crises that were not trivial but fundamentally and permanently important. Already that initial
ction of his had led to his own strained relations with his
ather, to Janet's unhappiness, to the unhappiness of Rosa-
nd, Tom, and Tom's mother. A little wind of dismay
eemed to blow through him. He only was happy, and in his
wn case, if anything touched Humphrey——

That thought paralysed him so finally that he stood where
e was, on the edge of the pavement just outside the Criter-
on Theatre, and for a moment was blind and deafened to
ll sound.

When he came to himself again he summoned a taxi. He
anted to escape from this spring air. It made him uneasy,
pprehensive. And he wanted to reassure himself about
anet. He did not wish to be uncomfortable about her. A
ttle ghost that he must exorcise. But ghosts were so elu-
ve.

He found them all having tea in the long drawing-room.
he figures, scattered, looked faded against the Morris wall-
aper, and the fires burned dimly. Yes, there they all were
s always—his mother, Janet, Miss Crabbage, Mr. Pomeroy,
aroline Marsh, old Mrs. Deedman from the Warrington
Iission, Lady Agatha Stanley, mother of most of the Lon-
on Crèches, the old Duchess of Moorsom, and the Dean
f St. Blum's, that tall and angular-faced ecclesiastic whose
rticles in the *Daily Messenger* were so widely read and so
ell paid.

Nearly everyone was talking, and Wildherne could s[ee] that his mother was very happy. Now was she in her eleme[nt] indeed. She knew just how to deal with all these peopl[e,] how to push them all into the positions that she wante[d] them to occupy. She would flatter Lady Agatha about h[er] crèches, argue with the old Duchess about foreign missio[ns] (because the old Duchess, who was looking like a pea-gre[en] haystack, loved argument), and congratulate the Dean [on] his brilliant rebuke to night clubs (in her private opinion h[e] should have been attending to his duties as Dean instead [of] earning money as a vulgar journalist). She was not insi[n]cere in these things, she meant what she said when she sa[id] it, because the Cause justified anything. Wildherne som[e]times called his mother the Little Jesuit, and to her face. Sh[e] liked the title.

But his mind to-night was set upon Janet. He wanted [to] remove his own intangible uneasiness. So when he had said [a] word to the pea-green Duchess, the Dean, and Mr. Pomero[y] he went over to where she was standing, a little in the shado[w] and alone.

The odd new feeling that during the last hour he ha[d] had about her caused her to appear to him a little change[d.] He valued her—oh yes, he did—immensely. Her height, h[er] carriage, the nobility of her brow, the beauty and tende[r]ness of her eyes, her repose and honesty, these were all he[r] as they always were, but to-night there was something [a] little touching, a little lonely too.

It was only chance that at the moment she should b[e] standing by herself outside the animated circle, but it was a[s] though there was truly some reproach for him in that.

Instinctively, putting his hand through her arm, he dre[w] her a little towards the light.

"Dearest," he began eagerly, looking into her face, h[is] back to the others, "you should have been there. She wa[s] wonderful."

"Yes, I do wish that I could have gone," she answere[d] gently. "I always seem just to miss her. It was the same la[st] autumn, when I was at Wintersmoon and I couldn't come u[p.] But to-day I had promised Katherine Mark to go with her t[o]

eet her brother-in-law. It had been arranged, and I couldn't
et out of it."

"Well, it *was* a pity," he went on eagerly. "She was better
han ever. She's improved the old ones, and somehow a
heatre enlarges her. It's marvellous the way she does it all
n her own, without any help at all."

"I'm so glad you enjoyed it," Janet said. "My afternoon
as interesting too. He was so nice and simple."

"He? Who?" asked Wildherne.

"Peter Westcott the writer. I told you this morning about
im, and you said you'd liked one or two of his books. He's
tterly unspoiled although he's had a lot of success. I *do* like
when people aren't spoiled."

Wildherne was irritated a little. Why was it that it was
nly strangers who showed interest in what you had been
oing? One's intimate friends and relations never cared at
ll. And he was not sure of this tendency of Janet's to mingle
n these Bohemian circles. And he was a little jealous, too,
ecause he was never invited. These novelists always made a
ass of women, and women always flattered them. Who was
his Westcott anyway?

But she did then a very charming thing. She led him right
way from the others over to the other fire where nobody
ast then was. She drew him down beside her on to the little
ofa. Holding his hand in hers and talking very low she said:

"I'm so glad you've come back. I've been thinking of you
ll the afternoon. I don't know why, but I haven't been able
o get you out of my head. Do you know, Wildherne, we
ren't alone enough. We aren't really. There is always some-
ne. Now let's have to-morrow entirely to ourselves. I've only
ne engagement, and I can easily break it. I'm sure you can
reak whatever you have. I want to take you to my old curi-
sity man. And in the afternoon we might go right away
omewhere. Haven't you been feeling the spring in the air
ll day? The streets have been simply shining with it. Oh,
Wildherne, let's have to-morrow to ourselves."

He was strangely touched. Her hand was trembling in his.
His heart was oddly beating. But he said:

"The only thing is, Janet, that I'd thought I'd go down to

Wintersmoon to-morrow morning. The boy's all alone dow[n] there. Of course, he's quite all right with Mrs. Bone an[d] Hignett, but it makes me a bit uneasy."

"We're going down the day after to-morrow in any case,[”] Janet said. "That's what we had arranged, wasn't it?"

"Yes, I know." He hesitated. Her trembling hand cause[d] his to close tightly over it.

"All right," he said, smiling. "That's a bargain. We'll hav[e] to-morrow all to ourselves."

When one has been granted by a friend some urgent desir[e] one hurries on to speak carelessly of other things, partly be[-] cause one wishes the request to seem not too important, an[d] partly because one is afraid that even now a refusal ma[y] come if one lingers on the dangerous ground. So Janet bega[n] eagerly now to talk of the weather, of little odds and end[s] of chatter, of poor old Mrs. Beddoes whose husband was i[n] bed with a fever.

Wildherne wondered at her agitation. It was suddenly a[s] though he did not know her at all. He had often made wit[h] her the mistake that all men who are very happily marrie[d] or are supremely devoted to one mistress make—he squeeze[d] all women into one pattern. His pattern was Diana.

A Diana not in love with him was the psychology, poo[r] young man, by which he tested Janet. Also because he ha[d] gone to Eton and Oxford, and had received therefore n[o] education, his imagination with regard to women was lat[e] eighteenth-century. He thought in terms of Lady Hamilto[n] or Lady Caroline Lamb. He was too old for the post-wa[r] generation of sexual frankness. He knew, in fact, nothin[g] about women at all.

But his heart was stirred by Janet to-night as it had neve[r] been before. Why? What moved him? She seemed to wis[h] to say something to him. It was as though she had some con[-] fession to make. He felt her heart beating close to his. It wa[s] almost as though she were threatened by some evil.

"Janet," he asked, almost whispering. "Are you unhappy[?] Is anything disturbing you?"

For a moment it seemed that she would speak. She stare[d]

to his eyes, confusing him. Then she drew back a little, smiled, and shook her head.

"No," she said. "Everything is all right. Everything except Rosalind, that is."

He shook his head impatiently. "Always Rosalind. What is it now?"

"No, you aren't fair to her, Wildherne. No one is."

"Fair to her! . . ." Wildherne checked himself. "No, perhaps I'm not. But she wasn't very amiable down at Winsmoon this last time. I don't envy Tom his job."

"Tom wasn't ever the right man for her. He has cared for her too much. Rosalind is always better with people toward whom she has to make the move. Wildherne, do you realise that Rosalind would never have married Tom had I not married you? That makes us a little responsible, doesn't it?"

This oddly chimed with his own thoughts of the afternoon, so he answered brusquely: "I don't see it. Rosalind couldn't have expected you to remain single for ever."

"No. But she would herself have married—more slowly, more cautiously—someone better suited to her than Tom had I still been there to keep her company."

But he shook his head impatiently. "Rosalind's old enough to manage her own affairs without our being responsible for her. That isn't our look-out."

He was aware that someone was listening. The talk from the other fireplace had been flowing so softly and evenly that it was as though he and Janet had been enclosed in some sheltered maze of their own. Someone now had broken in upon them. He looked up sharply, resentfully, and saw Caroline Marsh, her short-sighted eyes stuck into a book, standing under a lamp a pace away.

He bent forward and kissed Janet's cheek.

"Come, dear. We should be sociable a little and help mother." But for a moment, as they stood together before they moved forward, she put her hand on his arm:

"That's settled, then? We have to-morrow to ourselves?"

"Settled," he answered, his mind still on Caroline Marsh. To-day everything seemed doubly significant to him. Were

Ruth Draper's sharp eyes still sharpening his vision? Caro
line Marsh at least could have no significance. Janet disliked
her, and she in return disliked Janet, he supposed. But i
did not matter. Caroline Marsh was nothing, less than noth
ing.

They came into the circle by the fire and his mothe
greeted him with "Wildherne, come and listen. Mrs. Deed
man is telling us such interesting things about her Mis
sion."

Mrs. Deedman, who resembled a good-natured shark, al
teeth and kind intentions, continued in a trembling eage
voice about the two new billiard-rooms, the girls' reading
class, and the probable date for the opening of the new
lavatories. She addressed all her remarks to Mr. Pomeroy
feeling apparently that he would sympathise with everything
Miss Crabbage regarded her severely, thinking undoubtedl
that it was at her Duchess that Mrs. Deedman should b
looking.

"And so," Mrs. Deedman said, her teeth running forward
cow-catcher-wise, "of course we *had* to tell Mr. Bartholo
mew that that couldn't possibly be allowed. It wouldn't hav
mattered so much had it been only the younger girls———"

Wildherne, regarding the group, wondered, as so ofte
he had wondered before, how they could be so serious abou
it all, and then, after that, considered the amount of goo
they were doing in so many directions, and he, in spite o
noble intentions, a love of England and English poetry, wa
doing no good anywhere.

Then he reflected that this group was odd. It was possibl
at the head of all the groups of the kind in England, and it
actions, resolves, discussions rippled like the circles from
stone flung into a pond on and on to unmeasurable shore
Two Duchesses, Mr. Pomeroy, Miss Crabbage; and behin
them were not only all the workers for moral good in Eng
land, but also all those old families, noble and destitute
struck suddenly with poverty, lands sold and divided, thei
huge houses splitting into flats, but unchanged in them
selves, unaware of Jazz and Cocktails, very vaguely aware o
Bolshevists and Communism, believing in the things i

which they had always believed, standing fast to their traditions, refusing to see what they did not wish to see.

His people, the Purefoys, although not as yet penniless,
were like that. Could he and others of his generation turn all
this into something that would weld with the new post-war
world and make it finer, or must it go as people like Rosalind
and her friends wished it to go? Had he stuff enough in
him to preserve it for Humphrey and Humphrey's time? His
father, his mother, old Agatha Stanley, the old Moorsom
woman, Aunt Alice, how fine they were in their own fashion
with their integrity, their standards, their courage—could
he save them and perpetuate them? Yes, if he had Humphrey to fight for, and if he had Janet for his friend. He
turned round to look for her and found that she was gone.

He moved out of the circle as though to look for her and
almost walked into Caroline Marsh.

"Sorry, Caroline," he said. (What a clumsy creature she
was, for ever in the way!)

"That's all right, Lord Poole," she said in her silly giggling fashion, and then went on, blinking her sandy eyebrows at him. "When are you going down to Wintersmoon?
To-morrow morning?"

"No," he answered, thinking still about Janet, "day after
to-morrow."

"Oh!" she said.

"What do you mean by OH?" he asked her.

"Oh, nothing."

"Caroline, you are sometimes so maddening that murder
is the only cure."

She giggled again. She seemed always to be pleased by
the half-teasing, half-contemptuous attitude that he had now
for years adopted towards her.

"Really, Lord Poole! Murder! What a sensation there'd
be! Why, I'd be quite a celebrity at last!"

"Yes. That's the only way you're ever likely to be. Come
now, Caroline, what did you mean by saying OH?"

"I didn't mean anything. You always say I'm so silly—
well, there's a proof of it. Perhaps I was thinking of that
darling child all alone down there."

"Humphrey? Oh, he's all right."

"You never know." Her eyes danced maliciously. H
laughed at her and despised her. Well, here at least she ha
power over him and could spite that hateful Lady Poole .
well.

"He didn't look quite the thing to me two days ago.
wondered myself you let him go down."

"He was all right." Wildherne moved impatiently. "Wh
what did you think was the matter with him?"

"Oh, nothing. A little cold."

"Well, it's warmer weather now. Spring to-day. You ca
feel it in the streets."

"All the same," she turned away from him towards th
window, "if I felt about him as you do——"

He turned after her, catching her arm. "Look here, Care
line, is all this just a joke on your part, or is there somethin
in it?"

She looked up at him, blinking her eyes, and rubbing th
side of her nose with her fingers. "I know nothing. Ho
should I? But he's a dear little boy, and I'd like to be wit
him if I was his father."

She went off.

Nasty malicious creature, but, as he hurried back to sa
good-bye to the old Duchess, uneasiness was sweeping u
in him like an overwhelming wave.

She was wagging a finger at him. "You should take mor
interest in these things, Wildherne. Do you good. You'r
growing selfish."

"I love being selfish," he answered her with a smile.

"You weren't always. And if you're selfish long enoug
no one will love you."

"Oh, in these days," he answered, "it's only the selfish wh
are loved. They're so much less bother to everyone."

But meanwhile with every moment his alarm increased
That was probably true enough. The child had had a cold—
very slight, of course, but this sudden spring weather—*that*
the dangerous time! Who knew whether Mrs. Bone was tak
ing proper care? Odd how little Janet seemed to mind. Sh
would stay up here for weeks without any anxiety.

The child would be missing him. Even Caroline Marsh,
upid though she was, saw that. He saw Humphrey stand-
ıg on the lawn in front of the house, his legs apart, asking
ıe peacock where his father was.

Most people would call this silly sentimentality, of course.
ut then most people did not understand the special rela-
on there was between himself and his boy—the extraordi-
ıry relationship. Even Janet did not understand it.

The boy was needing him. He must go down to-morrow as
e had originally intended. Janet would not mind. They
ould have their day together later. Women never really
ıinded these things. They put up a little sentimental mask
ıd grinned derisively behind it. (When he said women he
ıeant Diana.)

Yes, he would go down to-morrow by the early morning
ain.

He was alone in the room with his mother and Miss
rabbage.

"Mother, dear, I think I'll go down to-morrow morning
ɔ Wintersmoon."

"Very well, dear. Is Janet going with you?"

"I don't know. I'll ask her."

Of course that was the way. Janet could come down with
im. They could have their day together at Wintersmoon
ıstead of in London. Exactly the same. Janet should go
ith him and inspect the new cottages at Betwhistle.

On his way upstairs to his room he paused at his father's
ɔor. Nothing was worrying him more just now than the
trange attitude that the old man wore to him. Their rela-
ons had never been so seriously strained in all their lives
ɔgether before. And of what it was all about Wildherne had
ɔt the slightest idea. And he was far too proud to ask.

But just because of the restraint, in an odd sort of way he
ɔved the old man more than ever. He went in. The Duke
ɾas as usual sunk in his huge chair, his white head bent over
ıis book. He looked up.

"Hullo, Wildherne!"

"Hullo, father! . . . By the way, I'm going down to
Wintersmoon early to-morrow morning."

The Duke put his book down. "To-morrow? But I though[you were here to-morrow."

"I've changed my mind."

"But Janet's just been in here telling me that you wer[going to have a splendid day in town together to-morrow."

"I know. But I've changed my mind."

"And Janet?"

"She can come down to Wintersmoon with me if sh[likes."

"Oh—if she likes. Very grand. Janet's not to be consulted[I suppose?"

Wildherne was irritated.

"Of course."

"And what of your promise to her?"

"My promise?"

"Yes. She asked you especially to have a day alone wit[her here."

"We can have a day alone at Wintersmoon, I suppose."

The Duke got up and stood, his legs spread, in front o[the fire. "You're not very intelligent or perceptive, are you[Wildherne?"

Wildherne was furious.

"I'm damned if I know what you mean, sir."

"No, and you don't know what women mean either. [know why you're going down. To coddle that boy of yours[If you thought of that wife of yours a little more and tha[boy of yours a little less it would do no harm."

"Thank you," Wildherne answered. "When I want you[advice, father, I'll ask for it."

He turned and left the room. Half way up the stairs he[met Janet coming down.

"Phew!" he cried to her, laughing. "I've just had a rating[Father's in a splendid rage."

"Why, what have you done?" she asked him.

"I only told him I was going down to Wintersmoon to-[morrow morning after all. It seemed to upset him terribly[By the way, I hope you don't mind, Janet. I'm a little anxious[about Humphrey."

"Oh, you promised!"

The disappointment in her voice was so acute that he was himself ashamed, and because he was ashamed he was angry.

"Why, what a fuss you're all making! For the matter of that, you can come down with me to Wintersmoon. We can have our day there instead of here."

"You promised," she repeated, her voice dull and colourless.

"I don't understand any of you," he answered, breaking past her up the stairs. "Whatever I do seems to be wrong."

Alone in his room her face haunted him. Why did she care so deeply?

Oh, well—his obstinacy was reinforced. She could come with him or not as she pleased. If a father mightn't go to see his own son——

Yes, indeed, things were at a pretty pass.

CHAPTER VI

THE DUKE IS UNHAPPY

THE Duke slept badly that night: nothing odd about tha
As he slipped through life sleep crept away from hi
wagging a finger at him: "You don't need so much of m
now. Don't complain. I've treated you well enough in th
past."

He had never needed very much, and had formed lon
ago the habit of walking through his three adjoining room
—the bed-room, the little dressing-room where Wildhern
had one night slept, the small breakfast-room—backward
and forwards wrapped in a high-collared dressing-gown o
white wool, thinking, talking aloud, sitting down for twent
minutes to read, talking aloud again: nothing new about thi

But to-night he was distressed and—something infinitel
rare with him—afraid. Afraid of what? Afraid, as one is a
three in the morning, of everything and of nothing.

This trouble with Wildherne had, for months now, in
creasingly distressed and irritated him, and in the cold chi
of three o'clock standing outside himself he cursed the Eng
lish reticences of himself and his son. Well, this reticenc
should continue no longer. Last night's short dialogue ha
determined him. Wildherne and he should at least under
stand one another. But understand what?

Here was the trouble that kept him, like an old growlin
bear, rambling up and down his cage. What if he were com
pelled to tell himself that Wildherne had bitterly disappointe
him? If facts forced him to see that Wildherne had bee
false to all his trusts—to his mother, his father, his wife—
had the main light and pride of his life forsaken him? Wha
else had he but his wife and his son? And if his son wa
not . . . ?

318

He was stricken with a cold shaft of that light that again and again breaks on all of us—the light of our absolute aloneness, so that the ties that we fancy that we have made, the work that we believe that we have sustained, all these fall from us.

His wife and his son? His wife? He saw—in this same chilly awareness—a fantastic picture of rows and rows of high-collared clergy, upright women, good women, energetic women, sitting in endless array back, back into cloudy distance. All so good, so staunch, so self-sacrificing, so honest—and so useless?

No, not useless for the good that they did, but useless to him, and oh! worse than useless, because of the cloud of business, preoccupation, arrangement, that they introduced between his wife and himself.

His wife and he loved one another. But did they? Now, in this clear morning light, did they? What is love? Is it this adjusted, reasonable, comfortable affection, so pliable that it can fit with no discomfort into the interstices of other preoccupations? When, now, did his wife and he face one another? What had their long life together brought them, his wife and he? Love?

It seemed in that cruel moment that he had neither wife nor son, that he had no one. It seemed also that all his life had been wasted. He had been given position and energies and sufficient wealth, and had done nothing at all with these things. He saw himself as an idle and lazy coward. Yes, coward, because for the last twenty years he had not liked the turn that the world was taking and so had stood apart from it, neither helping nor hindering.

And now he is to die. That personal consciousness of death. It is *he* who is going to die. No one else. The shiver of that personal consciousness. The sudden catch of the breath. Beneath his woollen robe he was cold. His body seemed to withdraw into itself, the skin dry and tight, and then to grow smaller and smaller until the woollen robe with the high collar stood up, stiff of itself and alive, more alive than the little pea-nut of a body detached inside it.

He will die, and soon.

He raised his white head and shook it like a lion who sniffs danger. And to-morrow he will have everything straight with Wildherne.

Next morning before nine, when they all breakfasted, Wildherne was gone. Janet was very quiet.

"I think, my dear," the Duke said, "I shall go down to Wintersmoon this morning by the eleven. Won't you come with me?"

"No, father, thank you. I shall go down to-morrow as we originally settled."

They were standing in his study. He put his hand on her shoulder.

"Don't take it too hardly, my dear, that he went down this morning. He wouldn't realise that that plan for to-day would mean so much to you. He's very young in some ways. He can only think of one thing at a time and he does adore that boy. Too much, as I tell him——"

"Ah," she said, smiling, "you needn't make excuses for him."

He felt that she had withdrawn herself from him that morning, from him and from all of them. Her pride was stiffening her. She would not be indebted to any one of them.

Suddenly he felt acutely his old age. He couldn't be bothered with any of them. They were too young for him and too selfish. He was tired, more tired than he had ever been in his life before. So he smiled at Janet, kissed her, and caught the train to Wintersmoon.

Those times in life when one is brought up sharply to be aware of one's short tenure of it are landmarks. With the Duke two had been memorable—once when, before his marriage, making some terms with an insurance company he had been medically examined by them. He had thought himself at that time in the very perfection of physical health, but they had discovered something wrong with him and had refused the policy. Most vividly he could recall his astonishment, sense of personal affront, hurt vanity, but above all a sudden precipitate looking down into a black, cavernous space, he insecure, helpless above it.

So later when in Switzerland he had actually for an hour

or more so hung above an unfathomable crevasse—plenty of
time then for thinking, but now the indignation, the astonishment was gone. All that was needed was a quick adjustment
to acquiescence.

Here now to-day, in the train, was his third occasion, the
definite certainty that he had not long to live. Whence it had
come, stealing towards him, greyly veiled through the night,
he did not know, but come it had. His life was almost done.

The day was very lovely; there are times when England is
more tenderly beautiful than any other country can ever be,
a time of small fields and thick shadowy trees, soil cultivated
through many centuries, roads that have run from point to
point for a thousand years, and over this ancient imperturbability the commencement of spring trembles and shines as
though it had never made its preparations before.

The sky this afternoon was flooded with light colour—
flooded because the shadows of primrose and shell pink
floated in over the pale blue like tides, sweeping forward
then again retreating, leaving the sky a shining marble shore
as the sand is when the tide has flooded.

The earth caught the reflection of this pale gold and rose,
the trees dark but glowing, the fields restless with light, the
hedges holding the faint spring sun so that the sense of glitter
was there, the suggestion of it without the actuality.

As the afternoon advanced bands of golden clouds
threaded their way through the watery tracks, and as the
land became darker the sky was lighter, washing in its surface colour to pale shimmering white, rosy above the horizon, daisy-tipped. The train became intimate with the country, the hedges, fields, and cottages clustering close to it,
watching its progress with a family interest, the lights in the
windows humorously greeting it. The day had been good.
You could hear the soil sleepily lie back, another day's work
towards spring well accomplished.

In the twilight the first stars were very bright, the air
having the freshness of running water. The bundles of
bullion had changed into the scattered gold feathers of a
gigantic bird. The ribs stretched in their wafers of trembling yellow and the feathers spread into gigantic patterns

and then suddenly were not. Light fled and the stars rushed out storming the sky, infesting the trees, and in the land all was dark save the quick white gesture of a running stream.

The Duke had an hour of passionate love for England, this soil, these fields, this country so faithful to him through all his life, always there for him with its tender, protecting care, never minding his own infidelities, so old that it was long past grief at the weak faithlessness of men, so strong that it could support for ever their feebleness.

Wildherne must serve England. When he himself was gone Wildherne would serve . . .

Yes, he and his son should talk to-night.

Meanwhile in darkening Wintersmoon Wildherne and Humphrey were utterly happy.

They were together and alone in the nursery. Mrs. Bone was not. The curtains were not drawn and the stars leaped among the trees. Humphrey and Wildherne were wrecked together on the square of green carpet in the middle of the nursery floor. No ships came that way; no signalling would be of any avail. Moreover, this island was volcanic and might at a moment's notice blow up or simply sink below the ocean never to appear again. A desperate spot, but can beggars be choosers when, the ship caught by a monsoon, they find themselves in a raging sea, nothing but a raft to cling to, and a poor sort of a raft at that?

The point really was that they were on this raft *together*. Nothing much matters then. And the nursery fire is warm.

Wildherne was lying flat on his back, his head on two cushions, and Humphrey was seated on his stomach looking for a rescuing sail. Humphrey took in so very much more than belonged to his years. Although he said but little it, was obvious that he had generations of experience behind him and that to be lost on a volcanic island was almost boring in its familiarity. And yet *not* boring, because the first and most glorious thing about Humphrey was his intense enjoyment of everything. He seemed to extract always the very last grain of pleasure from all things in life. If it was something he disliked—to be dressed by Mrs. Bone was a thing that he disliked intensely—he became cynical about it, cynical about the clothes that he must put on, cynical about Mrs. Bone, and above all cynical because he, at this moment physically rather feeble, must for that reason submit to Mrs. Bone's superior strength. But the time would come—and then Mrs. Bone would find him regarding her with a dry, cynical expression that would surprise her very much indeed!

With his father always he gave himself to sheer, absolute enjoyment. They would be, as they were now, completely wrapped in one another's company, Humphrey drumming his shoes on the floor, then leaning back right across his father, pinching his father's chin in his hand and regarding him wickedly out of the corner of his eye to see how he took it.

Wildherne's arm came round the boy and he held him there against his chest, Humphrey's round head hit— pumpetty-pump, pumpetty-pump—by the beatings of his father's heart.

The boy slipped on to the floor and then lay in the curve of his father's body, his head on his father's thigh, his father's arm thrown over his small round body. They both slept while the fire crackled, sputtered, flung up spires of flame then died, growing into ruby banks of light.

So the Duke found them. He stood in the doorway regarding them. How young they both seemed! Wildherne as young as his boy, but beyond that their kinship, their intimate oneness, leapt up at the old man. He had never been quite that with Wildherne. He had never seen a father and son quite so deeply united as Wildherne and Humphrey. This gave him a quick, odd twinge of loneliness; if he felt that now, looking down at them both asleep, how often must Janet have known it?

He could not bear to wake them and was turning softly away when Wildherne's eyes opened. He looked at his father without stirring, dreamily. Then he realised and jumped to his feet, bringing Humphrey with him.

"Hullo, father! What are *you* doing here? No idea you were coming down. Is everything all right?"

"Everything," the Duke answered, smiling.

"Janet?"

"Yes, quite all right."

"Oh, good . . ." he paused. "I'm glad you've come. Nobody met you at the station. Why didn't you wire?"

"No need to. I came up in Braddy Colethorpe's car. Don't hurry. I'll be in your room when Humphrey's disposed of. . . . Well, Humphrey? Got a kiss for your grandfather?"

Humphrey liked immensely his grandfather. He liked the roughness and tickling of his white beard; he liked also the smooth cheek above it, so that when you stroked it, it was like pulling a rabbit's ears. Held in his grandfather's arms he looked at his father. It was nice like this, warm with only men about.

And of course this was the moment when Mrs. Bone *would* appear just when he was secure.

"Now, Master Humphrey," she said, and his cynicism was gratified by perceiving, as he had so often perceived before, how instantly these two men yielded when that soft woman arrived.

He also surrendered. But later on he would show them. . . .

Wildherne in his room confronted his father. He was aggravated because he had been pulled out of his perfect happiness. Not one day was he allowed. They must come bothering. . . .

And then, looking at his father, he fancied him old and tired. It struck him, like a menacing tap just above the heart, that one day his father would die. It was characteristic of Wildherne that he had simply never faced that, making dreams always out of things as they were but never looking ahead except, again dreamily, at a poetic and star-shining England.

For ever so many months now he had been at odds with his father. At times this had made him acutely unhappy, but he had always allowed Humphrey to settle his uneasiness for him. The old man had some bee in his bonnet. That would right itself. But to-night suddenly he was aware that something serious was afoot, something that he would be compelled to face. And, oddly, he was glad. Perhaps in that moment of gladness the future Wildherne, the man Wildherne, the Wildherne who would matter to the world, was born.

"Father," he said. "You've come down here for some reason. What is it?"

"Yes," said the Duke. "I have. There's been something wrong between us during these last months and you know there has. Before we go to bed to-night we are going to clear it."

Wildherne said nothing.

"Well," broke in his father irritably, glaring at him. "Don't you know there has?"

"Yes," said Wildherne.

"I suppose you've liked it, enjoyed it. I suppose it's funny to you that our confidence which has lasted all our lives together should suddenly be broken. Funny! Yes! Most amusing!"

"No," said Wildherne. "There you're unfair, father. I've wanted many times to say something but you know it's hard for us both to speak our minds. We hate scenes."

"Yes, but we're not cowards," broke in the Duke angrily. "Fool though you are you're not a coward."

"Thank you," said Wildherne quietly. "And in what way particularly am I a fool just now?"

"I oughtn't to have said that. I take that back. You're not a fool. You're a damned selfish egoist, which is worse."

Wildherne flushed. "Exactly why?"

The Duke got up from his chair and paced the room.

"Now, you're not going to make me angry however hard you try. You're but a clumsy, ignorant boy who has no idea of other people's feelings."

"Ah, I see," said Wildherne, looking up at this father and smiling. "This is because I didn't stop with Janet to-day but came down here?"

"Was that kind?" his father asked, wheeling round and staring down at him.

"Perhaps not. It was my fault that I didn't realise at the time that it was going to hurt her, and afterwards when I did realise I was too—well, I suppose I was too proud. I did wrong. I'm sorry, and I'll apologise to Janet when she comes."

There was always something about Wildherne's honesty —and it was an Englishman's honesty—as though he had broken some sort of public school code of honour and therefore must own up—that stirred his father. He was in himself aware of just this same code.

But gruffly he said: "Yes, you should. She's coming to-morrow."

"All the same," Wildherne went on, "there's something more in it than this. You've been annoyed with me for months. Why?"

"For the same reason," the Duke answered. "Thinking only of your own wishes and feelings. Your damned selfishness."

"Well, I don't know," said Wildherne, thinking it out. "I wouldn't say that on the whole I'm more selfish than anyone else. We're all selfish."

"Yes, but we oughtn't to be—to those we love. One of the chief reasons that we love them is that they take us away from ourselves."

"You mean," said Wildherne, "that I've been selfish to Janet?"

"Yes. I do."

Wildherne considered this. "That I've failed her? That I haven't been all to her in our married life that I ought to have been?"

Wildherne considered this too.

At last he said: "I know you're a fair man, father—the fairest I know anywhere. I know you care for both of us. You wouldn't say this if you didn't think it just. But, upon my word, this time I think you're wrong. You don't know, you see, all the facts."

"The facts! What facts?" the Duke asked sharply.

"Oh, well . . ." Wildherne hesitated. "You see, Janet and I weren't exactly in love with one another when we married. All the trouble—if there's been any—has come from that. We did it with our eyes open. We made a kind of bargain. She wanted to make things better for Rosalind; I wanted a son. We liked and respected one another immensely. That's still, I hope, true of both of us. But love! That's another pair of shoes. We have neither of us felt that for one another, and I suppose never will, although, of course, you never can tell. I've sometimes wondered about myself. I keep myself in. Janet not loving me, it would be pretty terrible if I began to care in that way about her, wouldn't it, sir? And so all the more strongly, perhaps, I've adored Humphrey. I've always wanted a boy more than anything else in life, and then to have *such* a boy. . . ." His voice shook. "By God, I'm lucky. There's not many men get their desire so completely. And if sometimes, sir, I've seemed careless about Janet, it has been a little because I didn't want—well, to begin to care for her in any other way—in any way contrary to our original bargain."

Wildherne stopped and looked up at his father in very much the way he had looked up in the old days when he had committed some fault and had come for chastisement.

"I see." The Duke looked at him. "I suppose you consider yourself on the whole a bright, clever sort of fellow, someone with his eyes open and his brain working sharply."

Wildherne answered: "I'm a good deal what you've made me. You've influenced me more than anyone; I haven't seen a great deal of the world, always rather kept to myself. I'm stupid, of course, about a great many things—but my stupidities are largely yours. We're stupid mostly in the same way."

"Well," said the Duke, "that's a fair retort. So I've influenced you more than anyone else, have I? There's been no woman ever? You needn't tell me, of course, if you don't want to."

Wildherne nodded his head.

"Ah, now I understand. So you've been told at last. I wondered when that would happen."

"Yes. I've been told that you were in love with someone else when you married Janet."

"I was."

"And was that a decent, fair action—the act of a gentleman?"

"I told Janet everything. I told her that I had been in love with someone else for a long time. She accepted that. She wanted my friendship, not my love. . . ."

"Have I the right to ask," said the Duke, "whether you are still in love?"

"I am not," said Wildherne.

There was a pause. The Duke stood, his legs spread, his broad back square and, as sometimes happened, his beard seemed to swallow up his expression, to veil his emotion so that one could not tell his mood.

"Ah," at last said Wildherne, "so that's what's been troubling you. I might have guessed."

"Partly," said the Duke. "I think you might have given me your confidence earlier."

"I didn't feel it altogether my right," Wildherne said, "and then I didn't want to distress you. This lady cared for me only for a short while, but out of kindness suffered me. It has been the only love affair of my life, and it is all over —absolutely and entirely over."

The Duke said nothing.

"Do you remember, father," Wildherne went on, "the night I came up from Wintersmoon and made you spend the evening with me and slept in your dressing-room?"

The Duke nodded his head.

"That night I'd intended to go to her. I was terribly tempted. You helped me, and next day I learnt that Janet was going to have a child. I've never felt any temptation since."

"So Janet kept you."

"If you like. Janet and Humphrey together. Oh, you're so wrong if you think that I don't care for Janet. I do with all my heart. But she is like a friend; one isn't all the time wondering whether or no one's hurt a friend's feelings. That's the beauty of friendship; one trusts. So it's always been with Janet. I shouldn't be hurt if she wanted to break an engagement she'd made with me and went off with Mrs. Mark or Rosalind. And until lately she wouldn't have been hurt either. But lately—I don't know. She's so much more sensitive. I don't mean to be selfish, but of course Humphrey *is* very exciting to me. He's part of me as no one has ever been before. Not even you, father."

The Duke moved, sat down on the broad arm of Wildherne's chair, and put his hand on his son's shoulder.

"Wildherne, think for a moment. Don't you understand why Janet has been different lately, more sensitive, less happy?"

Wildherne smiled. He was terribly pleased that his father had come to him again. Not for months past had they sat close together like this, and now he knew how deeply he had missed that contact.

"To tell you the truth, father, I don't. I've been awfully puzzled. When we married she was so sensible about everything, in many ways more like a man than a woman. Of course her whole soul then was centered in Rosalind, and I've thought lately that some of her restlessness has come because she's unhappy about Rosalind's marriage, which isn't going very well, you know, and I think she feels responsible. And then sometimes I'm sure she's disappointed in me. She thinks I moon about too much. It isn't that she wants there to be lots of parties here, but of course other fellows in my position would have heaps of shooting and would do all kinds of things on the estate. I *am* doing more on the estate than she knows, but I think of the future more than of the present, the future of Humphrey and Wintersmoon, and then the future of England—how they can all work together. At first Janet loved to talk about everything, was as keen as I was; we seemed to have all our ideas in common. Young Seddon, too, had just the same ideas and was as keen as we were. Then everything broke up. Janet was different in some way, and I was always thinking about Humphrey and poor Tom—well, he's just been destroyed by his marriage—destroyed is the only word. As though he'd caught a painful illness.

"I dare say it's been largely my fault as well. I've been a bit disappointed in Janet, to tell you the truth, father. She has seemed to care so little for Humphrey. Of course she loves him. She's too fine a woman not to. But it's as though her mind were elsewhere all the time."

"Yes—and do you know why?" asked his father.

"No," said Wildherne.

"She loves you. She's madly in love with you. She has been so for a long time."

Wildherne laughed.

"Nonsense, my dear father. Now you're being romantic. I know Janet."

"You don't know Janet. You don't know her at all. I'm inclined to think you know nobody and nothing."

Wildherne half rose in his chair.

"But that's absurd, perfectly absurd."

"It's not absurd. She told me herself."

"She *told* you?"

"She told me. A short while before Humphrey was born."

"She *told* you?"

Wildherne got up. He paced the room, his head back. He wheeled round.

"*What* did she tell you?"

"She was very unhappy—in that hysterical state that women so often know before childbirth. I don't think she meant to speak to me, but—at last—she had to tell someone. We have always loved one another, she and I, from the first moment of our meeting. She implored me not to say anything to you. I've kept silent as long as I could, but it was impossible any longer. She so unhappy, you and I drifting apart, you so blind. You had to be told.

"She told me everything, how you had married without love, she thinking that she was absorbed in Rosalind and would never love anyone else, how it gradually came to her and she realised that she had never grown up, had never known at all what life was like. Then she knew that she loved you. She was horrified, she resolved to kill it. But she could not. It was too strong for her. She determined that you should never know, and indeed on her side still keep her feelings down to the last. She's a great woman. But she's all heart. She's longing for love. She's never had it; all her life she's never had it. The two people she has loved—her sister and yourself—have denied it to her. She would love Humphrey if he didn't seem to belong to you; if you weren't al-

ways telling her that he did. She has no one. I am the only
one in the world she can talk to and of what use is an old
man like me? . . . Now do you understand why she's unhappy?"

Wildherne couldn't speak. They were both silent for a
long while. At last Wildherne broke out:

"My selfishness. . . . My God, my selfishness."

Then again after a long space: "You should have told me
before. Why didn't you tell me before?"

Then again: "My selfishness . . ."

At last he came to the chair, sat down on it, covered his
face with his hands. After a while he looked up as though he
had come to some decision, sat back, leaning his head against
his father's shoulder, and so stayed looking out far beyond
the room.

CHAPTER VII

H ALKIN St. *April 7.*—I have so far miserably failed to do this in this Journal. When I began it it seemed an easy thing to do—to tell the truth, or rather to find out the truth, why I have failed so badly in this job that I undertook, what is lacking in me so that I have no power over people, can only want them and then see them slip away.

But I haven't succeeded. It is the hardest thing in the world to come face to face with oneself. I suppose one simply *will not* confess the truth. One is afraid to. One shrinks from what one sees. All the modern discoveries of Psycho-analysis and the rest do not, I imagine, even when one is very learned in them make one shrink less. They make one think more kindly of other people I suppose—that is *their* job. But one's meannesses and cowardices and selfishnesses, how hateful they look on paper if one truthfully puts them down!

So also when one is trying to tell any one about oneself what a grand romantic account one gives! Crimes and passions of course, but what grand big ones! How interesting one becomes as one talks; one's faults are more interesting and picturesque by far than other people's virtues!

But the real thing. . . . If, for example, I try honestly to give an account of myself, how I felt when Wildherne told me last night that he was going down to Wintersmoon instead of staying with me, was not my anger and disappointment largely wounded vanity? my charm so slender that he could leave me so easily; and a mean jealousy too, jealousy of my own baby two years old, whom I love with all my heart and soul and yet can be jealous of? And isn't my self-pity miserable and despicable? Am I not lying on the bed that exactly I made for myself with my eyes wide open and all my wits about me?

And I am grudging Wildherne his happiness. I know that Humphrey is the complete fulfilment of all his dearest dreams, that he hasn't got used to it yet, it's all so *wonderful,* and that if I joined with him in his happiness and thought of him and Humphrey and not of myself he would be so enraptured and would take me with him all the way.

Yes, take me as a friend, as a sort of jolly, good-natured chum who is pleased because he is pleased.

And I don't want that. God help me for the miserable weak woman that I am. I would rather now have nothing at all than that.

I love him wickedly. I love him possessively, greedily, self-ishly. I love him so that I want him in my arms, my lips on his, my arm holding him tightly, lost, the both of us, in an utter un-consciousness. I have never had that. No one will ever see these pages, so let me set it down—I have never been loved with passion, I have never known that last ecstasy of physical love. I have never given that final tenderness, that infinite compassion of adoring love to any one, because no one has ever wanted me to give it.

I did not know until that night in that hotel in London that I myself wanted to give it, but I can see now on looking back that there was something of that need in my love for Rosalind. I frightened her sometimes by what she called my sentimental-ity. It was my hunger, but I didn't know I was hungry.

I had never felt this terrible longing for anyone but Wild-herne, and now that I know that I have it, it devours me, making me always restless, unhappy, selfish, wicked. How often in the last year have I looked at Wildherne, longing to touch him, to put my hand against his cheek, to kiss him, mouth to mouth, both of us content, resting like that, mouth to mouth.

How could I have been such a fool as not to know that this would come? I was thinking only of Rosalind at that time, but I fancy now that from that, my first night when Wildherne lay with me and went to sleep, his head on my breast (but it might as well have been any other breast), the change began in me, although I did not recognise it until so long afterwards. . . .

When Grandfather went down to Wintersmoon this morn-ing and wanted me to go with him how I longed to go with him! My only thought was to see Wildherne, only to see him, to be near him, to hear his voice.

He is such a boy yet in so many ways, and I love that boy-ishness. I love the light in his hair, the red-brown of his cheeks, the smell of his country clothes, the way he has of walking, his head up, his arms swinging, all his body moving rhythmi-cally.

But I must kill this wickedness in me. I must kill it or leave him. I must train myself to realise that I shall always be a third to Wildherne and Humphrey, and I must take my place after them. I must get used to Wildherne wanting only Humphrey and Humphrey only Wildherne.

How wicked I am as mother! How many millions of women would envy me that child, and wonder that I could want anything in the world other than he! And I do love him. Oh, God, let me remember that, how dearly I love him with his sweetness and his courage and his fun.

But if I allow that love its liberty, then when Wildherne takes him or he goes to Wildherne I am doubly wounded, wounded because my husband loves my son! Yes, there is a confession to shame any woman ever born into this world.

I am writing melodramatically. I seem to those who know me to be so quiet and restrained, a little dull. I know just how they think of me. "Dear Janet! Lucky for her to have so quiet a temperament." Someone told me the other day that I was so restful—"in these turbulent times."

Grandfather knows differently and Katherine. These two alone in the world, and perhaps (how odd that it should be so) the old curiosity-shop man. Rachel has fallen away from me. She is too miserable about Tom. And Rosalind—Rosalind has other fish to fry.

Well, I will be quiet and controlled, just as I seem to be. One can conquer anything—I will conquer this.

But when like to-night I sit alone here, every one in bed, London watching like a spy, I am frightened of myself. Frightened of those sudden moods and impulses that jump out like animals from thickets.

I bought from old Zanti the other day a little Bokhara rug. It is a ragged little piece, but it is of a lovely shell-pink that breaks once and again into rose-red. It is in front of me as I write; on my writing table is the little silver tree that Rosalind gave me, and high on my mantelpiece is the great cherry-coloured bowl that Zanti gave me on my first visit to him. Of course it is not in actual physical fact there, and yet it is more there for me than anything else in the room. It shines, it glows; I can see every line of its pattern as it runs into darkness round the bowl. It is my most precious possession.

Well then, if I can sink myself in this beauty (imagined many people would say), if that little rug is a joy and happiness to me, if I have, as I have, people who love me, if I have health

and some power, if, more than all these and all of these in this,
I believe in the truth and continuance of my spiritual life and
that I am here, living thus, for my spiritual growth and education, surely, surely I can turn to the Power greater than myself,
the Power of love and beauty and all goodness, and rest in it
and trust it. But I cannot. I cannot. I want something *now*. I
want some one to love me *now*. I want Humphrey to turn to me
as though he longed for me. I want to be Wildherne's lover. And
I want to be Wildherne's partner, so that together we can do
something worthy with our lives, something for England, something for the happiness of the world.

Everything is held back. Nothing moves. I do not get closer
to Wildherne but farther from him. Humphrey does not want
me more as he grows older, but less. Rosalind does not want me
at all.

Luckily for me there is still Katherine. Dear Katherine!
After such a day as to-day it does me good to think of her.
She has found her solution, and found it in generous unselfishness. She has been able to lose herself utterly in other lives,
she is happy because she never thinks as to whether she is happy
or no. The point is that Philip should be happy or Peter or the
children. But then they all love her.

Thinking of her calms me. She is quiet like this night around
me now. So will I try to be.

WINTERSMOON, *April* 9.—I am so happy that I am afraid
to write it down lest it should run away from me even while I
write it.

And yet there is so little to tell. A movement, a word, a sign
from the one human being who can make a sign that means
anything to you and your world is changed, changed morally,
physically, spiritually. How platitudinous I should think these
words if any one else wrote them, but now I have experienced
them. I have had my sign! Peace on Earth and Goodwill to
Men. . . .

I left London yesterday morning in a violet haze—London
was I mean. And when I got out into the country everything
was pale and ghostly, but shot through with sun. I have no
power of description, but if I were a painter I would always
choose those weeks of early spring in England. No other
country quite has them, when we creep forward and slide back,
snowdrops and daffodils one instant, snowdrifts and showers
of hail the next, and slipped in between the storms and the

winds these wonderful most lovely hours when the faint mis
changes everything to fairy texture. There is a *shyness* over the
land that is adorable—the promise of something exquisite. Wha
matters if the promise is so rarely fulfilled? The trustfulness
of these days! But they remember, I suppose, the times when
the promise has been truly fulfilled—the regal Mays, the sump-
tuous Junes, the basking rich Julys.

It was just this shyness and this promise that was all over
the country yesterday. In spite of myself I had to be happy
How ridiculous that way that we take the good weather as a
compliment to ourselves! But I couldn't resist it. As I looked
out through that window at those soft colours, rose and pale
green, faint amber and trembling blue, when I saw how happy
everything and everyone was, the boy on the cart driving down
the lane, the geese waddling into their pond, the trees on the rise
of the field bearing their heads so proudly, the brown soil almost steaming with anticipation, how could it not seem meant
for me?

I resolved, as I sat there, on a thousand new rules for myself.
I used when I was young to despise so heartily people who were
for ever making new resolves and then breaking them. But
now I despise no longer for I am one of them. But at least, I
said to myself, I will be content with whatever Wildherne gives
me. I *must* be. And perhaps slowly he will care for me more. I
will make myself indispensable to him. I will be his councillor,
friend, father, brother, mother, sister—and the other, the lover
—it shall be beaten down, killed. . . . Others have done it, so
can I. The good omens still continued with me.

Hawes, with his round chubby smiling face, was there at the
station to meet me. Whatever I've failed in I've succeeded at
least in this, I've made the servants at Wintersmoon care for
me. I know they do. It isn't only lip service or hope of profit.
Hignett and Hawes, Forster and Mrs. Craddock, Mrs. Bone
and even poor old Mrs. Beddoes—they are my friends for life
and so am I theirs.

Indeed, I am easier in their company than in any other.
I could go round the world with Hawes and Hignett and know
neither alarm nor fear.

Everything was right up at the House, but would be righter
still, Hawes' smiling face assured me, now that I had come.

As the car ran forward through the country, the fields, the
lanes, the hedges seemed glad too. Although I don't belong to

this country I have come to love it. We ourselves are thick
with fields of the deepest green, dark lanes, clustered cottages,
but I am for ever conscious of the plain, so near to us, open
to the sky with no boundaries. The New Forest so near too,
the thickest and deepest of English country. The sea also so
near.

So beautiful was the day that I made Hawes stop at the
Lodge, and walked up through the Park. The grass was velvet,
the deer in farther fields seemed to keep pace with me as though
they, too, were welcoming me, the lower lake shone like one
glittering crystal shield under the trees whose branches had
that faint pink glow almost iridescent that they have in this
early Spring.

Just at the top of the hill, before the road turns towards the
House, you get that sudden view of Wintersmoon that is the
best of all. It stands all clustered together, one sentient being,
the Towers beautifully dignified. Seen thus its curve is the
most gracious thing, sweeping outwards with a gesture, controlled but very proud; its body is set square, four feet on the
ground, and then there is the farther curve, the old, old part of
it, bending away to the wood. The lawns flow like water from
terrace to terrace down to the band of dark trees, and behind
it the hill rises very gently to its thin stiff ridge against the
sky.

But it is beyond question its colour that is its chief glory. I
have never seen any other building anywhere that has quite
Wintersmoon's colour. Although so many parts of it are of
different dates, it is all harmonised into a mother-of-pearl
silver grey. Almost snow-white in places, but even then there is
a glow of silver-grey in its stone. It is so strong and yet so
delicate. So old and yet so alive.

This lovely spring afternoon it shone dimly like a cloud.
There was mist enough to shade it with the surrounding landscape. It had almost the texture of water, and you might expect
to find the trees reflected in it. It was so light that it would
not have astonished me to have seen it float away from the
lawns and sail like a fairy palace through the blue sky. The
stillness, as I stood there, was entrancing. Then I heard, very
distantly, the cry of the peacock.

I have tried very hard to put down something of the beauty
I felt on this particular morning, but of course I have missed
it. I haven't that gift at all. But it will always bring this day

back to me again when I read these pages, and no one else will
see them so no harm is done.

·So also will I miss the other beauty of this wonderful
day.

Wildherne came along the Terrace to meet me. When I
saw him coming my heart beat so that I was dizzy and the
Wintersmoon walls trembled. I was so afraid that by his very
first word he would fling me out of that beautiful world in
which I had been all the morning. By my fault—not his. Simply
because I had expected too much.

But with his kiss and grip of his hand I knew that there
was some change. It was nothing, and yet it was everything.
He was shy but tender to me, careful of me, putting his hand
through my arm as we walked to the house, not as before,
as though I were another man, but touching me gently, protecting me.

Then I said to myself: "Now, don't you cheat yourself here.
Don't be such a fool as to build on this. He is ashamed of
himself because he left you in London. When he has shown
you a little attention he will feel that he has done enough,
and will slip back into the old way again. Be grateful for
what you have, but don't persuade yourself that it means anything."

Then he took me astonishingly into the little drawing-
room, closed the door, put his arms round me and held me
close to him.

"Janet," he said, "I've been so selfish that I am ashamed. But
trust me. Let me show you that I love you."

He kissed me as he had never kissed me before. I cried
a little, and I'm not ashamed that I did. We stood together
cheek against cheek. I knew even then that much of this was
his kindness, his hatred of himself for having hurt me, it was
not love as men and women in love know love to be, but I was
contented—oh, how deeply, wonderfully contented!—with
what I had.

And how grateful—to something, someone high in heaven,
a heaven yesterday so distant now so close. How sentimental
Rosalind would think me if she read this! But it is true—exactly, and exactly true. I am writing it so close to the event
that there is no room for falsehood.

We went out, and Humphrey came running, tumbling,
scrambling to meet us.

And now how wonderful to know that nothing any longer

held me back from him. That getting right with Wildherne
had released all my love for my son. He rushed to me and
jumped up and down like a little animal.

Mrs. Bone was there.

"How is he?" I asked her.

She said that he had a little cough. It was nothing, but she
was keeping him in. The spring weather was so treacherous.

He took my hand and led me slowly up the wide stairs,
taking each step in that determined conquering way that he
has. Half-way up he turned to me with his proprietory smile
as though to reassure me that no harm should come to me
while *he* was about.

"I've a cough," he announced proudly once and coughed to
show me.

And all day that happiness continued. That night, last night,
was the most wonderful of all my life. When Wildherne slept
I lay there awake, my hand bent deep in his, my other hand
against his hair. And so I watched my darling.

I am so happy that I am afraid.

April 10, 4. 26 A.M.—I have put down the time exactly because that seems to control, to steady me, and I've been told
that I must try and get a little sleep now because I shall need
all my strength for the day. My strength. . . . Oh, God! No,
I must go on writing, otherwise I shall go back to the room,
and they have implored me not to do that. Wildherne won't
leave the room. He sits there watching Humphrey as though
at some moment he will be called on to save him. He must be
there but not I . . . what am I writing?

Was it only last night that I went to sleep so peacefully with
such happiness? Only two hours back that I woke to find Mrs.
Bone there: "Please, my lady, Master Humphrey is not well."
Temperature. Temperature. Temperature. Temperature. That
little man from Salisbury means well, but I have no confidence
in him. He says that as yet there is little to do. Bronchial
pneumonia. We kept him in yesterday because of his cold. I
thought his cheek was hot when I kissed him good-night, but
he was laughing, laughing about something Hignett had done.
And now so quickly. . . .

I've always hated the wall-paper of this room. It is the
wrong grey. I am always meaning to change it. Why don't I
do the things I intend to do? Oh, my darling, my darling. . . .
The house is noisy with little sounds.

Writing, writing. . . The stupidity. . . . If I go quietl
and open the door softly they can't mind. . . . I'm his mothe
. . . . Perhaps I can help him by being there. . . . If I g
quietly they can't prevent me. . . .

CHAPTER VIII

A PUFF OF WIND

YOUNG Humphrey died at ten minutes past four this Eleventh of April——

Mrs. Beddoes spoke the right word to Hawes:

"Barring my sister-in-law's youngest 'e was the jolliest kid I ever did see."

END OF PART III

PART IV

JANET, ROSALIND, AND WILDHERNE

CHAPTER I

AN OLD MAN IN A DRY MONTH

JOHNNY BEAMINSTER laid down his book with a sigh. It was *Pendennis* that he had been reading. He had thought that he would see what old Thackeray was like now, and what old Thackeray was like—well, there were points he could give to Mr. Martin Fairlawne, and points he couldn't. He was certainly rich and thick where Fairlawne was rather watery and thin, but on the other hand his moralisings how fearful, his snobbery how ghastly, his loose incoherent methods how inartistic!

The modern writer created less profusely, but he was more the artist, the poet. There was no human creature in any of Fairlawne's works so alive as old Pendennis, or the fair Rebecca, or the lovely Beatrix; but against that the writing, the symmetry, the beautiful evocation of London in such books as *The Plain Dealer* and *The Landowners!* Tit for Tat! And perhaps after all Tit suited our own age better.

It was of this same age, as contrasted with Mr. Thackeray's, of which Beaminster was really thinking. How oddly savage and naive and uncouth that mid-Victorian world appeared in these pages! A world in which the Claverings and the awful Altamont were even for a moment possible, a world of such snobbery that the highest in the land were snobs as gross as the pettiest shopkeeper, a world in its inconvenience and disorder and excitement over twopence-halfpenny pleasures quite incredible.

And socially—a world it appeared of vast eating and drinking, of ever recurring afternoon calls, a world in fact where it was "always afternoon" and where everybody had endless time for endless waste. So short a period and such a difference! Those night-long dinners, where were they now? Dancing and the motor car had killed them completely. That simple and, in spite of Bishop Colenso, unquestioning faith—what had psycho-analysis and modern science done to that?

The punctiliousness of calls and social observances, what did the young men and women say to those?

Yet in spite of the naïveté, the uncouthness, and the snobbery, Beaminster would have been more at home in Thackeray's world than he was in this present one. He was old. He was tired. His day was over. His world was done. And the boy whom he loved more than himself was mortally unhappy.

Things had gone badly with him that summer. Nobody had wanted him anywhere. Time had been when August was for him so stiff with invitations that it had been an agony of self-denial to make the choice. There had been old Moffat-Fortescue, to whose shooting he had gone year after year up in Perthshire. There had been the old Duke of Mixham (cousin by marriage of the old Duchess of Wrexe) up there at Loch Rannoch—what good times he had had with him. Or Charlie Ross down in Suffolk, or fat old Beeversides up in Arran. The old faces hung before him: Moffat-Fortescue, short, stocky, with the hunch in his shoulder and his chirrup of a laugh—dead of a cancer years ago; Mixham, thin, sallow, with that odd lift of the eye that looked so supercilious but meant nothing at all, tight with his money a bit, but otherwise one of the kindest—old Adela had been sweet on him once, but she was always too plain, poor Adela—Mixham liked pretty women; and Charlie Ross, large and fat and jovial, the best of hosts, adoring to make his friends happy, suddenly shooting himself, no one to this day knew why. Beeversides, wheezy, so corpulent that he could hardly manage his day's shooting, but a wit if ever there was one. What was that he had said once about the old Duchess and her ebony cane? something damned smart—everyone had quoted it—dead of heart failure.

So they were. All dead. All gone.

But now he was tumbling into the Thackeray strain. What were the words he had closed the book on? "This only we say—that a good woman is the loveliest flower that blooms under heaven; and that we look with love and wonder upon its silent grace, its pure fragrance, its delicate bloom of beauty. Sweet and beautiful!—the fairest and the most spotless! Is it not pity to see them bowed down or devoured by Grief or Death inexorable—wasting in disease—pining with long pain—or cut off by sudden fate in their prime? *We* may deserve grief—but why should these be unhappy? except that we know that Heaven chastens those whom it loves best; being pleased by repeated trials to make these pure spirits more pure."

Why did these words now seem to him the most ranting sentimental rodomontade? He who thirty years back would have read them with feeling and sympathy? Was this new world so wicked that it did not appreciate good women? No, he did not think so. Were there no good women left? There were as many as ever there had been. But, then, had there ever been any good women? Didn't we now find everyone, man and woman, so mixed in his or her qualities that this rapture about virtue seemed only childish and absurd? No. Bacon or Sir Philip Sidney on the virtues of the good and brave were as fine and true to-day as they ever had been.

No, there was something in that queer, stuffy, mixed, idealistic, selfish, self-satisfied, honest, humbugging, vulgar, emphatic, hypocritical, energetic mid-Victorian period that explained, in the reaction to it, the whole new world now rising over Beaminster's old body. How much closer to this new epoch were the Popes, the Swifts, Defoes, and Fieldings than the Thackerays, Dickens, Lyttons, Charlotte Brontës of the later time!

Beaminster looked down from his wide window. Piccadilly wriggled like a dry-skinned snake beneath him, down its back the line of traffic shining in the sun like a silver pattern in the skin stretched taut. This was a dry month. The Green Park was dry and brown. The cars, omnibuses, lorries seemed to pant as though with a flick of the snake's tongue. The summer was almost over, but here in its last moments this terrific mechanical world rolled on its tight shining wires; the levers were pulled, the little gleaming rods jerked backwards and forwards; soon with the fading light all the eyes, hooded by day, would be unveiled—a million glittering, staring eyes penetrating the London jungle, gleaming now here, now there, out of the depths of the thick fetid bush, and cowering, running for safety, hiding in sudden darkness, panting with apprehension, the little human beings would be allowed for the moment to pursue their plans.

But the day would come——

Beaminster laughed as he turned back from the window. Thackeray's rhapsody and that traffic! Yes, things had moved swiftly in the last fifty years, and he was tired, tired mentally, physically, spiritually. He would not be sorry when the end came.

But nevertheless he had an inexhaustible interest in life. He was vividly conscious of that as he stood in his pretty room. Things had gone badly with him that summer. Aches in his body, no communication with Tom, nowhere interesting to visit; but here he was looking forward with lively interest to his luncheon to-day with the Copley-Fawders. The Copley-Fawders! Very modern people. Why had they asked him? Oh, because he'd met Alice Copley-Fawder by chance at Christie's, and she, without anything especial to say, had brought forward an invitation instead of the weather. People were always in such a hurry these days that they hadn't time to think, and were as likely to ask you to dinner as to complain of the heat. That was why so many people had such strangely confused parties. They were not of his world, the Copley-Fawders, smart, new, here to-day, gone to-morrow. Never mind. He would show them that he could be up to them. . . .

The man came in to attend to the fire.

"Ever read Thackeray, Baxter?" Beaminster asked.

"Beg pardon, my lord?" Baxter said, looking up.

"Ever read any books by Thackeray?"

"Can't say I have, my lord. Not that I remember."

"What *do* you read, Baxter?"

"Well, my lord, can't say I've time for much except the paper. Look at a magazine sometimes, my lord."

"Well, you ought to. Widen your mind."

"Yes, my lord. You'll not be in to luncheon, you said?"

"No."

"That dark blue of yours, my lord, ain't good for much more. Wearing a bit thin, especially the trousers."

"All right, Baxter. I'll be back tea-time. That is, if I'm alive."

"Alive, my lord?"

"Never know. This damned traffic. Getting old, Baxter. Haven't you noticed it?"

"Can't say as I have, my lord. We're all getting on, my lord. These times wear you out, what with one thing and another. I can't carry a scuttle of coals as I used to—and those boys, they're never here when you want them. Not the boys they used to be."

"Nothing's as it used to be."

"No, my lord, I suppose it ain't."

No, nothing was quite what it used to be. And it never had been.

The Copley-Fawders lived in a house in Cadogan Place —a very smart little slim house which appeared to go in very slightly somewhere about the second floor, like a gay young man who is almost corseted but not quite. It was distinguished also from the houses on either side of it because of its bright and apparently fresh white paint, and all the windows had shining green borders. The door was a bright fresh green, and wore in its very centre a large brazen knocker representing a large fish swallowing a small one, and this shone so radiantly that it was difficult to look at.

Inside there was the same radiance. Everything gleamed and shone and glittered. The hall was so shiny and slippery that Beaminster found it difficult to walk with dignity as far as the staircase. The stairs were covered with carpet of bright orange; the wall was dead grey and hung with pastels by some very modern artist who was aware apparently of only three colours—orange, green, and purple.

A maid in a white uniform, so stiff and formal and glistening that she must surely have been poured into it, led Beaminster on to the first floor, and here at the entrance into

a long thin room he for an instant paused. The floor was a
shining surface of glassy black. The walls of the room were
of silver, and their only pictures were two of the most gor-
geous of M. de Smet's still life. The ceiling was a dark rich
blue, and on the white mantelpiece was a high gold clock.

How to cross this glassy sea with safety and honour?
Beaminster's old bones crept in their sockets. However, the
thing must be attempted. A very thin lady in a short white
frock, her hair cropped like a boy's (a fashion not yet at
that time general), was waiting for him. Near one of the
high slim windows certain people were grouped.

He achieved his adventure successfully. Alice Copley-
Fawder plainly was, for an instant, at a loss as to his iden-
tity. Then by what was for her obviously the luckiest of
chances, she fished him out of her entangled memory and
presented him to the others. The others were Althea Bendersley, Rosalind's friend, Major Hal Pinkerton ("Lobster"
to his intimates), and Clara Pundice, who was dressed exactly like a man, in a monocle, a high white stock, and a
green waistcoat with gold buttons. A moment later someone
else appeared. It was, of all people in the world, little Felix
Brun.

Beaminster was delighted to see a friend. In these first
moments he had been feeling very lonely indeed, the three
by the window continuing their amusing conversation as
though he didn't exist, and his hostess having introduced
him had remarked to the world at large, "My God, if that
isn't that damned telephone again!" and vanished into a
little room somewhere behind her.

Brun, however, did not miss his hostess. He navigated the
floor most successfully and then apparently knew everyone, kissing the hands of Althea Bendersley and Clara Pundice, saying "Bon jour, Major," and "Why, Beaminster, I
haven't seen you for an age."

Beaminster quickly realised, in fact, that since he had
seen Felix Brun last that social observer had in some subtle
fashion transformed himself into a citizen of the modern
age. He had always been modern enough, of course, but
when he had first returned to London he belonged still to

the pre-war fashion. Now no longer. Where lay the change? Difficult to say. He looked as old as the oldest hills, but he was nevertheless part of this present landscape, belonging to it and sharing in it. While Beaminster. . . . His very finger-tips told how dead and buried he ought, in Clara Pundice's eyes, to be.

Alice Copley-Fawder suddenly reappeared.

"We won't wait for Poppy Clay," she said. "She's always late, and it's an impertinence to bother about her."

So down to luncheon they went.

More colour in the dining-room. The walls were of shining green, and the only picture was a very modern portrait apparently of Alice herself in a tight black dress. Impossible to be sure that it was Alice.

Luncheon began under a burst of noise. Everyone screamed. Nobody listened. Beaminster had on one side of him Miss Bendersley, and on the other the empty chair reserved for Poppy Clay. He knew that lady by repute well. Who was there in London who did not? Mrs. Harrington Clay, immensely rich, interested in the arts, in politics, in social intrigue—everything. Immensely kind. To some immensely amusing, to others not so. Immensely energetic. He, Beaminster, was afraid of her. She talked so fast that he could never hear a word that she said. She knew so many things (superficially, her enemies said) that he always felt in her company a schoolboy ignorance. But he liked her for her generosity, her championship of her friends, her courage.

But he was afraid of her more than he liked her.

She came in a moment later. "Well, all of you! Alice, my dear, I'm late, of course, but this time I really would have been in time if . . . yes, I'm terribly hungry, of course. Old Fuzzy Wuzzy stayed and stayed. Oh, he came about Charlie Press. What do you think? He's got to do something about the boy—the trouble is the lad's an idiot. Complete. Nobody will have him, and I don't blame them, and it's no use Fuzzy saying that he'll be all right if there's only someone to look after him, but who *will* look after him? All the fuss just now is about the Crayton girl, and all I could say to Fuzzy was let them marry and have done with it, but Ma

Crayton's a horror, of course, and, as Fuzzy says, once you
let Ma Crayton in you let in all her friends. And so you do
But what does it matter? Let's talk of something else. How
are you, Clara, darling? Where's that nice young man of
yours? Beautiful manners, but you must stop him quoting
French poetry at you. He does it to show off his accent
Everyone has a French accent nowadays, so that is nothing
to be proud of. Tell him to give us some Czech. That migh
easily become the fashion. There's that delightful man
Kapek, and I'm sure there must be lots of others hidden
away somewhere. . . ."

No one talked to Beaminster. It was *his* duty to talk to
someone. He tried but, raising his voice, discovered that nobody heard it. He had noticed, during the last year, that
in houses like these, the *timbre* of conversation seemed to
have changed. Everything was pitched higher. From America, he supposed.

So he gave up his attempt, and rather sadly (because he
was a gregarious man and loved his fellow-creatures) devoted himself to his sole. Then there eddied round him conversation that was of the very first interest to him. In the
course of it he discovered no individuals, but words, bright
glazed, shiningly painted, rose and fell in the air like coloured balls tossed by a fountain—the pattern this time certainly his concern.

"Of course, my dear, it was too sad for anything, but
what could be worse than Poole shutting himself up in that
gloomy forsaken place and moping. . . ."

"He has her with him."

"Yes, and that's fun for him! Everyone knows that she
bores him to tears. She always has. He wasn't in the least in
love with her when he married her. Diana's been the only
woman in his life for years. And she's always been bored
with *him*. So there you are. . . ."

"Well, and I've always been bored with him too." This
Althea Bendersley. "Who wouldn't be? I saw quite a lot of
all of them at one time. The old Duchess took me up for a
bit and—well, anything at that time for free meals. But, my
dear, *what* meals! Pea soup, mince, and cabinet pudding. I

ssure you. And the house! I don't suppose you've ever been inside the Halkin Street house. All worsted work and sets of the classics, and a clergyman at every corner. You wouldn't believe unless you went there for a bit that there are still so many people left in the world *like* that. And the old Duke. . . ."

"Ah, the Duke!" Here Poppy Clay broke in. "You shan't say a word against him, Althea. He's a darling. Of course, I've never seen very much of him—nobody ever has—but he's too sweet for words, with his white beard and his adorable eyes and his soft voice. I've asked him again and again to come and see me, but he never would. I'd like to set him up in a corner of my dining-room and keep him there permanently. I don't blame him for not coming. Why should he? People like us are no use to him. He's worth the lot of us."

"That's all very well," Althea went on. "He may be beautiful to look at, but why shouldn't he have *done* something with his life? He's had the position and money enough, and he's done *nothing*—absolutely nothing."

"What would you have him do? Sit in the beautiful House of Lords and make long speeches? Have tea with you, Althea, darling, and back horses for you? He's much better as he is. At least he's remained *himself*. Which is more than most of us have done."

"Wildherne Poole isn't doing anything either," Althea went on. "Of course, it's terribly sad his losing his boy like that, and they say he was madly devoted to him and is simply going off his head down there, but Janet and the others ought to *rouse* him, make him travel for a bit. It's my belief it's that horrible house in Wiltshire; it just eats them all up, one after the other."

"I never *could* make anything of Janet Poole anyway," said Clara Pundice. "She's the dullest creature ever, and . . ."

"No, she's not," Althea broke in again. "Excuse me, Clara, you know nothing whatever about her. *I* do, because I've been Rosalind Seddon's friend for donkeys' years. Janet Poole's not my kind, of course. She's quiet and old-fashioned, but she's a good sort, if ever there was one. The mistake she

made was marrying young Poole for Rosalind's sake, and
she didn't do Rosalind any good after all."

("Good God!" thought Beaminster. "What a lot these
women know! Is there no privacy?" He felt a kind of cold
terror creep over him as he listened.)

"Anyway," said Clara Pundice in her slow, deep, detached voice, "your Rosalind, Althea, took on the wrong
young man in Seddon. Nice boy he was too, once."

"You can't blame Rosalind for that," Althea asserted, all
heat and energy. "The boy's been tied to his mother in the
most disgusting way. Of course, if Rosalind had wanted
to marry the *mother* . . ."

It was time here for Beaminster to speak. He raised his
voice above the babel.

"I beg your pardon," he said, "but Tom Seddon is a
very especial friend of mine, *and* his mother. I have a great
affection for both of them. . . ."

They had completely forgotten him. They remembered
now that the old man was Tom Seddon's especial guardian.
They were sorry. They had intended in no way to be unkind. Everyone had nice things to say about Tom Seddon.
The conversation was quickly changed.

But he sat there wretchedly until the meal was over. These
people whom he loved and knew, how oddly they appeared
when created by these others who were indifferent to them!
He had not lived all his life in London without realising,
often enough, this transformation that indifference made—
he had himself in his time gossiped enough—but now, in
his old age, he seemed less hardened; he had of late gone
into the world so little and had centered all his emotions and
energies upon one or two souls. And these women, why
could they not leave his own one or two alone? But why
should they? Everyone was a fair target. How often had
not he himself commented upon someone who meant nothing to him, who was like a coloured counter in an unimportant game? Yes, they were in their right. But he was
miserable as he thought of Tom and Wildherne and Janet
fighting their personal fates with all their tortured strength

—and then produced for the little slings and tiny poisoned arrows of this outside revolving world.

Luncheon was over. The women moved out of the room. Brun came up to him.

"Delightful house!" said little Brun. "When I think of the heavy, dreary rooms of pre-war London I'm amazed! Astonishing!"

"So you like new England?" Beaminster said.

"Enormously! But the change is incredible! One can talk about anything now, positively anything. There are no reserves. English people have become witty as well as bold. Hypocrisy has hidden her head and escaped to America."

"Yes," said Beaminster timidly. "But is it worth our while to become like the rest of Europe and lose our own characteristics? I rather liked us as we were."

"Ah, mon ami," said Brun affectionately, tapping Beaminster on the shoulder. "You must keep up! One mustn't drop behind! The way for old men like you and me to keep our health is to keep our brains, give them—what do you say?—five minutes' exercise every morning by the open window. No lamenting the past. That's fatal. One joins it as soon as one regrets it!"

Brun was himself obviously determined to keep even ahead of the times. He was bubbling with a vitality that was so modern that he might have bought it during the last five minutes at Lady Fitzgammon's new shop in Duke Street, the shop that sold coloured wigs, paste buckles, and *A Hundred Witty Stories from Esthonia*.

But how old was Brun? Centuries and centuries. And how many transformations of this kind had he not made in his time? The Harlequin of the ages.

"Well, hadn't we better join the ladies?" The Major, who had been examining the portrait of his hostess with the interest of a dog who sniffs at a stranger's trousers, summoned them.

Ten minutes later Beaminster was outside in the dry arid street.

He needed his courage. He was aware that, hovering over

him, was a cloud black and of a lumpy, unhealthy rotundity. Something threatened, and if he did not stiffen his back and defy—well, what would occur? Perhaps the end of every thing. Would that dismay him? No—not this afternoon. Life had no savour. What had he now in the world but Tom, and Tom was too proud to ask his help—and himself was too proud to give it unasked. To give it? How could he give it? Plead with Rosalind that she should be kinder?

He saw Rosalind as a lovely cameo. Hard, rose-coloured and deathly cold. And her scorn of him! No, that was no the way. . . . There was no way—and here was the end. He had not known for fifty years any religious beliefs. The moment had always been the thing, and now when the mo ment had lost its savour. . . .

He remembered poor Adela in her last illness, sitting there looking like a stork with jaundice and saying, "What a per petual scramble—and all for nothing!" Yes, even Adela had lost something of her pluck at the last.

Certainly he needed all his pluck this afternoon. How he had detested that luncheon party! Those shining, noisy, gossiping, heartless women!

But perhaps not. Little Brun had not found them so. "Al in the eye of the beholder!" The plain fact was that they had not wanted him, he had been in the way. And another plain fact was that they—and their kind—never would want him, never any more.

"Well, there were the other kind, the Purefoys and Med leys and Chichesters and Darrants. The mince-and-cabinet pudding kind. But did they want him either? They showed no signs of doing so. He had been twice to Halkin Street, but the Duchess had not been in any way interested in him. He thought of the Duke with pleasure. He liked *that* man. But there was another old castaway like himself. What had two old men to say to one another? And he liked Janet Poole, liked her extremely. But she did not like him. How could she when he hated her sister? Besides, she was involved deeply in her own trouble.

His mind turned then to the survivors in his own set. What relics! Crampton and Holly and Pitcher Warminster

nd Plug Forrest. Either crumbling away in their private
cubby-holes, watched greedily by male attendants or female
harpies eager for the pickings, or creeping day by day into
their clubs, snorting and whining and snoring. . . .

No, no. Not that, not that. . . .

He paused in his slow walk. He had come up the right
side of Knightsbridge and stood now just before the hospital
in front of the Hyde Park Tube.

He would cross here that he might escape that wide
troubled sea of traffic in front of the gates. At this moment
the traffic was held in leash, cars and omnibuses straining at
a pause. On an ordinary day he would have been across in
half a minute, but this afternoon he could not at once move,
and when at last something within him said "Go!" (he had
never before waited for that something), at that instant the
traffic was released and, like an army at the order of attack,
plunged forward.

He waited a moment longer and then moved. He went
five yards farther and then stopped. Something claret-
coloured and shining just missed him. He heard someone
shout. Then on every side of him the world was moving.
The very basis of the street was on the move. The trees of
the Park, the iron railings and the cabmens' shelter, they
were all moving too. And worst of all was the sound—the
sound of purring, grinding, whispering, lumbering, trembling machinery. He was involved—now in the very middle
—of a world of revolving wheels, hissing engines, rods sliding ever forwards and backwards.

The light grew dark overhead. The world was grey and
breathless like a great eye fixed upon him, derisively, to see
what he could do. And what he could do was exactly nothing.
His legs were trembling and his hand fluttered forward as
though to say "Keep off!" He dwindled smaller and yet
smaller, and a great arm was raised behind him to strike
him contemptuously in the back. . . .

With a mighty effort he moved forward and now he was
moving, it seemed to him, in and out of wheels. Huge wheels
like the surface of the globe, red flaming wheels like fiery
suns, sharp silver wheels edged like swords, heavy clumsy

wheels whose momentum nothing could stop, littl
wheels like biting animals. He ran a few steps, paused, ra
again.

Sweating, trembling, blind, deaf he knew that he ha
reached the central island.

He stayed there, his heart hammering so that he coul
hear nothing but that. A gigantic policeman appeared to b
looking at him with terrible severity. But the policeman wa
a human being. He had arms and legs and a large red face
Here at least was flesh and blood.

His heart steadied, his knees tightened. The army had ad
vanced. The road in front of him was shining and clear. H
crossed it quietly.

Nevertheless, as he reached the door of Number Ninety
he was still trembling and before his eyes a gigantic whee
rolled.

"Sir Thomas Seddon is waiting to see you, my lord."

He hardly took in the significance of that. Sir Thoma:
Seddon was waiting. Who was Sir Thomas . . . ? Tom
He turned to the man.

"Any letters?"

"Yes, my lord. I put them on your table."

Suddenly the iron cage that held the lift began to heave
at him. He sat down on the little wooden hall chair.

Baxter was deeply concerned. "Shall I bring you something, my lord?"

"No, no." He looked up and smiled faintly. "I'm all right.
Tired for a moment. Close sort of day."

With another mighty effort he pulled himself up. Slowly
he walked upstairs.

With his back to the high dark window-curtains Tom
Seddon was standing there staring sombrely into the
room.

He didn't move when Beaminster came in.

"Well, Uncle John," he said slowly. "Here I am
again."

The room was hot. The fire was lit, absurd for such a day
as this.

"Yes," said Beaminster gaily, "and about time too. I thought you'd given me up, Tom."

"I thought so also," said young Seddon. "I thought I'd given everyone up."

"How white he is!" Beaminster thought, a gripping ache at his heart. "And how foreign he looks!" was his second thought, "not English at all."

He went up to him and put his hand on his shoulder.

"Come and sit down. We'll have some tea." Tom came and sat down. Beaminster went on chattering, smiling, his eyes, in spite of his determination to be sensible, full of yearning affection. "I *am* so glad you've come. I've missed you a lot. In spite of having heaps to do you know. Been as busy as anything. Many times I've wanted to ring you up but I didn't like to take up your time, and then all day you're busy at the Foreign Office. I thought you'd come along to see me as soon as you were inclined—just as you have. Well, it's very jolly I'm sure. Now tell me about yourself. How have you been? You're looking a bit tired. Been very gay? How is your mother?"

"Mother's all right," Tom answered. "Not very pleased with me, I expect, although she hasn't said so. You see, Uncle John—I thought you might have heard—I've chucked the Foreign Office."

The great scarlet wheel edged in silver came rolling across the floor straight at Beaminster. He shifted in his chair to avoid it.

"What!" he said. "Chucked the Foreign Office! . . . Oh dear . . . No, I hadn't heard."

"I won't have any tea thanks," Seddon said as the man-servant came in.

"A whisky and soda then?"

"Yes. Thanks."

"But, Tom, explain. When did this happen? And why?"

"Last week. That's really what I came to tell you."

"But why?" Beaminster half rose then sat down again. "What's the matter?"

"I couldn't keep my mind on my work," Tom answered quietly. "I was no use. My mind wouldn't stick. They were very decent. They wanted me to take a holiday and come back. But I refused. What's the good?"

"What's the good?" Beaminster repeated. "But, good heavens, Tom, it's everything. It's your career. You were doing so well. . . . And, anyway, what are you and Rosalind to live on?"

Seddon rose, half filled his glass with whisky, put in a little soda.

"Rosalind and I are going to separate," he said.

Then Beaminster, seeing that the very worst had occurred, said quietly:

"Come, Tom. Tell me everything. You owe it to me."

"Tell you everything, Uncle John?" Tom answered, as quiet as he. "What is there to tell? Nothing. Except my weakness, my rottenness." Then he began to speak quickly, eagerly, as though the glass of whisky which he had already finished had released him. "Not that I pity myself or ask pity of anyone else. Don't you make that mistake, Uncle John. Not that I despise myself either. I haven't been able to shake off my obsession, that's all. My obsession that I must leave Rosalind. I want her. I've wanted her ever since I first saw her—and I've never had her. Not physically, you know. That's nothing. But the other way. They say nowadays that we have no souls. Well, I know that we have. I want Rosalind's soul and I can't have it. What's there in that? Plenty of men have wanted women before and not been able to have them. They've conquered their obsession. I haven't been able to conquer mine. That's all. It's been too much for me. Perhaps if I'd been all English I might have managed it. You English can manage things because you're all of a piece, but I'm not of a piece. My Russian blood laughs at the rest of me, and when I say, 'I can conquer this,' my Russian self says, 'Oh no, you can't.' . . . Yes, and you mustn't blame Rosalind. I forced her to marry me. She warned me. She knew she couldn't give herself to me. She will never give herself to anyone."

He came over to Beaminster, put his arm for a moment round the old man's neck: "Don't you worry, Uncle John.

Don't you worry. You've got nothing to worry about. You've always been damned good to me."

He filled for himself another glass of whisky, then sat down.

Now was the time for common sense. Now was the time for wisdom. No sentiment now. No emotion. No drama. Common sense.

But the old man was in spite of himself trembling. He had had a difficult day. He wasn't very well. He thought it would be easier if he didn't look at the boy's face. He stared into the fire.

"I see, Tom. I quite understand. Don't you think perhaps they are right at the Foreign Office, and that a little holiday would be the thing? Italy's very nice just now. Why not come to Rapallo or Amalfi for a bit with me? As a matter of fact, I want a holiday myself. I've been feeling the weather rather. What do you say?"

"Thank you, Uncle John. It's very jolly of you. I'll think about it." He got up, put down his glass on the mantelpiece and turned.

"I only looked in to tell you about the F.O.—and about Rosalind. I'll let you know how things go. I'll come in again soon and we'll talk about Italy."

He must keep him. At all costs he must keep him. "Oh, don't go yet. Stay and spend the evening with me. Have a little dinner here. I'm all alone to-night as it happens. (As though he were not alone every night!) Do stay. To please me."

Tom shook his head, smiling. "Afraid I can't. Things I must see to. But I'll soon be round again."

Beaminster went to him, put his hands on his shoulders, held him.

"Tom, please stay. The fact is I'm not very well myself. I don't quite know what's been the matter with me these last weeks. Expect I want a holiday too. Won't you stay to please me?"

Seddon was very kind. He put his hands on to Beaminster's. "Mustn't to-night, Uncle John. But I'm terribly sorry you're not fit. I'll look in to-morrow, and we'll arrange something."

Beaminster's eyes dropped. It was hopeless, for the moment hopeless. He let him go.

The boy smiled, nodded, and was gone.

What to do? Oh, what, what to do? See Rachel? See Rosalind? How useless he was, how *useless*.

But he must do something and at once.

He stood in the middle of the room at bay. An old man in a dry month.

CHAPTER II

JANET POOLE sat alone hearing the wind rise about the house. As always in these days she was listening for Wildherne, and the noise, the thud, the creaking and wailing of the trees made it difficult to hear. In the distance doors were banging, and the little scurries of smoke that blew fussily once and again from the open fire-place seemed themselves to have voices.

An hour ago she had left Wildherne sleeping in his room, had kissed the white weary face, and then had crept to her own sitting-room, lain down on the sofa, her door open, that she might hear his movements.

The little silver clock on her mantelpiece had chimed half-past four. The curtains were drawn, the lamps alight. And outside the storm growled.

She was glad of this respite. It seemed to her that she had not been alone for weeks, or, if alone, weariness had caught her so swiftly that she had had no chance for thought.

It was yesterday morning that the Duchess and Caroline Marsh had departed, but it seemed that it was only five minutes ago. Plenty in *that* to think about! Plenty in everything. . . .

She felt oddly tranquil and calm as she lay there, her thin arms so white behind her dark head and above her black dress. So much pity and sorrow and regret and unavailing anguish had been wrung from her heart that summer that there was no force for them any more, only force for her purpose, for her love, for her gathering power.

For herself, as regarded herself, the worst time had been some two or three weeks after Humphrey's death.

During the first days she had been dumb, asleep it seemed,

only awake about the immediate necessities of the hour, and above all about that watchfulness over Wildherne that had been from the very beginning her foremost duty.

Then, with a crash as though the walls of the house in front of her had been rent, Humphrey had appeared. For days and nights, nights and days, she had seen nothing but him, seen him in every phase and mood and action, seen him and his connection with her from that instant in the little London hotel when she had first been sure of his coming until that moment on the last night when he had turned on the stairs and told her of his cough.

And with every seeing of him there had been remorse and reproach, bitter, fierce, reiterated, savage. She had had no defence. She had not loved him enough; she had not watched over him; she had not loved him enough. Every instant of those moods of jealousy had returned to her, and under the pang of them she had bent her head ever lower and lower.

She had not, during this time, thought of Wildherne. She had seen only Humphrey.

She would have broken and collapsed, perhaps for ever, had it not been for Katherine Mark, for whom they had sent. Katherine had been the only one in the world who could save her. Rosalind had wanted to come; she had been prevented. But Katherine, with her quiet wisdom, her deep understanding, her tenderness and humanity, her strength and sanity, had known what to do.

What she had done was to show Janet that it was Wildherne of whom she must think, that Wildherne's danger was acute, and that no one could save him but Janet.

That was the amazing thing that Janet finally perceived, that that friendship and comradeship on which their marriage had been founded, that friendship and comradeship so often despised by her, was now the one hope of his safety. Even his father could not save him. It was for her and her alone.

And then most strangely it seemed as though Humphrey himself were helping her. She had no spiritualistic contact with him; she had no vivid consciousness that he was yet alive at her hand, and yet it seemed to her that someone who knew Wildherne and loved him was showing her what to do.

At first—for some weeks after the funeral—Wildherne was strangely quiet. He was quiet as a somnambulist is quiet who walks with stealthy steps and closed eyes towards some bourne known to himself alone.

He was from the first exceedingly gentle and submissive. It was as though his own secret purpose was so deep and strong that the little things on the surface might be eternally agreed upon.

He had grown—they were all aware of it—in the space of a night from a boy into a man, grown in this way that he was now formed and set and hardened into a shape concrete and defined.

He was especially sweet to Janet. From the very first it was plain that he felt that he had some especial relation to her that he had to no other.

It was when his father and mother came and tried to persuade him to leave Wintersmoon and go abroad that the first signs of his iron resolve were apparent.

He would not leave Wintersmoon, not for a day, nay, not for an hour. He was gentle to them all, but utterly resolved. Then he told Janet that he did not need his father and mother just then, and begged her to persuade them to return to London.

This was difficult. The Duchess especially, who had adored Humphrey, was convinced that she alone could properly understand Wildherne's need.

Nevertheless it was done. The summer came and Wildherne and Janet were alone.

It had been before this that she had had her own especial agony. And when, after her weeks of almost hopeless submission to it, she had risen again, borne up by Katherine's arms, it had seemed to her at first that without Katherine she could not live. She had felt a terror of remaining alone with Wildherne in this place. She had fought it, overcome it: the horror was pushed back, out of sight. Those August days were wet and cold.

With the coming of these dismal days the House seemed suddenly to droop. It hung its head. The woods draped their green in thin unsubstantial mist, the stone of the House lost its lustre and was ruffled on its surface as though it had been rubbed the wrong way. The air was close and warm under the cold spray of the thin rain. The House lost its heart.

Most strangely Janet felt this. It was maybe that her personal drama had narrowed down only to herself and Wildherne—that they two were shut up in this place, that Wildherne was in peril and must be saved and that his preservation depended on her as completely as though they were isolated on an uninhabited island, because they were thus cut off she was intensely conscious of the House.

She had been conscious of it of course from the first, but once it had been aloof, menacing, scornful. It had flourished its own past history as its own right to pride. She had wondered in the early days of her marriage when Wildherne had talked as though its future life depended upon *him*— upon Wildherne's and herself. Surely it was outside them, independent of them, spinning its own history out of itself, using the people who inhabited it as food for its life. You never really counted in its history until you belonged to its past—until you were dead, in fact.

But, of late, she had seen it in so many varying moods that she was not sure. And then there had come that wonderful moment—that marvellous moment of that wonderful day—when, returning from London, walking from the Lodge, she had seen the House in all its glory, so beautiful, so poignant, so superb, but yet so touchingly beseeching. She knew that it had wanted something of her then— that she and Wildherne had it in their power to make its future glorious or to hasten its sad decay.

Ever since Humphrey's death she had fancied—so odd do one's thoughts become at such a time under such an isolation—that it realised Wildherne's peril, that indeed it was acute, through all its floors, its stairs, its walls, with apprehension, and that the outward figures of its soul—Elizabethan Geoffrey, Francis Poole, beautiful Aubrey, even the

Dark Knight in Silver Armour—were waiting urgently for the issue.

So foolish can one's fancies become in this strange silent isolation!

The trouble was that no one knew what Wildherne was thinking. Since the moment when little Bamfield had stooped down and closed young Humphrey's eyes he had said no single word. No word of himself. His only utterance had been that he would not, not for a day, not for an hour, not for a moment, leave Wintersmoon. That was all.

The doctors—who had not of course examined him but had considered his case—had said that if he did not give way, break down, his brain would go, and often in the early hours of some dreadfully silent morning, Janet had wondered whether his brain had not already gone. Who could tell? Who could know?

He had never once uttered Humphrey's name.

He had been very busy. He had occupied himself with everything to do with the Estates. After Janet, his most constant companion had been Beresford. Wildherne, who had been always vague about business and affairs, was now accurate and persistent. He talked incessantly about this cottage and that, these fields and those, one repair and another. He frowned a little as he talked as though he were trying to remember something. He repeated details over and over again.

The third figure close to him was Hignett. Janet had at last during these months come to know what Hignett truly was, his loyalty, his common sense and, though no word foreshadowed, his heart.

About a week after Humphrey's funeral she had found him one day in one of the bedrooms. He was standing before the window looking out to the Park. In one hand he held some jacket of his master's, the other arm was across his face. He was crying, standing erect as though on parade, crying into his sleeve as a small boy might. He did not know that she had seen him.

She did not know, during those months, what she would have done without him. When complete weariness came over

her and she knew that she must rest or break, she had bee
able to surrender her guard to Hignett with absolute coi
fidence. He was never there when he was not wanted, l
never said anything to her to show that he understood, bi
she knew and he knew that, because they both loved Wild
herne as they did, the bond between them was made fc
life.

Then, only a fortnight ago, when the strain was at it
hardest, the awful thing had occurred.

The Duchess had insisted on coming down and of a
mistaken things she had brought Caroline Marsh with he

Janet had known, from the very beginning, that one da
Caroline Marsh would play her little part in this Purefo
drama, and now she had played it.

The Duchess had not felt over kindly towards Janet ove
the earlier dismissal, and on this second occasion she cam
determined to take things into her own hand.

Caroline Marsh on her side came determined to do Jane
any harm that she could.

The Duchess was not, in any case, suited for this oc
casion. She had dealt for so long in Cases and in Cause
that she was no longer clever about Individuals. She be
longed, too, to a period when Common Sense had been th
thing. She was sure that now it was Common Sense tha
Wildherne needed. He must be forced away from Winters
moon, sent somewhere abroad and, above all, he must b
forced to talk about Humphrey; it was time now that h
was used to the awful but quite inevitable fact of the poo
baby's death. It had been terribly, terribly tragic—no on
had adored Humphrey more than the Duchess—but thi
hanging on in the very place where the child had died, thi
dreadful silence—the worst policy that those who love
Wildherne could pursue.

When she had been a few days at Wintersmoon she ex
plained this to Janet and they had a quarrel, the first rea
quarrel that they had ever had. The grey turban had flashec
fire. Finally the Duchess had, in her anger, said that oi
course no one had been to blame for the poor child's death
but that, nevertheless, if proper care had been taken. . .

nd at that Janet's quiet eyes had flamed, and some unfor-
etable words had been spoken. Very sad.

Caroline Marsh had been present at this quarrel.

After that evening there could be no doubt but that Caro-
ne had done everything possible to incite the Duchess
gainst Janet. The Duchess was a good woman—honour-
ple, loyal and tender-hearted—but she was old and begin-
ing to be weary. Caroline Marsh had been with her for
any years; she knew her well; for the stupid, narrow-
inded, ignorant woman that she was she had a strange
ominating influence over her mistress.

So, with growing dislike for and disbelief in Janet, the
uchess pursued her plan. She could not help but see that
ildherne was ill at ease with her, and avoided any time
one with her. Nevertheless she persisted. She spoke to him
out leaving Wintersmoon, not once nor twice, but many
mes. He did not answer her. Had Caroline not been there
anet might have spoken with her so truly and with such
yalty that the barrier would have been broken down be-
veen them. But Caroline was always there.

Then, two nights ago, the catastrophe occurred. The four
f them were sitting after dinner together, Wildherne busied
s always now with rows of figures and plans of buildings.

The Duchess, her voice trembling a little, had begun. She
ad mentioned Humphrey's name. Then, frightened per-
aps at the silence, she had talked and talked—how sweet
umphrey had been; that no one had loved the dear little
ellow more than she; that his sudden death had been a
readful, dreadful tragedy; that no one had felt the darling's
ss more than she, but that we were all in God's hands;
at the Good God knew what was right for us; that He
ent these agonies to try us, to test us; that His Beloved
on knew our sorrows because He had suffered them all;
at it was therefore wrong of Wildherne, even a little
icked perhaps, to go on thus refusing to mention the lit-
e darling's name; that if this was partly the result of
anet's wish, then, indeed, Janet was terribly to blame. But
he was his mother and knew him as no one else could know
im, and that she now begged him, nay, ordered him, to

break this silence, to accustom himself to think and speak
of Humphrey. All was well with the darling boy. He was
in Paradise with God's saints, and Wildherne must not go
on grieving for him but must be brave and sensible. Yes,
brave and sensible. It was what she wished, what his father
wished, what they all, even Janet, must wish.

She stopped and there was an awful silence. Janet sat
there in an agony of terror, her hands furiously clasped. .

Then Wildherne looked up and at his mother.

"You must go, mother," he said. "Go back to London to-
morrow morning. You must not stay here just now. Later
perhaps, but not now. You must go to-morrow morning."
He got up and left the room.

Next morning the Duchess departed. Before she went she
said one word to Janet:

"It is you that have done this. You have separated me
from my son. I will never forgive you."

It would have helped Janet now could she have seen the
Duke. He had not come down again, but every week he
wrote to her. His letters were enchanting accounts of what
he had been doing and reading and thinking. He had that
gift, the most blessed given to letter writers, of being himself in his letters. He broke off in a temper (or at least a
pretended one), went on again in an excited passion over
Arabia Deserta or *The Dynasts* or *The Verney Letters,* or
chuckled like a child over one of his wife's projects or some
foolishness in the paper or some little street adventure, or
simply followed his own thoughts as though she, Janet, were
his other self.

In every letter there were messages to Wildherne, with
no allusion to his trouble that she could give him or no as
she felt wise.

During yesterday it had been her terror lest, after his
wife's return to London, the letters would cease. Janet knew
that he would not desert her, but some instinct of loyalty
might come in now and prevent him.

And then this afternoon there had been another letter
written late on the preceding evening, and everything was

he same. He made no allusion to the quarrel, but Janet
knew that he understood, yes, understood both his wife
and herself.

As she lay there she was thinking of him, how wonderful
he had always been to her, but how wonderful especially
he had been during these last two years. She thought that
perhaps he might say to himself: "My life's been a failure;
I've done none of the things with it that I ought to have
done. But now at the end of it I at least may do this—
keep these two together, help them to understand one another, out of my useless past help them to build their future."

As she lay there, half awake and half asleep, she was
aware that someone was standing there. Looking up she
saw that it was Hignett.

The alarm in his eyes drove her to her feet.

"My lady—I thought I ought to tell you. His lordship
has gone out."

"Gone out!"

"Yes, my lady. I saw that he wasn't in his room. Mrs.
Beddoes saw him go down the terrace about ten minutes
ago."

For an instant she listened. The house seemed to echo:
"Gone out. Gone out. His lordship's gone out."

With an instinct that came from something wiser than
herself she knew that this was Hignett's business.

"Quickly, Hignett. Will you find him? Go alone. There's
still some light left."

Hignett went. She stood there rigid, waiting.

Hignett, like all fit English servants of the sound old tradition, had feelings but no imagination, and his feelings were
subjected to his code. He saw exactly what was in front
of him, no more, no less, but he felt continually more than
he saw, and this, had he thought of it, would have distressed
him. So he thought as little as might be save about his daily
duties.

Nevertheless, throughout this sad and difficult summer he
had been so unhappy that a new little imp of imagination
had begun to stir in him. What to do to help his master!

How to help his mistress to help his master! How to b
there, watchful and on guard, and yet never in the way
Yes, there were things to think about here. His whole min
was given to them. He forgot even his little boy in Londo:

Now as he walked down across the upper lawn he wa
trembling. How had this happened? What if he should be to
late? And not only was the fear lest his own duty be be
trayed but also the anxiety of his own love. If, through a
these years of comparative happiness and prosperity he ha
cared for his master, how vastly had those affections bee
strengthened through this summer of trouble. Although I
would never, even to himself, have confessed it, considerin
it of the deepest impertinence, yet he had felt through thes
last months as though Wildherne were his own child.

Yes, an impertinence—but there, one's feelings were one
feelings and the only thing to do was to keep them dow:
Mrs. Beddoes, alone of the company below stairs, maintaine
that Hignett had a heart. And Mrs. Beddoes was a sent
mental old woman who cried at the bare mention of th
Royal Family in the daily papers.

A thin driving rain misted the scene. Between the tree
a faint, pallid light shivered under a grey, swiftly-movin
sky.

Wildherne was there. Hatless and without a coat he stoo
between the trees, his arms stretched, staring in front c
him. He saw Hignett, and without moving and speakin
as though he had expected him, said quietly: "Well, Hig
nett?"

"My lord, my lady sent me to ask you whether you woul
come in to tea. There's been a post, a letter from you
father. . . ."

"I was looking for something." Wildherne came up t
Hignett and put his hand on his shoulder. "Do you knov
Hignett, I am sometimes so tired that I simply don't kno'
how to bear it? It comes over me suddenly."

"Yes, my lord."

"And then another thing." He gripped Hignett's shoulde
"It's been a stiff time this year. There are things I don

ant to think about. I suppose there are things with every-
ody that they don't want to think about, but especially it
as been so with me—lately. Well, I sometimes, when I'm
red as I am now, feel as though those things would break
rough, a very thin board between them and me, you know,
 I come out here—to get some air."

The rain was driving down more fiercely now, slant-
ise, as though it liked slapping the faces of the trees.

Wildherne stood close to Hignett, almost leaning against
im.

"Won't you come in, my lord?" Hignett asked. "It's
aining pretty hard."

"Yes, in a moment." He turned round and, putting his
ands on Hignett's shoulders, looked into Hignett's face.

"Now tell me—man to man, you know—no master and
ervant business—do you think there's a God, Hignett?"

"Yes, my lord. I'm sure there is."

"You're sure, are you? That's good. So am I."

"Yes, my lord."

"Yes, and do you know what kind of a God He is?"

"Like one reads of Him in the Bible, my lord."

"Yes. He's a devil, a cruel devilish devil, loving to tor-
ure you, taking from you what you care for most just to
ave the fun of seeing you writhe. He plagued the Egyp-
ans, didn't He?"

"Yes, my lord."

"With serpents and fire and all sorts of dirty tricks. Well,
Ie found that so much to His taste that He's never been
ble to do anything else since. He loves it."

"Yes, my lord."

The rain beat down now torrentially, and all the trees
wayed and groaned and swayed again.

"There's another thing," Wildherne went on, looking at
Iignett with serious examining eyes, "another thing I'd like
 know. Why do you stay in my service, Hignett?"

"Why do I stay, my lord?"

"Yes, why should you? You've saved a lot of money.
Richer than I am, I expect. Why do you stay?"

"Because I'd rather serve you than do anything else with my life," Hignett answered, standing like a rock, the rain soaking his coat.

"Would you indeed?" Wildherne seemed to consider this. "Then you're fond of me?"

"Very, my lord."

"Fonder of me than most?"

"Than of anybody, excepting my boy."

"Indeed!" Wildherne nodded his head. "But why?"

Hignett hesitated. "I don't know, my lord. Because you're like you are," he added after a little thought.

"Because I'm like I am?" Wildherne laughed gently. "That's worth thinking over—seeing what I am. I'm glad you're fond of me, Hignett. I want friends—just now."

He gave him another look, then dropped his eyes.

"We'll go back. Give me your arm."

They walked back, through the rain, arm in arm.

Five minutes later Hignett appeared officially, an automaton, in front of Janet, who still stood where he had left her.

"His lordship is having a bath and will be with you shortly, my lady."

He said that he would have his tea on the table beside him while he worked. "You don't mind, do you?" he said, turning round in his chair and giving Janet a smile that was pathetic in its childish unhappiness.

"No," she said, smiling back to him, "of course not."

"You see, there's such a lot to do, such an awful lot to do." He ran his hand through a sheaf of papers.

"Why not take an evening off?" she asked him. "Go through them with Beresford in the morning."

"I should like to have them straight before to-morrow," sighing like a small boy who had school preparation in front of him. "I get so tired, you know. I was telling Hignett so just now."

Once more she had to sit and wait. Wait for what? She would not face the awful possibility. The men in whom she trusted most told her that for the moment this was the only thing to do. At any time the break might come, and f it came after some fit of irritation or forced distress there vould be active danger of the worst. She must wait. So she sat there quietly, loving him now and fearing for him now, mother as well as wife.

She sometimes, when as to-night the house within was very silent and without was lashed by the rain, fancied that Humphrey and Wildherne were now one. There were turns of the head that Wildherne made, movements of the hand— but she did not dare to pursue that thought too far. . . . If the ache for Humphrey was allowed to rise up in her then she could not stay where she was but must go out and walk the passages. . . . So that little figure was forbidden to enter.

"Speaking of Hignett." Wildherne turned round from his papers again. "I like Hignett."

"Yes," said Janet, "so do I."

"He says that he's fond of me, fond of me for myself, I mean."

"I'm sure he is."

"Funny thing," said Wildherne, "to be fond of me. I've been a pretty useless fellow. . . . That, you see, Janet," he went on eagerly, "is why I'm working at all this now. It's disgraceful how lazy I've been, how much I've neglected —yes, disgraceful."

He turned back and was busy again writing figures.

Janet sat quietly. It seemed that she was reading a book, but beyond the printed page her heart was a warring field of reproach, love, self-condemnation, fear, and then love again.

CHAPTER III

THE CHAPEL ON THE HILL

IT was from the moment when Hignett brought his master in from the wet garden that Janet knew that Wildherne's crisis—the crisis in the lives of both himself and her—was closely approaching

We look back afterwards upon such premonitions and find that everything that has accompanied them has for ever afterwards special significance for us. An evening of grey sky, across whose surface faintly pink clouds slowly and sadly wander, penetrated with thin rain and a little dying wind; a crowded street when, held on the kerb by the passing traffic, we see a woman, stout and comfortable, complacently seizing the moment for the powdering of her nose; a hotel room, untidy with discarded breakfast things, chill and comfortless, its tiny fire weighed down with piled-up coal dust; the sudden darkness of a theatre as the curtain rises, and an unknown world blazing with light is before us—these and such as these are more important possessions for us than our pictures, our clothes and unchanging furniture. They are the settings for our personal drama, only ours, and weighted for ourselves alone with eternal significance.

So now for Janet for ever the dim, slanting rain, the surroundings, furniture, noises of that room in whose centre for twenty minutes she had stood without moving, were to stand for the rising of the curtain on the chief drama of her life. The faint rustle of the fire, a cushion of gold brocade, the light of the lamp falling upon the little glittering silver tree on her writing-table, a book, a shabby Renan *Vi de Jesus,* fallen from the table to the rose-red carpet, none of these would ever be lost by her again.

376

She found, indeed, that everything was from that moment changed. It was as though not only she was now braced for the coming fight, but that all her surroundings were aware of it. She could not tell, strangely, whether they wished her well or ill, could only be sure that they were intensely aware of the importance of this conflict for her. It might be that some were with her and some against, but because she was so alone in this, because, too, her nerves were strained to their uttermost limit by the terrible summer through which she had just passed, she was abnormally aware of everything that touched her. Clothes and furniture, books and movements, and the sudden voices of clocks and bells, and above all of the house and its surroundings.

Walking on the morning that followed this evening among the trees below the lawns—it was a lovely morning of shining sun and brilliant air—she came unexpectedly upon a little stone statue of a naked Bacchus, vine-wreathed with protuberant paunch and a deriding leer. This had been found years ago in Italy by some earlier duke; it was shabby now with wind and rain; she had always been aware of its presence, had always disliked it, but never actively, with any conscious perception of it.

Now in a moment it seemed to have some especial significance for her. The sun shone upon its gross nakedness marking the streaks of rain, the droppings of birds, the shabby wearings of the stone; it seemed to Janet to have some particular malevolence for her, as though it would vent upon her especially its neglect and weary exile in this dreary, dark English country. She turned away from it with fresh fear at her heart.

Wildherne had during the last weeks resumed an old habit recently neglected, riding. Janet loved horses and everything to do with them, and she had always hoped that Wildherne would one day recover this pleasure. But their rides had not been the easiest part of her day, because during the course of them he was absolutely silent. When she talked he seemed not to hear her, and so she herself had fallen into long reveries, scarcely seeing the country through which they passed. It was on these excursions that Humphrey most persistently accompanied her. When in the house she could occupy herself with a hundred details, but now, passing through the quiet grey autumnal country, she seemed to be riding on a ghostly horse through a ghostly country and her baby was with her, so close, so insistent, that it was as though she could see his little body floating through the air in front of her just beyond her reach, but looking back to her, smiling gaily as he used to do, but always silent—the three of them silent—wraiths in the misty English air.

But it happened one afternoon when they had gone a little way, riding slowly side by side, that Wildherne began to speak. It was as though he were talking to himself, not looking at her, staring in front of him at the bare trees, the fields, sodden with rain, lit with pale evanescent sheets of thin sunlight. He talked about the estate, as now he was always doing, arguing with himself: "Yes, perhaps that's the thing to do," or "Everything takes so long. I must hurry the men up. Beresford is far too casual." Then suddenly, as though only that instant aware that she was with him, he turned towards her:

"You know, Janet, it's very good of you to come out with me like this. No one's ever been so good to me as you are. It must be so dull for you down here. Why don't you go up to London for a bit and enjoy yourself?"

"I'd rather be with you here," she answered quietly.

"Would you really? That's sweet of you. But I expect that's partly because you think I want looking after. I don't really, I've got plenty to do."

"Would you rather I went away for a little?" she asked him. "Does it irritate you my being here?"

She felt a great excitement. This was the first time he had spoken in any way about their relation to one another since Humphrey's death.

"No, of course, I wouldn't. I should miss you very much. It was only for your sake I suggested it. But you've had such a lot of me and my family since we married. Why don't you go up to London, not to Halkin Street, but to your friends the Marks, or to Rosalind, somewhere away from all the family affairs, to make a change?"

"I'd rather be here with you," she answered again.

"It's a funny thing," he went on, as though he hadn't heard her, "but we all of us—my father and mother and the rest of us—seem to be quite outside all modern life. I was reading the other night a novel—one of those books about modern London life—and it was full of dancing and jazz bands and smart young women. People were for ever mixing cocktails and having intrigues—up all night and the rest of it. I've been wondering. It's a funny thing, but I don't know a single human being like that, and none of the men or women I know live in the least like that. It exists, of course. I've missed it all. Not that I mind for myself, of course. I never had many friends anyway, father has always kept apart and mother wouldn't care for these people in any case, but for you . . . I'd like you to have some fun."

"That wouldn't be my kind of fun," Janet answered. "I should be at a loss in that world, awkward and stupid. I'm very happy as I am."

"I've always been shy," he went on, "all my life. There *is* a kind of shyness in our family. As soon as I begin to do something or meet someone new I distrust myself. They can't really want to know me, I say to myself. And I seem to talk so foolishly, to say such silly things. I think to myself, 'Well, you may think you like me, but when you see a little further into me you'll wonder that you ever wasted time over me.' When I'm at home here, in the house or in the fields, I don't think that. They've known me so long that they can't be deceived in me—and with some of the people about the place, Hignett and Beresford. And with you too, if I may say so. I always felt that about you, that you would understand and forgive—understand and forgive," he repeated.

They were going slowly uphill. The white road was like a long thin cord in the pale sky.

Janet longed to cry: "Oh, Wildherne, I love you so.

'Realise that. Build on it. Try and love me a little in return."

But the strange stillness of that autumn afternoon, broken only by the sound of their horses on the road and the flight of an occasional bird, weighted every word with heavy significance. At any instant she felt the crisis would break upon them; it must be his own action that produced it, not hers.

They had reached the hill-top and a stretch of country lay before them, grey and silver shot with the pale sunlight.

He began again as they started downhill, peering in front of him as though a thick veil of dusk hung between him and the landscape.

"There is something I must do, Janet, and I don't know what it is. I want to lose myself, my hateful, useless self, but I must find myself first. Then when I've seen what I am I can get rid of myself for ever. No one can help me. I'm very unhappy, Janet, but I'm like someone in a dream —a dream that won't break."

She felt a wave of poignant distress overwhelm her. In another moment she might collapse hopelessly. Perhaps that would be best for them both, but again her acute fear of what might come to them if she gave way made her steel herself. Their horses were now very close together; she put out her hand and touched his arm. He did not move away, but even came a little nearer to her, and they rode down the hill thus.

"Perhaps you shouldn't be too distressed, Wildherne," she said at last, "at your own idea of yourself. If we think of ourselves at all we must be frightened of what we are and of the things we do. What you say is true—that there's nothing that you could say or do that I wouldn't understand. Nothing. We are so much tenderer to those—we love—than we are to ourselves—that is why I like to be with you and will always."

It was the first time that she had ever told him that she loved him. She waited, her heart beating, for his next words.

But he had not, it seemed, heard her. He looked about him.

"I love this country, this pale misty country. Whenever I have been to North Africa or Egypt it has seemed wonderful at first, and then after a week or two I've longed for this, for the thin rain and the flowers wet in the hedges and the rare sheets of sunlight."

He spurred his horse and they galloped, the chill air beating about their faces.

As they galloped her soul rose within her like a bird. Her soul? Silly talk. Aren't we modern enough now to discard that ridiculous notion? Gas and ether—bones and nerves. But nevertheless it seemed at that moment like Janet's soul.

"Janet, let me out. I need air. I'm hungry, Janet, hungry for freedom and splendour. Janet, let me out!"

She dreamt, it might be, as they swung through the air, dreamt of pots and pans, of whirligigs and barrel organs, of nasturtiums that stray across the garden path and of wine-coloured carnations streaked with pink, of stockings and collars and tortoise-shell combs, and of the dead light in the corridor of Wintersmoon when, standing still on a cold night, you could hear the mice scratching.

Then through her dream came perhaps the whistle of defiance, the little shrill baby cry of that soul so justly squashed like a pea-pod by the modern mind.

"Let me out, Janet, and we'll see what we can do. Give me freedom so that I can fly through this winy wind and you can follow me. See what liberty you'll have, what new bravery and courage. Let me out! Let me out!"

This may be, and this may not be. Who can tell when, looking back on his journey down into the dark cellar, he wonders what he found there? Broken bottles and a blind bat, or the magpie's store; here a glittering pin, there a broken comb, a piece of tulle and a fragment of looking-glass, or nothing at all—only the coal and the coal dust and spiders' webs overhead. Anyway the journey into the cellar was little worth the while whatever old Grand-uncle Freud might fancy.

And Janet's dream, whether it led her upwards into the air or downwards into the cellar, was broken.

The horses were standing. The sunlight was all about

them, and in front of them on the rise of a green hill tha swung into open down was a little chapel.

"I don't remember," said Wildherne, "ever to have seer this before. Where are we?"

"I've no idea," Janet answered, laughing. "I don't know whether I was asleep or awake during that last ride. There's a village to the left down there. It might be Wintringham I never felt so lost in my life."

They tied their horses to a gate and walked towards the chapel.

It was a very old building. The strongest impression of it was that it was light and delicate; you wondered when you looked at it why, as it stood here in so exposed a place, it had not been blown away long before. The stonework shone in this sunlight with a faint pink colour, very old stone that all the weathers had loved and cherished and worked upon.

It was beautiful indeed in colour rather than in form, being a little square building with roof of faded red brick and a thin little tower like a pointing finger. The long lean windows looked as if they held fine old glass. There was no graveyard, no enclosure, no church notices on the little door. The road ran straight past it as though it knew it so well that there was no reason, at this late day, to pause.

They went in.

Within, everything was of the simplest. A little square phalanx of cane-bottomed chairs, an altar with two silver candlesticks, and a white bowl in which were fresh chrysanthemums amber-coloured. A wooden crucifix hung over the altar. The windows were of fine glass, old rich faded purple, dark blue, orange, crimson. Someone came here, someone tended it, but now the splashes of sunlight on the stone floor that seemed to move faintly like stirring water were the only life there. The silence was absolute.

Janet and Wildherne sat down.

Janet prayed. "O God, if Thou art God, help me. I have been very unhappy. I need some strength to be given me that I may help those whom I love when the time for my help comes. I know that my own strength is not enough.

I seem of myself to be nothing at all. If Thou art there, help me that I may be wise and strong."

She smiled, as though some happiness had suddenly come to her, and turned to Wildherne. He was staring, as so often during these last months she had seen him stare. His hands were folded on the back of the little chair in front of him so tightly that the knuckles stood out white and shining. His brow was knit in a frown, and his lips were parted as though he were about to speak.

Something deep and fierce was struggling in him. Far, far down in him a battle was waging. He looked like a man who was about to wake from some terrible nightmare. His lips moved; he gave a little moan and then sank, huddled, down from the chair on to the floor.

With a little cry she ran out into the sunlight. She remembered that at the side of the road through thick grass there ran a stream. She had with her a pocket metal cup that she always from long habit took with her on any expedition. She filled this with water. But when she returned she found that he was already recovering. His eyes, bewildered, were staring about him, and he was on his knees. She put her arm around him, supporting him.

"Where . . . ?" he asked. Then sighed. "How stupid of me! I've never done that before."

With her help he stood on his feet. He smiled at her. "Thank you. I've never done that before."

"Are you all right?"

He drank the water gratefully.

"Yes, of course. The place swam in front of me." He walked quite steadily to the door. "The air will put me right in a moment."

He looked back from the doorway. "Pretty little place. Come, Janet, we'll go home."

"Are you sure you can ride?"

"Why, of course."

There was great peace outside with the sunlight, the green hill, the horses pulling at the grass, the whisper of the running stream.

"Jolly little place. It must have been a bit close inside."

They mounted their horses and slowly rode down the hill. They went on for a mile or so, and then a sign-post pointed them home.

All the way back they rode together, her hand on his arm. But Janet saw in his face that the crisis in him had begun. He was waking.

He went early to bed that night. She lay awake for many hours. "Soon he will need me desperately. This is the culminating point of all our lives together. Nobody else can stand beside him now but I."

The door between their rooms was open. All through the long hours she heard his long steady breathing.

Next morning on the breakfast table there was a letter for her from Rosalind. Opening it she saw that it was longer than Rosalind's usual hurried scribbled note.

This was the letter:

MY DARLING MOPS—You'll be surprised to have a long letter from me, and indeed I'm surprised at writing it. Perhaps I shall tear it up and not send it. It's early in the morning—three o'clock—and for once in a way I can't sleep. Most unlike me, isn't it? I think one always tears up the things one writes at three o'clock in the morning, so probably I shall destroy this— no loss to you if I do. Well, my dear, what am I writing about? Oh yes, Tom and I have agreed at last—the first thing we've agreed upon for years—to separate. First he would, then he wouldn't, then he would. At last after a terrible row last night it's finished. I can endure it no longer, nor, poor boy, can he.

Janet, I've tried—really and truly I've tried. If, as a family, we have anything to pride ourselves on—of course you have, heaps of things—it is that we're honest, and I've always been honest to you at any rate, at least nearly honest. I'm telling you God's own truth—although as a matter of fact I don't believe at all in the Deity's honesty—when I tell you that I've tried with Tom, tried again and again. But everything I do to Tom seems to drive him mad. He wants me to love him in *his* kind of way, and I don't and can't—I never did and I never will. Call me hard and selfish if you like, I don't mind abuse a bit, and, after all, everyone sees one from a different angle. People see you as *they* are, not as *you* are, don't they? And

I know some who think me sentimental and soft. Perhaps I
am. Perhaps I am both soft and hard. At any rate to Tom
and his mother I seem the hardest and cruellest creature ever
born alive.

Anyway, darling Mops, my original sin was in marrying
him. I knew it. Oh, I knew it before I did it, but he wanted it
so badly, and I seemed so stray and unwanted, and *he* seemed
so gay and happy—and there you are!

But I'm not trying to defend myself. I don't believe in these
excuses. There we were, Tom and I, shut up together like mice
in a mouse-trap and no escape. He wanted different things
from life, utterly different things. He wanted the old things,
passion, soft soppy passion, and all the old ideas, no new ones,
everything to go on for ever and ever, as it always had done,
amen. And I wanted to move on, to take nothing for granted,
to see everything as it is without sentiment or tradition. I
loved him physically. Those were our happiest times at first.
We seemed to come together then as we did in no other way.
But even into that he brought in so many things that were
foolish. He must worship me, he said, and I can't bear to be
worshipped. Even you, you darling, used to irritate me in the
old days by that. I to be worshipped! Folly, and now you know
it. It grew worse with him instead of better. I moved on—how
can anyone put anyone's body, all alone by itself, so high?
But he stuck like a fly in the jam—stuck and refused to be
pulled out.

But why do I tell you all this when you know it all so well?
Perhaps because last night was the finish between me and Tom,
and I would like now to be fair to us both.

And then the mother. Oh, Mops darling, why couldn't you
have kept her away from us, at any rate for a bit until we'd
settled into some sort of relationship? She always hated me.
She never thought I was good enough for him. I wasn't, not
as she saw him, but why did she never try to understand me,
to show him better the way to deal with me? And why did I
never try to understand her? I couldn't. There was something
about her that seemed to me so foolish, one of those silly
women in a Turgenieff novel that he makes fun of. Of course
she *isn't* like that. You wouldn't have loved her for so long if
she had been that, but why didn't *you* try to bring us closer
together, you who loved us both?

But I'm not reproaching you. Poor dear, you've had your
own hands full.

But now, at three in the morning, Mops darling, I want you, want you as I've never in all my life wanted you before. I don't believe in leaning on people. I would be independent before everything else in the world, but now, just at this minute, I'm frightened, frightened of myself, of life, of everything. If I *don't* tear this up in the morning, won't you come to me, come just for a night, and scold me and bully me and put me just where I ought to be? I'm sure Wildherne can spare you for an hour or two.—Your loving sister,

ROSALIND.

Rosalind needed her. Never before in all their two lives had she appealed to Janet like this. It was for this that Janet had always longed, that Rosalind should need her help, and that she, Janet, should give it.

And now—she could not leave Wildherne.

Oh, what was she to do, what *was* she to do?

All that morning, through the breakfast talk with Wildherne, through the interviews with the housekeeper and Hignett, through the notes that she must write, through an inspection of flowers with the head gardener, this continued —*what* must she do?

Of course she must go to Rosalind. Rosalind was her first claim, always and for ever. All their youth together, all those countless things, those battles and parings and scrapings, those intimate talks, those sorrows and triumphs, all had led only to this. And even without these, was it not Janet's duty? Had not she been, in the main, responsible for this unlucky marriage? Would Rosalind have married Tom had Janet not married Wildherne?

No, she must go to Rosalind, and at once.

But Wildherne——?

Throughout that morning, although she had seen him only for that brief moment at breakfast, she was conscious of an odd suppressed excitement in him. A great change had come to him since yesterday morning. As he had left the breakfast table he had turned to her and said:

"Janet, I'm so glad you're here. I don't know how things would be without you."

And if she left him, even for half a day, what might happen while she was away? Supposing . . . Supposing. . . . She put her hand over her eyes to hide from herself a vision too awful for contemplation.

No, she must stay with him now whoever in all the world called her.

But Rosalind, of what was she afraid? Was it this man Ravage, or someone else whom Janet did not know? Or was it simply of life and her own impulses? Or was it fear for Tom and of what he might do?

Janet had seen so little of her lately. They had not had, in the last year, one confidential talk—and now this appeal. . . .

The afternoon came and she had reached no decision. Wildherne went off to the village with Beresford.

It was an afternoon of sweeping mist, and behind the mist there was a strange sombre glow as though from some distant conflagration. Against this light the house stood out like a white ghost—a ghost staring wistfully above the dank lawns to the hidden army of trees.

She paced the terrace, shifting from decision to decision. Then suddenly, as though in a vision, she saw Rosalind, waiting, afterwards with a shrug realising that Janet would not come, resolving some dreadful action. Behind her there were always two figures, shabby, motionless, Ravage and Tom, white-faced and desperate.

Yes, she would go to Rosalind. She called Hignett. She would send a telegram.

He came.

"Hignett, I want——" She broke off. "Hignett, speak to me as a friend. Tell me—to-day have you seen any change in Lord Poole?"

"Yes, my lady, I have."

"What exactly do you mean?"

"Well, my lady, he's terribly excited. It's my belief he's realising things for the first time, or will any minute. It was after you came in from your ride yesterday——"

"Yes."

"Well, my lady, it's hard to describe exactly, but I was in

his room when he was dressing for dinner and he took my
arm, held it tight. He was trembling, my lady, all over his
body, and he said, 'Hignett,' he said, 'don't leave me just
now, I'm frightened.' That's what he said, my lady. I asked
him whether he'd like me to sleep in his room. He said
no, he didn't want that. Only for me to be around. He looked
terrible tired, worn out."

"Yes," said Janet.

"If you'll excuse me, my lady, just these days he wants
watching. It's like the doctors said, it can go one way or the
other. No one can say which."

"Thank you, Hignett. Will you get me a telegraph form?"
When he brought it she wrote:

Dreadfully sorry, darling, Wildherne not well. Must stay
for the time. Will come the first moment possible. Writing.

The evening was quiet, and as usual Wildherne, after
dinner, worked at his figures and his maps of roads and
lanes and woods.

Janet pretended to read. Her ears were strained, as though
someone had instructed her that there would be some sound
that she must not, she *must* not miss. So she had been for
many months.

They parted at her door. He kissed her tenderly. He
looked, as Hignett had said, desperately tired. Then, astonishingly, she fell at once asleep. She was herself worn out,
and especially by her struggle that day.

She had a strange dream. She was with Rosalind, who
was pulling with naked hands at a thick stone wall. "It
must come down! It must come down!" she repeated again
and again. "Janet, help me!"

A cry broke in upon the dream. Janet heard it first in
her sleep, then, wide awake, she heard it repeated:

"Humphrey!"

She ran into the next room. She could see Wildherne
by the light of the flickering fire. He was sitting up, his
hands were raised, his eyes staring. He cried again and
again in a voice of agony:

"Humphrey! Humphrey! Humphrey!"

Her arms were round him; she could feel, beneath his jacket, that his body was damp with sweat.

"Wildherne, darling. Beloved. Wildherne. I'm here! We're together!"

He turned in her arms fiercely. "Humphrey's dead. Humphrey! Humphrey! My boy—my darling Humphrey! He's dead, he's dead. Oh, he's dead!"

She held him to her breast as though she were saving him from some furious enemy.

"Yes, Wildherne. Yes, he's dead. But I'm with you. I've lost him too. Wildherne, dearest, dearest. We've lost him together."

His voice broke:

"Oh, Humphrey! . . ." He turned his face to hers. "He's gone, he's gone. . . ."

He looked at her wildly, not seeing her, then burst into a torrent of tears.

He crouched in the bed, hiding his head on her knees. She stroked his hair, kissed him again and again, a queer odd triumph in her heart. He broke into unfinished words; his body heaved with great sobs. He flung up his head, starting away from her.

"Humphrey, come back!" he cried.

He waited, as though listening. Then he caught her to him with a fierce convulsive grasp. He pressed his face, wet with tears, against hers.

He did not speak again, only his body shook with sobs. And so, strained body to body, they stayed.

CHAPTER IV

JOURNEY IN RAIN

THE rain pelted. It came down maliciously, hitting the pavement with fury, kicking up its contemptuous heels, showing London, as it often had showed her before, that it could do anything with her that it pleased. And London surrendered, as she had always done since she was an insignificant gathering of mud huts on a yielding marsh. For centuries she had surrendered. In these days she gave up without a struggle.

And the rain could see no difference. London might boast of her advancing civilisation, her electricity, flaunting it now as she did in shapes and colours on the surfaces of her buildings, her traffic swift and gleaming and cock-sure—the rain dealt with it all in a moment and reduced everything, humans, lights and shadows, screaming chariots, to one muddled muddy significance.

The rain knew what it was doing, and was glad.

As the afternoon wore into thick humid dusk you might fancy that the old world was back again, the old world of marsh and mire, gigantic monsters peering through the gloom with leaden eyes, the gimcrack shoddy buildings sucking down into oblivion.

The rain had its way.

Rosalind, in her taxi, looked eagerly through the gloom for her Bloomsbury safety. Safety, that was what she needed, safety and Janet.

The panic that had dictated that letter early yesterday morning had persisted until now. She was afraid of she knew not what, she who had boasted that she feared nothing. Afraid of Tom, of Ravage, of life, but above all of herself. She could endure it no longer, this half and half,

390

this existence in which she was for ever on the edge of—what? She did not know. Janet would clarify everything for her. That was Janet's great quality, that she saw her way plain before her. Or did she? And was that what Rosalind wanted from her? Was it not comfort that, in spite of her fine talk, she wanted: comfort and kindliness and reassurance?

These last months with Tom had been frightful. His sudden disappearances, the change in him towards a desperation that moved Rosalind to an agony of irritation and an impotent pity. She must be rid of it all, of this present life of hers, and Janet must help her.

As she paid the taxi-man and felt for her latch-key she thought, with an almost wild sense of reassurance, that perhaps Janet was already there. She would have had the letter at breakfast, and if she left at once she could be here. She was sitting there by the fire—Rosalind could see her—leaning forwards towards the fire, her hands raised to catch the blaze. And then what a talk they would have! They would return, back, back, to their old relationship, together again as though none of these horrible years had intervened. And she would do what Janet advised her—if not altogether, then nearly. She would never take Tom back, of course, but, short of that, anything that would comfort him, make things easier for him, poor Tom. . . .

She cried to the maid, "Is Lady Poole here?"

"No, my lady. But there's a telegram."

She snatched it from the table and read it:

Dreadfully sorry, darling, Wildherne not well. Must stay for the time. Will come the first moment possible. Writing.

Wildherne, Wildherne, Wildherne! That idiot! Wildherne!—always Wildherne!

She read it again, then tore it into little pieces and flung it on the fire. That nincompoop, more woman than man, sitting down there in a sulk—fool! And Janet a fool too to humour him!

Oh well, then, if Janet didn't care enough for her to come, even for an hour, when she was in trouble! Oh well, then

—that was the end of that! So much for sisterly love, so much for all Janet's reproaches and protestations! No more Janet for her!

She was alone, then, absolutely alone. She could stand it. Oh yes, she'd show them whether she could carry her own weight or no! Catch her bothering Janet again. Not she. Never, never, never so long as she lived.

She stood in front of the fire, her face hardening. What a fool she had been to trust in Janet. One must trust no one. Go by oneself. That's what Ravage had always said, and he was right. At least one knew where one was with him. He never said a word more than he meant. No, and not so much as he meant. Well—she shrugged her shoulders— she would go her own way. This was a lesson. If she *was* alone she would *be* alone and would look after herself finely. How she despised herself for sending that letter! A moment of sentimental weakness. That incorrigible sentimentality always recurring, always urging her to foolishness— just as Ravage told her.

Her panic had left her. She was afraid of nobody and of nothing. There was nothing to be afraid of, and even though there were she could deal with it. Keep down your feelings and you could deal with anything—let them poke up their silly stupid noses and you didn't know where you were.

She raised her head. The bell had rung. Perhaps Janet had repented and come after all! Oh, if she had——! She moved eagerly to the door. That would be just like her, struggling with her duty to Wildherne and then, after all, loving Rosalind too much not to come to her. Her pride surged up again. After all, she meant something to Janet. Janet couldn't dismiss her as easily as that.

The door opened and Tom came in. At the sight of him Rosalind was afraid as she had never in her life been afraid before. He was neatly and tidily dressed—there was no disorder about him anywhere—but his eyes were crazy, eyes that belonged to no one, that had a determined frantic life of their own. His face was grey, his hair most carefully brushed, and he carried in his hand a pair of new bright brown gloves.

"Oh, Rosalind," he said quietly. "I hope you don't mind. I wanted to see you. Alice said that you weren't seeing anybody, but I had to see you. I told her so."

He softly closed the door behind him and then stood in front of it. Her wits were astray. She didn't know what she should do. Her only thought was that she should get help from somewhere. If he would move away from the door. . . .

She tried to speak easily.

"I wasn't expecting you, Tom. Why didn't you ring up? But as you're here come over to the fire and get warm. It's a pig of a day, isn't it?"

"No, thank you, Rosalind. I'll stay here if you don't mind."

The dull dead accents of his voice irritated her with that sense of aggravated impotent pity, and this irritation stayed, for a moment, a little of her fear.

"Well, what is it, Tom? There's really just now nothing for us to talk about."

"Do you think so? I can't agree. You mustn't think, Rosalind, that I've come here just to make a row. I haven't indeed. No row I assure you. I've been very unwell, but I'm better. Quite all right. Quite all right."

He didn't look at her but about the room, examining all the familiar things as though he were seeing them for the first time.

"I'm glad you're better. But do you think it's any *use* our seeing one another just now? I thought we'd decided about the main things. Let us meet a little later on when we've had time to think."

Then a wave of real pity moved her.

"Come, Tom, and get warm. You look so cold. Let's be sensible. You mustn't stay very long. Someone's coming to see me, but just for ten minutes come to the fire and let's be friends."

"No thank you, Rosalind. I'll stay here. Ravage, I suppose. But I'm more important than Ravage. He can wait. I'm your husband you see."

"Very well," she answered firmly. "But all the same I can't talk now. I'm tired and I've been soaked. I must change my things. I won't talk now. That's flat. You must go."

"Oh no, I won't go," he answered. "You've had things your own way a lot, but I'm going to have *my* way now. I'm coming back here altogether. It isn't right that you shouldn't live with your husband, neither right nor proper. I've come back for good."

"No you haven't," she cried; "let that be clear. I'll never live with you again, not for an hour. Whatever you threatened would make no difference. You can talk for ever. Now get away from that door and let me go."

He moistened his lips with his tongue.

"Yes, very well—but if you don't let me stay I am going to kill you—and then finish myself. I have a revolver here. I've thought it all out, I can assure you. Yes, I've thought it all out and I've decided that if you don't let me stay with you, you oughtn't to live. It wouldn't be fair. It wouldn't really. You're going and having a good time after what you've done. But if you let me stay it will be all right. I promise you it will."

He moistened his lips again and put his right hand into his coat pocket, letting his gloves fall to the floor.

Then she knew what terror was. For the first time she was with someone who was not sane, who had thrown away all the rules by which people played the game of life, all the rules of safety, decency, and civilisation. There was nothing to appeal to. He was living now in a world entirely of his own —he saw no other—and he was shutting her up with him.

She moved back to the wall and he said:

"At once, if you ring the bell or call out I'll shoot you. I've considered everything . . . the only sensible thing to do."

"Now that's nonsense, Tom. You know you won't do anything of the kind. That's silly talk—melodrama. How are things going to be better if you shoot both of us? I never heard such silliness."

"Yes, things wouldn't be better," he answered gravely, "but they wouldn't be worse. They couldn't be. You see, Rosalind," he went on gently, as though he were arguing with her about some unimportant trifle, "I can't go on suffering as I have been suffering. You oughtn't to ask me to.

I've had such a bad time that it mustn't go on any longer. It's your fault as well as mine. We're both to blame, so we both ought to suffer, oughtn't we? So it seems to me. Only fair. You haven't tried to help me as you might have done. You really haven't. Now I promise you that it will be quite all right if I stay. I'll be quiet and not bother you, no more than a husband has a right. Of course I won't let you be quite as free as before. That wasn't good for you. I see that now. A wife ought to listen to her husband sometimes, about her friends and so on. In the past you haven't listened to me enough, but still you shall have a lot of freedom—only we'll be more together. Yes, much more together," he repeated, smiling as though he was pleased at his own thoughts.

She had gathered now some strength. Oh, if only someone would come. Alice or anybody. The silence about them was awful. It was as though they two were alone in the middle of a hot and arid wilderness.

She tried to speak quietly.

"Yes, we'll see, Tom. I know that I've been terribly to blame in our not getting on together. I recognise that. I don't want to be unfair, and I'll do everything I can. But why don't you rest here? Have some tea and a sleep? You look so awfully tired. I'll go and have a bath and change my things and then we'll have a talk. We'll both see everything more in proportion."

She moved a little towards him.

"Oh no, you don't," he said, smiling again. "We must settle this now. No postponements. No, indeed. I'm not tired, thank you. At least not very. And it's all so simple. There's nothing to discuss. Either you're my wife again and we love one another and are happy as we ought to be or I end the thing for both of us. Perhaps that really would be better. Life isn't much fun, is it? No, life isn't much fun, that's certain. I used to think so once, but I was very young. Oh, I had great plans once, but they're all over, finished. No plans any more."

If only she could ring the bell without his seeing her; but his eyes, although they were ever wandering about the room, were ever still for a moment, yet never seemed to leave her.

She sat down.

"Well then—I've nothing more to say. Do what you please. You shan't stay here, make your mind up to that!"

He came forward into the room. "Oh yes, I will. You can't order me about any more, Rosalind, as you used. No you can't. My mind's made up."

He took a small revolver out of his pocket and looked at it. He regarded it gravely then put it back into his pocket.

And the sight of the revolver had the strangest effect upon Rosalind. She was in a moment swept with rage. Anger such as she had never known convulsed her. Why? She never afterwards, looking back, knew. The idiocy of it, the silliness —yes, Tom's silliness since the start of their life together, beginning with some sentimental sentence, ending with this revolver. And that *she* should be concerned in a scene like this, a tuppeny scene, a scene of sawdust, she . . . she . . . she. . . .

She crossed the room to him, then caught his shoulders and, trembling with rage, shook him until he nearly fell, stumbling back against the piano.

"You fool . . . you silly idiotic fool! You brainless ass . . . to come here . . . here . . . to me . . . with a thing like that . . . how dare you?"

She stepped away from him. He steadied himself, his knees bent, leaning back on the piano.

He said nothing; he stood there, his head hanging.

She stood there, panting, her hand to her breast.

"Now go," she said. "You've been fool enough. Go and let me never set eyes on you again."

He staggered as though he would fall. She was touched once more by her tiresome pity.

"Now . . . we can't talk after this. You see that we can't. I'll write to you—but for heaven's sake go now."

He said nothing. Then he looked at her. If he wished for his revenge he had it then.

She did not know what, afterwards, she was to suffer for that look.

With stooping head he turned and left her.

When she knew that he was gone she walked about the room speaking aloud. "To think that *I'd* stand that. . . . But how ridiculous! How silly! The two of us! Climax to everything. . . . I'll get away . . . I must. At once. . . . This place . . . I hate it. This beastly room. This *beastly* room. That's enough. That's settled it. Finished it."

As she moved she knocked on to the floor a large silver frame containing a photograph of Janet. She left it there. She had a wild impulse to break everything in the room. Everything. Smash it all up.

She sat down and wrote two notes. The envelopes were addressed one to Tom, one to Janet.

Then she went to the telephone.

"Is that you, Charles? Good. I'm coming round to see you at once. Yes, at once. I'm leaving this for good and all. Tom's been here—and for the last time I assure you. Are you alone? Good. We'll have to talk. . . . No, not now. Wait till I come."

She rang then for Alice.

Alice, who was pretty, clever, and without any morals to speak of, adored her mistress—or at least for the moment adored her. Her emotions were evanescent, whisky and soda emotions. She had always despised Tom and was quite on Rosalind's side in that affair. She fancied that the end had come, but she did not mind because very shortly she was going as mannequin somewhere. She had a charming figure. Rosalind's dresses fitted her perfectly. She hoped that Rosalind would go out that evening, because her at-the-moment lover, a chauffeur with some people in Curzon Street, would be coming round.

"Alice, I'm going to have a bath and change. Pack my bag. I shall be away for a night or two. If I'm away longer I shall write to you. Stay here until you get a letter from me. Do you understand?"

"Yes, my lady."

"And here are two notes. I want you to post them both to-morrow morning."

"Yes, my lady."

"Well then—all right. That's everything. Turn the bath on."

Alice looked at the silver frame on the floor. "There's been a row," she thought.

At the door she saw a pair of bright brown gentleman's gloves. She picked them up and laid them on the piano.

Rosalind, sitting back in the taxi, thought of nothing at all. She was so monstrously tired that thought was an eccentricity. But the few steps upwards into the Ryder Street building frightened her. "This is irrevocable," the long badly-painted hall with its ferns in green glazed pots said to her, "you've jumped—and you'll never go back. You won't be allowed to."

"No, you won't be allowed to," the fat pale-faced hall porter seemed to repeat to her.

"I'm going up to see Mr. Ravage," Rosalind said. "Would you mind looking after this bag for half an hour. I have to catch a train later."

"Certainly, Madam," the porter said, weary but admiring. "There's a beauty," he thought (he had not seen her before). Then considered his wife who was *not* a beauty, and a girl in a Lyons' tea-shop, a friend of his, who emphatically resembled this lady—"only, of course," he considered, "Amy dresses smarter."

Rosalind's fears (they had swept up and down all day, approaching and receding like waves on a shore) rolled forwards again as she stepped out of the lift. So bachelor this place was! Two men in their shirt-sleeves in the passage brushing coats and pressing trousers; suits of clothes hanging over the bannisters—rows of boots.

She had no place here. Ravage would think her a fool, yes, but he would be pleased. This was what for so long he had wanted.

How secret it all was here! You had to burrow if you wanted to get to Ravage! Up sudden little stairs, down thin squeezing passages, past mysterious whispering doors, so little light, so little sound.

Then he was at the door, and oh! she was glad to see him.

"Come in." He led her through into his funny sitting-room with the beams, the windows that faced such twisted roofs, such erratic chimneys.

"You're cold. Come to the fire. Beastly day, isn't it? Listen to the rain on the roof! Like a charge of cavalry. Well, what's it all about?"

She took off her gloves and warmed her hands. Then kneeling before the fire turned her face to him.

"I've had an awful afternoon. Tom arrived and with a revolver if you please!"

"Good God!"

"Yes—all that. He was half crazy. I was so sorry for him and so irritated and so frightened that I didn't know what to do. He threatened that if I moved one inch he'd shoot me and then himself. I think at first he meant it, but only at first. He isn't the sort really to do a thing like that. Well, what he wanted was to come back and live with me again. After all that we'd discussed it returned to this. I tried at first to be friendly, but when he produced the revolver I was so exasperated that I went and shook him. I was angrier than I'd ever been in my life. The silliness of it, Charles! The idiocy of it! Like a scene in a bad play—and it seemed such a shame that after all our efforts to be sensible it should come down to this sort of nonsense. . . . After I shook him he went away."

"Went away?"

"Yes, quietly, without a word, his head hanging. Then I could stand no more of it. Simply no more. I wanted to smash the furniture, everything in that beastly room that had seen so many silly sights, listened to so many quarrels. Beastly place—I'll never return to it. *That's* over anyway. So I came to you."

He looked at her. She was squatting now on the floor, her hands still towards the blaze. She seemed now to belong here. She had never been so before. And was lovelier, he fancied, than he had ever seen her.

"At last . . ." he murmured to himself and sighed.

"Let's have the truth," he said. "We don't humbug, you and I. What's the move now?"

"If you're willing," she said quietly, "I shall stay with you. Not here in London—at least not at first. Think of some place—but not abroad. We'll face it out at home. But only, of course, if you really want it that way. I know you'll say exactly how you feel. If you don't want it I shall go away by myself. But I've got to break with Tom so that there can be no going back—no going back ever."

"Want it?" he answered quietly. "I've wanted it for years."

"Good," she replied. "It's better for Tom too. It's been this uncertainty that's driven him mad. Once he realises that it's final he'll hate me and recover——"

"You realise," Ravage said quietly, "the other side of it. Many people will try to give you a bad time."

"Oh that!" she tossed her head. "Have I ever worried? Only Janet. . . . It will make her unhappy." Then her eyes hardened. "She could have done something . . . and she didn't. It's her look out." Then, turning round to him and half rising: "Charles, let's go at once—to-night. Let's leave this nasty town, get right away. Far. Where for a week or two we can be by ourselves."

"Certainly. Good. I like that." He thought a moment. "I know a place in the North. Cumberland. Near Keswick. I was there last summer for a bit. We could catch the night train to Carlisle—go on from there by motor."

"Fine," she stood up. "I brought a bag. It's downstairs." She went over to him and put a hand on his shoulder.

"Charles, no nonsense about the future. No swearing that we'll live together for ever, adore one another for ever—no silly promises!"

"Of course not," he answered, putting his hand on hers. "Truth always, Rosalind. Truth first and last."

"Truth first and last," she answered. She went over to the window and pushed it up. The sound of the rain came roaring into the room.

"What a night!" she murmured.

"I'll have some food up," he said. "You look dog tired. Go and lie down on my bed for an hour. Sleep a bit. I'll wake you."

"All right. I will."

When she was gone he moved to the fire.

"At last . . ." he said again, smiling to himself.

CHAPTER V

THE MOON OBSCURED

THE afternoon of wind and rain that saw Rosalind Seddon leave her Bloomsbury home found John Beaminster having tea cosily beside his fire at 90 Piccadilly.

He heard the rain drive against the panes and he was not going to stir—no, not he. On the little table at his side were two of those volumes of frank autobiography that were just at this time beginning to be very popular in London. One was by old Lord Nifton Pellew, who, in spite of being every day of eight-five, had a long chapter about his "Ambitions in Life," and the other was by that bright young fellow, Ambrose Augen, who had just seen his twenty-first birthday, but considered that the only fun in life left to him was to retail in public the confidences that had been generously given to him in private.

Beaminster, who was the least malicious of men, hoped nevertheless to get a good deal of instructive amusement out of Pellew's two fat volumes. Pellew had known everyone, and everyone, moreover, whom Beaminster had known. The Lady X who had been suspected of cheating at baccarat, the Lord Y who had seduced a dairymaid while financed by the ancient Baroness from Biarritz, these were no mysteries to Beaminster, who could cross all the Ts exactly.

As a matter of fact there was a great deal in the first volume about his own Beaminster family—many stories about the old Duchess, anecdotes about his brother Vincent and his brother Richard, the Prime Minister, allusions to his sister Adela, and even a veiled reference to that thorn in the Beaminster side, that vulgar scoundrel Frank Breton.

Had there ever been a social scandal within fifteen miles of him old Pellew would have had a sniff at it. And indeed he was, in these two rich volumes, frank enough about himself, telling the whole story of his intrigue with Lady Sibyl Carteret, and hinting pretty freely that in his younger days few bedroom doors were locked against him. Ugly devil, Pellew, too. Always was. Wonder how he managed it, thought Beaminster.

He expected also to obtain considerable entertainment from the young gentleman's volume. He had found that many of the names were new to him, but the air of deep disillusionment that penetrated the book was invigorating in one so young—pleasant too his frank assumption that everyone over thirty was done for.

"Everyone over thirty!" thought Beaminster. "And think of my age. My God!"

Then, as was often the case with him nowadays, he fell asleep and, when he woke, everything was changed.

He was muddled and confused and the oddest part of it was that he liked this confusion.

He knew that he was in his own place, and that his own things were about him. He could hear the rain lashing the windows; he recognised his possessions, his silver and pictures and the strange old fire-irons made from bayonets of the 1870 war. He recognised everything, but he was back among the scenes and characters of his earlier years.

He knew that he was here, in his old age, in 90 Piccadilly, dreaming here in his chair at the end of his days, but it was by no deliberate effort on his part that he called up these figures.

They were, it seemed, of their own freewill thronging the room, as alive as they had ever been.

They were reclaiming him; he recognised it with an easy happy laziness, glad, yes, glad indeed, that they had returned to him. He had been battling now for many months with a world to which he had not belonged, that he had not understood. But he was in his flat no longer! What a relief to be home once again in that vast-ceilinged, high-walled Portland Place house with its floors so soft to the tread, its intimate family silence, it breeding and leisure.

104 Portland Place! He was back there—the grim façade, the great hall door, the high shining windows.

Yes, there he was, a child again, climbing with difficulty the great stone staircase, so cold and white, so old too—as ancient, he used to think and as white as God Himself

And somewhere behind it was hiding his governess, Miss Cramp, with her heavy spectacles and strange light fuzzy hair and, behind her—behind her and behind the staircase—his mother!

Once again there crept all over him and through him that odd mixed feeling that his mother had always in his childhood produced for him, that mixture of fear and fascination. None of the others had had quite that feeling. Adela had been afraid of her but had understood her, Richard had been always too intent upon himself, his career, his possessions, to fear her, and Vincent had been a light flibbertigibbet—all things to all men and nothing long . . . a light weight. . . .

But for himself, here he was again! Miss Cramp had hold of his hand, he had paused at the door, and then with a little fluttering, terrified, wondering breath perceived once again that marvellous room, that astounding vision!

She hadn't been quite so old in those childish days, and yet how little, after all, she ever changed. He was advancing towards her now.

The strange room—dim and misty—with the long mirrors of old gold, the deep purple carpet, always a fire burning even on the hottest afternoon, the golden screaming cockatoo, and, most astonishing of all, there, as they had always been, one on either side of his mother's high-backed chair, the two green and white Chinese dragons, terrifying with their wide open mouths, cruel eyes, and large flat feet—terrifying and fascinating too.

And now his mother was speaking to him. "Well, little John"—that was what she always said; so small and so dominating, so sharp-nosed and eagle-eyed, with her little hand closed over her ebony cane. "Well, little John."

"Good morning, mother," and then he stepped forward and kissed her, tasting for an instant that dry, powdery, hot flavour, his little heart thumping, the cockatoo screaming, the dragons with their mouths wide open ready to devour.

"And how's John been this morning—good, I hope, Miss Cramp."

"Yes, your Grace—very good."

"That's right—not pulling Adela's hair any more?" and, with the question, the strange vibrating ghost of a laugh trembling through the air.

"No, mamma."

"That's right. And where's Richard?"

Where was Richard? Surely he's here and has been here all the time. And there are many other people in the heated misty room with him; he is standing quite close to his mother's chair, leaning his hand on the arm. But he is not a child, and John himself is no longer a child. There is Richard with his lofty white forehead, his head shaped like a pear, his long dark trousers and his high white collar, made so familiar to us, as was Gladstone's by the caricaturists.

There are others in the room, but only one now for John: Rachel is there.

Rachel, not as of late he has seen her, grave and old, reserved and sad, but Rachel as she was when she first came out into the world. Oh, how lovely to see her once again in her youth and beauty and happiness! Rachel with her dark hair and eyes, a faint flush of excitement—excitement at life and all that it promised—on her cheeks, Rachel looking at him with love and devotion.

But no, they were not in his mother's room any longer; they were in Rachel's own little room with the silver clock and the German water-colours and the photograph of Munich. He was sitting on the broad fat arm of her couch, looking out over the pale light that enwrapped so beautifully Portland Place in silence. She was telling him not to be so selfish. "But you *are* selfish, Uncle John. Of course you are. You think of us sometimes when you've nothing better to do, but you're made such a fuss of and are so spoilt by everyone that of *course* you think of yourself. That's the special danger of bachelors. If you don't look out you'll grow into a selfish old man whom nobody will love. Yes, you will."

He took the scolding very meekly, adoring to be scolded by her.

And then she talked about the coming-out ball which was to be this very next week, and how excited she was about it, and frightened too. Did he think that she would be all right and not do anything foolish? Why, of course he did. Yes, that was all very well, but she had been so much abroad, and it wasn't as though she were quite an English girl, and May Eversly had told her . . .

Then something is said about Roddy Seddon. He turns round on the chair and, balancing his stout body adroitly, puts his arm about her. Well, what about Roddy Seddon? Isn't he rather a nice young man?"

Yes, quite a nice young man—nothing out of the ordinary, perhaps—and an odd pang shoots through his pampered selfish body. Is he going to lose her? And so soon? Can she really care for this young man who isn't of course half good enough for her? . . .

But they are dancing. The band is playing. Here is the great ball-room, a glittering golden shell, packed, packed with moving figures. The walls are white, the ceiling gold, and on the white walls are the Van Dycks and the Lelys and Sargent's famous portrait of the Duchess.

Rachel is going to dance with him. She comes up to him, so happy, so triumphant, that he is almost frightened by her joy.

"Come, Uncle John. Don't let's dance. Let's talk. . . . Oh, darling Uncle John, I'm a success! I am really. I can put these young men in their places. They're frightened of me. They are indeed!"

And then she leaves him and he sighs: "She'll never be mine again."

The music fades, the lights of the ball-room die, and he is in his own rooms somewhere off Portland Place. Those old rooms, how nice to see them again with all the old things, the old photographs, the old silver, the high writing bureau piled with cards and invitations. Oh it is comfortable here, so quiet and peaceful. He *is* glad to be back again. He has been looking for this place for years, and had thought that he would never find it again.

He came back to it so naturally, settling down into his old shabby red leather chair, and there, just as she always was,

was Rose Lestrange standing before him twisting her necklace between her lovely hands, just as she always did when she wanted some money out of him.

He would let her have it, of course; so long as he was in love with them he gave them any thing they asked. And Rose had been the best of them all, and had lasted the longest.

How beautiful she looked with her masses of chestnut hair and her dress, that dim red one that he so well remembered, the shoulders puffed out, the tiny waist, the shoes peeping beneath the long heavy skirt.

"Well, Rose, what is it this time?"

It was the little diamond watch in the window of Cartier's. He'd been lucky at Newmarket that week—unlike his usual fate—so the watch was hers, and wasn't she pleased, and weren't they happy? He could feel her soft rounded cheek against his, his arms were round her—or was it Faith Penner? How odd! It *was* Faith, and he could hear her tiny chattering voice—like the tick of a clock, he always said— going on and on. She talked eternally. It was that, at the last, that he couldn't any longer stand, but when he broke with her she didn't seem to mind. She never minded anything very much so long as she had plenty to eat. But she was the best of all of them as mistress—little animal, a little animal. . . .

But now how the moon was shining, a great golden moon, round like a shield, almost filling the window.

The room was bathed in its light, a faint, misty, silken light, a light of silver and ivory, but dim so that, with all the figures moving in it, he could scarcely distinguish who were there.

All of them had come. Rose and Faith and Bella Harrowby, Clare Mackenzie, little Poppy Florence, large statuesque Lizbeth, Mary Breck, Anne Grace. . . . He leaned forward, staring, and with that movement they were gone.

Only the moonlight and, seated on the floor moving toy soldiers, a little boy in a sailor suit.

Tom! Ah, now he was happy. What did the rest matter if Tom were there?"

"Uncle John, do you think I could buy a cannon big enough to blow them all out of the window?" How odd he looked in the moonlight, pale and unreal. Ah, but here he was sitting on the floor, his head back against his uncle's knee, listening to *Hereward the Wake*.

He sat, staring into the moonlight, his eyes bulging with excitement.

"It's late, Tom. Time for bed."

"Oh, just another page. Go on to the next stop."

They always extended it that way and there wasn't a stop for pages. But Tom wasn't listening. He was looking at the full gold moon, and as he looked he changed, standing suddenly there in the window, a grown man, a child no longer.

"I love her, Uncle John, with all my soul. I must have her. I must"—and then, turning laughing, his body taut with his happiness: "It's all right, Uncle John, she loves me too. I know she does. I'm so happy I could explode!"

Yes, here was the centre of his life, the centre of all his hopes and fears; and although he was sure that the girl wasn't worthy of him, yet he must have her if he wanted her.

Nothing mattered but Tom's happiness. Nothing, nothing! And Tom must be happy. He had everything, looks and brains and health and strength. No one anywhere in the world like him!

But what was happening? The room was darkening. The great round moon was obscured. Heavy black clouds had covered it, and Tom was standing looking at him, so sad, so pale, so forlorn.

He would not speak, but only stood there, his eyes fixed, in some desperate despair.

The room grew darker. Tom was only a step away, but Beaminster could not get at him. He struggled, but something held him. "Tom, Tom! come nearer!"

But Tom did not move.

With a terrible effort that seemed to tear the very fibre of his heart he broke away.

Tom was there. He had touched him. Their hands were clasped. The room was flooded with light.

"It's all right, Uncle John. . . . Oh, wasn't that beastly! What a filthy dream! . . . But it's all right. Now we are free! We are free! Come on, come on, there's no time to lose!"

And hand in hand, so happy that there was no need of words, they ran together down the wide shining staircase out into the wide sunlit expanse of open plain.

Baxter came up to see that everything was right. There was no need for him to do this. Old Emily, who had been in these flats for hundreds of years, always came up at ten o'clock to turn the bed down and put in the hot-water bottle; but Baxter had grown fond of the old gentleman. This was the only flat into which he bothered to look before he went home to Vauxhall, where Mrs. Baxter would have his supper waiting for him; but he liked the old gentleman. And he hadn't been so well lately. Aged a lot in the last months.

So he went into the bedroom and saw that everything was right and cosy.

When he came out again into the little hall of the flat Herbert, the diminutive page-boy, was there.

"What is it?" he asked, pausing before he turned into the sitting-room.

"There's a constable here, Mr. Baxter."

Baxter opened the door of the flat and there, in the passage outside, was a policeman.

"Why, good heavens! . . ." he stared in his astonishment. There hadn't been a constable here since the robbery in Mr. Bettang's flat.

The police officer stepped very quietly into the little hall, closing the door behind him.

"Lord John Beaminster?" he asked.

"Yes?"

"Sorry to disturb the gentleman. Can I see him a moment?"

"Just now? He's going to bed. What's the trouble?"

"Sorry. Afraid I must see him for a moment. Won't keep him longer than I can help."

"What's the trouble?"

"Sir Thomas Seddon a friend of his?"

"Why, yes. A great friend. Anything wrong?"

"Shot 'imself—in his rooms in Jermyn Street. They found him 'alf an hour ago. Been dead sometime. You see, I wouldn't have bothered his lordship, but he left a letter addressed to 'im here. Only thing we could find."

"Shot himself? . . . Isn't that awful? And his lordship loved him like his own son. Oh, how ever will he stand it! O God! poor young gentlemen! And he's been terribly unhappy a long way back."

"Yes, so they tell me." The constable was touched. He showed his feeling by two short abrupt coughs. "Won't be longer than I can help," he said.

"But this will kill his lordship. He hasn't been very well lately anyway. Dear, oh dear! Who's to tell him?"

"Can't you prepare him a bit?"

"Oh, dear, isn't this terrible? Poor fellow! His lordship thought the world of him."

"Well, I'll stay out here till you've prepared him a bit."

Baxter very softly opened the sitting-room door. All was darkness save for the faint flicker of the fire. He switched on one of the lights, then stood hesitating. Very slowly he moved forward. He saw the back of Lord John's head over the chair.

"My lord," he said softly. "He's sleeping," he whispered to himself.

He moved into the room and saw his master lying back in the arm-chair, smiling in his sleep.

"I haven't seen him look so happy for months. What a damned shame!"

He came to the chair and touched the old man on the arm. "My lord!" he said. "My lord!—Sleeping like the damned —smiling and all."

He touched him again.

There was no movement. He put his hand on the heavy shoulder. The head rolled over a little.

"My God!"

He bent down and stared at the face, then quickly put his hand up and touched the forehead.

In a panic he started to the door.

"Constable, he's gone. . . . You're too late."

The police officer looked down on the smiling old man.

"Like as though 'e was sleeping," he said.

CHAPTER VI

JANET GOES NORTH

THROUGH the whole house ran a great new sense of happiness. Everyone felt it. A weight of apprehension had been lifted. The master was at last better. He had talked yesterday to everyone like a normal man. Grave, of course, and sad, but you weren't afraid of him any longer—and he wasn't afraid of you.

He had found Mrs. Beddoes polishing up the furniture, and had asked how her husband was. He hadn't spoken to her for months. Mrs. Beddoes was *that* pleased. . . . You might have supposed that it had been something in her own family.

Hignett, rising as he always did when his alarm clock struck six, switched on the light and sat on the edge of his bed in his night-shirt, stretching his arms and yawning and looking at his toes.

He listened to the House. Everything all right. He sighed a happy sigh. The only ornament in his room was a large photograph of his master. Taken, during the war, in his uniform. Nobody like him. Nobody. These Socialists could say what they liked, but when an English gentleman *was* a gentleman there was nothing in the world to touch him.

Nothing in the world to touch his master, and little in the world to touch his mistress. That he *must* say. Although, of course, women were different. . . .

As he shaved he hummed to himself. Hadn't felt so cheerful of donkeys' years. Although he had no imagination, nevertheless on these early mornings when everything was so silent he was bound to think of the house a bit. So large and so old. Pity they went about pulling down these old houses. Someone would be wanting to take a bit of this off to America, he shouldn't wonder. That's where all the money was. He'd been told that he could get a mint of money doing butler to some American gentleman. Kind people, too, he believed. But, please God, he'd stay with his master so long as his master needed him. Money wasn't everything. It was a good deal, though, and he was thankful he had something put by. His mind ran off then to his one and only artistic luxury. Organ recitals. If there was one thing in the world he adored, it was listening to a good organ. The only thing he missed down here. Well, he would be in London in a week or two, and then the Abbey could count on him. To hear a good organ rumbling through that old building! That was heaven.

It was at breakfast in the servants' hall an hour and a half later that he read the news. The papers were brought up with the letters from the station by motor. Hignett had, by immemorial right, first possession of the *Daily Mail*.

"Good God!" he cried.

"Why, whatever it is, Mr. Hignett?" said Mrs. Craddock. "Another of those murders?"

"Suicide this time," said Hignett. "Poor young fellow."

"Suicide. . . . Oh dear!" said Mrs. Craddock. "Whoever is it?"

"It's that young Seddon," said Hignett, "brother-in-law of her ladyship. O dear, this will mean trouble again."

Mrs. Craddock was greatly disturbed.

"It's as though there was a curse on them," she said. "What a year this *has* been, to be sure. Where did he kill himself, poor young gentleman?"

"His rooms in Jermyn Street," said Hignett. "He'd been dead two hours before they found him. Shot through the head. What'll her ladyship do now?—terrible fond of her sister as she is too."

"It won't worry Lady Seddon much, if you ask me," said Mrs. Craddock, tossing her head. "No good was ever going to come of that marriage. Didn't I say so from the first? You'll recall my words, Mr. Hignett. As fast as they were engaged I said, 'No good will come of *this* marriage,' I said. 'You mark my words,' I said, 'no good's going to come to anyone who marries *her*.' Selfish! That's what she was. Selfish! Was, is, and ever shall be."

Hignett got up, his face very grave.

"Not very different from the rest of her sex in that, Mrs. Craddock," he said. "I'd have given a hundred pound this hadn't happened just now—just when everything was turning right way up again. Upset her ladyship terribly. She's had enough trouble this last year without this."

As he went slowly upstairs about his business he felt, as through all this year he had so often felt, his impulse of protection over these two whose servant he was. As though they were children! One difficulty and trouble after another. They stood up to them; no giving in there. But they wanted looking after, and who was there to look after them save himself?

The Duke? Well, he was a married man, and we all know how free married men are! No, it was his job. He'd make them happy if he could—he would indeed.

Wildherne went off early that morning. He had business in Salisbury. Janet saw the car turn the corner of the long drive, then went in to her breakfast smiling. Last night had been wonderful. He had stayed with her, his head on her breast, sleeping like a child, softly, gently, without a dream. For hours she had lain there, her arms about him, staring into the thin, dim light, thanking whatever God there might be for her great great happiness.

Whether he loved her yet or not she could not tell. He came to her now as a child, in need of her, and as a mother now she was receiving him.

Seeing the letters on the breakfast table she instantly thought of Rosalind. Perhaps there would be a letter from her. Yes, there was one. Why, there were two! She tore open the first, still smiling, her mind, in spite of herself, still upon Wildherne.

This was a note, very short.

So you didn't come? Well, dear Janet, I don't blame you. How can I when I have myself been so bad? And now I am going to be worse. I am on my way this minute to Charles Ravage, and with him I intend to stay. Tom has just been here making a scene. Some sort of protection from his madness I've got to have, and Ravage is, I think, the best. Good-bye, my dear. Wildherne is lucky to have such a kind nurse.—Yours,

ROSALIND.

With trembling fingers Janet opened the second letter.

JANET DEAR—Forgive if you can my cross note earlier in the day. I'm afraid it's posted by now or I would stop it. I was distracted this forenoon. Tom had just been interviewing me, revolver in hand, and something had to be done. I am glad that I've come to Ravage. Try not to be too unhappy about this, but however unhappy you are it can, I am afraid, make no difference. Ravage understands me as no one in my life has ever done before. We understand one another, I think, and I fancy that we shall manage to achieve something together. Separated we are both useless.

We are going by the night train to Carlisle, then by motor to Keswick to some quiet place near there that he knows. He says that the Station Hotel, Keswick, will forward letters. I believe that I am taking now the first right step that I have ever taken.

There is one thing that you can do for me if you will. Go and see Tom. Drive into him that this that I am doing is irrevocable, absolutely and utterly. Tell him that I will not see him again until he has completely recovered from me and found some one much, much better. Most truly I wish him nothing but good, and now that I am free of him I want him to be happy. I want it more than anything in the world almost. If he can only realise that we never had any chance together, that it was fated absolutely from the first, but that there are so many in the world who will like him just as he is and understand him as I never could. You, for instance, with your kindness and goodness. Caring for the old things as he does. Befriend him, Mops darling. Never mind about me. I can look after myself. Save Tom.

I suppose you will hate me for doing this, but I have a hope that Charles and I are going to discover something more important than ourselves and lose ourselves in that.—Still your loving sister,

ROSALIND.

The letter fell from her hand on to the table: she stared out across the windows on to the terrace, but she saw nothing.

So the worst had happened, and happened because of her. Had she gone to London this could have been prevented. She knew that she could have stopped it. Surely a curse was on

her, so that whatever she did tragedy resulted. Better that she
had died. . . .

But these last months had stiffened her. Whatever her
fate she would do battle. She raised her head and saw suddenly the terrace and lawns bathed in sunlight, and the sky
above them a pale translucent blue.

She must go at once to Rosalind, without an instant's de-
lay. The eleven train, and then the night express.

She fixed her mind upon this. Nothing beyond. She must
get to Rosalind: after that she would see what to do.

She ate some breakfast, then rang for Hignett. His first
look when he came in was to the newspapers. There they
were, still folded one upon another, untouched. She had not
then seen the news.

"Hignett, I must go at once to London. By the eleven. Will
you order the little Daimler? I don't know when I'll be
back."

She had heard, then, by letter.

He sighed as he went off to find Hawes. He wished he
could do something. But what could he do? In any case there
would be his master to look after. He was always pleased when
he and his master were left alone. More intimate somehow.

Janet left a note for Wildherne:

My DARLING—I've had a letter from Rosalind. She's gone
off with Charles Ravage. I know you'll understand that I must
find her and see what I can do. You know how deeply I feel
that all this trouble is my fault. They have gone north, and she
tells me that the Station Hotel, Keswick, is their address. I'll
write at once as soon as I get there, and you know that I'll
return as soon as I possibly can.—Your loving

JANET.

She reached the train without looking at the newspaper.
In the house she had no time, and at the little station there
was no bookstall.

When the train moved off her orderly sensible mind began
to reassert itself. There was still much for her to do. She
had, even now, great influence over Rosalind. The thought
came to her that she would go first to see Tom and discover
from him exactly what had happened.

Then as she thought of Tom the oddest relief came to her. She had expected to be overwhelmed by the tragedy of his position. She was not. She knew that against all her proper instincts and righteous desires something in her—with which indeed she had nothing to do, as though it had been merely an unaddressed and unidentified "lodger for the night"— told her that it was an excellent thing that Rosalind and Tom were at last rid of one another, and that they ought to have been rid of one another long ago.

She realised that almost since the day of their marriage there had been, unrecognised until now, but always present, irritation—irritation not with Tom or with Rosalind, but rather with the situation. And now the situation was changed.

The awful scandal that there would be because Rosalind was living with Ravage that she, Janet, would face. She wouldn't like it. She was more old-fashioned than Rosalind, and the Duke and Duchess were more old-fashioned still.

It would upset most dreadfully the Purefoy clan, and at that Janet felt again an odd and quite unexpected little twinge of pleasure. Let them be upset. Not, of course, the Duke and Duchess; but the Duke, she fancied, would not mind very greatly. His tolerance was as broad as his figure, and his sense of humour broader than either.

She discovered then—it was as though the whirr of the train was gently urging her forward into these investigations—that she was not as deeply concerned about this catastrophe of Rosalind's as she ought to be. She was not feeling it in a bewilderment of distress and dismay as she ought to, and the reason, yes the reason was—Wildherne.

She realised with a flood of happiness that rose up in her heart, do what she would to prevent it, that beside the fact of Wildherne's safety and new need of her nothing anywhere so deeply mattered.

Mattered of course. Rosalind terribly mattered. She was going now to do everything in her power, everything for Rosalind, everything for Tom that she could do. But that old dreadful unhappiness, that unhappiness that she had known so often when she lived with Rosalind, the unhappiness of the first year of her married life, the unhappiness before Humphrey was born, the awful unhappiness of these last months, that was gone from her for ever. Through those hours of last night when Wildherne had lain asleep in her arms she had been given that for which all her life unknowingly she had longed. Nothing, nothing, no terror nor disaster of the future could rob her of these hours.

She was now a woman completed, fulfilled; she had known, for however short a space, love maternal, physical, spiritual, fulfilled and utterly satisfied. She had Wildherne for her own now, even though the thing that he gave her was not the love that once she had longed for.

He was hers, and the rest of the world had stepped back a pace; life had no longer quite the power that it had had over her before.

She went straight to Halkin Street. She wanted to see the Duke before finding Tom. To her distress she learnt that the Duke was down at Purefoy; he would return that evening. Her Grace was there. Would she see Her Grace? Yes, she *would* see Her Grace, although her courage faltered for a moment.

She needed her courage indeed when she stood waiting in the long drawing-room with the faded Morris wall-paper, a fire smoking drearily in the high fire-place, the sets of glassy-fronted classics surveying her with chill indifference, the great sea of dull carpet untravelled, you might suppose, in all its ancient history by any cheerful traffic.

There are some rooms into whose heart the very deadliest of London's atmospheres has penetrated. London at its chokiest and stiffest and most wearisome was here—the London of long empty Sunday afternoons, of barren streets and hostile primness, the London that would kill all intruders, all innovation, all change, the London of the Victorian properties and tyrannies and prejudices.

"I'd have died if I'd had to live in Halkin Street much," Janet thought. "And now I'm going to be scolded—if, indeed, she comes down at all. Perhaps she'll send Caroline with a message."

But a moment later she came herself, very stiff, very cold, all grey turban and ceremony.

"Well, Janet," she said. "This is an unexpected pleasure."

But Janet saw at once that she was in distress, and when she was in distress there was something touching and helpless about her, some revival of that pretty childishness that had, so many years ago, won the Duke's heart. This was the side of her that Janet could never resist. When she was in trouble she seemed to lose her official dignity, her attitude as standing as symbol to a world of organised charity and disciplined ceremony. She was simply a little bewildered woman whose heart was eternally forcing her to feelings that, for the proper carrying out of all her duties, were only too tiresomely in the way.

Janet went straight up to her, put her arms around her and kissed her.

"I know you're furious with me. I know you will never forgive me. But be patient with me. I take so long to learn. I had to come to you for advice and help, so forget for a moment all the bad things I've done and help me."

"Of course you had to come to me," said the Duchess tearfully. She hesitated a moment then kissed Janet in return. "Is Wildherne all right? There isn't awful news about him too?"

"Wildherne's all right," Janet answered. "Then you know about Rosalind? How have you heard?"

"About Rosalind?" said the Duchess. "What about Rosalind?"

"Why, I thought it was that that had upset you. Rosalind has left Tom and gone off with Mr. Ravage, Charles Ravage, a man she's known for a long time."

"Gone off! Then *you* haven't heard?"

"Heard what?"

"Haven't you seen the papers?"

"No! Why? I left Wintersmoon at once, as soon as I had Rosalind's letter."

"Then you don't know about Tom?"

"Tom!" Janet stood trembling. Was there yet more trouble?

"No. . . . What's happened?"

The Duchess caught Janet's hand. "My dear, he was found dead in his rooms last night. He shot himself."

Janet looked about her, bewildered.

"Killed himself?"

"Yes. Shot himself with his revolver. He'd been dead some hours when they found him. It appears that he had been to see Rosalind in the afternoon, and that they had a dreadful quarrel, came straight back, shut himself in and—shot himself. He'd locked the door. They had to break it in. . . . Ah, that's where Rosalind is! They couldn't find her last night and the maid didn't know where she'd gone."

"Oh Tom! Poor, poor Tom! What he must have suffered!" The tears fell down Janet's cheeks unchecked. She could see nothing but Tom's unhappiness, so unhappy, so alone . . . poor, poor Tom. . . .

The Duchess went on, finding now some pleasure in the drama of the event.

"Wherever she's gone she'll have to come back again, I'm afraid. They'll want her for the inquest. They won't be very nice to her about it all, but she doesn't mind criticism. They ought never to have married, never."

"Did he—did Tom leave no message for anyone?" Janet asked.

"Oh yes," the Duchess went on moved by Janet's tears, and suddenly sitting down beside her and taking her hand. "That's another sad thing. The only person he left anything for was Lord John—Beaminster you know. There was a note addressed to him. The police took it round to his rooms, and what do you think? They found him dead in his chair—died in his sleep. Just as well, poor man. He adored Tom. He never could have stood the blow. And so he died without knowing. And they say there was such a happy smile on his face when they found him."

Janet looked up. "Yes, that was better. His dying like that. He had been so unhappy about Tom for a long time. He came once to see whether I couldn't do anything." Then she sprang to her feet. "Oh, but Rachel! Rachel! How could I forget her! I must go to her, at once, at once. . . . Oh, how *could* I forget her?"

She was hurrying away, but the Duchess stopped her.

"Hadn't you better wait a moment, my dear, and telephone. Perhaps she won't see anyone just now."

"Yes, you're right. I'll go and telephone."

As, after five minutes, she came back into the room the Duchess realised that there was something new in Janet, some control and maturity that had never been there before.

Janet was older, nearer herself. She suddenly felt that in the future she would like to consult Janet, tell her about her affairs, ask her advice. It was true that she had been very tiresome not long ago about Wildherne, but then, after all, she was his wife. Would the Duchess, in her younger days, have allowed anyone to interfere with her care for the Duke? No, most certainly she would not.

So, almost timidly, she came up to Janet and stood close to her, putting her hand on her arm.

"Well?" she asked.

"Yes, she'll see me," Janet answered quietly. "I'll go there now. And then if I may, mother dear, I'll come back and have a little dinner here before I catch the night train. I must see Rosalind at once. At once. Do you know when the inquest is to be?"

"No. I haven't heard. Janet. Listen, dear. I'm sorry I was cross about Wildherne. All these sad things happening makes one ashamed of being cross about anything."

"Mother dear." Janet kissed her. "I was cross too. It was a difficult time. Wildherne is better—much, much better. Last night he talked about Humphrey, on and on, as though he would never stop. I don't like his being alone down there all the same. I don't know how many days I shall be away. Won't you go down and stay?"

"Yes, dear, I will. Of course I will. Would you mind if Miss Crabbage went with me? You see there are some things to arrange. . . ."

"Why, of course! Take Caroline Marsh too if you like. Now I must go."

They kissed again and Janet went.

We all of us know how a succession of unusual events, springing up as they sometimes do in a sequence of highly-

painted jack-in-the-boxes, can turn life into a fantasy whose
unreality is beyond emotion. We move in a dream and, when
the fantasy is over, we, returning to real life, wonder at our
iron endurance or our cynical indifference or our philo-
sophic stoicism. Mountains have been paste-board; we have
crushed them in our hands. Torrents have been piddling
brooks, and over them we have cast our shoes. The gold
apple of Paris has been awarded, before a sleeping audience,
to the goddess of a suburban pantomime.

It was thus with Janet now and the world, as she walked
the short distance through the Park to Rachel's rooms in
St. James' Court, assisted her. The air was cold and a little
bitter like the taste of silver on the tongue. A thin half moon
was like a piece of painted orange cardboard. Everything
moved, as it sometimes does in London, on soundless wheels.
The movement through the air resembled the soft sliding of
a revolving platform, as though the stage-hands of the Deity
were rolling the scene away, having had quite enough
of it with its puppet-like marionettes, its Statue of the good
Queen with the bulging muscles of gigantic Colonials, the
Royal Dollshouse with its shabby façade, the bright loz-
enges of colour, here a flower, there a lady's hat, here a
sentinel and there a cloud pink with boredom taking its rest
among the branches of a toy tree. Only, far away over there,
out beyond one's reach, Westminster was real, huddled,
silver grey under a soaring canopy of golden cloud. Maybe
in Westminster the audience was assembled waiting between
the acts for the vanishing of this tinsel scenery, sucking
oranges or chocolates as the case might be, condemning the
puppets and yawning over the programmes.

This same unreality accompanied Janet into Rachel's
rooms. It was perhaps that the emotions of her crisis with
Wildherne had drained her of all superficial feeling. The
true feelings were there—her abiding love for Rachel, her
pity and tenderness for her, her deep compassion for Tom's
tragedy, the guilty probings of her own responsibility, the
longing to help in any way that she might; but she could
not weep, and words would yield themselves only to perfect
sincerity.

But Rachel wanted neither tears nor words. She had, during the last two years, withdrawn from almost every human contact in the fight to preserve her son. Janet had been Rosalind's sister and that had been enough for separation.

Rachel, half Slav, had been acquainted with Destiny since her birth. The worst, the absolute uttermost worst, had occurred. She had lost, in circumstances the most tragic, the only human being left to her. She had rebelled until the issue was certain. Now, in silent acquiescence, she greeted her Fate.

She kissed Janet quietly. She spoke, without any emotion, of the inquest, the funeral. Janet knew that she had lost her, not because she bore any grudge or felt any bitterness, but because she was now a dead woman, incapable of love, of fear, of desire.

"You'll see Rosalind?" she asked quietly.

"Yes," Janet said.

"I want you to give her a message from me. Tell her not to reproach herself, to regret nothing. Tom's death was not her doing. While he lived I would have made things right if I could. In my heart I knew that nothing would put it right. Tom was cursed, as I all my life have been cursed. If it had not come this way it would have come some other. . . ." She continued as though she were speaking to herself. "When I was a child, trembling with fear before my grandmother who hated me, I used to feel like a mouse in a trap. I would escape sometimes, but only for a moment —back into the trap I went. And my grandmother knew it. She knows it now. This conclusion must satisfy her. She has been waiting for this for so long. At this instant how delighted she must be!

"I thought I had escaped during the first months of my marriage. I soon discovered my mistake. Then again when Tom was born, and sometimes during his childhood. And at the beginning of our friendship, Janet. Always I have gone back. At last the trap is empty. No piece of cheese to tempt me, no live mouse to be tempted."

Janet touched Rachel's hand. It was so cold that after a moment she drew her own back again.

"If only Tom had never met Rosalind," Janet said. "If only he had never seen her! It was a poison in his blood and Rosalind knew it. It was because she wanted to be kind that she married him. . . . If only I had been wiser, stronger, more far-seeing." Then after a moment's hesitation she pleaded. "Dear Rachel, don't give up. Wait until this has passed a little. Think of Tom as he used to be and then take these last two years as a disease that attacked him—and now perhaps—how do we know? It may be true— he is his old self again, happy and ambitious and healthy. And even if that isn't so at least he's quiet—better than the last two years. . . ."

"Think of Tom as he was?" Rachel repeated. "When I had hopes for him and desires, when, fool as I was, I even sometimes imagined that he would escape and grow into a fine happy man. Think of that? No thank you, Janet. Not if I can help it. And as for his being active in some impossible heaven, the best that I can hope for him is that he is nothing. Nothing . . . and for myself too."

Janet tried once again.

"But, Rachel, don't put yourself off from us all. After a little come down to Wildherne and me. I love you as I always did and as I always will. Don't be alone, Rachel. That is the worst of all. At present I am so far away from you that you can scarcely see me, but later on you will want a friend. Let me be there then."

"Not to be alone!" Rachel answered. "Dear Janet, you don't change. Always simpler than life deserves. You're so English, and once I loved you for just that. But now—how am I not to be alone? I'm a dead woman and I'm glad of it. Peace at last. So think of me sometimes, but don't come to see me, don't write. You've no place with ghosts, my dear. You've still got much to do and a full life to live. . . . At least I have my boy again. I've been two long years without him."

She moved away and seemed to vanish into the hollows of the dimly-lit room. Was there anyone there?

"Good-bye then, Rachel."

There was no answer. Janet saw a dark shadow against the wall. Suddenly afraid, she hurried away.

CHAPTER VII

THE SEA-CAPTAIN WALKS HIS DECK

THE Duke, returning from John Beaminster's memorial service, found them all at luncheon—the Duchess, Miss Crabbage, Caroline Marsh, Mr. Pomeroy, Mrs. Canter (head of Rossin College at Oxford), old Lady Weddon, and Mary Fort who ran the League of Social Service.

Mr. Pomeroy had the gift of being at his ease wherever he might be; nevertheless, perhaps to-day he was relieved to see the Duke. A great many ladies on every side of him. He was sometimes glad to see a man, a real man, even though, as he always recognised, real men were never *quite* real men when he was with them.

An odd thing had happened to the Duke at Beaminster's memorial service. He had suddenly all in a moment felt, pressed close to his nostrils, an intense savour of the joy and happiness of life. It was not altogether perhaps what you would have expected.

He had liked Johnny Beaminster although he had never known him well, and had most certainly felt the tragedy of poor Tom Seddon's death. Lucky the old man had gone the way he had without knowing. Without knowing? Did he know now? Was he with Seddon now? Were they together in the definite positive way of recognition and discussion, laughter and warm friendliness?

It was then that the hot joyous savour of life had come to the Duke. Sitting there in the middle of the Sloane Street Church, pressed about on every side by black-coated friends and acquaintances all looking so much more solemn than they really felt, listening (or rather not listening) to the sonorous reading of the lugubrious lesson, it was just then this came to him.

He knew—he had known ever since that train journey down to Wintersmoon—that he had not long to live, but that knowledge seemed now only to add to his happiness. Indecent of him to be happy there at such a time, but he could not help it. Life was good, life was terribly good. Failure though in so many ways he had been, in the very fact of that failure there was something enthralling. That failure was part of him. Because he was a certain kind of man so he had been unable to move in certain directions. Part of his personality. Part of his soul. And he saw his soul, like a bright-tinted little bird, fluttering from tree to tree, shivering in the gale, triumphantly breasting the sun, sighting a worm on a new patch of ground or a twig for the nest. . . . Marvellous this life whether there were another or no. He felt as though he had never truly lived in all his days before.

It might be, he thought as he walked home through the pale gold day across whose sheen a few shining grey flakes of snow were slowly falling, that it was the knowledge that Wildherne was at last better that made him happy. He had arrived home in time last night to have dinner with Janet before she started on her night journey northwards and, behind her sorrow at Tom's death and her distress about Rosalind, he saw that in her heart a steady fire was burning—the fire of her love for Wildherne, the hope that at last after all this trouble he was coming to her.

Yes, it might be that—because these two whom he loved so much had at last a chance of happiness. But no—he knew, as he raised his head, saw that bright glitter of the blue, felt the cold wet smudge of a snow-flake on his cheek—it was more than that, something that life held that went beyond individuals and individual lives.

He sat down at the table and conversation flowed on around him.

Mary Fort was explaining her next move. She was a stout woman of forty with a round red face like a Dutch cheese and large wide open startled eyes naked of eyebrow.

"You see, Mr. Pomeroy, it isn't enough simply to have the building in Maddox Street. Of course that does *some-*

thing. But fifty bedrooms are nothing at all. Only the beginning of what we need. And the modern girl demands so much liberty which, if you understand what I mean, only involves still sharper supervision of another kind. So that the staff is quite inadequate. Of course the Bazaar will do something. . . ."

"What date did you say it was?" asked the Duchess.

"Fourteenth, fifteenth, sixteenth of December. Of course, we hope that people will buy their Christmas presents there and we ought to have some really nice things. . . ."

"I think I could manage the fifteenth. . . ."

"The *fifteenth,*" said Miss Crabbage, "is the Parminter Committee Day. I don't know that it would really *matter* your missing *one* committee."

"Oh, if you'd only open it on the fifteenth," cried Miss Fort, her eyes nearly bulging out of her head. "It would be too wonderful. Mr. Pomeroy will tell you how desperately in need we are. Aren't we, Mr. Pomeroy?"

Mr. Pomeroy raised his kindly glance from the sole that he had been carefully dissecting and, smiling, answered: "I don't know of anything anywhere in London that deserves more hearty support. And excellent work. Quite excellent."

"Well then," said the Duchess briskly. "I really think I can miss the Parminter Committee for once. I'd like to help you, Miss Fort. I'm sorry I can't come on the opening day, but we have a meeting here that afternoon at which I must be present."

The Duke was thinking: "I'll get down to Wintersmoon to-morrow. How excited I am! As though something wonderful were going to happen! Or perhaps it's happening now. I'm so hungry I could eat fifty lunches!"

But he must attend to old Lady Weddon who was bored, preferring Bridge to Charities.

"Well, Duke, you're looking remarkably fit. How's Wildherne?"

"Wildherne's very well. Down at Wintersmoon."

"Ugh! I wouldn't be in the country this time of year. Harry and I are off to Cannes end of the week, thank God. Harry's lumbago's been bothering him."

"Sorry to hear it," said the Duke. "How's Alice?"

Oh, Alice is all right. Crazy about hunting. She's in Leicestershire now with the Stopfords. I had a letter from her this morning. They're a bit afraid of the frost."

And the Duke was thinking: "Strange how light it is this morning. Never seen the sun so bright in here before."

"Jolly thing," he said aloud. "Snow in sunlight. Coming along just now prettiest thing I ever did see."

Miss Fort's eyes started violently in his direction.

"I suppose you wouldn't come with the Duchess on the fifteenth?" she asked. "It would be such a help! Of course I know it's a lot to ask . . ."

Smiling, he shook his head.

"No bazaars for me, Miss Fort, thank you," he said. "It's an old man's privilege, you know. Needn't go to bazaars any more."

He thought: "Poor Johnny Beaminster. Everyone's forgotten him already. Nobody's even asked me what I've been doing this morning. But it's all right. Beaminster's not minding."

Soon he was free and was alone in his adored study, the door tightly closed, the books gathering around him, the fire blazing, his chair waiting for him.

"Yes, life's splendid to-day," he thought. "I suppose it's my digestion."

On the book-rest beside his chair was Bradley's *Shakesperian Tragedy*. As he took the book into his hand he sighed with a glorious content. Five minutes later he was asleep.

He carried his happiness with him into his sleep. He dreamt: his dream was about everything and about nothing. He was happy because he was all right, and not only was he all right but everything else was all right too. He was happy because some question that had been puzzling him for ever so long was solved. How puzzled he had been! He roared with laughter as he remembered his agonizing struggles to settle this great question, and now it was settled without any trouble at all. Why, during all this time, had he never thought of this so obvious solution?

Why, any one of these things scattered around him afforded an answer. All kinds of things . . . large green cabbages, crooked chimneys that belched grey smoke, a mountain with a cherry-tree in blossom, a roll for a pianola in its elastic band and neat narrow box, a Tang horse with a curly tail, the bulging eyes (detached and rolling like marbles up and down the floor) of Miss Mary Fort, Burton's *Anatomy of Melancholy* (his own copy in eighteenth-century calf), Caroline Marsh in bathing costume, the sun red and flaming, two mackerel wobbling towards the lake that shone like a silver shield on the other side of the daisy-sprinkled meadow, Mr. Pomeroy without any clothes on (how thin and sharp his spine-bone!) leading a reluctant lamb by a bright pink ribbon, an oak-tree tugging at its own roots, and five clouds rosy and round standing to attention before God's unlifted finger. And God Himself? He could not see Him. He was just round the corner behind the mountain. But God was all right. There was no doubt about God. He would come over the mountain in a moment and show His cheery face. But everyone knew that He was all right. Only possibly Mr. Pomeroy was a little uncertain.

"To think that I should have worried all that time!" he exclaimed aloud, and saw his wife leading a flock of geese across the meadow. Although he was naked he went to meet her without any sensation of shyness, and at that moment the five rosy clouds burst into song, and indeed sang so beautifully that the Duchess forgot her geese and sang too. "What a darling she is!" he thought, looking at her there in the middle of the daisies in a dress that might have been lent her by one of Botticelli's angels.

The sun rolled up the mountain side and everything became glorious. God's cheery face appeared over the mountain's brow. . . .

The Duke woke, rubbed his eyes, and saw that Wildherne was standing beside him and had his hand on his shoulder.

"Why, good heavens, I've been asleep!" he sputtered reluctantly, then, rolling right back into the middle of this world as it is, exclaimed:

"Wildherne! What the devil . . .!"

"Sorry I woke you, father!" Wildherne said. "But I'd got to see you before I go on——"

"Go on!" said the Duke, still thinking of the rosy clouds and the Duchess like a Botticelli angel. "Go on where?"

"I've come up," Wildherne answered quietly, "after Janet."

"Janet went north last night."

"Yes, I know. I'm going north after her."

"Yes . . . well . . . that's all right," said the Duke. "Sit down, my boy, and tell me about things. I'm still half asleep. I'll be all right in a minute."

"I've only got about half an hour," Wildherne said. "There's an afternoon train to Carlisle. I'll stay the night and go over to Keswick in the morning. That's where Janet is."

"Yes, I know. She dined here last night. She's in great trouble about her sister."

Wildherne nodded his head. "I know. That's why I'm going after her. "If she's in trouble I want to be with her."

The Duke looked at his son. The boy was changed. Always thin, he seemed now emaciated, but it was not the emaciation of weakness. As he stood there, grave and quiet, the Duke saw him at last a man. Always before there had been some kind of appeal for help from somebody, as though he could not make up his mind unless someone else strengthened him.

Now he had an odd look of standing alone. The change was perhaps in his eyes, soft in colour as they had always been, but now unwavering; no more that hesitating glance and that charming but rather timid smile. The lines of his mouth were altered. He looked desperately tired, and with something of that dim other-place vision that men sometimes have when they have just completed some most arduous work or surmounted some hazardous peril.

"Sit down, my boy, you look tired."

"I am tired—physically," Wildherne answered, drawing a chair close to his father's. "But I can't rest until I know that Janet is all right. Bad luck this—about poor Seddon."

"Yes, isn't it, poor boy."

"Father, tell me what Janet said to you."

"She didn't say very much. She thought that she ought to go to Rosalind at once. Rosalind went off with that man Ravage—before she knew about Tom, of course."

"Did he know that she'd gone off?"

"No, apparently he didn't. He went to see her and made a scene. Janet says that he had a revolver and threatened all kinds of things. Anyway he frightened Rosalind so badly that as soon as she'd got rid of him she went off to Ravage. And he went back and shot himself. He was pretty well off his head, I imagine!"

"Poor devil!"

"Janet reproached herself. She'd had a letter from Rosalind asking her to go up and see her and she didn't go."

"Yes, she stayed with me. I didn't know, of course. I was pretty queer just then. I don't know what would have happened to me if Janet hadn't been there." Wildherne waited a moment, then went on:

"Was Janet awfully miserable yesterday when she was here?"

"No. She was unhappy, of course, dreadfully unhappy about poor Tom and terribly anxious about Rosalind. But not miserable. She's been through so much this year that she's beyond being miserable, I fancy. And then—you are more to her now, you know, than all the rest of the world put together. She felt that you and she had come together during this last week as you never had before."

"That's true, of course." He hesitated a little, then went on: "Father, I've been through a damned queer time. If I say something about it now, shall we make it a bargain between us that we never speak of it again—never so long as we live?"

"Certainly. You needn't speak of it now if you don't want to."

"I'd like to, because you're the best friend I've ever had except Janet. But after this I want to begin life absolutely afresh—as though simply I'd never lived before. I feel like that, too. Everything looks new to me, the streets, the houses, you and mother. I shouldn't know where I was or where I was going if someone, who'd been there before, as it were, weren't always whispering to me, 'Now turn to the left. That's the train you've got to catch. Cross that street.' It's exactly as though I'd come from another planet."

"Yes. I can understand that."

"When the boy died, I wasn't sorry or angry or anything. I died too. It was literally that. My body went on functioning, but I'm sure I don't know why it did. There was nothing to make it. One of the chief arguments against the survival of personality after death I believe is that when your brain ceases to work—if you become an idiot through disease or an accident—you are no longer a person, your individuality goes. Well, I know now that that isn't true. My brain did cease to function except in connection with little trivial details, about the house and the estate for instance, things that had nothing to do with my personality at all, because when I had been normal and active those were the things I'd never thought of. My personality was buried just as though the whole of Wintersmoon had crashed in on it, and my brain without my personality was going on just as a clock ticks because it was wound up, but it worked quite meaninglessly, busy about nothing. Do you understand that?"

"Absolutely," said the Duke.

"Although I was crushed under all this débris, father, still I was apprehensive, dreadfully afraid. That fear never left me. I was increasingly conscious of it as the days went on. The sort of fear that you have in dreams, without reason or argument. Of course I never reasoned, because I hadn't got my brain to reason with, and yet I was sure, just as you are in a nightmare, that one day I would make some awful discovery. I preferred to be dead if I had any choice in the matter, but about this apprehension I hadn't. The fear was nothing to do with me. It came from outside, just as you see a thunderstorm advancing over the hill."

He shivered and laid his hand on his father's knee.

"It was that that made me cling to Janet. She seemed to be my only safety. I didn't know why, but I had the kind of reassurance that if she was near I wasn't in such terrible danger. Hignett a little too. Right through all the smash

I felt that these two loved me and wouldn't let any harm come to me if they could help it. You know that sometimes when you're under an anaesthetic a sort of consciousness goes with you all the time if someone you love was with you when you went under."

His father nodded his head.

"I can see now that Janet understood this marvellously. I don't know how she did, unless it was because she loved me so deeply, but she just stayed quietly beside me, never asking questions or disturbing me, only defending me by being there."

He paused, breathed a great sigh.

"Oh, father, how wonderful she's been to me! I can never now do enough for her in return. . . . But I'll try. God knows I'll try."

Then he went on:

"I never thought of the boy all those months. I never missed him nor needed him. I wasn't aware that I'd ever had a son. I only knew that one day soon something awful was going to happen to me.

"Then I began to move, to stir. It was something like the pain when a limb's been tied for a long time and then the blood begins to run again. I was in terrible pain, mental pain. I didn't know why, but I was so frightened I couldn't sleep, and never moved without expecting some horror. It came all in a moment. I had been out riding with Janet. We came to a little chapel somewhere, and while I was sitting there it was as though a thousand voices broke into my ears crying, 'It's coming! It's coming! Look out! It's coming!'

"It was like a fight then—against what I didn't know. I was being urged to kill myself, to prevent this awful thing that was coming getting me. I meant once to finish it. I went down into the wood. I was going to drown myself. Hignett found me. That was before the chapel, though.

"But that night after the ride I went up to bed, undressed, and just as I lay down everything broke. I knew what it was. Humphrey was dead. . . . Never mind. . . . I can't—I can't . . . Janet. . . ."

He fell on his knees, buried his head in his father's lap. The old man put his arm round him and held him, looking about the room as though he defied all the powers of life and death to touch his dearly loved son.

"I'll go with you to the station," the Duke said. "Say good-bye to your mother and we'll be off."

They didn't say very much in the taxi. They passed a placard that said, "Franc up again." The Duke was very indignant.

"Can't understand those French. All of them refusing to pay their taxes and then expecting to balance their Budget. Then they blame us for helping them to win the war. Can't understand the French. Never could. Aren't natural to me somehow." Then he said abruptly:

"Hignett all right?"

"Splendid," said Wildherne.

"It's all very well for you to say 'Splendid,' but I miss him a damned sight more than you imagine. Why shouldn't I have him a little too? I'm sure he doesn't want to be down at Wintersmoon all the time."

"Why, of course, you shall have him for a bit, father."

"Then he'll be complaining all the time because he isn't with you. Extraordinary thing one can't get a decent man-servant these days. Such a pack of idiots!"

"Are you coming to Wintersmoon for Christmas, father?"

"Your mother wants to go to Purefoy."

"All right. We'll come to Purefoy."

The Duke grunted: "Good boy. Your mother will be pleased."

The Duke hated stations, the noise and racket, and especially he hated Euston, which, with all its business, seemed to have a dead inside. So he saw his son into a carriage, shook hands with him, said "Give my love to Janet," and strode away.

He got out of his taxi at the corner of Piccadilly Circus. He would walk home from there.

Although he would never confess it to anyone, he was as

pleased as a child with Piccadilly Circus. Like Johnny Beaminster, he felt as though it were all his own creation. Moreover, he had no high aesthetic feelings about the ugliness of
modern improvements. Quite the contrary.

He was over now on the Lower Regent Street corner in
front of the shop that has the beautiful leather bags, those
bags with the heavy silver fittings that are so beautiful to the
beholder and so ungrateful to the possessor.

There was a great congress and push of people and everyone so soon as he touched the magic circle seemed to be en-
riched by it and transformed. The Circus itself was a pool of
shifting colour, and in its centre was the island with
Eros, slim and dark beneath hurrying clouds of silver grey.
On the opposite side of the pool rose the rocks: up and
down their changing surfaces flashed and vanished and
flashed again whirls of ruby colour, lines of diamond light,
figures in blue and gold, a gigantic bottle spurting out its
liquor, a bicycle with flashing wheels, and words of flame
hissing madly their message against the running clouds.

.On the opposite bank these shining colours were reflected
in dull reds and golds; windows in the rocks caught their
sheen. The omnibuses came thundering forward, splashing
into the pool and went charging away. The pool and the
rocks seemed themselves to swing to some mysterious rhythm
as though the little figures in the air conducted them. Light
flashed upon the darkness, and the darkness lifted its hunched
shoulders into the light, and the clouds rushed past leaving
a pale, faint, shell-like sky behind them.

But it was the people whom the Duke loved. So soon as
the lights flashed upon their faces they seemed to respond.
Some of them hastened, others waited on the pool's brink
hesitating, others crossed its shifting waters with slow confident step as though they commanded the pool and could
order its waters to flow as they wished.

The Duke loved them. He seemed to-night to be a companion of them all. None of them were strange to him, and as
they, laughing, elbowed past him or stopped beside him to
wait for the ominbuses to plunge past them, he felt as

though, did he speak to anyone of them, he would receive a friendly and understanding answer.

A young man, a young woman on his arm turned round and asked:

"Could you tell me, sir, the best way to Shaftesbury Avenue?"

"It's just there," the Duke answered. "On the opposite side of the Circus. By the theatre there."

"Thank you, sir." The young man smiled, and the young woman smiled too.

"Going to the theatre?" the Duke said, smiling back at them.

"Yes. The Palace," the man answered.

"That's at the top of Shaftesbury Avenue on the left."

"Thank you kindly, I'm sure," said the young man.

"Bit early for the theatre, isn't it?"

"Well, you see, we're new to London. Standing in the queue's part of the fun—or so my wife thinks."

They both laughed and then, seeing that the policeman were holding back the traffic, plunged forward.

He felt now, as on one or two other occasions when he had been in a crowd, happy and excited, or moved and reverent, as though it would not be difficult to solve the world's problems. One wave of the hand would do it. One pass-word. . . . But what pass-word? Ah, he didn't know. No one knew. But if someone would only discover it. . . .

He walked homewards still enwrapped in that strange happiness that had been with him ever since the morning.

He thought of his wife with deep and desirous love. What if at times she had seemed so far from him, to understand him so little? It had been his fault more than hers. He had, all his life, shut himself up *in* himself. He had tried too much to judge her by himself, to criticise her because she did not respond to the things in life that moved himself. He had wanted too often that she should have his character instead of her own. There was an innate shyness in him that held him back.

Ah, it was cold! The snow was beginning to fall again,

and now the flakes were mysterious against the swiftly darkening sky.

Home again, he was glad to find a large fire roaring in the long drawing-room and his wife seated close to it reading, her spectacles forward on her nose, her skirt pulled up a little showing her short round legs.

He bent down, kissed her, then sat beside her.

"Well, dear, had a nice afternoon?"

"Yes, dear thank you." She put the book down on her knee and stared into the blaze.

"I've had a jolly afternoon. I don't know why, but I've been especially cheery all day. Digestion, I daresay. Or it may be seeing that boy well again. He and Janet will go on finely now. . . . Rum thing, I've felt younger to-day than I've felt for years. Do you know, Mamie, I've been too shy all these years of talking to you. It's a bit late now, isn't it? But I don't know. Life's so strange it's never too late to talk about it. . . . I've lived a long while as lives go, but it doesn't seem five minutes since my father took my breeches down and gave me a hiding for bathing in the lake at Wintersmoon when he'd told me not to. And if it *seems* like five minutes, it may be that's all it is. How do we know? I know when I was a kid I was crazy to make things—ships, houses, anything you like. And now here I am at the end of my life and I haven't made anything at all. Unless it's Wildherne, perhaps. And yet to-day I don't mind. I feel as though I wasn't meant to worry. Life's so damned beautiful that my being a failure isn't of any account. I'm glad I've had a chance of sharing in it, even though I haven't done much with it.

"So many things I might have done. Politics, all sorts. And the War too. Thought I was working hard, but now I look back I might as well have been dead for all the good I did. The trouble is, Mamie, I've been shy of getting close to people. Felt they mightn't want me. Even with you I've felt that. We haven't been as close as we might have been, and that's been my fault. That doesn't mean I haven't loved you. Indeed I have, but I've been shy of telling you so. If we ever have a chance of looking back on this little episode, I shouldn't wonder if the oddest thing of all isn't that we missed so many chances of getting closer to people, to those we loved. Afraid of making a fool of myself. As though it mattered. Who cares? I seem to see it all clearly to-night Such a beautiful day as it's been, and all the people this evening in the streets were as jolly as anything. . . . I'd like to talk to you a bit more than I have done—about ourselves. I don't really know you, and you don't know me. Funny thing when we love one another. . . ."

He looked at her timidly, then took her hand in his.

She looked up at him, smiling. "Yes, dear? . . ." Then she added, turning her gaze back to the fire: "It would be excellent if I could only persuade Mary Fort to come on that East End Housing Committee. She's just what we want, and even if she doesn't come often her name will be something. She more or less refused to-day, but I think if I write her a personal letter. . . ."

CHAPTER VIII

JANET, as she turned from the Lake road, lifted the latch of the gate and started up the hill, had to drive her determination forward. What was the use? *What* was the use?

Yesterday had been a tragedy. She could yet see the two of them standing in front of that dead mouse-faced farm like idols watching, without a flick of the eyelid, her departure out of their lives.

Because that was what it had been, that was what, at that particular moment, she had intended it to be!

She had herself been at fault in going at once to them yesterday morning, wearied out as she was. There had been the long night journey to Carlisle, sitting up in the stiff uncomfortable carriage, the search early in the morning for a motor, the desperately cold thirty miles' drive, the arrival at the Station Hotel at Keswick so early when the maids were lighting the fires and sweeping the floors. Then, after a bath and some breakfast (everyone was as kind as possible), she had, mistakenly, chosen to walk out to Watendlath. The walk had been beautiful, the air like fresh icy water about her head, but the last little climb up to the farm had seemed almost more than she could manage.

And then to find them both as they were, set, rigid, icy as the air blew about them!

Janet had always detested the thought of Ravage, and she found now that she detested his actual presence no less. He made no move at all to propitiate her. He had stood there at Rosalind's side, mean, shabby, scornful, regarding her of course as an interfering, sentimental, stupid woman—and his enemy.

And sentimental was just what she had been, although she resolved so determinedly not to be! Rosalind, amazingly beautiful, had shown no pleasure at seeing her. They had not embraced. After a few minutes Ravage had gone, but his shadow remained between them. They had sat in the farm parlour, clean but, in spite of its fire, cold, dead, over-loaded with photographs, ferns, and crochet. Janet had seen no sign of anyone else about the farm. Rosalind herself had opened the door to her.

Everything had gone wrong—everything. Janet knew Rosalind well enough to realise that she was suffering, and that, because she was suffering, she would arm herself in triple brass.

She was suffering, probably, more than in all her life she had suffered before, and because Janet knew that, she was, against all her earlier determination, against all her reason, all her wisdom, sentimental.

Alone with Rosalind she forgot, as she always had for-gotten, everyone else, even Tom—and then, when Rosalind showed no movement at the evocation of Tom's memory, Janet could think only of Tom, of his torture and misery and wretched, lonely, abandoned end.

The thought of Tom had been more than she could bear, and so, foolishly, unwisely, she had cried out, "Have you no feeling for him? No thought of what you have done?" and after that there was no hope.

Janet had fancied that she had heard Ravage's sardonic chuckle. It was characteristic of him that his personality should be more keenly felt in his absence than in his pres-ence. . . .

Yes, it was hopeless.

They had parted without a word of kindness, without any hope of the future.

"Good-bye, Rosalind."

"Good-bye, Janet."

At first she had resolved not to return. Of what use was it? Ravage would be there counter-acting at every step any move that Janet might make. Physically she felt that she could not force herself to face him any more. But when in the evening, sitting alone in the hotel, she had gone over it again and again, one thing above all others forced her back. On the next evening Rosalind and Ravage were going to London for the Inquest. Rosalind would have to surmount the most hateful hours of her life. The whole world would be against her. She would suffer the first realisation of something of what her life was now going to be. Janet could not, no, she could not, allow her to meet this without some word of love from herself. How much of all this had not been her own doing? Was she to share none of the responsibility?

And so she was returning. At the first bend of the hill she stood, looked back, and received some cheer.

The scene was wonderfully beautiful. She was standing where one of the tumbling, hurrying streams reached the path, passed under it, then broke into foam beyond it. Behind her lay Derwentwater, laced with a feathery pattern of trees that almost obscured it. Above Derwentwater Skiddaw humped its shoulders, scattered with a thin powder of snow. The sky was grey with little pools and rivers of watery blue. All the colours were faint. There was no wind. The day seemed to be holding its breath, but beyond the thin strip of Bassenthwaite a streak of violent light like a sword slashed the water. Here was just the beauty that Janet needed, not violent, not so commanding as to be above human weakness, but kindly, with its finger on its lip as though it said, "Friend, be patient. Everything has its rule and its order. Despair is never justified."

She pushed onward, over the little bridge that spanned another tumbling river, up through the thickly clustered trees, with a new hope. To-day she was not so weary. She had slept last night in spite of her distress. Tom's figure to-day was more distant. She was wiser than she had been yesterday. She would not stay long, but only assure Rosalind that she loved her and would always love her whatever might befall.

Then, passing a squat bungalow on her right, she came to the open common and there, standing back on her left in the hollow of a hill ridged with rock like a ruined castle, was the mouse-faced farm, its white-washed porch sharp against the grey like an open mouth. And there, at her side in the path, as though an apparition risen from the ground, was Rosalind!

Janet was so happy at sight of her that she could only hold out her hands and cry, "Rosalind! You expected me?"

"I thought you would come," Rosalind answered gently. "We couldn't leave it as we did yesterday. I would have seen you to-night before we caught the train if you hadn't come. Look! Shall we walk up and down here? It is fine springy turf, and all so open and clear—if it isn't too cold for you?"

"No, it isn't cold," Janet answered. "It is lovely here. So quiet. Only the stream."

They started to walk up the slope together. On their left were fields sheltering under the hill, and on their right open common, very fresh and green, that ran down to the trees clothing the rocks above the Lake.

Before they started up the hill they had to jump from stone to stone over a stream that rushed and sported under trees between deep green banks. On the open grass everything was free and clear. They two seemed alone in a deserted world.

"Janet, I was unkind yesterday," Rosalind said. "I was afraid of my own feelings—afraid of what you might make me say. It may be that now we must go quite different ways —it may be. I don't know, but at least, even though we never see one another again, we must love one another. Think of me as wicked, cruel, what you like, but never that I don't love you."

Janet answered: "I came to say something of the same kind, although if you want me, Rosalind, we needn't separate. Your world—no, that I should never be at home in, nor would you ever in mine, but that doesn't keep *us* apart— not if you want us to be together."

Rosalind turned and looked at Janet.

"What I wanted to say to you yesterday, what I was afraid to say, was this. Tom's death is a relief to me. I know it's horrible, that everyone will blame me for it, that in any case his life was a tragedy because of me—I know this is all true, but, chiefly, I am relieved that he is dead.

"If he had lived and been happy, then how glad I would have been. I think nothing else would have made me so glad. But had he lived and gone on being unhappy, then it would have been dreadful—unbearable—more than either he or I deserved."

"Poor Tom," Janet said. "And what is so awful is that now everywhere people are saying 'Poor Tom, poor Tom' —to be pitied by everyone, by strangers who never saw you, acquaintances who never cared for you, friends who once believed in you—that's the worst thing, the very worst thing of all. . . ."

"Yes, that is perhaps the worst thing. At least no one will pity me. They'll have other things to say. But I feel now —Janet, you'll think it awful—as though I'd come out of prison. And that prison has lasted from the very moment that I told Tom I'd marry him. There was my crime. Everything afterwards came from that. And everything before it led up to it. I was weak, vain, selfish, and most evil of all, frightened. I wanted to be safe. I knew that I didn't love Ravage, but I *did* love the things that he stood for, and I knew that I loved them so much that if I didn't take care I'd go after those things, and that then life would be difficult and many people would criticise. And so I funked it and married Tom for safety. And, after all, it's come to the same path in the end. You can't escape it. You may wriggle as you like, you've got to go your destined way."

"That's a selfish doctrine, Rosalind," Janet answered. "We were both selfish. I wanted to keep you, and so I was glad for you to marry Tom, although I was always afraid. But it was selfish—yes, in both of us."

"Of course I'm selfish," Rosalind answered; "and I'm selfish because I wanted something finer than myself. Now at last I can forget myself. I can work in the world of ideas and of facts. I've rid myself of all human ties. Ravage is a fellow-worker, but we are free of one another, thank God, free as though we had never met. He cares for ideas more than for any human being, and so shall I—save only you,

Mops dear. I can't shake you off. I shall never shake you off. I knew that yesterday after you had gone."

"Does he care only for ideas?" Janet asked. "Are you sure? He didn't look at you yesterday as though you were only an idea. Are you sure, Rosalind?"

"For the moment, perhaps, there's something personal between us," Rosalind answered. "We are both in a mess together for one thing. . . . But even if we do care a little, our work means more to us, far, far more."

"And what is your work to be?" Janet asked.

"To help to rid the world of shams, of hypocrisy and sentimentality—above all, of the past, the rotten, clogging, hampering past." She flung her arms out towards the hills and the Lake. "To build a new world when we've destroyed the old!"

She looked so young, so simple, so childishly beautiful as she said this that Janet felt for her suddenly the old protecting maternal love that so often in the old days had led her to do so many foolish, useless, defending things.

There on the top of the hill, where the whole world could see them if it pleased, she put her arms round her and kissed her.

At that kiss Rosalind melted. She clung to Janet, holding tightly to her.

"Oh, Janet, I shall always see Tom's face as he looked at me that last time before he went. Oh, what have I done? What did I do? Why couldn't he have seen that I meant him no harm, but only good? Why couldn't he have waited and learnt to forget me? Oh, if only I had said something to keep him from that . . . that despair. . . . I said it was a relief that he is dead, but I shall see him looking at me until I myself die. . . ."

Then, with that swift movement that was so like the old Rosalind of years ago, she drew herself away.

"But I'm not afraid. I will take what comes. There is something far grander than myself that I can work for. A new world to be built. What does my little twopenny story matter? It belongs to the past and will be swept away with the rest."

Then, smiling almost timidly, she put her arm through Janet's. They were standing now above the deep-bedded stream.

"Do you remember, Mops darling, the little silver tree I once gave you the night you told me you were going to marry Wildherne?"

"Of course I remember."

"Have you still got it?"

"Of course I have it."

"Well, look at that sometimes and remember that, however far apart we get in the things we think and do, I love you always, just as I did when I gave it to you. Perhaps in our different ways we are working for the same thing—trying to make something—a silver tree—one more beautiful thing in the world than there was before we came into it."

"Yes," Janet said. "I don't doubt that."

"Now cross the stream. I'll stay this side. I'll write to Wintersmoon. Kiss me good-bye. Now over you go. Good-bye. Good-bye."

When she reached the bungalow Janet looked back. Rosalind stood there, stiff, motionless, as though she were carved of black marble. Behind her the green grass, the brown naked trees, the grey sky, all were more free than she. Janet waved her hand, but the figure remained motionless. Tiny flakes of snow were beginning to fall. Janet hurried on her way.

She wanted Wildherne. Thank God she had not lost Rosalind, but Rosalind didn't need her. Even now, in the heart of her crisis, she didn't need her. Nobody needed her but Wildherne.

And it might be that after all that need of his had been imagined by her. As she faced, at the brink of the hill, the still grey lake bordered by the still grey hills, that old loneliness—always the fear of her life—once more threatened her. Wildherne seemed terribly far away. He had seemed to cling to her those last days, but might that not be because he was climbing out of illness? When he was well again would he want her any more than he had done in the early days of their marriage, want her as anything more than companion? Oh, she must be loved, be loved by someone, by something, and by someone who needed her.

To be needed was the thirst of her very soul—shy, diffident, self-judging, at the heart of these things was the *passion* to be loved; and if, after all, she was to be alone again —could she bear it?

She was in a world of ghosts. The thin trees, the bare brown hill, the misted lake, the faint chilly snow-flakes, all these were shadowy forebodings. Ah, why was Wildherne so far?

She was at the gate, her hand on the wooden latch, and there, coming down the Lake road, was Wildherne! Wildherne's ghost—of course his ghost! The ghost walked as he did with his swinging measured step; the ghost saw her and cried out in no ghostly voice, "Janet! Janet!"

Weakly in a whisper she answered, "Wildherne," and then ran down the road and straight without faltering into his ghostly arms.

"I left London yesterday afternoon—went in to see father, caught the train, had a beastly long cold journey, stayed the night at Carlisle, motored to Keswick this morning, had some breakfast, they told me where you'd gone, and I came after you."

He told her all this breathlessly, his arm around her, her hand inside his coat where she could feel from the beating of his heart that he was real true flesh and blood, no ghost made of mist and snowflakes.

She cried a little. "I can't help it. I was just thinking. You seemed so far away, and it's all been so difficult."

"Rosalind?" he asked her.

"Oh, it's all right. She is going to meet whatever comes to her. And she loves me still. This hasn't separated us. But she's on her own now. She doesn't need me or anyone else. And after leaving her I began to imagine that nobody needed me. You were so far away, and then suddenly you were here! . . . But why, Wildherne, darling? Why, when I was coming back to-morrow?"

"I couldn't bear to think of you up here when I knew it would all be so difficult, and that man Ravage . . . and besides, I hated our being apart—even a day. I'm lost without you. Everything's wrong if you aren't there. I'm not alive." He drew a deep breath, holding her arm tightly in his. "If we live to Methuselah's age and are together all the time it will never be enough!"

They walked down the road towards Lodore.

They came to the corner where, looking back, you have the whole sweep of the view, the full lake, Catbells and its neighbouring hills, and at the end above the trees the Keswick roofs, St. John's pointing finger, Skiddaw.

They stayed and looked, at their feet a field deeply green, a little landing-stage almost submerged by the flooding water. The snow was falling so gently that it was as though the air whispered. On Skiddaw's central point, that rose from its enfolding shoulders like the rounded stamen of a flower, a shining, brilliantly white cloud rested.

This cloud, that glittered like a great pile of frozen snow, dominated all the scene. It gave Skiddaw the appearance of great height, and the thin spray of snow spread on the shoulders of the surrounding hills seemed to catch also this glitter which slowly advanced from shoulder to shoulder.

Under the hill the Lake was grey as a bird's wing without a ripple. Then, as though the glittering cloud gave the word of command, the surface of the Lake began to move. Ripples ran in shudders from bank to bank. The ripples broke also into light, flashing in broken lines like quicksilver. Everything began to stir. Little waves splashed against the wooden landing-stage. The green field caught the glow, and behind the naked trees shining shadows, as though a sun burned behind mist, gathered like thin silver gauze.

The sky broke and fields of pale blue shone out; the water caught the blue and seemed to tremble with joy at the sudden colour. But the white silver cloud did not change. It stayed there, like a God ordering the universe.

Janet thought that now all was well with the world. She saw Rosalind, standing dark and motionless, facing her destiny. She saw everyone alive, moving, creating. She had come to the end of that movement that she had started by accepting Wildherne. To everyone involved by that action the crisis had come. Now a new cycle would begin. Always movement, always creation. And perhaps, after all, she and Rosalind were not so far apart.

She pressed Wildherne's arm:

"Isn't this beautiful? And there's Wintersmoon waiting for us. Wintersmoon that Rosalind and her world are going to pull down, and that we and our world are going to create new beauty from—if we can. There'll be a struggle, and I suppose that neither of us will win. But out of the struggle something wonderful may come!"

As she uttered the word "struggle" great joy filled her. Standing there, this beauty around her, Wildherne at her side, she savoured life with a burning intensity—life so vivid, so confusing, so dramatic, so touching, so creative, and at the last so mysterious. To make something out of it before one went, one thing brave, lovely, of good report. . . .

With a happy sigh she turned away from the Lake, that was now one shining glory, to Wildherne.

THE END